高等学校英语应用能力考试系列丛书

高等学校英语应用能力考试导学

Guide to
PRETCO

编委会主任：余丽华

编委会成员：梁育全　杨世强　林德福　熊晓雯　赵 红

主　　 编：赵 红

副 主 编：王 艳　欧阳敏

编　 者：高 辉　王秋菊　尹文山　木鸿英

　　　　　任莉平　赵东丽　苏幼敏

A 级
Level A

外语教学与研究出版社
FOREIGN LANGUAGE TEACHING AND RESEARCH PRESS
北京 BEIJING

图书在版编目(CIP)数据

高等学校英语应用能力考试导学. A级／赵红主编 .— 北京：外语教学与研究出版社，2008.5
ISBN 978 - 7 - 5600 - 7547 - 1

Ⅰ. 高…　Ⅱ. 赵…　Ⅲ. 英语—高等学校：技术学校—水平考试—自学参考资料
Ⅳ. H310.42

中国版本图书馆 CIP 数据核字 (2008) 第 071796 号

出 版 人：于春迟
责任编辑：付分钗
封面设计：刘　冬
出版发行：外语教学与研究出版社
社　　址：北京市西三环北路 19 号 (100089)
网　　址：http://www.fltrp.com
印　　刷：北京国防印刷厂
开　　本：787×1092　1/16
印　　张：14.5
版　　次：2008 年 6 月第 1 版　2008 年 6 月第 1 次印刷
书　　号：ISBN 978 - 7 - 5600 - 7547 - 1
定　　价：23.90 元 (含 MP3 光盘 1 张)
＊　　＊　　＊

前　言

为了贯彻《高职高专教育英语课程教学基本要求（试行）》（简称《基本要求》和《高等学校英语应用能力考试大纲和样题》（简称《大纲和样题》），云南省外语教学与考试指导委员会对本省高职高专英语教学进行了调研，并组织长期从事英语教学的老师编写了《高等学校英语应用能力考试导学系列丛书》，本系列丛书包括《高等学校英语应用能力考试导学——A级》、《高等学校英语应用能力考试导学——B级》和《高等学校英语应用能力考试导学——写作》。

本书为《高等学校英语应用能力考试导学——A级》，全书共分四部分。第一部分为各种题型的解题思路、技巧、专项训练及解析；第二部分为六套模拟试题。第三部分为专项训练及模拟试题听力原文；第四部分为模拟试题答案及解析。听力录音另附 MP3 光盘。

本书的特点：

1. 针对性强。按照考试大纲及命题规律针对每种题型进行分析讲解并组织相应题型进行专项训练，可以使广大考生快速进入备考状态并达到事半功倍的效果。

2. 难易适度、重点突出。针对实考项目设置的专项强化训练；从真题中选取例子进行解析，联系实际，讲、练结合，帮助考生举一反三，融会贯通。

3. 实用性强，难点复现率高。重要考点和难点以各种不同题型形式在专项训练中复现，使考生在训练的过程中对自己的薄弱环节得到强化及巩固。

本书由赵红担任主编，王艳、欧阳敏担任副主编，其中王艳、王秋菊编写了听力部分；木鸿英、尹文山、赵东丽、赵红编写了语法词汇及改错题部分；高辉编写了阅读理解部分；欧阳敏、任莉平编写了英汉翻译部分；苏幼敏老师编写了模拟试题。

由于编写水平有限，疏漏与错误之处在所难免，敬请读者不吝批评指正。

编　者

2008 年 3 月

目　录

第一部分 专项训练

Part I   Listening Comprehension

听力理解主要测试考生理解所听对话、会话和简单短文的能力。要求考生能听懂日常和涉外业务活动中使用的结构简单、发音清楚、语速较慢（每分钟 120 词左右）的英语对话和不太复杂的陈述，理解基本正确。常见的听力理解题型主要有简短对话、简短会话和短文三种类型，主要以日常生活和实用交际性内容为主。词汇限于《基本要求》中的"交际范围表"所列的全部听说范围。

1 简单对话和简短会话的解题思路及技巧

简短对话和简短会话的解题思路

纵观近几年考试的情况，听力理解的出题形式有了一定的变化，由原来的纯客观型试题转为主客观兼顾型试题。简短对话和会话题型仍以客观测试为主，以选择题为考查方式。

简短对话主要测试考生理解简短对话的能力。对话中的内容并不复杂，出题形式相对稳定，多数情况下是对第二说话人的说话内容进行提问。在所问的问题中大多数是以WH- 引导的特殊疑问句，主要内容包括考查逻辑推理、判断、数字计算、因果关系、请求建议五类题型。

简短会话题由两段较长的对话（一般为 5 个回合）组成，每篇后有 2-3 个问题，两篇共 5 题。会话的选材多为情景对话，涉及旅行、宾馆、海关、飞机、签证、保险、饮食、求知、购物等各个方面。简短会话的题型同简短对话基本一致，也可分为前面提到的五类题型。

对于简短对话和简短会话，解题时听者应首先预览选项，对篇章进行预测；边听边做记录；听到提问，确认预测，修正预测，做出正确判断。

简短对话和简短会话的解题技巧

该类型的解题技巧按照前面所说的五类题型来进行分解。

● 逻辑推理题

e.g.（2002年6月真题）

W: Sir, I've come to complain about the skirt I bought in your shop yesterday.

M: What's the matter with it?

Q: What's the probable relationship between the two speakers?

A. Boss and secretary.　　　　　　B. Husband and wife.

C. Salesman and customer.　　　　D. Doctor and patient.

[解析] 对话中，skirt, bought, shop是三个重要的关键词，在商店里买了裙子并对此进行投诉，双方的关系肯定是售货员和顾客。因此很容易判断出C就是正确答案。

e.g.（2004年6月真题）

M: Madam, what are you going to order?

W: Just a cup of coffee and a sandwich.

Q: Where does the conversation most probably take place?

A. In a bookstore.　　　　　　　　B. In a bank.

C. In a snack bar.　　　　　　　　D. In a library.

[解析] 地点推断题。根据关键词order, a cup of coffee and a sandwich可以推断出对话发生在快餐店，故答案为C。

　　在这类题中，对话发生的时间、地点及说话者的身份往往没有明确提到，所以，在听这类对话时，要特别注意说话人的态度、语气和关键词语，以便做出正确判断。

e.g.（2005年6月真题）

M: Where have you been, Mary? I didn't see you the whole morning.

W: Peter took me sightseeing around the city.

M: I see. Are you doing anything this evening?

W: Nothing special. But I'm leaving for Shanghai tomorrow morning.

M: Good. Could you come to my house this evening? We're having a small party.

W: I'd love to. Is there anyone I know?

M: Yes. I've also invited Peter.

W: That's great. I'll be there.

M: Please come by around six if you can.

W: OK. See you then.

Q1: What was Mary doing this morning?

A. Sightseeing around the city.　　　B. Attending a meeting.

C. Shopping in the city.　　　　　　D. Giving a party.

[解析] 细节题。对话开始男士问Mary到哪里去了，一上午都没见到她，Mary回答说Peter took me sightseeing around the city，这就是答案所在。另外，选项B和C都未出现过。Mary是受男士邀请参加party的，并非举办的party。故正确选项为A。

Q2: When will Mary leave for Shanghai?

A. This afternoon.　　　　　　　　B. This evening.

C. Tomorrow morning.　　　　　　D. Tomorrow afternoon.

[解析] 细节题。答案在 Mary 的回答 But I'm leaving for Shanghai tomorrow morning 中。对话中的时间状语是考试的重点，故正确选项为 C。

Q3: Where can Mary meet Peter again?

A. At the party.　　　　　　　　B. At the meeting.

C. In the office.　　　　　　　　D. In the hotel.

[解析] 推理题。对话中男士邀请 Mary 参加今晚的聚会，并说 I've also invited Peter，这是答案的关键所在，Mary 会在聚会上见到 Peter。另外，选项 B、C 和 D 都未在对话中出现过。故正确选项为 A。

● 判断题

　　判断题型是听力考试对话部分最难的一类题。它不仅要求考生听出每一个词及其基本内容，还要通过上下文、字里行间、语境等来判断说话人的行为方式、目的，从而正确理解对话。这类题中通常是对第一说话人的提问或谈到的看法，第二说话人不直接回答，而是婉转地表达自己的意思，而且对话中很少有判断各种逻辑关系的信号词。听者要善于从特定的词语中推断、悟出潜台词，注意说话人的语气、语调和出现的短语、谚语、格言等，从上下文推测其含义。

e.g.（2006 年 6 月真题）

W: I've got a few things for Mary.

M: A few? It seems you have bought the whole supermarket for her.

Q: What can we learn from this conversation?

A. The woman has bought a few things for the man.

B. The woman has bought a lot of things for Mary.

C. The woman has bought nothing for Mary.

D. The woman has bought a few things for herself.

[解析] 判断题，考查学生对重复反问句的推理判断能力。从男士的反问句 "A few?" 的语气及句子内容可推测女士为 Mary 买了许多东西，而不是仅仅几样。故正确答案为 B。

e.g.（2006 年 6 月真题）

W: Excuse me?

M: Yes, madam. Can I help you?

W: Could you tell me where the bank is?

M: It's upstairs across the coffee bar.

W: Thanks. Do you know what time it is open?

M: It should be open now. It opens at 8 a.m.

W: Good. And can you tell me how often the buses leave for the city center?

M: Every half hour. And you just miss one.

W: Oh, dear, then I have to wait for another 30 minutes. Thank you very much.

M: That's OK.

Q1: Where is the bank?

A. Upstairs.   B. Downstairs.

C. Right behind the woman   D. Across the bus stop.

[解析] 判断题。从对话中 "It's upstairs across the coffee bar." 可知银行是在往前走的方向，
在咖啡厅的对面。upstairs 是关键词，可以推断出答案是 A。

Q2: How often do the buses leave for the city center?

A. Every ten minutes.   B. Every other hour.

C. Every hour.   D. Every half hour.

[解析] 细节题，考查学生对对话中的问题与答案的快速捕捉。对话中有问题 "…how
often the buses leave for the city center?" 和答案 "Every half hour." 听者应迅速熟
悉四个选项，并根据所问问题找出答案，选择正确答案 D。

● 数字及计算

　　数字计算中涉及数字方面的内容比较多，主要包括：年代、年龄、日期、时间、
价格、数量等几类。在听这类对话时，听者可以事先将四个选项的数字浏览一下，听
的时候就有一定的重点。把听到的数字及相应的关键词记下来，然后根据提出的问题
做出正确的判断。

e.g.（2005 年 1 月真题）

M: Can I rent a room for two weeks? I'm not sure whether I will stay for a whole month.

W: Yes, 150 dollars a week, but only 400 dollars a month.

Q: How much will the man pay if he rents the room for two weeks?

A. $150.   B. $200.

C. $ 300.   D. $400.

[解析] 这是一个租房的场景对话，房租和租房的时间是考试的重点，有时候房租要根据
租房的时间进行计算。根据女士说的 150 dollars a week, but only 400 dollars a month
计算出问题中两周的房租是 300 美元，因此判断出 C 是正确答案。

● 因果关系

　　此类题型要求考生正确判断事物发展的前因后果，这种问题大多数提问原因。考生只
要按照做听力题的常规方法去做，即浏览选题、细听原文、对照预测、做出判断。听时注
意对话中含有的一些表示因果关系的词汇：because, for, since, due to, that is why, so, so that,
in order to, therefore, as a result of。

e.g. （2002 年 12 月真题）

M: Terry starts work at 6 o'clock.

W: So he has to get up early.

Q: Why does Terry get up early?

A. Because he has to go outside.   B. Because he has to work early.

C. Because he has to catch the bus.   D. Because he has to have breakfast.

[解析] 对话中出现了表示结果的提示词 so, 说明之前第一说话人所提到的 Terry starts work at 6 o'clock 就是 Terry 必须早起的原因，故答案为 B。

● 建议及请求

    建议题要求考生掌握建议的各种表达方式，这种对话的常见形式是用 Why don't you…, Why not…, You'd better…, You should…, How about…, Would you like…, I suggest…, Shall we… 等句型表达建议及请求，而建议及请求的内容通常是考查的重点，根据建议选择正确选项。

e.g. （2003 年 12 月真题）

M: Shall we go to the airport to meet Dr. Smith this afternoon?

W: Oh, I forget to tell you he has put off his trip.

Q: What do we know about Dr. Smith?

A. He has changed his plan.   B. He has canceled his trip.

C. He is arriving this afternoon.   D. He forgot to arrange his trip.

[解析] 根据关键句型 Shall we 可知这是考查请求建议的，对话中男士问是否去机场接 Dr. Smith，女士回答说"我忘记告诉你他推迟行程了"，根据关键词 put off 可知 Dr. Smith 是改变计划了，而不是取消计划了，故答案为 A。

② 简单对话和简短会话的练习及解析

Section A Short Dialogues

Directions: *This section is to test your ability to understand short dialogues. There are 50 recorded dialogues in it. After each dialogue, there is a recorded question. Both the dialogues and questions will be spoken only once. When you hear a question, you should decide on the correct answer from the 4 choices marked A, B, C and D given below.*

Example: *You will hear: W: Are you catching the 13:15 flight to New York?*

                     M: No. I'll leave this evening.

                     Q: What are the two people talking about?

You will read: A. New York City.

               B. An Evening Party.

               C. An air trip.

               D. The man's job.

From the dialogue we learn that the man is to take a flight to New York. Therefore, "C. An air trip" is the correct answer. Now the test will begin.

● 逻辑推理题

1. A. On the second floor.   B. On the third floor.

   C. On the right side.   D. Next to the stairs.

2. A. In the bookstore.   B. In the department store.

   C. In the library.   D. In the hotel.

3. A. At the airport.   B. At the hotel.

   C. At the station.   D. At the bus stop.

4. A. He really doesn't want to buy a house.

   B. He plans to buy a house in a little while.

   C. He will have enough money for a house soon.

   D. He doesn't have enough money for a house.

5. A. He thinks it's very crowded.   B. He thinks it's a big city.

   C. He likes the buildings of Paris.   D. He likes modern buildings of Paris.

6. A. Boss and secretary.   B. Waitress and guest.

   C. Doctor and patient.   D. Husband and wife.

7. A. They were both businessmen years ago.   B. They were schoolmates.

   C. They are very good friends.   D. They are professors of a university.

8. A. He has no idea.

   B. He has no preference.

   C. He'd rather have the party on Tuesday morning.

   D. He'd rather have the party on Friday afternoon.

9. A. Cold and windy.   B. Warm and sunny.

   C. Cloudy and windy.   D. Rainy and cold.

10. A. The plan should be discussed again in the next meeting.

    B. The woman should have supported him at the meeting.

    C. His back hurts during the meeting.

    D. He agrees that it was a good meeting.

● 判断题

11. A. To talk with Mrs. Robbins.   B. To make a complaint.

    C. To make a phone call.   D. To do some shopping.

12. A. To see Peter.   B. To talk to his doctor.

    C. To meet his friend.   D. To visit Professor Johnson.

13. A. He dislikes it because of too much violence.

    B. He likes it because of too much violence.

    C. He thinks it's very interesting.

    D. He thinks it's very boring.

14. A. She wants the man to call her back.

    B. She wants the man to ask Smith to call her.

    C. She wants to leave a message for the man.

    D. She wants Smith to take a message for her.

15. A. Who are going to attend the meeting?

    B. When is the meeting going to be held?

    C. Where is the meeting going to be held?

    D. What is to be discussed at the meeting?

16. A. To ask Tom to be their tutor.   B. To take Tom to a doctor.

    C. To talk with Tom about his study.   D. To study English with Tom.

17. A. To attend a meeting.   B. To clean the office.

    C. To hold a party.   D. To have a rest.

18. A. The tour was worth the time but not the money.

    B. The tour was not worth the time or the money.

    C. The tour was worth both the time and the money.

    D. The tour was worth the money but not the time.

19. A. Alice does not know much about electronics.

    B. Alice is unlikely to find a job anywhere.

    C. Alice is likely to find a job in an electronics company.

    D. Alice is not interested in anything but electronics.

20. A. The company has trouble printing a schedule.

    B. The schedule has been misprinted.

    C. The speakers arrived at the station late.

    D. The train seldom arrives on time.

● 数字及计算

21. A. One.   B. Two.   C. Three.   D. Four.

22. A. 20 minutes.   B. 25 minutes.   C. 50 minutes.   D. 55 minutes.

23. A. $40.   B. $90.   C. $108.   D. $120.

24. A. 25.   B. 75.   C. 100.   D. 125.

25. A. 7:15.   B. 8:15.   C. 9:15.   D. 2:00.

26. A. 8:00 a.m.   B. 8:15 a.m.   C. 8:30 a.m.   D. 8:45 a.m.
27. A. $12.   B. $8.   C. $5.   D. $4.
28. A. $14.   B. $25.   C. $28.   D. $50.
29. A. At 1:40 p.m.   B. At 1:50 p.m.   C. At 2:00.   D. At 3:50.
30. A. $39.95.   B. $39.9.   C. $40.   D. $45.

● 因果关系

31. A. He didn't like the present.   B. He didn't have television.
   C. He got home too late.   D. He was busy with his studying.

32. A. She will have a meeting.   B. She will buy a ticket.
   C. She will go to the movie.   D. She will meet her sister.

33. A. He finished his chemical research paper last semester.
   B. He'll finish his chemical research paper in a few minutes.
   C. He never does his assignments early.
   D. He always does his assignments late.

34. A. He doesn't have spare time.   B. He doesn't have enough money.
   C. He doesn't like traveling.   D. He doesn't like going with them.

35. A. She likes typing very much.   B. She learns to read and write at six.
   C. She types faster than her mother.   D. She has a long experience of typing.

36. A. The man didn't come with his wife.
   B. The man didn't let her know his trip in time.
   C. She doesn't want to leave so early.
   D. She doesn't want his wife to leave with him.

37. A. Because the new apartment is cheaper.   B. Because he needs a quieter place.
   C. Because the present apartment is too small.   D. Because he needs a better place.

38. A. Because its style is out of fashion.   B. Because its color fails to match her.
   C. Because it suits her very well.   D. Because it seems too bright for her.

39. A. Because the film is frightening   B. Because the film is interesting.
   C. Because the film is disappointing.   D. Because the film is extraordinary.

40. A. His mother is ill.   B. His sister is ill.
   C. He has been ill for several days.   D. He has to look after her sister.

● 建议及请求

41. A. It's time to clean up her room.
   B. It's time to listen to the weather report.
   C. There's no need to wait for her.
   D. There's no need to fetch his umbrella.

42. A. Go out to work.　　　　　　　　　B. Listen carefully to John.

　　C. Be calm and patient.　　　　　　　D. Do the easiest thing.

43. A. She suggests the man should look at the advertisement.

　　B. She suggests the man should not look at the advertisement.

　　C. She suggests there be no new advertisement.

　　D. She suggests that the advertisements be useless.

44. A. To let their children do as they pleased.

　　B. To leave their children at home.

　　C. To tell their children some stories.

　　D. To sing some songs for their children.

45. A. To get some travel information.

　　B. To help him to carry his luggage.

　　C. To tell him the way to the luggage office.

　　D. To look after the luggage for him.

46. A. Waiting in the line.　　　　　　　　B. Not going to the movie today.

　　C. Coming back for a later show.　　　D. Coming back in ten minutes.

47. A. He will go out with the woman.

　　B. He will ask the woman to post his letter.

　　C. He will write a letter after taking a walk with the woman.

　　D. He will wait until the woman comes back.

48. A. To have a birthday party.

　　B. To join in a birthday party.

　　C. To invite all his classmates to his party.

　　D. To invite a few of his classmates to his party.

49. A. To travel abroad.　　　　　　　　　B. To visit China.

　　C. To cook food.　　　　　　　　　　D. To eat outside.

50. A. He only knows one way to get to the bookstore.

　　B. He doesn't know how to get to the bookstore.

　　C. The bookstore is a bit far away.

　　D. The bookstore is around the corner.

答案及解析

● 逻辑推理题

1. **B** 女士想要找约翰的公寓，男士说约翰住在三楼，所以女士应该再上一层楼，答案为 B。

2. **C** 判断谈话发生的场合，由对话中的 keep the books 和 return 可推断谈话主题是借书，显然谈话发生场所是图书馆，故答案为 C。

3. **B** 就地点提问，根据对话中的关键词如 bill 和 room number 可以判断这个对话发生在酒店。故答案为 B。

4. **D** 男士问 Bill 计划买房子了吗，女士回答几乎没有，因为 a house is beyond his means，也就是说他没有足够的钱买房子，故答案为 D。

5. **C** 本题关键在于男士对巴黎的印象，首先是 It's interesting 可以看出他还是喜欢巴黎的，然后继续说明自己对这个城市的特殊喜好，所以可以推断出他喜欢巴黎的建筑。故答案为 C。

6. **B** 就人物关系提问，根据对话中的关键词如 order 可以判断这两个人应该是饭店里服务员和客人的关系。故答案为 B。

7. **B** 就人物关系提问，根据对话中的关键句 I haven't seen you since we graduated from the university 可以判断这两个人应该是同学。故答案为 B。

8. **B** 女士问男士聚会是周二早上开还是周五下午开，而男士的回答是你安排的我就满意，说明自己并没有什么特别的要求，故答案为 B。

9. **A** 男士说前两天非常冷，女士说天气预报说下周会有更多的雪并伴有强风，所以可以推断出天气将是又冷又有风，故答案为 A。

10. **B** 关键在于理解男士的话，back up 的意思为支持，男士的意思是既然女士同意他的观点，就应该在会议上支持他才对。故答案为 B。

● **判断题**

11. **B** 男士说要找服务部门，要找经理，可以判断出男士要找经理投诉，故答案为 B。

12. **D** 男士问女士是否愿意去看望彼得，女士说愿意，但是她先要去拜访约翰教授，故答案为 D。

13. **A** 关键在于理解男士不喜欢这部电影的原因，男士说的 No 是对女士问题的否定回答，其后通常会说否定的原因，此时要留意其后的内容 I thought it showed too much unnecessary violence，而 A 是对此句的同义转述，故答案为 A。

14. **B** 从女士的话中可以听到女士希望男士带个信给史密斯，请他回来后给女士打电话，故答案为 B。

15. **D** 关键在于理解女士回答了男士的话 Yes, I did 后，由 But 引起的句子 I'm still not quite sure what the meeting is about 说明女士希望知道会议的内容，故答案为 D。

16. **C** 女士说汤姆英语不好，也许需要一个家庭教师辅导他，男士回答也许是的，但是他认为应该先和汤姆谈一谈，所以他们有可能要去和汤姆谈谈他的学习，故答案为 C。

17. **A** 男士请女士明天帮他打一些文件，但女士说恐怕不行，因为据说会议可能要开一整天，由此可以推断出女士明天可能要参加一个会议，故答案为 A。

18. **B** 从女士的话 It was worth neither the time nor the money 中可以看出女士认为这次旅行时间和金钱都不值，故正确答案为 B。

19. **A** 关键在于理解女士的话，女士说除了电子学 Alice 什么都好，也就是说她对于电子学一无所知，故答案为 A。

20. **D**　女士说我们被告知火车又晚点了，男士说为什么铁路公司还要那么麻烦地印时刻表，从男士的话中可以看出是在抱怨，可能因为火车经常晚点，故答案为 D。

● **数字及计算**

21. **C**　男士说想要借两本小说和一本书，一共三本，故答案为 C。

22. **C**　女士问男士在交通不拥挤时驱车回家需要多长时间。男士说只需 25 分钟。但是如果在下午 5：30 以前不能离开办公室，有时就需要 50 分钟。问男士在高峰时间驱车回家需要多长时间，故答案为 C。

23. **C**　男士说一双鞋 40 美元，3 双总额 120 美元，但是总额可以有 10% 的折扣，即 12 元的折扣，所以女士应该付 108 美元，故答案为 C。

24. **B**　女士说共有 100 个学生，其中四分之一来自美国，其余的来自欧洲，故答案为 B。

25. **C**　男士说因为桥断了，7:15 的火车要推迟两小时，所以火车应该 9:15 到，故答案为 C。

26. **B**　男士问会议几点开始，女士回答 8:30 开始，我们还有 15 分钟到那儿，所以现在应该是 8:15，故正确答案为 B。

27. **A**　女士说她以为寄一封快递是 8 元，男士说过去是，但现在价格已经上涨了 4 元，所以现在寄一封快递应该是 12 元，故答案为 A。

28. **C**　男士说一件 T 恤衫 28 元，两件 50 元，而问题问一件 T 恤衫价值多少钱，故答案为 C。

29. **B**　问的是演讲什么时候开始，而对话中女士说到 It will begin at 1:50，故答案为 B。

30. **A**　关键在于理解女士的话，女士说今天这双鞋特价，只要 $39.95，昨天还是 $45，故答案为 A。

● **因果关系**

31. **C**　女士问男士是否喜欢昨晚总统的电视演讲，男士说不幸的是他回来得太晚了而没有看到。故答案为 C。

32. **D**　男士问是否和他去看电影，女士说很想去，但是她必须去车站接她妹妹。故答案为 D。

33. **C**　关键在于理解男士没有完成研究论文的原因，原文中男士说 I always seem to put things off until the last minute，而 C 是对此句的同义转述，故答案为 C。

34. **B**　关键在于理解男士不去杭州的原因，从男士的话中可以得知是因为没有足够的钱，故答案为 B。

35. **D**　女士说从她六岁起母亲就开始教她打字，所以可以看出她打字快的原因是她打字的经历很长，故答案为 D。

36. **B**　关键在于理解女士生气的原因，从女士的话 I wish you had told me your departure time earlier 中可以知道女士生气是因为男士没有及时让她知道他的行程，故答案为 B。

37. **B**　关键在于理解男士搬家的原因，男士说 My roommate plays the radio all night long, and I can't sleep well，由此可以看出他需要一个安静的地方，故答案为 B。

38. **B** 男士说式样不错，但和年龄搭配，颜色似乎太深了，由此可以得知男士不喜欢这条裙子的原因是颜色和女士的年龄不配，故答案为 B。

39. **C** 男士说那部电影几乎让他睡着了，说明他对那部电影很失望，故答案为 C。

40. **D** 女士问男士为何没有完成家庭作业，男士回答因为他母亲病了几天，他不得不照顾他的妹妹，故答案为 D。

● 建议及请求

41. **D** 男士说把伞忘在房间里了，要回去取。女士说不用麻烦了，天气预报说中午天就要晴了，故答案为 D。

42. **C** 考查原因，女士说她对约翰非常生气，因为他从不听她的话。男士说别着急事情会解决的，可以看出男士建议女士冷静、耐心，故答案为 C。

43. **A** 女士在向男士提建议，用到了常用的提建议句型 Why not have a look at the advertisement? 因此可以判断出女士是建议看一下广告，故答案为 A。

44. **A** 男士用了提建议的句型 Why don't we leave that for themselves? 意思是说让孩子自己做决定，故答案为 A。

45. **D** 男士问女士能否把行李留在这里几个小时，女士说为什么不把它们放到行李寄存处，由此可以推断出男士希望女士帮他照看行李，故答案为 D。

46. **C** 男士用到了建议的句型 Why don't we come back for the next show? 由此可以看出男士建议看下一场电影，故答案为 C。

47. **A** 女士建议 Why don't we go sighting? 男士说 Would you like to wait for me a few minutes? 可以看出男士愿意和女士一起出去，故答案为 A。

48. **C** 男士说要邀请一些同学参加他的生日晚会，女士说不能只邀请一些，否则其他人会生气的，因此可以看出女士是建议男士邀请所有的同学，故答案为 C。

49. **D** 男士建议 Shall we have something special for a change? 女士提出 How about Chinese food? 可以推断出他们有可能要出去吃饭，故答案为 D。

50. **C** 女士问你能告诉我怎样到达书店吗，男士回答当然可以，但是路太远了。从男士的话中可以得知到书店的路程很远。故答案为 C。

Section B Short Conversations

Directions: *This section is to test your ability to understand short conversations. There are 20 recorded conversations in it. After each conversation, there are some recorded questions. Both the conversations and questions will be spoken two times. When you hear a question, you should decide on the correct answer from the 4 choices marked A, B, C and D given below.*

Conversation 1

1. A. Renting a house.   B. Letting a house.

  C. Selling a house.   D. Talking about a rented house.

2. A. To see other house.   B. To see the rented house again.

   C. To buy some furniture.   D. To bargain with the house owner.

3. A. Friends.   B. Husband and wife.

   C. Newly-married couple.   D. Landlady and tenant.

Conversation 2

4. A. He is born wise.

   B. He is a very good boy.

   C. He is still too young to do anything bad.

   D. He will grow up to be a wise young man.

5. A. Disappointed.   B. Surprised.

   C. Amused.   D. Annoyed.

Conversation 3

6. A. From her office.   B. From her home.

   C. From a library.   D. From a tea house.

7. A. Because she is not in at the moment.

   B. Because she is at work in her office now.

   C. Because she is out for lunch now.

   D. Because she is busy with her English now.

8. A. Because she wants to invite Cathy to tea.

   B. Because she wants to leave Cathy a message.

   C. Because she wants to say hello to Cathy.

   D. Because she wants to find out if Cathy has her English dictionary.

Conversation 4

9. A. A housewife.   B. A customer.

   C. An air hostess.   D. A receptionist.

10. A. In a travel agency.   B. In the booking office of the airport.

    C. At the woman's home.   D. At the reception desk of a hotel.

Conversation 5

11. A. She isn't very well.

    B. She feels lonely living in Britain.

    C. She has some trouble with her study.

    D. She is not accustomed to the weather in Britain.

12. A. Because Mary's English is too poor.

    B. Because she never speaks first.

    C. Because English people hate to be talked to.

    D. Because she often asks stupid questions.

13. A. English is very hard for foreigners to learn.

    B. English people are hard to make friends with.

C. Mary is not interested in speaking English.

D. Mary is a foreigner, coming to Britain to learn English.

Conversation 6

14. A. To borrow a book.　　　　　　　　B. To mail a book.

    C. To buy a book.　　　　　　　　　D. To return the book.

15. A. In the classroom.　　　　　　　　B. In the bookstore.

    C. In the woman's house.　　　　　　D. In the library.

Conversation 7

16. A. In three weeks' time.　　　　　　B. In a few days' time.

    C. On July fourth.　　　　　　　　　D. On August third.

17. A. Because she wants to relax there.

    B. Because she has never been to the beach.

    C. Because she wants to save some money on lodging.

    D. Because it is cooler there in August.

18. A. At home.　　　　　　　　　　　　B. At the beach, too.

    C. He is not going to have one.　　　D. He has not thought about it yet.

Conversation 8

19. A. The tree was broken.　　　　　　　B. One of its branches fell down.

    C. The tree was cut down.　　　　　D. All the leaves fell down.

20. A. Worse.　　　　　　　　　　　　　B. Terrible.

    C. Good.　　　　　　　　　　　　　D. Wet.

Conversation 9

21. A. In the spring.　　　　　　　　　　B. In the summer.

    C. In the autumn.　　　　　　　　　D. In the winter.

22. A. Sacramento.　　　　　　　　　　　B. San Francisco.

    C. San Diego.　　　　　　　　　　　D. San Barbara.

23. A. Because it is her favorite city.

    B. Because that's the place where they fall in love.

    C. Because that's the place where her parents-in-law live.

    D. All of the above.

Conversation 10

24. A. She will take a bus.

    B. She will take a train there.

    C. She will be picked up at the station.

    D. She will be picked up at her own house.

25. A. Around 7 p.m.　　　　　　　　　　B. Around 7:30 p.m.

    C. Around 8 a.m.　　　　　　　　　　D. Around 8:30 a.m.

Conversation 11

26. A. In the hotel.   B. In the restaurant.
    C. In the hospital.   D. In the snack-bar.

27. A. He wants to have lunch in the hotel.
    B. He wants to order some foods for lunch.
    C. He wants to have breakfast in his room.
    D. He wants to eat something immediately.

28. A. 7:00 a.m.   B. 7:30 a.m.
    C. 8:00 a.m.   D. 8:30 a.m.

Conversation 12

29. A. In the supermarket.   B. In the subway.
    C. At the railway station.   D. At the airport.

30. A. Because he is not Mr. Smith's friend.
    B. Because he is not in the city this moment.
    C. Because he is very busy.
    D. Because he is in hospital now.

Conversation 13

31. A. For a volleyball match.   B. For a basketball match.
    C. For a football match.   D. For a baseball match.

32. A. Tomorrow evening.   B. This afternoon.
    C. This evening.   D. Tomorrow afternoon

33. A. Because she has something else to do.   B. Because she hates the players.
    C. Because she is rather tired.   D. Because she is not interested.

Conversation 14

34. A. In a beautiful garden.   B. In a camp.
    C. In the mountains.   D. In a town.

35. A. Because there is no pollution.   B. Because there is a beautiful lake.
    C. Because there is a cabin.   D. Because there is a beautiful garden.

Conversation 15

36. A. They are planning to watch a movie.
    B. They are planning to eat out.
    C. They are planning to spend the weekend there.
    D. They are planning to go climbing.

37. A. It will be the man's birthday.
    B. It will be the woman's birthday.
    C. It will be their 10th wedding anniversary.
    D. It will be their 15th wedding anniversary.

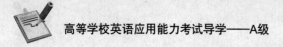

Conversation 16

38. A. 2 days.　　　　B. 3 days.　　　　C. 4 days.　　　　D. 5 days.

39. A. 15 years old.　　B. 16 years old.　　C. 17 years old.　　D. 18 years old.

40. A. He will go shopping.　　　　　　B. He will write a letter.

　　C. He will prepare the meal.　　　　D. He will have a party.

Conversation 17

41. A. At home.　　　　　　　　　　　B. At a store.

　　C. At school.　　　　　　　　　　D. At the railway station.

42. A. She doesn't know where to repair the walkman.

　　B. She isn't sure how much the walkman costs.

　　C. She doesn't know how to use the walkman properly.

　　D. She isn't sure how long the batteries can be used.

Conversation 18

43. A. An engineer.　　　　　　　　　B. A salesman.

　　C. A secretary.　　　　　　　　　D. A teacher.

44. A. At a store.　　　　　　　　　　B. At a university.

　　C. In a primary school.　　　　　D. In a company.

45. A. For two years.　　　　　　　　B. For three years.

　　C. For half a year.　　　　　　　D. For one year.

Conversation 19

46. A. It has no problem at all.　　　　B. It doesn't have an alarm.

　　C. The surface of the clock is broken.　　D. The alarm button doesn't work.

47. A. Because it wasn't sold in this store.

　　B. Because there is nothing wrong with the clock.

　　C. Because the man doesn't have the receipt with him.

　　D. Because the saleswoman does not like the man.

Conversation 20

48. A. His children.　　　　　　　　　B. His wife.

　　C. His friend.　　　　　　　　　　D. His mother.

49. A. A tablecloth.　　　　　　　　　B. A handkerchief.

　　C. A blouse.　　　　　　　　　　D. One of the above.

50. A. Expensive.　　　　B. Fair.　　　　C. Cheap.　　　　D. Costly.

答案及解析

Conversation 1

1. **D** 推理题。根据对话中出现的关键词 rent, house, bedrooms, kitchen 等，可推断出他们谈论有关租房的事。故排除 B、C，而根据男士的问话 "Tell me about it. What

about the inside? Is there any furniture yet?"可知男士是在询问女士所租的房子情况，故选 D。

2. **C** 细节题。根据对话中 "Is there any furniture yet?"，"No. We can go shopping tomorrow." 可知女士下一步是要买家具，故选 C。

3. **B** 判断说话人的关系。对话中，男士询问所租房事宜，女士做了详细的说明，并且还提到两间卧室，一间给他们自己，另一间给孩子住，故选 B。

Conversation 2

4. **D** 细节题。男士问 "He's a wise young man. How old is he?" 女士回答 "He's six months old today. But he'll grow up to be a gentleman." 可知女士对自己的孩子充满信心和期待，故选 D。

5. **C** 推理题。在对话一开始男士误认为女士有一个大孩子，因此在最后当他得知女士的孩子只有六个月时，认为自己前面的问话很逗，故选 C。

Conversation 3

6. **B** 细节题。男士问 "And where are you calling from?"，女士回答 "130, Rose Avenue"，告知男士自己的家庭地址，因此可知女士是从家里打来，故选 B。

7. **A** 因果关系题。根据对话 "Is Cathy there?"，"No, I'm sorry, Cathy is out." 可知是由于 Cathy 现在不在家，故选 A。

8. **D** 因果关系题。女士要男士帮她问 Cathy 是否拿着她的英语词典，并且让她在喝茶时把词典带上。这是女士打电话的目的所在，故选 D。

Conversation 4

9. **B** 推断题。女士问 "How soon do I have to leave my room"，男士回答和问话 "…by 12 noon…" 和 "which room is it, madam?" 等句子可知他们的关系一定是客人和服务员，故选 B。

10. **D** 推理题。他们的对话中出现的 leave, room, departure, keep your room 等词和词组，可知对话是发生在酒店，故选 D。

Conversation 5

11. **C** 因果关系题。从对话的问答 "What's the matter, Mary? You don't look very happy." 和 "I'm not. I'm worried about my English." 可知女士不愉快的原因是由于她的英语学习不顺利，故选 C。

12. **B** 因果关系题。从女士说 "But… English people never speak to me" 和男士的反应 "You should speak first." 可以得知原因在于女士没有主动开口讲话，故选 B。

13. **D** 推理题。在四个选项中，A 是说英语对于外国人来说很难学，B 项说难以和英国人交朋友，和 C 项 Mary 对讲英语不感兴趣，会话中并未提到。只有 D，Mary 是到英国来学习英语的外国人符合会话的内容，故选 D。

Conversation 6

14. **C** 细节题。听者可从对话开篇的第一句话得到答案 "I've been trying to get that book for some time."，并且在很多时候动词 get 往往是 buy 的意思，故选 C。

15. **B** 地点推断题。通过听整篇对话可以知道对话是发生在这个女士买书时，故选 B。

Conversation 7

16. **B** 细节题。男士问 "When is your vacation going to start, Barbara?"，女士回答 "I'll be leaving on the third of July."，男士又说 "…that's only a few days from now."，虽然女士给出了具体的时间，但选项中 C 和 D 均不是所提到的时间，从男士的后面这句话可知女士度假的时间在几天后，故选 B。

17. **A** 关系题。女士说 "This time I'd like to go to the beach. I need a real rest."，由此可知女士选择海滩的目的是为了运动和放松，故选 A。

18. **D** 细节题。女士问 "Where are you planning to take your vacation?"，男士回答 "I don't know. I should think about it now." 说明他还没有考虑这个问题，故选 D。

Conversation 8

19. **B** 细节题。女士说到 "Do you know that big tree in front of my house? One of the biggest branches came down in the night."，这就是答案所在，came down 和 fell down 这里都是指 "树枝折断掉落下来"，故选 B。

20. **C** 细节题。女士最后一句话说 We had a fine March after all，故选 C。

Conversation 9

21. **A** 细节题。对话开始男士问 "When are you getting married?"，女士回答 "In the spring."，因此得知女士将要在春天举行婚礼，故选 A。

22. **B** 细节题。男士接着问说 "Where's the wedding going to be?"，女士回答 "We're not sure yet. Perhaps in San Francisco."，由此可判断他们有可能在 San Francisco 举行婚礼，故选 B。

23. **C** 因果关系题。女士说到他们有可能在 San Francisco 举行婚礼，男士说 "I remember Adam's parents live there, don't they?"，由此可知女士选择 San Francisco 是由于她的公公、婆婆住在那里，故选 C。

Conversation 10

24. **C.** 细节题。在对话中女士问男士 "How do I get to your house from the station?"，男士回答 "Well, call me when you get to the station and I'll pick you up there."，这就是答案所在，男士将来接女士，故选 C。

25. **B.** 细节题。问题涉及时间，根据对话 "What time do you plan to arrive at the station?" "I plan to get there around 7:30 p.m."，很容易听到答案，故选 B。

Conversation 11

26. **A** 地点推断题。根据对话中的可以听到的关键词 breakfast, served in your room, menu 可以推断出场景是在宾馆饭店的房间，服务员在问房客如何吃早餐和吃什么。故选 A。

27. **C** 细节题。从对话一开始房客就问服务员 "Can I have breakfast in my room?"，所以可以知道他想在房间用早餐。故选 C。

28. **D** 细节题。在对话中服务员问房客 "And at what time would you like it?"，他回答道 "About half past eight, I think."，所以很容易得到答案 8:30。故选 D。

Conversation 12

29. **D** 推断题。从对话中可以听到 from England, to pick you up, a good flight, luggage, 从这些关键词中可以推断出对话场景发生在机场。故选 D。

30. **C** 因果关系题。在对话中 Terry Wang 告诉 Mr. Smith "Mark is much occupied this morning, so he asked me to pick you up.", 所以可知 Mark 没有来是因为他今天早上很忙。故选 C。

Conversation 13

31. **C** 细节题。在对话中男士告诉女士 I've got two tickets for a football match this afternoon, 问题的答案在对话的开头第一句，听时很容易捕捉到 football match。故选 C。

32. **B** 细节题。在对话的第一句出现了关键词 tickets, for, this afternoon, 答案很明显就是 this afternoon。故选 B。

33. **D** 因果关系题。虽然这个对话很长，但是所问问题的答案在前面几句话里就能找到。第一句中男士问女士 "Why don't you come?", 女士回答 "Uh, no, thanks. I'm not interested in it." 则是她犹豫不决的原因，故选 D。

Conversation 14

34. **C** 地点推断题。问题的关键是 "where…live", 在对话中有女士所说的关键词句 "Welcome to the mountain!", 男士问 "How long have you been in this place?", 主人欢迎客人用 welcome, 而男士的问题更是加大了这种可能性，那就是女士住在山里。故选 C。

35. **B** 因果关系题。在对话中当男士问女士 "How long have you been in this place?", 女士不仅回答了男士的问题，而且还说 "I like the beautiful lake here most.", 这就是她住在这里的原因。故选 B。

Conversation 15

36. **C** 细节题。此题的关键在最后的协商结果中，男士说 "Great idea! It'll be just like old times", 由此可以知道他赞成女士的提议 "Don't you think it might be a good idea to spend this weekend there?", 所以他们最终是要按照女士的提议做。故选 C。

37. **D** 细节题。问题说的是他们要去度周末的那一天，而在对话中跟问题本身相衔接的是 our 15th wedding anniversary, 故选 D。

Conversation 16

38. **D** 计算题。在对话中可以听到 "22" 和 "26" 这样的数字，女士对儿子说 She is coming by car on the 22nd and staying here until 26th, 从这句话中我们可以计算出 Aunt Alice 从 22 号呆到 26 号。故选 D。

39. **C** 细节题。从妈妈的回答 "Cynthia is 15. Fay is older, she is 17." 中可知，故选 C。

40. **A** 该题为细节题。问题涉及时间 immediately, 儿子对妈妈说 "Prepare the list, mother. I can go shopping."。故选 A。

Conversation 17

41. **B** 地点推断题。关键在于在这个场景里发生了什么事，对话中的女士说 I bought this walkman here yesterday, 从这一句话可以推断事情发生在商店。故选 B。

42. **C**　细节题。通过听整段对话，可以知道男士在教女士如何使用 walkman，而女士在说明来意时说 but I don't know how to use it，经过信息筛选可以得到答案，故选 C。

Conversation 18

43. **D**　细节题。男士一开始便提出该问题，女士回答 I worked first as a teacher in a primary school，可以知道她的第一份工作是做教师，故选 D。

44. **D**　细节题。从对话可以知道 Sandy 的第二份工作是在一家公司的销售部门，故选 D。

45. **B**　计算题。开始 Sandy 说做小学老师的时间是："That lasted for two years. Then I was promoted to deputy schoolmaster."，做了"Oh, about a year"，在这期间 Sandy 一直呆在 primary school，故选 B。

Conversation 19

46. **D**　细节题。会话中男士说到 The alarm button doesn't work，由此可知闹钟的具体问题是出在按钮上，故正确答案为 D。

47. **C**．因果关系题。男士在会话中说到 we can't replace your clock without the receipt，由此可知闹钟不能换的原因是男士没带收据，故答案为 C。

Conversation 20

48. **D**　细节题。在对话中第一句话就有了 I'm thinking of buying a gift for my mother，故选 D。

49. **D**　细节题。会话中女士建议男士买些诸如手帕、桌布、衬衣等丝织品，男士说"That's a good idea! Where can I buy them?"，说明他会去买上面提到的东西，但是具体是什么，会话中还不得而知，但是丝织品是肯定的，故选 D。

50. **B**　细节题。男士问的是价格是否很贵，对话中女士说 the prices are very reasonable，在四个选项中只有 fair 跟 reasonable 意思相近。故选 B。

3　听力短文的解题思路及技巧

　　短文部分的听力主要考查考生从一大段信息中抓取关键信息的能力。短文涉及面较广，包括文化教育、风土人情、历史地理、新闻报道、医学科技、人物传记等。

　　短文听力测试满分为 5 分。要求考生在大概 3 分钟的时间里听完一篇文章，并且要听懂大意，记住并理解具体细节，然后在 15 秒钟内针对所提问题，写出正确答案。考生要取得较好的成绩，不仅要具有较高的听力能力，还须掌握一些听力技巧。

短文理解的解题思路

● **了解并熟悉提问方式**

本部分试题所提问题主要有以下两种类型：

主题

What is the main idea of the passage?

What does the passage mainly talk about?

Which of the following is the best title of the passage?

Which of the following statements best expresses the main idea?

What does the passage mainly suggest?

细节

Which of the following statements is (not) true?

Which of the following is (not) mentioned in the passage?

According to the passage what / who / when / which / why / how did / was / would…?

What can you (not) infer from the passage?

● **读问题，重分析**

听音前通过读问题预测短文的主题，并通过分析问题确定关键信息点。

● **听重点，重理解**

在听音过程中，集中精力听清楚含有关键词或短语的信息，并注意理解，联系上下文及问题来确定答案。

短文理解的解题技巧

这部分特别要注意答题的顺序，遵循"读—听—答"的顺序是制胜的关键。

● **听前**

阅读问题，预测短文主题和分析关键信息

利用播放 Directions 的时间，快速阅读所给出的五个问题，抓住问题或下面不完整的回答中所暗示的关键词或短语，预测短文的主题，通过分析问题确定关键信息点。例如：

（**2007 年 6 月真题**）

1. What does your doctor usually advise you to do when you're quite sick?

   To ＿＿＿＿＿＿ .

2. What does the speaker think of following a doctor's advice?

   Following a doctor's advice is not always ＿＿＿＿＿＿ .

3. What will keep a sick man working when he should have gone to bed?

   The stress of his ＿＿＿＿＿＿ .

4. What will happen to the person who doesn't take medicines properly?

   The medicines will do the person ＿＿＿＿＿＿ .

5. How should a person rest during an illness?

   He should rest both his body and ＿＿＿＿＿＿ .

预测短文主题

[解析] 根据五个问题和回答中反复出现的 doctor, advice, sick, medicines, illness 等词，我们可以预测，将要听到的短文主要讲一个人生病后医生通常会建议怎么做，病人对此建议的看法，药物服用不当会产生什么后果，以及一个人生病时应该如何修养。预测出这些信息后，我们在听音时就会有所准备，不会紧张。

关键信息分析

[解析] 根据第1题的提问和回答，我们知道这道题的关键信息是 doctor usually advise you to do，因此听音的重点是含 doctor's advice 的句子；第2题的关键信息是 what does the speaker think 和 following a doctor's advice，因此我们在听到1题中提到的 doctor's advice 后，要特别注意 speaker 对此建议的看法；第3题的关键词是 stress，要特别注意含 stress 的句子；第4题的关键信息是 not take medicines properly；第5题的关键信息是含 rest 和 during an illness 的句子。判断出这些关键信息有助于我们在听音时集中精力，抓住重要信息。

● 听中

边听边记，抓住关键信息

通过听音前的问题分析，我们已基本可以确定短文的大意和所需要抓取的关键信息。在听音过程中，集中精力听清楚含有关键词或短语的信息，并适当地做一些笔记，记下重要信息，如时间、地点、人物和事件等。本部分录音要播放两遍，因此两遍录音听力的重点也要有所区别。

一听：抓住重点，确定部分答案。第一遍要根据读问题分析出的重点进行辩听，抓取重点词前后的关键信息。这时不要着急填写答案，可以用略写等形式记录下部分答案关键点。

二听：核实答案，攻克部分难点。在听完一遍之后要对听音的结果做个大致的梳理。在第二遍录音播放时核实已经听出的答案确实无误，然后将注意力放在那些难懂的句子和问题上。即便还未彻底理解，也要尽可能记下关键信息的发音。

● 听后

根据所听到的内容，准确答题

听音结束后，根据听音过程中所做的笔记，认真地填入单词，完成答句。对于部分未能答出的试题，要回过头来想想文章的主题，根据主题和已经记录下的关键信息的发音进行推测，填入一个合理的答案，尽可能不要在试卷上留空。另外，填写答案时特别要注意单词的拼写，注意字迹工整，所填答案不得超过三个词，否则可能前功尽弃！

4 听力短文的练习及解析

Section C Short Passages

Directions: *This section is to test your ability to comprehend short passages. you will hear 10 recorded passages. After each passage, you will hear five questions. Both the passages and questions will be read two times. When you hear a question, you should complete the answer to it with a word or a short phrase (**in no more than 3 words**).*

Passage 1

1. What are the applicants going to have in almost every case of job hunting?

   They are going to have _____.

2. How long does an interview usually last?

   It usually lasts for _____ minutes.

3. What is the most important thing the interviewer wants to know about the applicants?

   The most important thing is what _____ the applicants are.

4. Which question will be asked if the applicants once worked somewhere?

   The question will be "Why did you _____?"

5. What should the applicants remember to do when taking an interview?

   To dress formally, talk politely, respond quickly and _____.

Passage 2

6. What is a library?

   A library is a place where _____.

7. What can we get from libraries?

   We can get all kinds of _____.

8. What kinds of books are available?

   There are fiction, nonfiction and _____.

9. What do the students go to the library to do?

   Students go to the libraries to study and to write _____.

10. If one is in a hurry, how can he get the information?

    He can _____.

Passage 3

11. Why was the old man walking in the subway?

    Because he was looking for _____.

12. What did the old man see lying on the seat?

    He saw _____ lying on the seat.

13. What did the old man ask?

    The old man asked whether the seat _____.

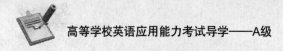

14. What did the old man say when the subway started?

The old man said the owner of the bag must have _____.

15. What did the old man want to do?

He wanted to _____ out of the window.

Passage 4

16. What are people confused about?

People are confused about what type of food is healthy, and what kind of food may

_____.

17. What is important for people?

_____ is important for people.

18. What kind of food can prevent many different diseases?

Doctors believe that _____ can usually prevent many different diseases.

19. What's the result of eating more meat and other high-fat foods?

Meat and other high-fat foods are bad for our health, which may _____.

20. To enjoy many years of healthy life, what should we do?

We should _____ now.

Passage 5

21. What's the difference between life in one country and another?

The difference between life in one country and another is _____.

22. In an English village, what does a person know about his neighbors?

A person knows _____ about his neighbors.

23. How about people in a large city like London?

They often do not know _____ well.

24. How do people in London feel, particularly after work?

People living in London often feel _____.

25. If people walk through the streets in the center of London on a Sunday, what is it like?

It is like _____.

Passage 6

26. In the United States, what question is top secret?

In the United States, _____ is top secret.

27. How do people think about inquiring about one's property?

It is also considered _____ about one's property.

28. What can't you ask when someone shows you something that he has bought?

You can't inquire about the _____.

29. What would people in the United states feel if you ask their age?

They will feel _____ , especially ladies and the old.

30. What should we do before going to the States?

We should get familiar with the American idea of _____ .

Passage 7

31. How many parts are there in the conversation when you talk with a new friend?

Usually there are _____ parts in the conversation.

32. What's the first part?

The first part is _____ .

33. In the second part, what can't you ask your new friend?

You cannot ask about private or _____ .

34. What's the third part of the conversation?

The third part of the conversation is the _____ .

35. In the third part, what can we talk about with a new friend?

We can tell our new friend that we're happy to _____ him or her.

Passage 8

36. What's the most important goal in the advertising industry?

In the advertising industry, _____ is the most important goal.

37. How can the messages go around the world by advertising?

Messages can go around the world _____ .

38. What're the problems of international advertising?

The problems of international advertising are _____ .

39. To avoid problems in translation, what must we consider about?

We must also consider differences in _____ .

40. What does an advertisement mean if the product is not suitable for the market?

It means _____ even it is the best advertisement.

Passage 9

41. What kind of product is the salesman promoting?

_____ .

42. What is the most outstanding feature of the new device?

It is _____ .

43. Why is the new product called Easy-Click?

Because it is very _____ .

44. What do we know about the size of the new model?

It is _____ .

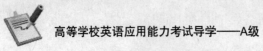

45. Where are the products available?

　　_____ .

Passage 10

46. When was the White House completed?

　　The White House was completed in _____ .

47. Who was James Hoopen?

　　James Hoopoen was _____ of the building.

48. What happened to the building during the War of 1812?

　　The building _____ .

49. Why were the walls painted white?

　　The walls were painted white to cover _____ .

50. Who was the first president of the White House?

　　_____ was the first president of the White House.

答案及解析

Passage 1

1. **an interview**　　问的是求职者在找工作时都要做什么。在文章的开头第一句 Almost in every case of job hunting, you are going to have an interview，可知是 an interview。

2. **15 to 30**　　由问题和答案的其他部分可知这里需要填入表示时间的数词。文中提到 An interview usually lasts for 15 to 30 minutes，故答案为 15 to 30。

3. **kind of person**　　问面试者最想了解应聘者的哪个方面，根据听力的具体内容我们可以知道面试考官希望了解应聘者的学历、知识、经验以及表达能力，然后提到 the most important of all, what kind of person they are，故答案为 kind of person。

4. **quit your job**　　问如果应聘者曾在别处工作过，会被问到什么问题，原文中有：If you once worked somewhere, they would asked, "Why did you quit your job?"，故答案为 quit your job。

5. **think wisely**　　根据文中 When taking an interview, remember to dress formally, talk politely, respond quickly and think wisely, 可以填入答案。

Passage 2

6. **books are stored**　　问什么是图书馆。在原文中开头第一个句子就是图书馆的定义，A library is more than just a place where books are stored, 由此可知答案。

7. **information**　　问我们能从图书馆获得什么。文章中第二个句子说到 A library is a source of information，故答案为 information。

8. **reference books** 由问题和答案的其他部分可知这里需要填入和 fiction, nonfiction 同样的名词。原文中提到了 That information may come from books such as fiction, nonfiction, or reference books, 故答案是 reference books。

9. **research papers** 问学生通常去图书馆做什么。原文中提到了 Students go to library to study and to write research papers。故可得出答案。

10. **telephone the librarian** 问如果一个人很忙，他怎样获得信息。在原文的最后一句 People who need information in a hurry can telephone the reference room at many libraries 中可得到答案。

Passage 3

11. **an empty seat** 由问题和答案的其他部分可知这里需要填入名词词组。根据 "An old man was walking in the subway, looking for an empty seat." 可得出答案。

12. **a small handbag** 由问题和答案的其他部分可知这里需要填入名词词组。老人突然看见一个空座，A small bag was lying on the seat，故得出答案。

13. **was empty** 由问题和答案的其他部分可知这里需要填入从句中的谓语部分。根据 "Is this seat empty?" asked the old man. 可得出答案。

14. **missed the subway** 由问题和答案的其他部分可知这里需要填入动词词组。地铁开车后，老人说道，He has missed the subway, 据此可写出答案。

15. **throw the bag** 由问题和答案的其他部分可知这里需要填入动词词组。说完这些话后，he took the bag and was about to throw it out of the window，据此写出答案。

Passage 4

16. **hurt their health** 由文章开头第一句话 Sometimes people are confused about what type of food is healthy, and what kind of food may hurt their health, 可知人们经常感到困惑哪些食物是有益健康的，哪些食物有可能伤害到健康，所以此处应该填 hurt their health。

17. **A healthy diet** 根据第二段第一句话 A healthy diet is important for people，可得出答案。

18. **fruit and vegetables** 原文中第二段直接提到了 doctors believe that fruits and vegetables can usually prevent many different diseases, 医生认为蔬菜和水果能防止许多疾病。

19. **lead to obesity** 原文中提到了 meat and other high-fat foods are bad for our health, which may lead to obesity, 可以知道吃太多肉和高脂肪食物的后果就是导致肥胖。

20. **improve our diet**　根据文章最后一段倒数第二句话 To enjoy many years of healthy life, we should improve our diet now, 可以知道，为了享受许多年的健康生活，从现在起我们就应该改善我们的饮食习惯，所以此处应该填 improve our diet。

Passage 5

21. **not great**　文章第一段第一句话就提到了 The difference between life in one country and another is quite often not so great as…, 所以此处应该填 not great。

22. **almost everything**　根据文章中的句子 In an English village, everybody knows everybody else; 可以知道在英国的乡村里，一个人对于邻居的情况是了如指掌，所以此处应该填 almost everything。

23. **each other**　在介绍了乡村的情况后，作者又对比了大城市如伦敦 "In a large city like London…people often do not know each other well"，人们通常互相都不认识，所以此处应该填 each other。

24. **very lonely**　原文中直接提到了 People living in London are often very lonely, particularly after work, 生活在伦敦的人通常会感到孤独，尤其是在下班后。

25. **an empty town**　在倒数第二句话提到了 If you walk through the streets in the center of London on a Sunday, it is almost like an empty town, 周日如果你穿过伦敦市中心的街道，整个城市就像一座空城，所以此处应该填 an empty town。

Passage 6

26. **one's income**　第一段就介绍了在美国有一些问题是不能问的，然后第二段接着说 In the United States, one's income is top secret, 一个人的收入是绝顶机密，故此处填 one's income。

27. **impolite to inquire**　原文中第三段第一句话提到了 It is also considered impolite to inquire about one's property, 在美国询问别人的财产被认为是不礼貌的，所以可得出答案。

28. **price**　原文中第三段提到了当一个美国朋友给你看一些他刚买的东西时，你可以说些赞扬的话，but don't inquire about the price, 但是不能询问价格，所以此处应该填 price。

29. **unhappy**　原文中第四段提到了在美国，不能问别人的年龄，If you do, they will feel unhappy, especially ladies and old. 故此处应该填 unhappy。

30. **personal privacy**　文章最后一段提到了 It is, therefore, advisable to get familiar with the American idea of personal privacy before going to the States, 去美国之前最好先了解一下美国人关于个人隐私的观念，所以此处应该填 personal privacy。

Passage 7

31. **three**　　从文中第一句话 When you talk with a new friend, usually there are three parts in the conversation 可以知道，当你和新朋友交谈时，一般谈话应包括三个部分。

32. **greeting**　　原文中直接提到了 The first part is greeting，可知谈话的第一部分为问候。

33. **unpleasant things**　　文中提到了谈话的第二部分为谈话本身，这部分可以谈论一些不重要的事情，比如天气、运动、娱乐等等，然后接着说 But it's not the time for you to ask about private or unpleasant things，所以不应谈论私人或不愉快的事，此处应该填 unpleasant things。

34. **leave-taking**　　文中直接提到了 The third part of the conversation is the leave-taking part，可知第三部分为告别。

35. **have met**　　文章最后一句话提到了 In this part, you tell your new friend that you're happy to have met him or her and then the conversation comes to an end，所以此处应该填 have met。

Passage 8

36. **selling products**　　由文章第一段最后一句话 selling products is the most important goal 可知销售产品是广告最重要的目标。

37. **at high speed**　　原文中第二段第一句话就说到了，通过广告，信息能高速传到世界各地，所以此处应该填 at high speed。

38. **language and culture**　　原文中直接提到了 the problems of international advertising—problems of language and culture，国际广告最大的问题是语言和文化的问题，故此处应该填 language and culture。

39. **laws and customs**　　文中提到了为了避免翻译的问题，国际广告必须针对不同的国家选择不同的广告方式。然后又说 Besides, they must also consider differences in laws and customs，还应考虑法律和习俗的差异。

40. **nothing**　　原文中倒数第二句话提到了 The best advertisement in the world means nothing if the product is not suitable for the market，如果产品不适应市场，那么世界上推销得再好的产品也毫无意义，故此处应该填 nothing。

Passage 9

41. **wireless mouse**　　由原文中第一段最后一句话 our newly-developed wireless mouse 可知这篇广告推销的是一种无线鼠标，所以答案为 wireless mouse。

42. **wireless**　　该题提问的是这种新装置最突出的优点是什么，从原文中的句子 What makes this new product special is it is wireless 可知这个鼠标最大的特别之处就在于它是无线鼠标。

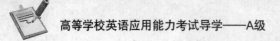

43. **easy to use**	由原文中句子 You will find this new model extremely easy to use, and that's why it's called the Easy-Click 可以知道，因为这种鼠标使用起来非常方便，所以被称为 Easy-Click，所以此处应该填 easy to use。
44. **small**	根据文中第三段的句子 though it is small itself 可知这种鼠标本身是很小巧的，所以此处应该填 small。
45. **the chain stores**	该题问的是在哪儿可以买到这种产品，根据最后一句话 Buy one now at our chain stores and click easy，可以知道，顾客可以在连锁店买到这种新型的无线鼠标，所以此处填 the chain stores。

Passage 10

46. **1799**	根据文中的第二句话 it was completed in 1799，可以知道白宫是 1799 年完成的。
47. **the designer**	由原文 James Hoopen, an architect, designed the building，可知 James Hoopen 是个建筑师，他设计了白宫，联系问题及给出的部分答案，此处应该填 the designer。
48. **was burnt**	从文中的句子 during the War of 1812, the English burnt the building 中可知，在 1812 年战争中，英国人放火烧了这幢建筑，所以此处应该填 was burnt。
49. **the smoke stains**	文中提到了白宫重建后，The gray stone walls were painted white to cover the smoke stains，据此得出答案。
50. **John Adams**	原文中直接提到了 The first president living in the White House was John Adams in 1800，由此可知白宫的第一个主人是 John Adams，所以此处应该填 John Adams。

Part II   Structure

　　语法题主要测试考生运用和掌握语法结构、词法和词性（词形变化）的能力以及对书面语的理解和运用能力。测试范围限于《基本要求》中的"词汇表"和"语法结构表"所规定的全部内容。常见的语法题型主要测试动词的时态和语态、介词、连词、限定词、形容词和副词的比较级和最高级、虚拟语气、非谓语动词、复合句、倒装句和强调结构、主谓一致等。

① 语法结构题的解题思路及技巧

　　本部分包括 Section A 和 Section B 两部分。

　　Section A 部分一般是 10 个选择填空，本部分的解题原则：首先是从语法角度来考虑，"语法第一，语义第二"。从题型结构看，常见的题型主要有辨认题、近义词辨析题、语境理解题和固定搭配题。

　　Section B 部分有时是 10 个单句填空题，考点为语法结构和词性变化两种类型，要求考生根据句意选出最佳答案，填入空白处。词汇命题范围为《基本要求》中 3,400 个左右的单词以及由这些词构成的常用词组来测试考生词性转换和语法结构的能力。词性变化主要包括动词、名词、形容词和副词四大类实词之间的转化，主要考查学生对词汇和构词法的掌握程度及常用的前、后缀；语法测试的范围主要是：动词的时态和语态、非谓语动词、形容词和副词的比较级、虚拟语气、主谓一致等。依据是《基本要求》的语法结构表。

Section A 的解题思路

● 辨认题

1) 在正确理解题干内容的基础上，首先应确定词性即名词、动词、副词、形容词或其他；

2) 排除词性与题干结构不相符的选项；将剩下的选项放入题干进行检查，并最后确定选项；

3) 检查所确定的选项在意思、内容和语法结构等方面有无不妥之处。

● 近义词辨析题

1) 认真理解题干的内容和含义；2) 根据题干提供的信息，选择最佳答案；3) 还应根据词性进行比较。

● 语境理解题

　　从题干中寻找解题的语境线索，并注意其逻辑与搭配关系。

● 固定搭配题

1) 读懂题干，寻找搭配线索；2) 考虑是否是固定用法；3) 考虑语境线索；4) 核查题干内容与搭配项在逻辑上有无不妥之处。

Section A 的解题技巧

● 同义词、近义词辨析

　　应认真理解题干的内容和含义，确定所需填的词并从意思与用法两方面进行对比，选择正确答案。例如：

1. Every hour on the hour the CCTV _____ the latest news.

　　A. announced　　　　B. broadcast　　　　C. reported　　　　　　D. published

　　[解析] 答案为 B。announce: 宣布；broadcast: 播出；report: 报告；publish: 出版。根据题干的内容正确答案为 B，句意是："每小时的正点中国中央电视台都播出最新报道。"

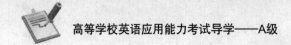

2. There are some more topics to discuss, _____ the problem of pollution.

A. generally   B. especially   C. exactly   D. probably

[解析] 答案为 B。generally: 一般地，通常地，普遍地；especially: 特别，尤其；exactly: 确切地，精确地；probably: 很可能，大概。根据词义 B 为正确选项。句意是："还有另外的几个主题要讨论，特别是污染问题。"

● 语境理解题

应把握"语义线"、"语法结构线"和"逻辑线"的关系，根据题意选出符合上下文关系的词或短语。例如：

1. _____ we have all the materials ready, we should begin the new task at once.

A. Since that   B. By now   C. Since now   D. Now that

[解析] 答案为 D。从前后两句的逻辑关系看，前半句是原因状语从句，所以应选相应的连词。since 可作连词，但不和 now, that 搭配；而 by now 是介词短语，不合语义。句意是"既然我们把所有的材料准备好了，就应该立即开始执行这项新任务。"

2. You sang well last night. We hope you'll sing _____ .

A. more better   B. nicely   C. still better   D. best

[解析] 答案为 C。从第二句看，more better 结构不成立，应改为 much better；而其他选项均可搭配，但不符合题意。第一句意为"唱得好"，第二句"希望唱得更好"才符合逻辑。

● 固定搭配题

首先读懂题干，分清固定结构、短语或惯用法，根据题意进行选择。例如：

1. They said they had been _____ from China for several decades and did not understand the Chinese people and their way of life.

A. cut out   B. cut down   C. cut away   D. cut off

[解析] 答案为 D。cut out: 割去，删去；cut down: 砍倒，削减；cut away: 切下，逃走；cut off: 切断，阻断。cut off 符合句意。

2. I don't mind _____ the decision as long as it is not too late.

A. you to delay making   B. your delaying to make

C. your delaying making   D. your delay to make

[解析] 答案为 C。mind 和 delay 后都常接名词或动名词，mind 在句中的意思是"介意，反对"，相当于 feel annoyed or upset about。本句话的意思："只要不拖得太晚，我就不反对你们延迟做出决定。"

● **排除法**

根据题干与句意，注意时态、语态和语气之间的关系，逐个排除，最终确定正确选项。例如：

1. This kind of glasses _____ comfortably.

    A. is worn   B. wears   C. wearing   D. are worn

    [解析] 答案为 B。先排除 C，wearing 不能作谓语，A 和 D 为被动语态用法，不能选择，只有 C 是正确答案。

2. While people may prefer television for knowing about the news, it is unlikely that television _____ the newspaper completely.

    A. replaced   B. have replaced

    C. replace   D. will replace

    [解析] 答案为 D。本句的意思是："虽然人们可能喜欢靠电视获得最新消息，但电视完全取代报纸是极不可能的。"此句是对将来情况的预测，故用一般将来时，而不能用过去时、现在完成时和一般现在时，故 A、B 和 C 均应排除。

3. It is suggested that everyone _____ a five-minute talk at the party.

    A. give   B. gave   C. will give   D. have given

    [解析] 答案为 A。由 It is suggested that 引出的主语从句，其谓语要用虚拟语气，用"(should) + 动词原形"表示。故应排除 B、C、D 选项。

Section B 的解题思路

1. 熟悉语法、词法的基础知识，并能够准确理解和灵活运用。
2. 认真分辨词汇的词性，避免因词性判断失当影响结果。
3. 熟练掌握英语中某些固定的习惯用法。尤其是注意固定搭配中的介词和副词，通过对介词和副词用法的掌握来达到正确应用的目的。
4. 分析备选词，确定选项。

    总之应遵循字不离词，词不离句的基本原则。对整个句子的意思或需要表达的意图进行分析，准确地把握该词在句中的含义，就能作出正确选择。

Section B 的解题技巧

● **构词**

    按照构词法分清单词的词根、前缀、后缀和派生词。如：由 able(形容词) 可以派生出 enable, disable, ability, disability, disablement, disabled 等。例如：

1. It's very (thought) _____ of you to offer me a job in your company.

    [解析] 答案为 thoughtful。本题考核词形转换，要求根据句意得出 thought 的形容词形式 thoughtful。本句意为：您在您的公司里给我安排了一份工作，考虑得真是周到。

2. Your behavior shows that you are a well (education) _____ person.

[解析] 答案为 educated。本题测试过去分词的用法，应填入 educated，过去分词在句中作定语。本句意为：你的行为表明你是一个受过良好教育的人。

● 同义词、近义词

英语中往往同一个意思可以有多个意义相近或意义相同的词和多种相近的表达方式。如：pastime 的近义词有 amusement, diversion, entertainment, hobby, pleasure, recreation and sport 等。例如：

1. I felt (thank) _____ to my girlfriend for having supper together with me.

[解析] 答案为 thankful。根据题意，空格处应填写形容词，因此应把动词 thank 变为形容词 thankful。本句意为：我非常欣慰我的女朋友和我共进晚餐。

2. Her parents felt (pleasure) _____ when their daughter made big progress in her final exam.

[解析] 答案为 pleased。空格处需填入形容词作主语补足语。本句意为：女儿期末取得好成绩时，她父母非常开心。

● 联想记忆法

将记忆、理解新词与巩固、复习旧词有效地结合起来。例如：由 wind（风）可以联想到 breeze（微风），gale（强风），gust（阵风），typhoon（台风），cyclone（旋风），tornado（龙卷风）和 hurricane（飓风）等。

● 结构

考生不仅要理解题意，更要有针对性地对语法结构、句式特点进行必要的分析思考。例如：

1. If you don't take measures at once, things will go (bad) _____ .

[解析] 答案为 worse，本题测试形容词比较级，空格处 bad 应用比较级 worse。本句意为：如果你不马上采取措施，事情会越变越糟。

2. It is necessary that he (be) _____ called back immediately.

[解析] 答案为 (should) be，在 it is necessary (important/suggested) that 这类句型中，主语从句的谓语用 should＋动词原型，should 可省略。本句意为：他有必要马上回电话。

② 语法结构题的练习及解析

Section A

Directions: *In this section, there are 50 incomplete sentences. You are required to complete each one by deciding on the most appropriate word or words from the 4 choices marked A, B, C and D given below.*

1. If we had had a map with us, we _____ the person who lost his way.
   - A. hadn't found
   - B. hadn't been found
   - C. would found
   - D. would have found

2. I don't care _____ she is beautiful. I care _____ she is honest or not.
   - A. if...if
   - B. whether...whether
   - C. if...whether
   - D. whether...if

3. When Lily asked me whether I had been to China, I told her, "_____ enough money, I would have visited China."
   - A. Have I
   - B. I have
   - C. Had I had
   - D. I had

4. So important _____ which Edison had given us that we could not live without them.
   - A. the electrical inventions were
   - B. the electrical inventions was
   - C. was the electrical inventions
   - D. were the electrical inventions

5. He reached the station _____ only _____ that the train had just left.
   - A. exhausting, learning
   - B. exhausted, to learn
   - C. exhausted, learning
   - D. exhausting, to learn

6. It was impossible to avoid _____ by the stormy weather.
   - A. being much affected
   - B. having much affected
   - C. to be much affected
   - D. to have been much affected

7. Most of the people in the group felt rather disappointed at their traveling abroad. They said it _____ better organized.
   - A. might have been
   - B. must have been
   - C. had to be
   - D. ought to be

8. "I'm in a hurry, but where is my dictionary? I remember _____ it in your drawer."
   "Don't ask me. Remember _____ your things in my drawer anymore."
   - A. putting...not putting
   - B. putting...not to put
   - C. putting...not put
   - D. to put...not putting

9. _____ , all your problems will be solved if you use the computer.
   - A. How difficult is not a matter of
   - B. The matter is difficult if no
   - C. It does not matter if the difficulty
   - D. No matter how difficult

10. Mr. Black _____ we have a sincere respect, is quite outstanding in the field of natural science.
    - A. of whom
    - B. for whom
    - C. on whom
    - D. for that

11. Not one of us has a clear idea _____ to do.
    - A. what the others want
    - B. that the others want
    - C. which do the others want
    - D. what do the others want

12. _____ , he managed to find time to go to see a doctor.
    - A. As he is
    - B. As he was busy
    - C. Busy as he was
    - D. Busy as he is

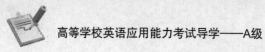

13. He has very poor life habit, and he also said he was used to going to bed late, _____ ?

    A. didn't he   B. did he   C. wasn't he   D. was he

14. Research _____ all over the world into the possible cause of cancer in the past few years.

    A. was made   B. had been made

    C. has been making   D. has been made

15. When we reached the port, we knew the ship hadn't arrived yet. We _____ .

    A. needn't have hurried   B. needed not to hurry

    C. had not needed to hurry   D. didn't need to hurry

16. After I took the Japanese culture course, I knew that the culture and customs of Japan are a little bit like _____ of China.

    A. what   B. that   C. ones   D. those

17. I heard Mrs. Brown had a heart attack, I wonder how she has been _____ in hospital.

    A. getting off   B. getting across

    C. getting on   D. getting through

18. After a long time's hard work, I will have a _____ vacation to go to Beijing.

    A. two weeks   B. two-weeks'   C. two-week   D. two-week's

19. When you _____ , I know for certain that you will feel much better.

    A. are waking up   B. have been waking up

    C. wake up   D. have woken

20. He suggested that everyone of us _____ at the meeting.

    A. shall present   B. present   C. be present   D. presented

21. The little boy _____ the road when he was hit by a bus.

    A. was just crossed   B. was just crossing

    C. just cross   D. had just crossed

22. —I saw Mary in the hospital yesterday.

    —You _____ her, she is away from Beijing.

    A. must not see   B. can't have seen

    C. mustn't have seen   D. couldn't see

23. On seeing the skirt, I will pay $40 for it; it's worth _____ .

    A. all that much   B. that much all   C. that all much   D. much all that

24. According to the map, I know this street is three times as _____ as that one.

    A. long   B. longer   C. longest   D. the longest

25. The little boy is only 5 years old. He needs _____ .

    A. being looked after   B. looked after

    C. looking after   D. to look after

26. The elephant ought _____ hours ago by the keepers.

    A. to be fed   B. to feed   C. to being fed   D. to have been fed

27. When we lose confidence on our study, our teachers often persuade us that the harder you study, _____ knowledge you will get.

　　A. the harder　　　　B. harder　　　　C. more　　　　D. the more

28. He spends all his spare time collecting stamps. He says that by the end of the next year, he _____ 3000 pieces.

　　A. will have collected　　　　　　B. is going to collect

　　C. will be collecting　　　　　　D. is about to collect

29. Although an old lady of 70, her grandma is still fond of reading _____ .

　　A. stories of childrens　　　　　　B. children stories

　　C. childrens' stories　　　　　　D. children's stories

30. The Olympic Games, _____ in 776 B.C., did not include women players until 1912.

　　A. first playing　　　　　　　　B. to be first played

　　C. first played　　　　　　　　D. to be first playing

31. Mary often attempts to escape being fined whenever she _____ traffic regulations.

　　A. having been broken　　　　　　B. was breading

　　C. has been broken　　　　　　D. breaks

32. It's high time we _____ something to stop road accidents.

　　A. did　　　　B. are doing　　　　C. will do　　　　D. do

33. We are happy everything will go smoothly as _____ .

　　A. to be planned　　　　　　　B. planned

　　C. being planned　　　　　　　D. having planned

34. We had to wait for a long time to buy these CDs, _____ ?

　　A. had we　　　　B. hadn't we　　　　C. don't we　　　　D. didn't we

35. _____ to miss the plan, he got to the airport an hour earlier.

　　A. Not to want　　　　B. To want　　　　C. Not wanting　　　　D. Wanting

36. We think it possible _____ their production plan in a few weeks.

　　A. for them to fulfilling　　　　　　B. for their fulfilling

　　C. for them to fulfil　　　　　　D. for them fulfill

37. _____ from the top of the hill, the city looks even larger and more beautiful.

　　A. Seeing　　　　B. See　　　　C. To see　　　　D. Seen

38. They _____ their work ahead of time without our help.

　　A. haven't completed　　　　　　B. wouldn't have completed

　　C. weren't completing　　　　　　D. shall have completed

39. Only when he had handed in his writing paper, _____ he had made several grammatical mistakes.

　　A. would he realize　　　　　　B. he realized

　　C. has he realized　　　　　　D. did he realize

40. Whether it is a good solution depends on _____ .
    A. how you look at it   B. what you look at it
    C. you look at it   D. that you look at it

41. Can you imagine the ugly _____ famous as an actor?
    A. boy becoming   B. boy become
    C. boy to become   D. boy's becoming

42. She told us the reason _____ she didn't pass exam, _____ made everybody laugh.
    A. why…that   B. why…which
    C. why…what   D. which…that

43. Hardly _____ when a loud explosion was heard.
    A. the train had started   B. the train had been started
    C. had the train started   D. did the train start

44. We were friends, _____ I mean that he was easy with me and I liked him and was easy with him.
    A. by which   B. by whom   C. with which   D. with whom

45. _____ room is very nice, but the room is very dirty.
    A. Mary's and Lily's   B. Mary and Lily's
    C. Mary's and Lily   D. Mary and Lilys'

46. Open a magazine or turn on the television, you _____ a lots of current information.
    A. are often getting   B. often get
    C. will often get   D. have often seen

47. It's absolutely necessary that the problem _____ in some way or other.
    A. is settled   B. has been settled
    C. was settled   D. be settled

48. The number of the trucks produced in our factory this year _____ in yours.
    A. is more than that   B. are more that those
    C. is larger than that   D. are larger than those

49. In order to put everything in order, Mary put away her _____ in the upstairs room.
    A. summer's clothes   B. summer clothes
    C. summers' clothes   D. summer cloth

50. Having been delayed by heavy snow, _____ .
    A. they arrived late
    B. it is impossible for them to arrive on time
    C. it led to them being late
    D. their friends thought that they would be late

答案与解析

1. **D** 虚拟语气。由 if 从句的时态可知，这是一个表示与过去事实相反的虚拟语气。

2. **C** 宾语从句。if 与 whether 引导的宾语从句时，若宾语从句是肯定句，if 和 whether 可互换；若宾语从句是否定句就只能用 if 而不能用 whether 引导。

3. **C** 虚拟语气。这是一个省略 if 的表示与过去事实相反的虚拟条件句，需用倒装结构。

4. **D** 倒装句。so 开头的句子谓语部分要倒装，而且主语 inventions 是复数形式，所以用 were。

5. **B** 分词与不定式。exhausted 作主语补足语，表示主语状态，意为"感到筋疲力尽的"，而 exhausting 的意思是"令人筋疲力尽的"。only to do 表示"结果却……"。

6. **A** 动名词。avoid 后面必须接动名词，根据题意要用被动语态。

7. **A** 情态动词。might have + 过去分词，表示"可以做而实际未做"，有责备的意味，用于肯定句中。

8. **B** 动名词与不定式。动词不定式表示还没有发生的动作，动名词表示已发生了的动作。

9. **D** 状语从句。no matter 引导让步状语从句，how difficult 后面省去了主语 they 和系动词 are，因为该主语和主句中主语 all your problems 相同。

10. **B** 定语从句。have respect for sb. 意为"对……表示尊敬"，句中 For whom we have a sincere respect 是定语从句，作 Mr. Black 的定语。

11. **A** 宾语从句。此句是由 what 引导的从句。what 在从句中作宾语。

12. **C** 让步状语从句。在由 as 引导的让步状语从句中，必须把主语的补语或状语等放在从句的句首。

13. **A** 反意疑问句。在反意疑问句中，凡带有宾语从句、定语从句的主从复合句，都应根据主句的谓语动词来决定其反意疑问部分的形式。

14. **D** 被动语态。从时间状语 in the past years 判断，该句应该用现在完成时态；research 作主语，其谓语应用被动式。

15. **A** 情态动词。"needn't + have + done"表示本来不必做某事而实际已经做了；"didn't need to do"表示不需要做某事。

16. **D** 代词。在替代时，one/ones 只代可数名词，可指人或物，可带前置定语；而 that/those 既能代不可数名词，也可代可数名词，定语要后置，另外，that 指物，those 指人、物均可。

17. **C** 介词短语。How Mrs. Brown has been getting on 即布朗太太的情况如何。get off 意为"从……下来"；get across 意为"使通过"；get through 意为"通过"。

18. **C** 数词。数词与名词之间有连字符时，名词用单数，另外这里表示的是多长时间的假期，并不需用所有格。

19. **C** 时态。在时间从句中可用一般现在时表示将来。

20. **C** 虚拟语气。在表示命令、建议、要求等动词如：suggest, ask, require, demand, order, command, persist, insist 引导的宾语从句要用虚拟语气，要用"should + 动词原形"，should 可以省略。

21. **B** 时态。用过去进行时表示过去某个时间正在进行的动作。

22. **B** 情态动词。must + have + 过去分词，意思是"想必，一定……"。表示对过去已发生的事情进行肯定推测判断，其否定句应用 can't/couldn't have done，而不能用 mustn't。

23. **A** 限定词。代词、冠词等通称限定词，从排列顺序上看，分前位、中位及后位。前位限定词有 all, both, half, twice 等；中位限定词有 a/an, the, this, that, these 等；后位限定词有 one, last, next, another, such, many 等。

24. **A** 比较级结构。这是一个表示倍数的结构：倍数 + as + 原级形容词 + as + 被比较对象。

25. **C** 动名词。英语中有些动词后接动名词的主动形式，表示被动的意思，这些动词有 need, require, deserve 等。这些动词还可以接动词不定式的被动形式，表示的意思相当。

26. **D** 情态动词。这是一个"ought to + have + 过去分词"的结构，表示过去本应该而实际上并未做的事，并含有责备的意思。句中主语是 the elephant，所以要用被动语态。

27. **D** 比较级结构。在比较级的结构中"the more…, the more…"表示"越……就越……"。

28. **A** 时态。用将来完成时表示将来某时间之前将完成的动作。

29. **D** 名词所有格。所有格为名词作定语，常表示材料或特性，或表示一类人或物，所有格作定语也可以表示所有权关系或特性（如本题的 children's stories）。

30. **C** 分词。主语与非谓语动词之间是被动关系，因此应用过去分词，它相当于一个非限制性定语从句 which were first played。

31. **D** 时态。用一般现在时与 often 连用，表示习惯性动作。

32. **A** 虚拟语气。It is (high, about) time that 结构中用虚拟语气，动词形式一般用过去式表示该做某事或早该做某事了，有时用"should + 动词原形"，但 should 不能省略。

33. **B** 分词。非谓语动词与句子的主语 everything 是被动关系。

34. **D** 反意疑问句。当句子的谓语是 have to 时，其附加疑问句的助动词根据时态用 do 或 did。

35. **C** 分词。现在分词表示原因，等于 because he didn't want。

36. **C** 形式宾语。句中的 it 是形式宾语，真正的宾语则是带逻辑主语的不定式结构，其构成形式是"for + 名词 / 代词 + 不定式"。

37. **D** 分词。作状语的分词短语的动词 see 与句子的主语 the city 是被动关系，用过去分词表示条件。

38. **B** 虚拟语气。有时有些句子假设的条件不通过条件从句表达出来，而隐含在某些介词短语里，如 without, but for（要不是），这类句子叫含蓄虚拟条件句，要用含蓄虚拟结构，含蓄虚拟结构为"could / might / would + V 原形 / have + 过去分词"。

39. **D** 倒装句。"only + 副词 / 介词 / 从句"放在句首时句子需用倒装。

40. **A** 宾语从句。how 引导的宾语从句，作介词 on 的宾语，从句主谓顺序不颠倒。

41. **A** 动名词。imagine 后面可以跟动名词或跟带现在分词的复合结构作宾语，一般来说，如果宾语是名词，多用"名词普通格 + 现在分词 / 动名词"，如果宾语是代词，既可以用"代词宾格＋现在分词／动名词"，也可以用"形容词性的物主代词＋现在分词／动名词"。

42. **B** 宾语从句。定语从句的先行词是 reason，其关系副词用 why。which 引导非限制性定语从句。

43. **C** 倒装句。在英语中以否定形式或否定意义的副词开头的句子要求部分倒装，这些副词是 hardly, barely, little, seldom, scarcely, never, not until 等。

44. **A** 定语从句。mean...by...（说……的意思是……），by 后接的 which 就是指 we were friends。

45. **B** 所有格。谓语用了单数，说明两人共用一个房间。两者共用的，只在后面一个名词后用所有格。

46. **C** 时态。从句为表示条件的祈使句，主句谓语应用一般将来时。

47. **D** 虚拟语气。在"It is ＋形容词＋that"的结构中要用虚拟语气，结构为"should ＋动词原形"，should 可以省略。这种结构的形容词包括 important, essential, advisable, surprised 等。本句的从句中的语态为被动语态。

48. **C** 主谓一致。"the number of ＋名词"作主语应按单数处理，number 的大小不能用 more 来表示。

49. **B** 所有格。名词作定语与所有格作定语的区别在于：前者无所属关系而后者表所属关系。

50. **A** 分词短语。having been delayed by heavy snow 是分词短语作状语，根据语法结构判断，分词短语的逻辑主语应该是主句的主语，所以 they arrived late 既符合语法结构的要求又合题意。

Section B

Directions: *There are 50 incomplete statements here. You should fill in each blank with the proper form of the word given in the brackets.*

1. That street corner is a very (desire) _____ place for you to open a new store.

2. The little girl gave an (extreme) _____ wonderful performance at party last night.

3. I think that our head teacher is always very (reason) _____ .

4. Her only (complain) _____ is that she sometimes didn't get enough heat in her apartment.

5. It's very (thought) _____ of you to stop and give me a lift.

6. The (argue) _____ went on for the whole day as neither side would give in.

7. Food and clothing are (universe) _____ human needs.

8. The college student has decided to devote (her) _____ to helping disabled persons.

9. Laid-off staff and workers（下岗职工）should consider looking for some jobs in a (reality) _____ way.

10. We can come to some (arrange) _____ with her about the matter.

11. There's a severe (short) _____ of low-cost housing in the city.

12. The young man is very well (qualify) _____ to teach high school mathematics.

13. We are busy (prepare) _____ for the final examination, so I cannot come to see you.

14. The scientists study carefully and record the (frequent) _____ of earthquakes in this region.

15. With the fast (develop) _____ of compulsory education (义务教育), people should pay special attention to good manners.

16. Besides (commerce) _____ value, collecting stamps also has artistic value.

17. The books and magazines in the bookstore are (classify) _____ by subject.

18. The solider was punished for (obey) _____ orders.

19. He didn't know how to express after listening to the (excite) _____ news.

20. Because of lasting drought this spring, the farmers were (doubt) _____ about the dream of a good harvest.

21. The lecture was so moving that every student listened (attention) _____.

22. Students should (strength) _____ their sense of self-confidence.

23. Mountaineering (登山运动) is agreeable as well as (health) _____ to human beings.

24. We've made up our minds to (buy) _____ the house.

25. She was such a (consider) _____ person, always asking how I'm feeling.

26. The next-door neighbor told her not (practice) _____ her violin near the window.

27. I get the (impress) _____ that she's rather shy.

28. We can take the (numerous) _____ 115 bus to our college.

29. For a (various) _____ of reasons, the economy of our country is growing at its fastest rate this decade.

30. He pressed the button, and the machine (immediate) _____ started working.

31. (frank) _____ speaking, we don't think your plan is practical.

32. It is well-known that monkeys and dolphins are very (imitate) _____.

33. He has kept denying the (true) _____ that he would murder his wife.

34. Are you saying that (simple) _____ because I'm here?

35. They wrote us a letter, (confirm) _____ that they had received our check.

36. His behavior shows that he is a well (education) _____ person.

37. If you want to sell your product, you must (advertisement) _____ it.

38. It is well known that smoking is (harm) _____ to one's health.

39. To be a good nurse or a good sales woman, you need great (patient) _____.

40. The (argue) _____ went on for two hours as neither sides would give in.

41. When you (sharp) _____ an object you make its edge very thin or you make its end pointed.

42. My (decide) _____ to drop out of the college was entirely my own.

43. The city library is going to be (formal) _____ opened tomorrow.

44. Sometimes it is more difficult to find (qualify) _____ manager than to get financial support.

45. The (nature) _____ resources of a country include rich soils, thick forest, mineral resources, tourist industry and plentiful plant and animal life.

46. You may accept our (propose) _____ or against it.

47. It is (danger) _____ walking on thin ice in winter.

48. English differs (great) _____ from Chinese in pronunciation and grammar.

49. He made a few (care) _____ mistakes in his examination.

50. There are a lot of (similar) _____ between the Chinese culture and Japanese culture.

答案与解析

1. **desirable**　空格前面有副词 very，后面有名词 place，所以空格处缺少一个形容词作定语。desire 的形容词形式为 desirable，意为"需要的，需求的"。

2. **extremely**　空格处须填入一个副词来修饰 wonderful，extreme 的副词形式为 extremely。

3. **reasonable**　测试名词转换为形容词。题中给出的是名词，空格前是系动词，空格处应填入形容词作表语。

4. **complaint**　测试动词转换为名词。complain 的名词形式是 complaint。

5. **thoughtful**　考核词性转换，要求根据句意写出 thought 的形容词形式 thoughtful。

6. **argument**　要用 argue 的名词，即 argument。

7. **universal**　空格前为系动词，空格后为名词，根据题意应填形容词 universal，意为"普遍的"。

8. **herself**　测试反身代词的用法。devote oneself to doing sth. 为固定搭配。

9. **realistic**　根据题意要把名词 reality 变成形容词 realistic。

10. **arrangement**　根据题意空格处需填入 arrange 的名词单数形式（arrangement）。

11. **shortage**　测试词性转换后形成的固定短语 a shortage of，意为"不足，短缺"。

12. **qualified**　要求能根据上下文的意思写出 qualify 的形容词形式 qualified。

13. **preparing**　英语中"忙于干什么"用固定搭配词组 be busy doing sth. 来表示。

14. **frequency**　根据题意要用 frequent 的名词形式 frequency。

15. **development**　此题考查的 develop 的名词的用法，develop 的名词为 development。

16. **commercial**　根据题意空格处应填入形容词 commercial 作定语。

17. **classified**　空格处需填该词的过去分词，测试的是被动语态。

18. **disobeying**　考查构词法。obey 加上前缀 dis- 表示违反。又由于空格前有介词 for，所以应填入 disobeying。

19. **exciting**　应填形容词作定语。

20. **doubtful**　构词法。be doubtful about 意思为"对……感到不确定"。

21. **attentively**　该句应该用 attention 的副词形式。

22. **strengthen**　主句缺谓语动词。

23. **healthy**　as well as 前后词性应保持一致。

24. **buy**	make up one's mind to do sth. 意为"下定决心做……，打定主意做……"。
25. **considerate**	空格处应填入形容词 considerate，意思为"考虑周到的，体谅的"。
26. **to practice**	动词不定式形式。tell sb. not to do sth. 意为"告诉某人不要做某事"。
27. **impression**	名词作宾语，impress 的名词形式为 impression（印象，感想）。
28. **number**	测试形容词转换成名词的用法。
29. **variety**	空格处需填入名词，构成短语 a variety of，意为"许多，大量"。
30. **immediately**	空格处需填入副词 immediately 作状语。
31. **Frankly**	测试形容词转换成副词的用法，frankly speaking 构成现在分词做习惯用语，意思是"坦白地说"，修饰整个句子，作状语。
32. **imitative**	空格处应填入形容词作表语。
33. **truth**	考查形容词转换成名词。
34. **simply**	根据题意空格处需填入副词 simply，意为"仅仅"。
35. **confirming**	测试现在分词的用法。本句中 confirming 作伴随状语。
36. **educated**	测试过去分词的用法，空格处填入 educated，其作用相当于形容词在句中作定语。
37. **advertise**	空格前为情态动词，其后应填入动词形式 advertise。
38. **harmful**	be harmful to sb. 意思是"对某人有害"。
39. **patience**	根据题意，应该把形容词改为名词。
40. **argument**	要用 argue 的名词，即 argument。
41. **sharpen**	空格处需要一个谓语动词，因此应把形容词 sharp 变为动词 sharpen。
42. **decision**	my 是形容词性物主代词，后面应跟名词，to drop out of the college 这一不定式短语是作定语修饰名词的，因此应填入 decide 的名词形式 decision。
43. **formally**	本句中 open 是谓语动词，应使用副词来修饰它，所以用 formally。
44. **qualified**	qualify 的形容词形式为 qualified，修饰 manager。
45. **natural**	nature 的形容词形式为 natural，用来修饰 resources。
46. **proposal**	此句宾语应该是名词，propose 的名词形式为 proposal。
47. **dangerous**	系动词 is 后面应带形容词，因此应填写其形容词形式 dangerous。
48. **greatly**	differ 是谓语，后面跟的应该是副词，great 的副词形式是 greatly。
49. **careless**	从空格后的 mistakes 来判断，空格中应该是个反意形容词来修饰它的。
50. **similarities**	此句 similar 的名词为 similarity。

③ 改错题的解题思路及技巧

在全国高等学校英语应用能力 A 级考试大纲中，Part II Structure 的 Section B 部分，有时为改错题，每题的分值是 1 分，满分为 10 分。改错题考试范围包括高职高专教育《基本要求》语法结构表中所列的所有语法项目。主要考查考生对语法知识点的掌握情况以及用词的准确性。

解题思路

● 正确理解句意

读懂句子的意思，是解题的第一步。例如：

Stressful environments <u>lead to</u> unhealthy behavior <u>such as</u> poor eating habits, <u>which</u> <u>in return</u>

               A   B   C   D

increase the risk of heart disease.

[解析] 答案为 D。此句中 lead to（导致），such as（诸如），in return（作为对……的报答）是固定短语，in return 放在句中显然不符合句意，应改为 in turn（转而，进而）。本句意为：充满压力的环境会导致诸如不良饮食习惯等的不健康的行为方式，继而增加了患心脏病的危险。

● 从选项涉及到的语法点正确分析句子结构

各个选项都可能涉及到语法的正误，比如动词的主动、被动，动词的时态；各词的单复数；一些固定搭配等。例如：

After <u>graduated</u> from high school, my son <u>decided to</u> work <u>for</u> a year before continuing his <u>education</u>.

    A   B   C   D

[解析] 答案为 A。本题中，graduated 为过去分词作状语，decide to do 为短语固定搭配，介词 for 后面加时间段，看到 education，要想到名词的分类和单复数变化。此题中，my son 和 graduate 之间是主动关系，要用现在分词 graduating。故 A 选项为错误项。

解题技巧

● 动词的常用时态和被动语态

改错题中改动部分经常集中在现在完成时、过去完成时、现在完成进行时、将来完成时等时态中。动词的被动结构也经常作为考点。例如：

I have been studying here for three years, by the next summer I <u>will graduate</u>. (will have graduated)

● 非谓语动词

简单句中，除一个谓语动词外，其余动词为非谓语动词。这些非谓语动词以现在分词、过去分词和不定式的形式出现。现在分词 v-ing 表示主动或正在进行的动作；过去分词 v-ed 表示被动或已经完成的动作；不定式表示未完成的动作。例如：

The old man carrying a basketful of apples was run down by a car when <u>crossed</u> the street. (crossing)

● 虚拟语气

重点掌握非真实条件句的结构和虚拟语气在从句中的用法。例如：

The doctor suggested that both of them <u>would spend</u> 20 minutes doing the job. (spend)

● 句子结构

改错题主要可以从以下几方面来思考：1) 名词单复数；2）主谓一致；3) 单词的词性与其在句中的功能；4) 复合句中连接主句和从句的关系词或引导词的运用等。例如：

1. The surroundings which a child grows up in usually <u>has</u> an effect on his development. (have)

2. I know nothing about the accident except <u>which</u> I read in the newspaper. (what)

● 固定结构（固定句型、固定短语、固定搭配）

所谓固定结构是指英语中一些不能随意更改的习惯表达。固定短语中的词不能随意删减，固定搭配要前后一致。例如：

Many children spend most of their time <u>to watch</u> TV. (watching)

● 易混淆的词或词组

易混淆的词既包括词意相同或相近的同义词、近义词，也包括外形相似、意义有别的词组。易混淆词或词组的辨析也是改错题中不容忽视的部分。例如：

The article attracted <u>considerate</u> interest from scientists who study physics. (considerable)

④ 改错题的练习及解析

Directions: *There is an error in each of the following sentences marked with A, B, C and D. You are required to mark out the error.*

1. The fire started in the basement and <u>quickly</u> spread to <u>the first</u> floor, <u>where</u> it destroyed all the
   　　　　　　　　　　　　A　　　　　　　　B　　　　　C

   <u>furnitures and equipments</u> in the language lab.
   　　D

2. What <u>do</u> you think we <u>shall do</u> if it <u>will rain</u> on the day <u>fixed</u> for the sports meeting?
   　　A　　　　　　　　B　　　　　　　C　　　　　　　　D

3. My mother doesn't <u>care</u> much <u>for</u> <u>sweets</u> and <u>so</u> do I.
   　　　　　　　　　　A　　　　B　　C　　　　D

4. It is <u>simply</u> strange that <u>such an accident</u> <u>should be happened</u> <u>in the University</u>.
   　　　　　A　　　　　　　　B　　　　　　　C　　　　　　　　D

5. I'm sure <u>of</u> they <u>will make</u> rapid progress in English if they <u>study</u> <u>much</u> harder than before.
   　　　　　A　　　B　　　　　　　　　　　　　　　　　C　　D

6. The hotel <u>that</u> we worked <u>for practice</u> at the end of <u>last term</u> was <u>built</u> several years ago.
   　　　　　　A　　　　　　B　　　　　　　　　　C　　　　　D

7. The new <u>chemistry teacher</u> together with his students <u>are</u> going to <u>pay a visit</u> to our factory
   　　　　　A　　　　　　　　　　　　　　　　　　B　　　　　　C

   <u>next week</u>.
   　　D

8. The plan supported those who wished to have more chance to travel.
           A   B   C   D

9. Because she had not been able to hear well, the old lady asked that the question was.
               A   B   C   D

10. She denied the rumour which she had been visited by the police in connection with the recent crime.
    A   B   C   D

11. The picture was bought at a very low price, but it has turned out to be a valueless painting.
               A   B   C   D

12. She had trouble finding out that the capital of the country lay in the coastal area or in the mountains.
               A   B   C   D

13. The residents, all of their homes had been damaged by the flood, were given help by the Red Cross.
              A   B   C   D

14. Like a magazine, a newspaper has a content guide that indicates where is each feature.
  A   B   C   D

15. The experiment is very expensive, but if we succeed, we would be able to make production more
                               A   B   C

    efficient.
    D

16. Even although Mary is studying music now, she is planning to spend one year studying Chinese.
        A   B   C   D

17. Because of the recent accidents, our parents forbid my brother and me from swimming in the
    A   B

    river unless someone agrees to watch over us.
         C   D

18. Nowadays, almost every household has different kinds of electrical equipment to relieve
             A   B   C

    manual labor.
    D

19. The fact whether most people believe nuclear war would be madness does not mean that it
        A   B   C

    will not occur.
    D

20. Nothing in recent years has so greatly changed the economy of China with the development
    A   B   C   D

    of the market economy.

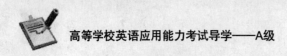

21. It is <u>reported</u> that by the end of this month the output of cement <u>in</u> the factory <u>will be rising</u> by
        A   B   C   D
    about 10 %.

22. <u>A</u> UN report says that the world population will pass <u>six millions</u> <u>by the end of</u> the <u>twentieth</u>
    A   B   C   D
    century.

23. He felt unhappy, <u>because</u> he was <u>deeply</u> displeased by <u>that</u> <u>had occurred</u> that day.
                      A   B   C   D

24. <u>When</u> and <u>by whom</u> this interesting novel was written is a matter of <u>discussing</u> <u>among</u> scholars.
    A   B   C   D

25. Be that <u>when</u> it may, her first <u>journey</u> to America <u>gave her</u> a very <u>deep impression</u>.
            A   B   C   D

26. <u>If</u> you want a new book on <u>current</u> affairs, the person you want <u>to talk</u> is the librarian <u>who</u> is
    A   B   C   D
    wearing glasses over there.

27. <u>A</u> daughter of <u>Mrs. White</u>, who <u>had been</u> in the United States <u>for</u> two years, came back home
    A   B   C   D
    yesterday.

28. Romanticists show life <u>as being</u> more emotionally <u>excited</u> and <u>satisfying</u> than it <u>normally is</u>.
                          A   B   C   D

29. The teacher <u>worked out</u> a new method <u>in which</u> the students <u>can</u> memorize new words <u>quickly</u>.
                A   B   C   D

30. The manager has promised <u>replacing</u> the <u>digital camera</u> if anything <u>goes</u> wrong in the first six
                            A   B   C
    <u>months</u>.
    D

31. The meat is not ready <u>yet</u> and it <u>already</u> has to <u>be cooked</u> for <u>another</u> five minutes.
                          A   B   C   D

32. <u>Seeing from the top of the hill</u>, the house <u>appeared to be</u> much smaller than it <u>seems</u> to us when
    A   B   C
    we look at it <u>on the street</u>.
                  D

33. Don't you think it's <u>high</u> time someone <u>tells</u> him to <u>stop behaving</u> <u>like</u> that?
                        A   B   C   D

34. Many people stop <u>to smoke</u> because <u>there is</u> a lot of evidence that smoking is <u>the main</u> cause
                    A   B   C

of lung cancer.
　　D

35. So badly he was in the traffic accident that he was sent to hospital for treatment.
　　A　　　　　　B　　　　　　　　　　　　　C　　　　　　D

36. As time went on, she suffered such heavy losses that she was forced giving up her business.
　　　　　A　　　　B　　　　　　　　　　C　　　　　　　　　D

37. Living in a new city, he felt lonely at first, but after a time he got used to live alone and even
　　A　　　　　　　　　　　　　B　　　　　　　　　　　　　　　　C

　　got to like it.
　　　　D

38. On being asked if he had had any good food in Germany or not, he answered "Terrible".
　　　　A　　　　B　　C　　　D

39. The greater the population there is in a locality, greater need there is for water, transportation, and
　　　　　　　A　　　　　　B　　　　　　　C

　　disposal of refuse.
　　　　D

40. The advantages of computerized typing and editing are now being extending to all the written
　　　　　　　　　　　　　　　A　　　　　B　　　　　　　C　　　　　D

　　languages.

41. She studies hardly in order to be one of the best students in her class.
　　　　　　　A　　　B　　　　C　　　　　D

42. Before she died the old lady who lives next door to the drugstore used to feed her pigeons
　　A　　　　　　　　　　　B　　　　　　　　　　　　　　　C

　　three times a day.
　　　　D

43. He wrote few letters to some of his family, but he sent a few cards to some of his friends.
　　　　　　　　　　A　　　　B　　　　　　　　C　　　　　D

44. The firemen managed to get there enough quickly to save the burning house.
　　　　　　A　　　　B　　　C　　　　　　　　D

45. Under no circumstances a student should disobey the school discipline.
　　A　　　　　　　B　　　　C　　　　　　D

46. She had worked on this essay for 20 minutes but she has written only about a hundred words.
　　　　A　　　　　　　B　　　　　　　　　　　C　　　　　　　D

47. Human beings are using the natural resources so rapidly over the years that some of them are
　　　　　　A　　　　　　　　　　　B　　C

　　almost gone.
　　　　D

48. The <u>company's</u> training plan <u>was designed</u> to help the employees <u>improve</u> <u>its</u> work—habits and

         A   B   C   D

    efficiency.

49. If you want <u>to travel</u> from Beijing <u>to</u> Hong Kong, you <u>didn't need to take</u> <u>a passport</u>.

                            A   B   C   D

50. The message <u>will be</u> that neither the market nor the government is capable of <u>dealing with</u> all of

                A   B

    <u>their</u> uncontrollable <u>practices</u>.

    C   D

答案与解析

1. **D** 改为 furniture and equipment。furniture（家具）和 equipment（设备）都是不可数名词，没有复数形式。

2. **C** 改为 rains。if 引导的条件状语从句中，从句用现在时表示将来。

3. **D** 改为 neither。因为句子的前半部分是否定句，要表示相同的否定含义须用 neither。

4. **C** 改为 has happened 或 happened。happen 不用于被动语态。

5. **A** 改为 that。形容词 sure 之后可接宾语从句，用 that 引导。

6. **A** 改为 where。where 是关系副词，在定语从句中作地点状语时用，在本句中 where 所带的从句作为定语修饰 hotel，相当于 in which。

7. **B** 改为 is。由 with, together with, as well as 等连接的短语，谓语动词的单复数取决于连词前的短语。

8. **A** 改为 was supported by。主语 the plan 与谓语动词 support 之间是被动关系，计划被人支持，要用被动语态。

9. **C** 改为 what。what 引导宾语从句，在句中作表语。

10. **B** 改为 that。引导同位语从句，说明 rumour 的内容。

11. **D** 改为 invaluable。本题考点是形容词的词义，valueless 是"没有价值的"，invaluable 是"无价的，极其贵重的"。

12. **B** 改为 whether。跟后面的 or 搭配使用。

13. **A** 改为 whose。本题考点为定语从句，由"代词/名词 +of +whose"结构引出定语从句。

14. **D** 改为 where each feature is。因为是由 where 引导的宾语从句，故应为陈述语序。

15. **B** 改为 should/were to succeed。本题考点是与将来事实相反的虚拟语气，从句中用 should/were to + V- 原形。

16. **A** 改为 even though 或 even if。用来引导让步状语从句。

17. **B** 改为 to swim。forbid sb. to do sth. 意为"禁止某人做某事"。

18. **C** 改为 appliances。equipment "设备"，是不可数名词；家用电器的正确表达为 electrical appliances。

19. **A** 改为 that。that 引导同位语从句，作 the fact 的同位语。

20. **D** 改为 as。因为句子前面部分的 so 应和后面的 as 相呼应。

21. **C** 改为 will have risen。by the end of this month 提示要用将来完成时。

22. **B** 改为 six billion。基数词六十亿的正确表达为 six billion。billion 的复数形式，用于 billions of 短语中，意思是"数以十亿计的"。

23. **C** 改为 what。what 引导的从句作介词 by 的宾语，意为"那天所发生的事"。

24. **C** 改为 discussion。当动词有同根或同形的名词时，应采用其名词形式。

25. **A** 改为 as。be that as it may 是固定搭配，表示让步，意为"即便如此"。

26. **C** 改为 to talk to。第一个 to 是动词不定式的小品词，talk 在这为不及物动词，要带宾语时应加介词 to。

27. **B** 改为 Mrs. White's。a daughter of Mrs. White's 的意思是怀特夫人的一个女儿。考点为名词的双重属格。

28. **B** 改为 exciting。因为跟情感有关的动词，其 -ing 形式表示"令人……的"，而 -ed 形式表示主语（通常是人）"感到……的；觉得……的"。

29. **B** 改为 by which。本题考点为定语从句的引导词，先行词为 a new method，介词 + which 引导定语从句。学生通过新方法来记单词，通过某种方法用介词 by 而不是 in。

30. **A** 改为 to replace。在动词 promise 后常用动词不定式。

31. **B** 改为 still。already 用于完成时态中，句子的后半句中有 has，但不是完成时态，容易混淆。

32. **A** 改为 Seen from the top of the hill。非谓语动词的逻辑主语要与主句的主语一致。在本句里主语房子本身不会发出看的动作，所以只能用过去分词表示被动含义。

33. **B** 改为 told。本题考点是虚拟语气。It is (about/high) time that 后的定语从句，表示委婉的提议或建议，谓语动词用过去式。

34. **A** 改为 smoking。在 stop 后用动词不定式，表示停下来去做某事；用分词，表示停止做某事。句中表达的是目前要戒烟，所以应用现在分词。

35. **B** 改为 was he。当 so...that... 结构中的 so 用于句首，加强语气时，用部分倒装结构。

36. **D** 改为 to give up。be forced to do sth. 是固定搭配。

37. **C** 改为 used to living。be/get used to doing 是固定短语，意为"习惯于，适应于"。

38. **B** 改为 whether。whether 和 if 都可以引导宾语从句，但如果从句中带有 or 或 or not，一般只用 whether，而不用 if。

39. **C** 改为 the greater need。考点为"the + 比较级 + ... + the + 比较级"，意为"越……就越……"。

40. **C** 改为 extended。being 后接动词的过去分词，表示被动。

41. **A** 改为 hard。hard 用作形容词，意思是"困难的"，用作副词，意思是"努力地"；hardly 是副词，意思是"几乎不"。

42. **B** 改为 lived。因为现在所谈到的老太太已经去世。

43. **A** 改为 any。few 表示否定概念，any 用于否定句、疑问句中，some 用于肯定句中。

44. **C** 改为 quickly enough。enough 的位置在名词前、形容词和副词后。

45. **B** 改为 should a student。介词短语在句子开头，句子须倒装。

46. **A** 改为 has been working。现在完成进行时表示现在以前这段时间里一直进行的动作，该动作可能仍在进行；过去完成时表示在过去的某一时间之前已经完成的动作。

47. **A** 改为 have been using。用现在完成进行时表示"一直……至今"。

48. **D** 改为 their。work 指代的是 employees 的 work，因此需将 its 改为 their。

49. **C** 改为 needn't have taken。表示过去做了某事，但是没有做的必要。

50. **C** 改为 its。本题考点为一致关系，neither... nor... 后面接的是单数名词，代词要用单数 its 而不是 their。

Part III Reading Comprehension

本部分测试考生从书面文字材料获取信息的能力。阅读总量为 1,000 词。

每套题包括 5 项阅读任务，其中第一、第二项为选择题，2 篇文章，共 10 题；第三项为填空题，1 篇实用性文章，共 5 题；第四项为匹配题，1 组实用性的专业术语，共 5 题；第五项为简答题，1 篇实用性文章，共 5 题。本部分测试的文字材料包括一般性阅读材料（文化、社会、常识、科普、经贸、人物等）和应用性文字，如信函、技术说明书、合同等，测试考生从书面文字材料获取信息的能力，实用性文字材料约占 60%。

阅读材料涉及的语言技能和词汇限于《基本要求》中的"阅读技能表"所列的全部技能范围和"词汇表"中 3,400 词的范围；除一般性文章外，阅读的应用文限于《基本要求》中"交际范围表"所规定的读译范围，如：函电、广告、说明书、业务单证、合同书、摘要、序言等。

1 阅读理解题的解题思路及技巧

解题思路

● **主旨题**

这种题考查学生对所读文章的全面理解和综合概括能力，考生在答题时必须考虑全文，从整体上把握文章大意。

● **细节题**

目的是考查考生查找或阐述文章中某个或某些具体细节的能力。

● **推理题**

目的是考查考生根据上下文对文中信息进行分析、判断、推理的能力。

● 语意题

　　考查考生根据上下文判断、猜测文章中某个词汇、短语或句子意思的能力。

● 填空题

　　要求考生根据材料提供的信息完成句子。文章大多为广告、海报、通知、说明书等，填写部分一般均为细节题。

● 匹配题

　　主要考查考生匹配英语的专门术语及对应的汉语意思。内容多为和人们生活相关的某一领域的专门术语，如：标牌用语、服务用语、广告用语等。

● 简答题

　　要求考生用正确、简洁的语句回答所提出的问题或补足不完整的句子，题材大多为应用文，如广告、商务信函、产品说明书等。该部分问题多为细节题。

解题技巧

● 主旨题

　　主旨题主要考查考生对主题思想的掌握，对文章的中心思想的理解程度。常见的提问形式有：

The passage is about…

The passage is primarily concerned with…

The main idea of the passage is…

The best title for this passage would be…

What is the purpose of the passage?

Which statement best expresses the main idea of the passage?

What does the passage mainly discuss?

Which of the following best summarizes the main idea of the passage?

　　主旨句一般在段首或文章的开头，或者文章段末或文章结尾，也有极少数文章的主旨句出现在文间或段落的中间。如果没有明显的主题句，则需对全文内容进行分析、归纳、概括，才能得出文章大意。同时还要注意：段落中出现转折时，该句很可能是主题句；作者有意识地反复重复的观点通常是主旨；首段出现疑问句时，对该问题的回答就是文章主旨。文章主旨常伴有一些提示词，如：therefore, thus, but, however, in short 等。例如：

Mountain climbers around the world dream about going up Mount Qomolangma（珠穆朗玛峰）. It is the highest mountain in the world. But many people who have climbed the mountain have left waste material that is harming the environment.

A team of Americans is planning the largest clean-up effort ever on Mount Qomolangma. They will make the risky trip up the mountain next month.

The team of eight Americans will be guided by more than 20 Sherpas of Nepal (尼泊尔夏尔巴人). Their goal is to remove all the trash (废物，垃圾) they see. They will spend two months cleaning up the mountain by gathering oxygen bottles, fuel containers, batteries, drink cans, human waste and other kinds of trash. They are expected to remove at least three tons of trash in large bags.

Team leader Robert Hoffman is making his fourth trip up the mountain. He says he hopes to bring Everest to the condition it was in before the first successful climb 50 years ago. He says he hopes the effort will influence other people to clean up the environment closer home.

Human waste on Qomolangma is a major concern. So the clean-up team will take along newly developed equipment to collect and treat human waste. Over the years, the waste articles have polluted the mountain. In the warm season when the ice melts, the polluted water flows to Nepali villages below. The problem has gotten worse in recent years because climbing Qomolangma has become more popular.

What is probably the best title for this passage?

A. A Risky Trip up Mount Qomolangma
B. Pollution on Mount Qomolangma
C. Mount Qomolangma Clean-up Effort
D. Robert Hoffman and His Clean-up Team

[解析] 答案为 C。题干意为"最合适这篇文章的标题很可能是……"。该题为主旨题。从文章可以看出整篇文章都是在围绕对珠穆朗玛峰的一次清扫工作展开，因此 C 项正确。A 项和 D 项只是描述了局部细节，不能涵盖文章内容；B 项说珠穆朗玛峰的污染问题，概括内容过宽。

● 细节题

细节题就是对原文的具体叙述、事实依据或具体数据等提出问题，考查考生理解文章中的具体信息和快速查找有关信息的能力。常见的提问句式有：

Which of the following belongs to the third tip that the author has given?

According to the passage, what do people have strong desire for?

By saying that "…" in the passage, the author means...

The reason for… is that…

Which of the following can be the cause of…?

The author mentions the following EXCEPT…

有时细节题也以填空题的形式出现，如给出一个不完整的句子，考生根据文章内容选择一个正确的选项补全所缺内容。例如：

In the survey findings, some Americans regretted _____ .

When the author saw the play for the second time, he was _____ years old.

Low efficiency of the system is mainly caused by _____ .

细节题在阅读理解中占较大比重，在历年考试题中，细节题大约占到 50%，实际内容也较广。细节题一般可以在文章中直接或间接找到答案，关键还要理解题干。

解题时注意细节题干扰选项的几种情况：部分正确，部分错误；是原文信息，但是不是题目要求的内容；符合常识，但不是文章内容；与原句的内容极为相似，只是在程度上有些变动。例如：

There are some problem areas for international students and immigrants studying in the United States. Making friends is a challenge (this is also true for some American students). Many colleges and universities offer a variety of student clubs and organizations where both foreign-born and native American students have a greater chance of meeting people with shared interests. Information about these out-of-class activities is often posted in the student center and listed in the student newspaper. Sometimes foreign students and immigrant students find Americans to be "cliquish" (有派性的) (Americans find some non-U.S. born students to be cliquish as well). If people feel separated from the social aspects of American college life, they should actively seek people with shared interests. It's unlikely that students will make friends just by passing people on the campus.

Foreign or immigrant students may feel confused during the first few weeks at a new school because they do not understand the system and are not willing to ask questions. Many students do not take advantage of the numerous services offered on campus that assist students in developing new skills and social groups. Some colleges offer students tutorial (辅导的) support in such subjects as writing, language study, computer skills, and other basic subjects. Students who appear to be most successful in "learning the ropes" are those who can solve problems by taking the initiative to ask questions, locate resources, and experience new social situations.

In the United States, students can find friends with the same interests by _____ .

A. making friends on the campus   B. reading the students newspaper

C. visiting the student center   D. joining the student clubs

[解析] 答案为 D。题干意为"在美国，学生能找到志趣相同的人做朋友是通过……"。该题为细节题。由第一段第三句"Many colleges and universities offer a variety of student clubs and organizations where both foreign-born and native American students have a greater chance of meeting people with shared interests."可知，学生通过学校提供的学生俱乐部和组织与自己兴趣相投的人交朋友。因此 D 项正确。

● 推理题

推理题主要是考查考生根据上下文对文中信息进行分析、判断、推理的能力，一般在原文中没有现成的答案，要求考生不仅要理解文章，还要理解文章的隐含意义和深层意义，领会作者的言外之意。常见的几种提问形式有：

We can learn from the passage that…

From the passage, we can infer that…

What does the author imply?

It can be concluded that…

From the last sentence of the passage, we can learn that…

The author's purpose of writing the passage is…

推理题干扰选项的几种情况：是原文的简单复述，而非推断出来的结论；把直接表达当作间接推理；看似从原文推断出来的结论，然而实际上与原文不符，如因果倒置、手段变目的等；根据考生已有的常识是正确的，但却不是基于文章；推理过头，引申过度。例如：

（2004 年 6 月真题）

In many countries in the process of industrialization, overcrowded cities present a major problem. Poor conditions in these cities, such as lack of housing, inadequate sanitation（卫生）and lack of employment, bring about an increase in poverty, disease and crime.

The over-population of towns is mainly caused by the drift of large numbers of people from the rural areas. These people have become dissatisfied with the traditional life of farming, and have come to the towns hoping for better work and pay.

One possible solution to the problem would be to impose registration on town residents. Only officially registered residents would be allowed to live in the towns and the urban population would thus be limited. In practice, however, registration would be very difficult to enforce（推行）; it would cause a great deal of resentment（不满）, which would ultimately lead to violence.

The only long-term solution is to make life in the rural areas more attractive, which would encourage people to stay there. This could be achieved by providing encouragement for people to go and work in the villages. Facilities in the rural areas, such as transport, health and education services should be improved. Education should include training in improved methods of farming and other rural industries, such as transport, health and education services should be improved. Education should include training in improved methods of farming and other rural industries, so as to develop a more positive attitude towards rural life. The improvement of life in the villages is very important, because the towns themselves cannot be developed without the simultaneous or previous development of the rural areas.

In the author's view, solving the cities' problem of overcrowding by strict registrations is _____ .

A. practical   B. possible

C. not realistic   D. not sufficient

[解析]　答案为 C。题干意为"作者认为通过严格人口注册来解决城镇人口问题……"。该题为推理题。根据第三段最后一句"In practice, however, registration would be very difficult to enforce." 可知这种方法在现实中很难推行，因此不现实，故正确答案为 C。practical: 实用的；possible: 可能的；sufficient: 充分的。

● 语意题

语意题是考查学生根据上下文推断句子意思的能力，同时考查学生的词汇量。常见的提问方式有：

The word/phrase/sentence "…" in line…means…

By saying that "…", the author means…

The word "…" stands for…

What is the meaning of "…" in line/paragraph…?

考生除了掌握大纲要求的词汇和一定数量的短语外，掌握必要的做题技巧也是很重要的。猜测词汇语意时，可以使用构词法，根据词根、词缀判断词意；也可通过找同义词、反义词或在上下文中找出其派生词的方法推断其含义；还可通过找同位词，或上下文中有可能有类似该词出现的句子的平行结构，找出其中和该词处于同一位置的词去推测。有些词一词多义，要通过阅读，正确理解该词在文中的意思，从而得出正确答案。例如：

（2003 年真题）

Most of us grow up taking certain things for granted. We tend to assume that experts and religious leader tell us "the truth". We tend to believe that things advertised on television or in newspapers can't be bad for us.

However, encouragement of critical thinking in students is one of the goals of most colleges and universities. Few professors require students to share the professor's own beliefs. In general, professors are more concerned that students learn to question and critically examine the arguments of the others, including some of their own beliefs or values. This does not mean that professors insist that you change your beliefs, either. It does not mean, however, professors will usually ask you to support the views you express in class or in your writing.

If your premises（前提）are shaky, or if your arguments are not logical, professors personally point out the false reasoning in your arguments. Most professors want you to learn to recognize the premises of your arguments, to examine whether you really accept these premises, and to understand whether or not you draw logical conclusions. Put it this way: professors don't tell you what to think; they try to teach you how to think.

On the other hand, if you intend to disagree with your professors in class, you should be prepared to offer a strong argument in support of your ideas. Arguing just for the sake of arguing usually does not promote a critical examination of ideas. Many professors interpret it as rudeness. The word "shaky" (Line 1, Para. 3) most probably means "_____".

A. creative   B. firm   C. false   D. weak

[解析] 答案为 C。题干意为"第三段第一行中 shaky 一词的意思是……"。该题为语意题。shaky 的动词形式是 shake，"动摇"的意思。根据第三段第一行 "…professors personally point out the false reasoning in your arguments" 可以推断出 shaky 在文中的意思与 false 相近。

● **填空题**

阅读理解中的填空题，要求考生根据材料提供的信息完成句子。文章大多为广告、海报、通知、说明书等，填写部分一般均为细节题，在已测试的题型中，细节题几乎占了 100%。考生做题时应注意题目要求，从文章中找到答案。例如：

（2002 年 12 月真题）

Before making a speech, we often need to make brief speaking notes. You can put them on cards no smaller than 150×100 mm. Write in large and bold letters that you can see at a glance, using a series of brief headings to develop the information in sufficient details. The amount of information you include in your notes will depend on the complexity（复杂性）of the subject, your familiarity with it, and your previous speaking experience. Here are some steps for you to follow when preparing brief speaking notes.

First, you should write a summary, or an outline, of the project to be reported and the results achieved. Then an introduction follows. This includes background information and purpose of the project. Next comes discussion. In this part, what has been done, how it has been done and the results achieved should be dealt with. At the fourth step, you have two choices: one is the conclusion if the project is completed. The other is the future plan if the project is still in progress. At last, a summary should be prepared. In this part, you should have a brief summing-up, plus a question-and-answer period.

Speaking Notes Preparation

Words to be written: in ____1____ letters

Means of developing information: using a number of ____2____.

Steps of making speaking notes:

1) work out an outline

2) write ____3____

3) deal with the subject

4) draw ____4____ at the end of the project, or make a ____5____ if the project is not finished

5) have a summary

[解析]　本文是一篇关于怎样准备演讲笔记的介绍文。

1. **large and bold**	由第一段第三句 "Write in large and bold letters that you can see at a glance, …" 可直接从文中找到答案。	
2. **brief headings**	由第一段第三句 "…using a series of brief headings to develop the information in sufficient details." 可直接从文中找到答案。	
3. **an introduction**	文章第二段介绍步骤。由第二段第二句 "Then an introduction follows." 可得到答案。	
4. **a conclusion**	本题的文字描述与原文稍有不同，但意思与原文是一样的。由第二段第六句，第四个步骤 "At the fourth step, you have two choices: one is the conclusion if the project is completed. The other is the future plan if the project is still in progress." 可得到答案。	
5. **(future) plan**	题解同 49。	

● 匹配题

匹配题主要考查考生匹配英语的专门术语及对应的汉语意思。内容多为和人们生活相关的某一领域专门术语，如：标牌用语、服务用语、广告用语等。考生在解题时应注意与所给的单词、词组或短语相关的专业领域，判断选项属于哪方面的内容，根据题目中的中文找出相对应的英文选项。先做把握比较大的，逐一选择。例如：

A. — Waiting and Boarding

B. — Luggage Delivery

C. — Inspection and Quarantine

D. — Getting a Board Pass

E. — Security Check

F. — Domestic Departure

G. — Over-sized Luggage Checked-in

H. — Goods Prohibited to Be Hand-carried

I. — Duty-free Articles

J. — Customs Declaration Form

K. — Quantity Allowed to Take

L. — Regulations on Restriction of Liquids

M. — Temporary Boarding ID Card

N. — Guide to Outgoing Passengers

O. — Goods Prohibited to Exit the Country

P. — Restriction of Hand Carry-on Articles

Q. — Detection Passage

Example:（L）限带液体物品的规定　　　（C）检查与检疫

1.（　）离港旅客指南	（　）领取登记牌
2.（　）禁止携带出境的物品	（　）大件行李托运
3.（　）候机 / 登机	（　）禁止随身携带的物品
4.（　）限带物品数量	（　）检查通道
5.（　）海关申报表	（　）免税物品

[解析] 这是一列机场用语。答案分别为：

1. N, D　　2. O, G　　3. A, H　　4. K, Q　　5. J, I

其中各项的意思分别如下：

A. — Waiting and Boarding 候机 / 登机

B. — Luggage Delivery 行李托运

C. — Inspection and Quarantine 检查与检疫

D. — Getting a Board Pass 领取登记牌

E. — Security Check 安全检查

F. — Domestic Departure 国内航班出站

G. — Over-sized Luggage Checked-in 大件行李托运

H. — Goods Prohibited to Be Hand-carried 禁止随身携带的物品

I. — Duty-free Articles 免税物品

J. — Customs Declaration Form 海关申报表

K. — Quantity Allowed to Take 限带物品数量

L. — Regulations on Restriction of Liquids 限带液体物品的规定

M. — Temporary Boarding ID Card 登机临时身份证

N. — Guide to Outgoing Passengers 离港旅客指南

O. — Goods Prohibited to Exit the Country 禁止携带出境的物品

P. — Restriction of Hand Carry-on Articles 限带随身物品

Q. — Detection Passage 检查通道

● 简答题

简答题要求考生用正确、简洁的语句回答所提出的问题或补足不完整的句子，题材大多为应用文，如广告、商务信函、产品说明书等。该部分问题多为细节题。考生在答题时要读懂问题，抓住关键词，用正确、简短的语言概括地回答问题。答案大多在原文中可以找到，应尽可能利用原文中的关键词，用简短的英语回答问题。例如：

(2005 年 6 月真题)

Dear Sirs,

Today we have received your bill for 150 name-bearing (刻有名字的) crystal vases (花瓶) which you sent us the other day.

We had ordered these vases on condition that they should reach us by the end of June. But they arrived here 15 days behind the schedule.

The customers refused to accept the goods because they arrived too late. Since the vases bear their names, we cannot sell them to other customers. So we asked the customers again and again to take the vases, and finally they agreed to accept them, but at a price cut of 30%.

You may understand how we have lost the customer's confidence in us. In this situation, we have to ask you to compensate for the loss we have suffered. We are looking forward to hearing from you soon.

Yours faithfully,

G. Pastry

1. What was the problem with the delivery of the vases?

   They arrived 15 days _____ .

2. When did the vases actually arrive?

   In the middle of _____ .

3. Why couldn't the vases be sold to other customers?

   Because they were bearing _____ of those who ordered the vases.

4. In what condition did the customers accept the goods?

   At a price cut of _____ .

5. What was the purpose of this letter?

   To ask the supplier to _____ for the loss they have suffered.

[解析]

1. **behind the schedule** 由第二段第二句 "But they arrived here 15 days behind the schedule." 可得到答案。

2. **July** 由第二段第一句和第二句 "...they should reach us by the end of June. But they arrived here 15 days behind the schedule." 可得到答案。

3. **names** 由第三段第二句 "Since the vases bear their names, we cannot sell them to other customers." 可得到答案。

4. **30%** 由第三段最后一句 "...they agreed to accept them, but at a price cut of 30%." 可得到答案。

5. **compensate** 由第三段最后一句 "In this situation, we have to ask you to compensate for the loss we have suffered." 可得到答案。

② 阅读理解的练习及解析

Directions: *This part is to test your reading ability. There are 5 tasks for you to fulfill. You should read the reading materials carefully and do the tasks as you are instructed.*

Task 1

Directions: *After reading the following passages, you will find 25 questions or unfinished statements below. For each question or statement there are 4 choices marked A, B, C and D.*

Passage 1

It is the duty of every man to work. The lazy man wastes his time and his life is of no use to himself or to others. The man who is too lazy to work is the man who is generally most ready to beg or steal. Every one when he is young should learn some useful work.

But it is not enough that one should learn some kind of work. He should work hard, and not waste his spare minutes or half hours. "Work while you work and play while you play" is as good a rule for young people as for the old.

There is no better aid to diligence than the habit of early rising, and this, like all other good habits, is most easily formed in youth.

There is an English saying "Lost time never returns." This means that everybody must be diligent, and must make a good use of his time. One must study hard when he is young, so that he may succeed in his life and become useful to his country.

I have never heard that those who are diligent will become beggars, but I know that lazy fellows will become beggars. Therefore, I should say that diligence is the mother of success.

1. The best title of the passage could be "_____".
   A. Learn to Work   B. Diligence
   C. Early Rising Is a Good Habit   D. Students Should Study Hard
2. According to the passage, which of the following statements is NOT true?
   A. Habits are easily formed when one is young.
   B. Old people can easily form the habit of getting up early.
   C. One should be diligent.
   D. A lazy man is likely to be harmful to society.
3. From the passage, we can conclude that _____.
   A. diligence can always help one to achieve success
   B. laziness always leads to theft
   C. "Lost time never returns" is a law of physics
   D. youth is the only important period in life
4. According to the passage, the best way to make a person diligent is _____.
   A. to make good use of his time   B. to learn some useful work
   C. to work hard   D. to get up early
5. From the passage, we can guess that the author of the passage is _____.
   A. a lazy man   B. a beggar   C. a diligent man   D. a writer

Passage 2

The American definition of success is largely one of acquiring wealth and a high material standard of living. It is not surprising, therefore, that Americans have valued education for its monetary value. The belief is widespread in the United States that the more schooling people have, the more money they will earn when they leave school. The belief is strongest regarding the desirability of an undergraduate university degree, or a professional degree such as medicine or law following the undergraduate degree. The monetary value of graduate degree in "nonprofessional" fields such as art, history, or philosophy is not as great.

The belief in the monetary value of education is supported by statistics on income. Ben Wattenberg, a social scientist, estimated that in the course of a lifetime a man with a college degree in 1972 would earn about $380,000 more than a man with just a high school diploma.

Perhaps this helps to explain survey findings which showed that the Americans who wished they had lived their lives differently on some way regretted most of all that they did not get more education.

6. What most Americans like most about higher education is _____.

    A. its cultural value   B. its monetary value

    C. its moral value   D. its material value

7. According to the passage, which of the following statements is NOT true?

    A. Americans take success as acquiring wealth and a higher material standard of living.

    B. In American people's mind's eye, education has its monetary value.

    C. Education is the only way to acquire wealth.

    D. A person's income is related to his schooling.

8. The passage says that people have stronger desire to _____.

    A. study medicine   B. study history

    C. study law   D. both A and C

9. In the survey findings, some Americans regretted _____.

    A. not having much education

    B. having too much unnecessary education

    C. living differently

    D. earning $380,000

10. In this passage, the writer wanted to show us _____.

    A. the earlier you start to work, the better you live

    B. education is very important in the American society

    C. people with little education are looked down upon by others everywhere in the United States

    D. Americans take money seriously

Passage 3

Student participation in the classroom is not only accepted but also expected of the student in many courses. Some professors base part of the final grade on the student's oral participation. Although there are formal lectures during which the student has a passive role (i.e., listening and taking notes), many courses are organized around classroom discussions, student questions, and informal lectures.

A professor's teaching method is another factor that determines the degree and type of student participation. Some professors prefer to control discussion while others prefer to guide the class without controlling it. Many professors encourage students to question their ideas. Students who object to the professor's point of view should be prepared to prove their positions.

In the teaching of science and mathematics, the controlling mode of instruction is generally traditional, with teachers presenting formal lectures and students taking notes. However, new educational trends have turned up in the humanities and social sciences in the past 20 years. Students in education, society, and history classes, for example, are often required to solve problems in groups, design projects, make presentations, and examine case studies. Since some college or university courses are "practical" rather than theoretical, they pay more attention to "doing" for themselves.

11. Part of the final grade of the student may be based on _____.
    A. the student's oral participation
    B. the student's written scores
    C. the student's attitude in learning
    D. the professors' formal lectures

12. Participation in the classroom is not only accepted but also expected of the student in many courses EXCEPT in _____.
    A. science and mathematics
    B. the humanities and social sciences
    C. informal lecture courses
    D. discussion courses

13. From the passage we know that education in the humanities and social sciences _____.
    A. has not changed much
    B. pay attention to students' studying instead of teachers' teaching
    C. is much more important than that of science and mathematics
    D. has become more practical than theoretical

14. The main reason why some professors ask students to make presentations and lead discussions is that _____.
    A. these professors are often not well prepared before class
    B. these professors want to stress "doing"
    C. these professors want to test the students' abilities
    D. these professors are not willing to teach theory

15. Which of the following statements is true according to the passage?
    A. Student participation is not common in the classroom in many courses of society.
    B. Some professors want to control the classroom discussion.
    C. Some professors usually want the students to take part in the teaching of science and mathematics.
    D. New educational trends have turned up in natural sciences such as chemistry.

Passage 4

A few minutes ago, walking back from lunch, I started to cross the street when I heard the sound of a coin dropping. It wasn't much but, as I turned, my eyes caught the heads of several other people turning too.

The tinkling sound of a coin dropping on pavement is an attention-getter. It can be nothing more than a penny.

We are surrounded by so many sounds that attract the most attention. People in New York City seldom turn to look when a fire engine, a police car or an ambulance comes screaming along the street.

At home in my little town in Connecticut, it's different. The distant wail of a police car, an emergency vehicle or a fire siren brings me to my feet if I'm seated and brings me to the window if I'm in bed.

It's the quietest sounds that have most effect on us, not the loudest. In the middle of the night, I can hear a dripping tap 100 yards away through three closed doors. I've been hearing little creaking noises and sounds which my imagination turns into footsteps in the middle of the night for 25 years in our house.

I'm quite clear in my mind what the good sounds are and what the bad sounds are.

The tapping, tapping, tapping of my typewriter as the keys hit the paper is a lovely sound to me. I often like the sound of what I write better than the looks of it.

16. The sound of a coin dropping makes people _____.

    A. think of money   B. look at each other

    C. pay attention to it   D. stop crossing the street

17. People in New York _____.

    A. don't care about emergencies   B. are used to sirens

    C. are attracted by sounds   D. don't hear loud noises

18. The writer _____.

    A. sleeps next to the window   B. has lived in Connecticut for a long time

    C. believes in ghosts   D. is interested in fire engines

19. How does the author relate to sounds at night?

    A. He imagines sounds that do not exist.

    B. He exaggerates quiet sounds.

    C. He thinks taps should be turned off.

    D. He believes it's rather quiet at night.

20. What kind of sound does he find pleasant?

    A. Tinkling sound of a coin dropping.   B. Clinking sound of keys.

    C. Tapping of his typewriter.   D. Creaking sounds.

Passage 5

Short stories tend to be less complex than novels. Usually, a short story will focus on only one incident, has a single plot, a single setting, a limited number of characters, and covers a short period of time.

In longer forms of fiction, stories tend to contain certain core elements of dramatic structure: exposition (the introduction of setting, situation and main characters); complication (the event of the story that introduces the conflict); rising action, crisis (the decisive moment for the main characters and their commitment to a course of action); climax (the point of highest interest in terms of the conflict and the point of the story with the most action); resolution (the point of the story when the conflict is resolved); and moral.

Because of their short length, short stories may or may not follow this pattern. Some do not follow patterns at all. For example, modern short stories only occasionally have an exposition. More typical, though, is an abrupt beginning, with the story starting in the middle of the action. As with longer stories, plots of short stories also have a climax, crisis, or turning-point. However, the endings of many short stories are abrupt and open and may or may not have a moral or practical lesson.

Of course, as with any art form, the exact characteristics of a short story will vary by author.

21. Longer fictions tend to _____.

    A. focus on one incident   B. have a limited number of characters

    C. cover a short period of time   D. contain more core elements

22. In long fictions, _____ core elements are mentioned in the passage.

    A. 4   B. 5   C. 6   D. 7

23. The crisis element in a fiction means _____.

    A. the introduction of the main characters

    B. the event that introduces the conflict

    C. the decisive moment and the main characters commitment to the action

    D. the point of the story when the conflict is resolved

24. Plots of short stories _____.

    A. are almost the same as longer stories   B. only have an exposition

    C. have an abrupt beginning   D. only have a climax or turning point

25. Which one is NOT true according to the passage?

    A. Some short stories may not have a moral or practical lesson.

    B. All long fictions and short stories follow the same pattern.

    C. The exact characteristics of short stories may be different from each other.

    D. Novels are usually more complex than short stories.

Task 2

Directions: *This task is the same as Task 1. The 25 questions or unfinished statements are numbered 1 to 25.*

Passage 1

The School of Computer Science invites applications from outstanding faculty candidates. This year we have a special interest in applicants with interests in Robotics, as described in "The Robotics Institute Position Description", and in *Learning Science and Educational Technology*, described in the "HCI Institute Description".

All faculty candidates are expected to have a strong interest in research, outstanding academic credentials, and an earned Ph.D. Candidates for tenure-track appointments should also have a strong interest in graduate and undergraduate education. The highly selective undergraduate and graduate programs in the School of Computer Science draw top students from around the world. Carnegie Mellon also has an expanding presence with campuses and teaching opportunities in Silicon Valley, Qatar, and Greece. Further information about the School of Computer Science and its programs may be found on the SCS home page.

Applications should include curriculum vitae, statement of research and teaching interests, copies of 1-3 representative papers, and the names and email addresses of three or more individuals who have been asked to provide letters of *reference*. Applicants should arrange for reference letters to be sent directly to the Faculty Search Committee (hard copy or email), to arrive before January 15, 2007. Letters will not be requested directly by the Search Committee. All applications should indicate citizenship and, in the case of non-US citizens, current visa status.

1. Applicants for job in the School of Computer Science need to _____.
   A. have interest in Robotics
   B. invite applications from outstanding faculty candidates
   C. have interest in computer
   D. have an expanding presence with campuses

2. If you need more information about the School of Computer Science, you can _____.
   A. make an appointment with the school authority
   B. find it on the SCS home page
   C. write a letter to the Search Committee
   D. go to Silicon Valley, Qatar, and Greece

3. Applications should include the following EXCEPT _____.
   A. representative papers
   B. curriculum vitae
   C. statement of research and teaching interests
   D. plans on undergraduate and graduate programs

4. The word "reference" Line 3, Para. 3 means _____.
   A. a comment that mentions something or someone
   B. the process of looking at something in order to get information
   C. a statement from someone who knows you that gives information about you
   D. a number that shows someone where they can find information that they need

5. Which one of the following is NOT true according to the passage?
   A. The applicant must be US citizen.
   B. In references, you need to offer the names and email addresses of three or more people.
   C. Reference letters should arrive before January 15, 2007.
   D. All applications should indicate citizenship.

Passage 2

Wal-Mart Stores, Inc. was founded by American retail legend Sam Walton in Arkansas in 1962. Forty-four years later, Wal-Mart serves more than 176 million customers per week. It is the world's largest private employer and retailer with over 1.9 million associates worldwide and more than 6,800 stores in 14 countries.

Wal-Mart came to China in 1996. In China, the first Supercenter and SAM'S CLUB were opened in Shenzhen, Guangdong Province. Today, there are 83 units in 46 cities, with a total investment of over RMB1.7 billion. Across China Wal-Mart employs over 38,000 associates.

As an outstanding corporate citizen, Wal-Mart actively gives back to the community and has donated funds and in-kind support worth more than RMB26 million to local charities and welfare organizations over the past ten years.

Wal-Mart firmly believes in local procurement. The people in Wal-Mart recognize that by purchasing quality products, they can generate more job opportunities, support local manufacturing and boost economic development. Over 95% of the merchandise in their stores in China is sourced locally. They have established partnerships with nearly 20,000 suppliers in China. At Wal-Mart, they always work with their suppliers to grow together. In the August 2006 Supplier Satisfaction Survey published by Business Information of Shanghai, Wal-Mart ranked first across several supplier satisfaction indexes.

Additionally, Wal-Mart directly exports about US$9 billion from China every year. The export volume by third party suppliers is also estimated to be over US$9 billion.

6. Wal-Mart owns more than _____ stores in the world.

    A. 176 million   B. 1.9 million   C. 6,800   D. 83

7. The first Supercenter and SAM'S CLUB in China were opened in _____.

    A. Guangzhou   B. Shenzhen   C. Beijing   D. Shanghai

8. Which one of the following is NOT true?

    A. Most goods in Wal-Mart are produced in the local area.

    B. Wal-Mart has actively donated funds to local charities and welfare organizations over the past ten years.

    C. The first store of Wal-Mart was established in Shenzhen in 1996.

    D. Wal-Mart can also generate job opportunities and boost economic development.

9. Wal-Mart exports about _____ from China every year.

    A. RMB1.7 billion   B. RMB26 million

    C. US$9   D. not mentioned in the passage

10. According to a survey by Business Information of Shanghai, Wal-Mart _____.

    A. was first across some supplier satisfaction indexes

    B. is the world's largest private employer and retailer

    C. was one of the stores that sold quality products

    D. Partnerships established by Wal-Mart were most in China

Passage 3

To write an effective business report with efficiency, a three-stage approach is recommended:

1) Case Analysis

2) Report Planning

- Develop a report outline (i.e., the overall structure of your report) by identifying particular headings and subheadings. The framework structure may be helpful, but you may use another structure if it presents your analysis in a better fashion.

- List the ideas associated with each heading and subheading. Group related ideas where possible and then arrange them in a logical order.

- Plan exhibits.

- Plan the introduction and the conclusion (but do not use phrases such as "The Introduction", "The Conclusion", or "The Main Body" as the headings).

3) Report Writing

- Use the outline you developed in stage 2. Write the first draft.

- Develop one paragraph for each idea or topic. Write a strong opening sentence for each paragraph, which will indicate the conclusions you made at the case analysis stage.

- When presenting more than three facts or numbers at one time, consider whether a table or chart might communicate the information better in fewer words.

- Avoid redundant or overblown words.

- Be concise! When 6 words will replace 14 words, let them do so!

- Check grammar, spelling, and punctuation.

- Number the pages.

- Write draft 2, correcting errors, wordiness and unnecessarily pretentious words.

- Proofread draft 2. It's a good idea to have another person do this. Correct/improve as necessary.

- Are exhibits labeled and numbered, and in the order they are mentioned in the report?

11. The passage gives tips for _____.

    A. writing a business letter   B. writing a memo

    C. wiring a business report   D. writing a letter of recommendation

12. The second stage of the approach recommended in the passage is _____.

    A. case analysis   B. report planning

    C. plan exhibits   D. reporting writing

13. When you have more than three facts or numbers to be presented at one time, it might be better to _____.

    A. use a table or chart

    B. describe in fewer words

    C. to use 6 words to replace 14 words

    D. avoid redundant or overblown words

14. In writing the first draft, points for attentions are the following EXCEPT _____.

    A. develop one paragraph for each idea or topic

    B. check grammar, spelling, and punctuation

    C. number the pages

    D. correct errors, wordiness and unnecessarily pretentious words

15. Which one of the following sentences is NOT true according to the passage?

    A. Ideas should be associated with the headings and subheadings.

    B. Related ideas are grouped and arranged in a logical order.

    C. Replace each 14 words with 6 words.

    D. Develop one paragraph for each idea or topic.

Passage 4

    All employees have a contract of employment, although it might not be in writing. What is a contract of employment? A contract of employment is an agreement between an employer and an employee. Your rights and duties, and those of your employer, are called the "terms" of the contract.

    The contract doesn't have to be in writing, but you're entitled to a written statement of the main terms within two months of starting work.

    The contract is made as soon as you accept a job offer, and both sides are then bound by its terms until it's properly ended (usually by giving notice) or until the terms are changed (usually by mutual agreement).

    The employment rights you have will often depend on whether you are classed as an "employee", "worker" or "self employed". This depends on the type of contract you have with your employer.

    If you are an employee, you must get a "written statement of employment particulars" setting out some of your main terms. Your employer must give you this within two months of starting work. The statement must include: pay, hours of work, pay arrangements, and notice period, information about disciplinary and grievance procedures.

16. A contract of employment is _____.

    A. a written agreement signed by the two parties concerned

    B. an agreement between an employer and an employee

    C. an agreement containing the rights and duties of the employer

    D. an agreement containing the rights and duties of the employee

17. The word "term" in the last sentence of the first paragraph means _____.

    A. fixed or limited period of time

    B. period during which a Court holds session

    C. conditions or items offered or agreed to

    D. mode of expression

18. If the terms of a contract will be changed, _____.

    A. it is usually done within two months of your work

    B. it is usually done as soon as you accept a job offer

    C. it is usually by giving notice beforehand

    D. it is usually agreed by both sides

19. The employment rights you have often depend on _____.

    A. the type of contract you have with your employer

    B. whether you are classed as employer or employee

    C. your struggle with the boss

    D. the intention and wishes of the employer

20. _____ would be the best title of the passage.

    A. Contracts of Employment: Introduction

    B. How to Write a Contract of Employment

    C. What Is a Contract of Employment?

    D. What Should Be Included in a Contract of Employment?

Passage 5

Writing a resume in English can be very different than in your native tongue. The following points outline a standard resume format.

Begin resume by writing your full name, address, telephone number, fax and email at the top of the resume.

Write an objective. The objective is a short sentence describing what type of work you hope to obtain.

Begin work experience with your most recent job, include the company specifics and your responsibilities—focus on the skills you have identified as transferable.

Continue to list all of your work experience job by job progressing backwards in time. Remember to focus on skills that are transferable.

Summarize your education, including important facts (degree type, specific courses studied) that are applicable to the job you are applying for.

Include other relevant information such as languages spoken, computer programming knowledge etc. under the heading: Additional Skills.

Finish with the phrase: REFERENCES Available upon request.

Your entire resume should ideally not be any longer than one page. If you have had a number of years of experience specific to the job you are applying for, two pages are also acceptable.

21. Objective in a resume means _____.

    A. your resume is uninfluenced by personal feelings or opinions

    B. your purpose for writing the resume

    C. your resume is impartial

    D. the type of work you want to get

22. Work experience should be arranged _____.

    A. with your recent job at the beginning

    B. with your first job at the beginning

    C. with the most transferable job at the beginning

    D. not mentioned in the passage

23. Relevant information is listed under the heading of _____.

    A. Work Experience   B. Education

    C. Additional Skills   D. References

24. The meaning of the word "reference" in the second paragraph from the bottom is _____.

    A. a statement about a person's character or ability

    B. note or direction telling where certain information may be found

    C. instance of referring

    D. turning to or going to someone for information

25. Your resume is better to be written on _____.

    A. one page   B. two pages

    C. three pages   D. any pages according to your job experience

Task 3

Passage 1

Directions: *The following is an advertisement. After reading it, you should fill in the blanks marked 1 through 5 in the table below. You should write your answers briefly (in no more than 3 words) on the Answer Sheet correspondingly.*

    Welcome to the American Red Cross Advertising Press Room! Thank you for helping to share our lifesaving message with the public by supporting our public service advertising program. Please use any of these PSA as you wish, being mindful of the expiration dates corresponding to some of them. Visit us again to check for retired or new ads.

    Radio, print and online PSA are available here for download in print- or broadcast-ready format. TV spots are also available for preview. To order a broadcast-quality Beta SP tape, please contact your local chapter. National broadcasters can request a tape from the Advertising Office.

    For more information please contact the Advertising Unit:

    Advertising@usa.redcross.org

Public Service Advertising (PSA)

The American Red Cross Advertising Pressing Room thanks those who help to share their ____1____ with the public by supporting their ____2____ program.

When using any of these PSA, you may be mindful of the ____3____ corresponding to some of them.

Radio, print and ____4____ are available for download in print-ready format.

For a broadcast-quality Beta SP tape, you can contact the ____5____.

Passage 2

Directions: *The following is an application letter. After reading it, you should fill in the blanks marked 6 through 10 in the table below. You should write your answers briefly (**in no more than 3 words**) on the Answer Sheet correspondingly.*

6123 Farrington Road
Apt. B11
Chapel Hill, NC 27514
January 11, 2005

Taylor, Inc.
694 Rockstar Lane
Durham, NC 27708

Dear Human Resources Director:

I just read an article in the News and Observer about Taylor's new computer center just north of Durham. I would like to apply for a position as an entry-level programmer at the center.

I understand that Taylor produces both in-house and customer documentation. My technical-writing skills, as described in the enclosed resume, are well suited to your company. I'm a recent graduate of DeVry Institute of Technology in Atlanta with an Associate's Degree in Computer Science. In addition to having taken a broad range of courses, I served as a computer consultant at the college's computer center where I helped train computer users on new systems.

I will be happy to meet with you at your convenience and discuss how my education and experience match your needs. You can reach me at my home address, at (919) 233-1552, or at krock@devry.alumni.edu.

Sincerely,
Raymond Krock

The letter is written to _____6_____ of Taylor, Inc. for a position as a(n) _____7_____ at the new computer center.

Taylor is a company producing both _____8_____ documentation.

The writer's qualification includes: has an Associate's Degree in _____9_____; served as a _____10_____ at the college's computer center.

Passage 3

Directions: *The following is an advertisement. After reading it, you should fill in the blanks marked 11 through 15 in the table below. You should write your answers briefly (in no more than 3 words) on the Answer Sheet correspondingly.*

South Coast Style is a regional lifestyle magazine. It promotes the ideal lifestyle. It showcases the rich and abundant experience living on or visiting the South Coast. The magazine offers South Coast communities a publication to herald the unique country/coastal culture and showcases the array of interesting people, picturesque places, magnificent homes & gardens as well as the first class products & produce found in the region.

South Coast Style offers businesses an upmarket platform for advertising goods and services, directly to a tightly targeted market. *South Coast Style* is a resource for consumers seeking information on fine dining, great get-aways, selective shopping and exciting experiences.

South Coast Style covers stories from Austinmer to Eden and is distributed via news agents and selected retail outlets in affluent Northern & Eastern suburbs of Sydney, ACT, Wollongong, Illawarra, and South Coast of NSW. *South Coast Style* magazine is also presented to visitors via prestige accommodation outlets in Wollongong and the South Coast.

South Coast Style **Magazine**
The magazine showcases the rich experience living on or visiting _____11_____. It offers businesses a platform for _____12_____. It is also a resource for consumers advertising _____13_____ on food, shopping and entertainment.
The magazine is distributed via _____14_____ and _____15_____ in affluent Northern & Eastern suburbs.

Passage 4

Directions: *The following is memorandum. After reading it, you should fill in the blanks marked 16 through 20 in the table below. You should write your answers briefly (in no more than 3 words) on the Answer Sheet correspondingly.*

Memorandum

To: Director

From: Pierre Aries

Date: Sep. 3, 2003

Subject: Reducing Staff

    I have several proposals for cutting down on office staff. First, I suggest that we eliminate the full-time position of order clerk, since there is not enough work to occupy him throughout the month. Orders and requests for sales information are heaviest at the end of the month; in contrast, there is little to do in the first two weeks of each month. Therefore, I recommend that we hire temporary help for the last two weeks of each month and give the orders from the first of the month to the sales department to process.

    Second, now that our systems are completely computerized we no longer need a computer programmer on staff. It's true we will need computer programming services occasionally in future, for instance, when we revise our hilling system. In such cases, however, we can hire a freelance programmer. Third, I suggest that I share my secretary with the assistant office manager, thus eliminating one secretarial position. Although this will increase the managerial workload, I feel we can handle it. Moreover, we can always hire temporal help to get us through particularly busy periods.

    If these suggestions are followed, we should he able to save approximately $26,000 in the coming year in salaries alone. In addition, I believe these changes will result in greater work efficiency.

The memo is written by _____16_____ on proposal for _____17_____ office staff. His suggestions are:

1) eliminate the full-time position of _____18_____;

2) do not need a _____19_____ on staff; since the systems are completely computerized; and

3) share his secretary with the assistance office manager, thus eliminating one _____20_____ position.

Passage 5

Directions: *The following is a reference letter from an employee's manager. After reading it, you should fill in the blanks marked 21 through 25 in the table below. You should write your answers briefly (**in no more than 3 words**) on the Answer Sheet correspondingly.*

    I have known John Smith for the past year while he has worked as an Accounting Assistant in the Company Accounting Office. I have been consistently impressed by both John's attitude towards his work and his performance on the job. His interpersonal and communication skills have allowed him to develop productive working relationships with both our clients and our staff. John has the listening and interviewing skills necessary to extract information from our clientele while performing financial assessments.

John possesses solid writing skills which have enabled him to compose quality correspondence. He also has the analytical skills to diagnose problems and devise viable solutions. His ability to remain unflustered during frenzied periods like tax season proves his ability to work well under pressure.

I recommend him for employment without reservation. Please let me know if you need further information.

Reference Letter from Manager

John Smith once worked in the ____21____. His ____22____ skills have allowed him to develop working relationships with both clients and staff. His writing skills have enabled him to compose ____23____. His analytical skills have enabled him to ____24____ and ____25____.

Task 4

Passage 1

Directions: *The following is a list of terms commonly used in positions. After reading it, you are required to find the items equivalent to those given in Chinese in the list below. Then you should put the corresponding letters in brackets on the Answer Sheet, numbered 1 through 5.*

A. — Accounting Assistant

B. — Copywriter

C. — Legal Adviser

D. — Personnel Manager

E. — Maintenance Engineer

F. — Sales Supervisor

G. — Securities Custody Clerk

H. — Bond Trader

I. — Financial Controller

J. — Project Staff

K. — Simultaneous Interpreter

L. — Business Manager

M. — Cashier

N. — Administrative Assistant

O. — Electrical Engineer

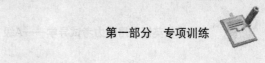

Example: （C）法律顾问　　　　　　　　（I）财务主任

1. （　）人事部经理	（　）业务经理
2. （　）销售监管	（　）证券交易员
3. （　）出纳员	（　）维修工程师
4. （　）电气工程师	（　）行政助理
5. （　）（项目）策划人员	（　）文字撰稿人

Passage 2

Directions: *The following is a list of terms used in public signs. After reading it, you are required to find the items equivalent to those given in Chinese in the list below. Then you should put the corresponding letters in brackets on the Answer Sheet, numbered 6 through 10.*

A. — Office Hours

B. — One Street

C. — Buses Only

D. — No Entry

E. — Filling Station

F. — No Visitors

G. — Lost and Found

H. — No Admittance

I. — Toll Free

J. — No Honking

K. — Safety First

L. — Wet Paint

M. — Fragile

N. — Insert Here

O. — Split Here

Example: （C）只准公共汽车通过　　　（I）免费通行

6. （　）单行道	（　）失物招领处
7. （　）闲人免进	（　）禁止入内
8. （　）此处撕开	（　）易碎
9. （　）游人止步	（　）禁止鸣喇叭
10. （　）油漆未干	（　）此处插入

Passage 3

Directions: *The following is a list of terms used in airport. After reading it, you are required to find the items equivalent to those given in Chinese in the list below. Then you should put the corresponding letters in brackets on the Answer Sheet, numbered 11 through 15.*

A. — Check in area (zone)

B. — Departure airport

C. — Domestic flights

D. — Luggage reclaim

E. — Reclaim belt

F. — Luggage from flights

G. — Inquiries

H. — Lost property

I. — Return fares

J. — Airports shuttle

K. — Emergency exit

L. — Flight connections

M. — Airport lounges

N. — Left baggage

O. — Queue here

Example: （C）国内航班　　　　　　　　（I）往返票价

11.（　）行李寄存		（　）机场休息室
12.（　）机场班车		（　）失物招领
13.（　）办理登机区		（　）到港行李
14.（　）取行李传送带		（　）取行李
15.（　）转机处		（　）安全出口

Passage 4

Directions: *The following is a list of terms used in price term. After reading it, you are required to find the items equivalent to those given in Chinese in the list below. Then you should put the corresponding letters in brackets on the Answer Sheet, numbered 16 through 20.*

A. — freight

B. — wharfage

C. — world/international market price

D. — landing charges

E. — customs duty

F. — custom valuation

G. — import surcharge

H. — discount/allowance

I. — return commission

J. — spot price

K. — indicative price

L. — wholesale price

M. — customs valuation

N. — port dues

O. — net price

Example: （C）国际市场价格　　　　　　（I）回佣，回扣

16. （　）批发价	（　）参考价格
17. （　）净价	（　）港口税
18. （　）进口附加税	（　）折扣
19. （　）海关估价	（　）关税
20. （　）卸货费	（　）码头费

Passage 5

Directions: *The following is a list of terms used in public signs. After reading it, you are required to find the items equivalent to those given in Chinese in the list below. Then you should put the corresponding letters in brackets on the Answer Sheet, numbered 21 through 25.*

A. — Reduced Speed Now

B. — On Sale

C. — Handle with Care

D. — Road Up. Detour

E. — Guard Against Damp

F. — No Smoking

G. — Admission Free

H. — Seat by Number

I. — Complaint Box

J. — No Bills

K. — Hands Off

L. — Staff Only

M. — No U Turn

N. — Hands Wanted

O. — No Littering

Example: （ C ）小心轻放　　　　　　　　（ I ）意见箱

21. （　） 本处职工专用	（　） 免费入场
22. （　） 不准张贴	（　） 减速行驶
23. （　） 勿乱扔杂物	（　） 请勿触摸
24. （　） 禁止掉头	（　） 对号入座
25. （　） 马路施工，请绕行	（　） 招聘

Task 5

Passage 1

Directions: *Read the following advertisement. After reading it, you are required to complete the statements that follow the questions (No. 1 to No. 5). You should write your answers (**in no more than 3 words**) on the Answer Sheet correspondingly.*

AOL® Wallet makes shopping online faster and easier for you. When you shop on AOL, you can have checkout forms automatically filled in with your billing and shipping information. You enter your information one time, and then AOL® Wallet will enter it for you in the future.

To make things more convenient, if you currently pay for your AOL monthly service with a credit card, you can use that billing information in your AOL® Wallet. Your information will be stored and ready for you when you want to make purchases. AOL® Wallet allows you to store up to 10 credit cards and 50 shipping addresses so you don't have to search for the right credit card, or scramble to find that old birthday card with your sister's return address label when you're making your purchases. It's all available for you in your AOL® Wallet.

AOL takes online privacy very seriously and we will never disclose AOL® Wallet User Information except to complete an online purchase you have requested or as permitted by law. We also value your safety and security, so we've taken the extra step of protecting your AOL® Wallet with your Account Security Question, which you may have created when registering for AOL or when logging into the AOL service.

If you don't already have an Account Security Question, you can sign up for one at AOL Keyword: Account Security Question.

1. What can AOL® allow you to store?

AOL® allows us to store up to _____ and 50 shipping addresses.

2. What does AOL take seriously and will never disclose AOL® Wallet User Information except on your request or as permitted by law?

AOL takes _____ very seriously.

3. What does AOL value?

AOL values the user's _____.

4. What may you have created when registering for AOL or when logging into the AOL service?

We may have created _____.

5. What is AOL keyword for signing up for an Account Security Question?

The AOL keyword is _____.

Passage 2

Directions: *Read the following passage on How to Write a Business Letter. After reading it, you are required to complete the statements that follow the questions (No. 6 to No. 10). You should write your answers (**in no more than 3 words**) on the Answer Sheet correspondingly.*

The first paragraph of a typical business letter is used to state the main point of the letter. Begin with a friendly opening; then a quick transition to the purpose of your letter. Use a couple of sentences to explain the purpose, but do not go into detail until the next paragraph.

Beginning with the second paragraph, state the supporting details to justify your purpose. These may take the form of background information, statistics or first-hand accounts. A few short paragraphs within the body of the letter should be enough to support your reasoning.

Finally, in the closing paragraph, briefly restate your purpose and why it is important. If the purpose of your letter is employment related, consider ending your letter with your contact information. However, if the purpose is informational, think about closing with gratitude for the reader's time.

6. What does the first paragraph of a typical business letter do?

The first paragraph usually states _____ of the letter.

7. What should one do after a friendly opening?

He/she should write _____ of the letter.

8. In which paragraph do you go into detail?

In _____.

9. What are the forms the supporting details may take in the second paragraph?

They may take the form of background information, statistics or _____.

10. How will one end his letter if the purpose of his letter is employment related?

He will end his letter with his _____.

Passage 3

Directions: *Read the following passage on Library Instruction Room Use. After reading it, you are required to complete the statements that follow the questions (No. 11 to No. 15). You should write your answers (**in no more than 3 words**) on the Answer Sheet correspondingly.*

Goddard Library has an enclosed room on the 2nd floor that can accommodate up to 25 people for library instruction or for student group study.

- Equipment in the room: there are 5 tables, 25 chairs, 1 very small white board, and a projection screen. The person or group who reserves the room is responsible for contacting the appropriate departments (Media Services, IT, etc.) for any and all of their media and computer networking needs for their session.
- Person(s) who reserve the room are also responsible for returning any media/computer equipment that they borrowed.
- Person(s) who reserve the room are also responsible for returning the room to its prior condition including cleaning the white board and collecting any generated trash.
- Reservation requests must be made at least 48 hours in advance of the day and time that the room is needed. You will receive an e-mail or a telephone call confirming your reservation of the available room.
- Library instruction takes precedence over all other activities.
- Regular, weekly meetings of non-library classes/organizations will not be permitted, due to the irregular nature of library instruction appointments.
- A weekly schedule of upcoming classes will be posted both on the doors of the room, and on the Library's website in the Library Instruction section.
- Reservations can be made during the academic year by contacting Sondra Bentz, Jen Boone, or Mary Dennison at: 285-723.

11. What is the equipment in the library room?
    There are 5 tables, 25 chairs, 1 small white board, and _____.

12. When must the reservation requests be made?
    They must be made _____ in advance.

13. What will you receive for confirming your reservation?
    An e-mail or _____.

14. Where will be the weekly schedule of upcoming classes posted?
    It will be posted on the _____ the room and on the Library's website.

15. Which number can one dial to make reservations?
    One can dial _____ to make reservations.

Passage 4

Directions: *Read the following passage. After reading it, you are required to complete the statements that follow the questions (No. 16 to No. 20). You should write your answers (**in no more than 3 words**) on the Answer Sheet correspondingly.*

The *Wall Street Journal* Honored With
Two Pulitzer Prizes in 2007:
Public Service and International Reporting

Distinction, Authority and Trust

The *Wall Street Journal* takes great pride in our belief that we serve a public trust—that our highest calling as a news organization is to unearth issues so that they can be effectively addressed.

That mission was once again rewarded with two Pulitzer Prizes in 2007: one for Public Service (for the brilliant investigative and analytic work on stock options backdating) and a second for International Reporting (for our work on China and the strain that their astonishing growth is putting on its people and its environment).

These awards represent the 15th and 16th Pulitzer Prizes the Journal's news department has received under Paul Steiger, who became managing editor in 1991. The *Wall Street Journal* has received 33 Pulitzers to date.

Our readers have come to expect this kind of value from us, and we will continue to bring it to them because we believe it is our most important role, providing the ideal environment for our advertisers.

16. What are the two Pulitzer Prizes the *Wall Street Journal* honored with in 2007?

   The two prizes are _____ and International Reporting.

17. What is the *Wall Street Journal*'s highest calling as a news organization?

   It is to _____ so that they can be effectively addressed.

18. What has the magazine done to get the prize for Public Service?

   They have done the brilliant _____ work on stock options backdating.

19. Who was the managing editor in 1991?

   _____.

20. How many Pulitzers has the *Wall Street Journal* received to date?

   It has received _____ Pulitzers to date.

Passage 5

Directions: *Read the following production introduction. After reading it, you are required to complete the statements that follow the questions (No. 21 to No. 25). You should write your answers (**in no more than 3 words**) on the Answer Sheet correspondingly.*

Product Introduction MP211

NEC Electronics has developed the MP211, an application processor for mobile phones that features three CPUs and a DSP on a single chip, enabling multimedia processing such as digital terrestrial broadcast reception, videophone replay, and music replay, with modest power requirements. Proprietary software technology allows the CPU cores to perform processing in parallel, and through optimum task allocation between three CPUs according to the used application, high performance and low power consumption are both realized.

Further reductions in power consumption have been achieved by optimizing the MP211 for cellular phone terminals, a product category for which maximizing battery life is essential, through fine power management according to usage conditions, including the use of separate power supplies for the internal circuits and the selective implementation of a sleep mode for specific circuits.

The MP211 also features a high-performance DSP design based on the digital signal processor technology accumulated over many years by NEC Electronics. Among other things, this DSP supports H.264 decoding essential for digital terrestrial broadcast reception, encoding and decoding for various formats such as MPEG-4 and JPEG, enabling the use of a large array of multimedia applications through software processing only, without any additional dedicated hardware.

21. Which company developed MP211?

    _____.

22. What is MP211?

    It is a(n) _____ for mobile phones.

23. What allows the CPU cores to perform processing in parallel?

    _____ technology.

24. What has been achieved by optimizing the MP211 for cellular phone terminals?

    Further reductions in _____.

25. What did the high-performance DSP design base on?

    It based on the _____ technology accumulated over many years by NEC Electronics.

答案及解析

Task 1

Passage 1

1. **B** 题干意为"该文章最恰当的标题是……"。该题为主旨题。文章所提到的工作、早起、努力学习都是围绕勤奋的主题展开，B 项正确。

2. **B** 题干意为"根据文章内容，下列哪一项不正确？"该题为细节题。由文章第三段可以看出，早起及其他好习惯，都较容易从年轻时养成，因此不正确的一项为 B。

3. **A** 题干意为"根据文章可得出……的结论"。该题为推论题。文章第四段可以看出，任何人都必须勤奋，年轻时努力学习，这样才能取得成功；最后一段也说到勤奋是成功之母。文章提到懒惰的人可能会成为乞丐或小偷，但 B 项懒惰总是导致偷盗过于绝对化；"Lost time never returns."是一句谚语，而非 C 项的物理学定律；由文章第二段可以看出工作的法则既适用于年轻人，也适用于老年人，因此 D 项"青年是生命中唯一重要的阶段"不恰当。

4. **D** 题干意为"根据文章内容，使一个人勤奋的最好方法是……"。该题为细节题。由文章第三段可以看出，有助于勤奋的最好方法是早起的习惯，因此 D 项正确。

5. **C** 题干意为"根据文章内容，我们猜测文章的作者是……的人。"该题为推论题。作者通过文章来表达他的观点，即"勤奋是成功之母"，可见作者不会是一个懒惰的人或乞丐，而是一个勤奋的人。C 项正确。

Passage 2

6. **B** 题干意为"大多数美国人喜欢高等教育主要是因为其……"。该题为细节题。由文章第一段第二句可以看出，美国人重视教育是因为其金钱价值。B 项正确。

7. **C** 题干意为"根据文章内容，下列哪一项不正确"。该题为细节题。从文章可以看出，美国人普遍认为所受学校教育越多，毕业后就可能挣到越多的钱，但文中并未提到教育是唯一获得财富的途径，因此选 C 项。

8. **D** 题干意为"文章说到人们更愿意学……"。该题为细节题。由文章第一段第四、五句可以看出，人们最强烈的愿望是获得医学或法律的学位，而艺术、历史、哲学等"非职业"领域学位的货币价值就没有这么大了。D 项正确。

9. **A** 题干意为"根据调查发现，一些美国人为……感到遗憾"。该题为细节题。由文章第二段最后一句可以看出，一些希望他们所过的生活和现在不同的美国人遗憾他们没有接受更多的教育，因此 A 项正确。

10. **B** 题干意为"作者在文章中想告诉我们……"。该题为主旨题。从文章可以看出，美国人对成功的定义是获得财富和拥有较高的物质生活水平。美国人普遍认为教育是达到成功的最好的途径，因此教育在美国社会中非常重要。其他 A、C、D 项文中均未提到。

Passage 3

11. **A** 题干意为"学生的部分最后成绩可能会根据……"。该题为细节题。由第一段第二句可以看出，一些教授根据学生的口头参与来评定学生的部分最后成绩，因此 A 项正确。

12. **A** 题干意为"（教授们）不但接受而且期望学生在课堂上的参与，但……课程除外"。该题为细节题。由第三段第一句可以看出，自然科学和数学的教授方法主要还是传统的老师讲、学生记的方式，A 项正确。

13. **D** 题干意为"通过文章，我们知道人文学科和社会学科的教育……"。该题为推论题。由第三段可以看出，人文学科和社会学科在过去 20 年出现了新的教育趋势，一些大学课程更重实践而非理论，因此 D 项正确。

14. **B** 题干意为"一些教授让学生做演讲、主持讨论的主要原因是……"。该题为推论题，由文章可以看出，一些课程出现了新的教育趋势，更注重实践而非理论，因此这些教授的授课方式是注重学生的实践能力，即"动手能力"。B项正确。

15. **B** 题干意为"根据文章内容，下列哪一项正确"。该题为细节题。多数采用新的教育方法的课程为人文学科和社会学科的课程，因此A项"社会学课程学生参与不常见"可以排除；多数采用传统教育方法的课程是自然科学和数学的课程，因此C项"一些教授通常让学生参与自然科学和数学的教学"可以排除；新的教育趋势是出现在人文学科和社会学科，D项是出现在如化学等自然学科中，显然不对。根据第二段第二句，"一些教授更喜欢控制讨论，而另外一些教授喜欢引导而非控制讨论"可得出B项正确。

Passage 4

16. **C** 题干意为"硬币落下的声音使人们……"。该题为细节题。由第二段第一句"当我回头看时，我看到一些人也在回头看"和第二段第一句"硬币落在人行道上的声音是注意力的集中点"可以看出，C项正确。

17. **B** 该题为细节题。由第三段第二句"当消防车、警车或救护车在街上呼啸而过时，纽约人很少回头看"可以得知，他们已经习惯了这样的声音，因此B项正确。

18. **B** 该题为推论题。由第四段第一句可以看出，作者以前是生活在康涅狄格；第五段作者说到在他的家乡，他25年来都听着深夜吱吱的声音，因此B项正确。

19. **B** 题干意为"作者是怎么提及夜晚的声音的"。该题为推论题。由第五段第二句可以看出，作者能听到隔着三道关着的门，一百码外的滴水的龙头，采用了夸张的手法，因此B项正确。

20. **C** 题干意为"他认为什么样的声音愉悦"。该题为细节题。由最后一段第一句"打字机的键在纸上轻敲的声音对我来说是一种可爱的声音"可得出C项正确。

Passage 5

21. **D** 题干意为"较长的小说往往……"。细节题。由第二段第二句"在更长结构的小说中，故事往往包含某些戏剧结构的核心要素。"得知，D项"包含更多核心要素"正确。

22. **C** 题干意为"在长篇小说中，本文章提到几个核心要素"。该题为细节题。由第二段可以看出，一共提到6个，分别是：说明、冲突、危机、高潮、解决、寓意。因此C项正确。

23. **C** 题干意为"小说中危机是指……"。该题为细节题。由第二段危机要素的解释可以得知，危机是指主要角色及其某个行动决定性的时刻，因此C项正确。

24. **A** 题干意为"短篇小说的情节为……"。该题为细节题。由第三段第四句"和长篇小说一样，短篇小说的情节也有高潮、危机或转折点"可得出，A项正确。

25. **B** 题干意为"根据文章,下列哪一项不正确"。该题为细节题,由第三段第一、二句"短篇故事可能会也可能不会依照小说的结构。一些短篇故事完全不遵循结构。"可得出，B项正确。

Task 2

Passage 1

1. **A**　题干意为"计算机科学学院的应聘者需要……"。细节题。由第一段第二句得知，学院感兴趣的是对自动化有兴趣的应聘者，因此 A 项正确。

2. **B**　题干意为"如果你需要关于计算机科学学院更多的信息，你可以……"。细节题。由第二段最后一句可得知计算机科学学院更多的信息可在 SCS 首页找到，因此 B 项正确。

3. **D**　题干意为"求职信需包含以下信息，除了……"。该题为细节题。由第三段第一句可以看出，作者所需提供的信息未提到 D 项。

4. **C**　题干意为"第三段第三行 reference 一词的意思是……"。语意题。文中 reference 的意思为"（关于品行、能力等的）证明、介绍"，因此 C 项正确。

5. **A**　题干意为"根据文章内容，下列哪一项不正确"。细节题。由第三段最后一句可以看出，求职者需表明国籍，非美国人公民需表明目前的签证状况，因此 A 项正确。

Passage 2

6. **C**　题干意为"沃尔玛在全球拥有……多家店"。细节题。由第一段最后一句可以得出，沃尔玛在 14 个国家拥有 6,800 多家店，因此 C 项正确。

7. **B**　题干意为"沃尔玛在中国最早的超市和山姆俱乐部是在……"。细节题。由第二段第二句可得知，沃尔玛在中国最早的超市和山姆俱乐部是在深圳，因此 B 项正确。

8. **C**　题干意为"下列哪一项不正确"。细节题。由文章可知，沃尔玛建于 1962 年，于 1996 年来到中国，而并非最早是在 1996 年建在深圳，因此选 C。

9. **C**　题干意为"沃尔玛每年从中国出口……"。细节题。由最后一段第一句可得知，沃尔玛每年从中国出口约 90 亿美元，因此 C 项正确。

10. **A**　题干意为"根据上海《商业信息》报的调查，沃尔玛……"。细节题。由第四段最后一句可得知，沃尔玛在供应商满意指标中排名第一，因此 A 项正确。

Passage 3

11. **C**　题干意为"文章给了……的建议"。细节题。由第一段第一句"要写好一份有效的商务报告，建议遵循以下三个步骤的方法"，可得知 C 项正确。

12. **B**　题干意为"文章所推荐方法的第二步是……"。细节题。由第一段可以得知，第二步是规划报告，因此 B 项正确。

13. **A**　题干意为"当你有超过三个的事实或数列要同时呈现时，最好……"。细节题。由第三步"写报告"中的第三小点可以看出，当要同时呈现超过三个的事实或数列时，可考虑采用表格或图表，因此 A 项正确。

14. **D**　题干意为"在写初稿时，需要注意以下几点，除了……"。细节题。由第三点"写报告"中可以看出，"改正错误，删除多余的、不必要的词"是在第二稿中要做的，故选 D 项。

15. **C** 题干意为"根据文章，下列哪一项不正确"。细节题。由文章可以看出，建议在写报告时要简洁，作者举例说"当6个词可以替代14个词时，就进行替代"。其意思并不是凡是14个词都用6个词代替。因此选C项。

Passage 4

16. **B** 题干意为"雇用合同是……"。细节题。由第一段第三句"雇用合同是雇主和雇员签订的协议"可得出，B项正确。

17. **C** 题干意为"第一段最后一句中 term 一词的意思是……"。语义题。该词在上下文中的意思为"条件、条款"，因此C项正确。

18. **D** 题干意为"如果合同的条款要改变，……"。细节题。由第三段可以得出，合同变动通常需双方同意，因此D项正确。

19. **A** 题干意为"你所拥有的就业权利通常取决于……"。细节题。由第四段可得知，就业权利取决于和雇主签订的合同的类型，因此A项正确。

20. **A** 题干意为"文章最好的标题是……"。主旨题。由第一段可以看出文章主要是介绍什么是雇用合同，以下均围绕此主题展开，因此A项正确。

Passage 5

21. **D** 题干意为"简历中的目标是指……"。细节题。由第三段可得知，目标是一个很短的句子，描述你希望得到的工作类别，因此D项正确。

22. **A** 题干意为"工作经历应该怎么安排……"。细节题。由第四段第一句"以最近的工作开始写工作经历"，因此A项正确。

23. **C** 题干意为"相关信息列举在……标题下"。细节题。由倒数第三段可以看出，相关信息列举在"其他技能"下，因此C项正确。

24. **A** 题干意为"倒数第二段 reference 一词的意思是……"。语义题。reference 在文中的意思是"证明人，介绍人"的意思，因此A项正确。

25. **A** 题干意为"你的简历最好写在……"。细节题。由最后一段可以看出，简历最好不超过一页，因此A项正确。

Task 3
Passage 1

1. lifesaving message   由第一段第二句 "Thank you for helping to share our lifesaving message with the public by supporting our public service advertising program." 可得到答案。

2. public service advertising   同1。

3. expiration dates   由第一段第三句 "Please use any of these PSA as you wish, being mindful of the expiration dates corresponding to some of them." 可得到答案。

4. online PSA　　　　　由第二段第一句 "Radio, print and online PSA are available here for download in print- or broadcast-ready format" 可得到答案。

5. local chapter　　　　由第二段第三句 "To order a broadcast-quality Beta SP tape, please contact your local chapter." 可得到答案。

Passage 2

6. Human Resources Director　由信件开头的称呼 Dear Human Resources Director 得到答案。

7. entry-level programmer　由第一段第二句 "I would like to apply for a position as an entry-level programmer at the center." 得到答案。

8. in-house and customer　由第二段第一句 "I understand that Taylor produces both in-house and customer documentation." 得到答案。

9. Computer Science　　由第二段第三句 "I'm a recent graduate of DeVry Institute of Technology in Atlanta with an Associate's Degree in Computer Science." 得到答案。

10. computer consultant　由第二段第四句 "I served as a computer consultant at the college's computer center where I helped train computer users on new systems." 得到答案。

Passage 3

11. the South Coast　　由第一段第三句 "It showcases the rich and abundant experience living on or visiting the South Coast." 得到答案。

12. goods and services　由第二段第一句 "*South Coast Style* offers businesses an upmarket platform for advertising goods and services, directly to a tightly targeted market." 得到答案。

13. seeking information　由第二段第二句 "*South Coast Style* is a resource for consumers seeking information on fine dining, great get-aways, selective shopping and exciting experiences." 得到答案。

14. news agents　　　　由第三段第一句 "*South Coast Style* covers stories from Austinmer to Eden and is distributed via news agents and selected retail outlets in affluent Northern & Eastern suburbs of Sydney, ACT, Wollongong, Illawarra, and South Coast of NSW." 得到答案。

15. selected retail outlets　同 4。

Passage 4

16. **Pierre Aries**　　　　由信头 "From: Pierre Aries." 得到答案。

17. **cutting down on**　　　由第一段第一句 "I have several proposals for cutting down on office staff." 得到答案。

18. **order clerk**　　　　　由第一段第二句 "I suggest that we eliminate the full-time position of order clerk, since there is not enough work to occupy him throughout the month." 得到答案。

19. **computer programmer**　由第二段第一句 "Second, now that our systems are completely computerized we no longer need a computer programmer on staff." 得到答案。

20. **secretarial**　　　　　由第二段第四句 "Third, I suggest that I share my secretary with the assistant office manager, thus eliminating one secretarial position." 得到答案。

Passage 5

21. **Company Accounting Office**　由第一段第一句 "I have known John Smith for the past year while he has worked as an Accounting Assistant in the Company Accounting Office." 得到答案。

22. **interpersonal and communication**　由第一段第三句 "His interpersonal and communication skills have allowed him to develop productive working relationships with both our clients and our staff." 得到答案。

23. **quality correspondence**　由第二段第一句 "John possesses solid writing skills which have enabled him to compose quality correspondence." 得到答案。

24. **diagnose problems**　第二段第二句 "He also has the analytical skills to diagnose problems and devise viable solutions." 可得到答案。

25. **devise viable solutions**　同 4。

Task 4

Passage 1

这是一列职务职位常用术语

1. D, L　　　2. F, H　　　3. M, E　　　4. O, N　　　5. J, B

A. — Accounting Assistant 会计助理

B. — Copywriter 文字撰稿人

C. — Legal Adviser 法律顾问

D. — Personnel Manager 人事部经理

E. — Maintenance Engineer 维修工程师

F. — Sales Supervisor 销售监管

G. — Securities Custody Clerk 保安人员

H. — Bond Trader 证券交易员

I. — Financial Controller 财务主任

J. — Project Staff（项目）策划人员

K. — Simultaneous Interpreter 同声传译员

L. — Business Manager 业务经理

M. — Cashier 出纳员

N. — Administrative Assistant 行政助理

O. — Electrical Engineer 电气工程师

Passage 2

这是一列公共标志的用语

6. B, G   7. H, D   8. O, M   9. F, J   10. L, N

A. — Office Hours 办公时间

B. — One Street 单行道

C. — Buses Only 只准公共汽车通过

D. — No Entry 禁止入内

E. — Filling Station 加油站

F. — No Visitors 游人止步

G. — Lost and Found 失物招领处

H. — No Admittance 闲人免进

I. — Toll Free 免费通行

J. — No Honking 禁止鸣喇叭

K. — Safety First 安全第一

L. — Wet Paint 油漆未干

M. — Fragile 易碎

N. — Insert Here 此处插入

O. — Split Here 此处撕开

Passage 3

这是一列机场用语

11. N, M   12. J, H   13. A, F   14. E, D   15. L, K

A. — Check in area (zone) 办理登机区

B. — Departure airport 离港时间

C. — Domestic flights 国内航班

D. — Luggage reclaim 取行李

E. — Reclaim belt 取行李传送带

F. — Luggage from flights 到港行李

G. — Inquiries 问讯处

H. — Lost property 失物招领

I. — Return fares 往返票价

J. — Airports shuttle 机场班车

K. — Emergency exit 安全出口

L. — Flight connections 转机处

M. — Airport lounges 机场休息室

N. — Left baggage 行李寄存

O. — Queue here 在此排队

Passage 4

这是一列价格术语

16. L, K   17. O, N   18. G, H   19. M, E   20. D, B

A. — freight 运费

B. — wharfage 码头费

C. — world/international market price 国际市场价格

D. — landing charges 卸货费

E. — customs duty 关税

F. — custom valuation 海关估价

G. — import surcharge 进口附加税

H. — discount/allowance 折扣

I. — return commission 回扣

J. — spot price 现货价格

K. — indicative price 参考价格

L. — wholesale price 批发价

M. — customs valuation 海关估价

N. — port dues 港口税

O. — net price 净价

Passage 5

这是一列公共标志用语

21. L, G   22. J, A   23. O, K   24. M, H   25. D, N

A. — Reduced Speed Now 减速行驶

B. — On Sale 大减价

C. — Handle with Care 小心轻放

D. — Road Up. Detour 马路施工，请绕行

E. — Guard Against Damp 防潮

F. — No Smoking 禁止抽烟

G. — Admission Free 免费入场

H. — Seat by Number 对号入座

I. — Complaint Box 意见箱

J. — No Bills 不准张贴

K. — Hands Off 请勿触摸

L. — Staff Only 本处职工专用

M. — No U Turn 禁止掉头

N. — Hands Wanted 招聘

O. — No Littering 勿乱扔杂物

Task 5

Passage 1

1. **10 credit cards**　　由第二段第三句 AOL® Wallet allows you to store up to 10 credit cards and 50 shipping addresses 可得到答案。

2. **online privacy**　　由第三段第一句 "AOL takes online privacy very seriously and we will never disclose AOL® Wallet User Information except to complete an online purchase you have requested or as permitted by law." 可得到答案。

3. **safety and security**　　由第三段第二句 "We also value your safety and security, so we've taken the extra step…" 可得到答案。

4. **Account Security Question**　　由第三段第二句 "…so we've taken the extra step of protecting your AOL® Wallet with your Account Security Question, which you may have created when registering for AOL or when logging into the AOL service." 可得到答案。

5. **Account Security Question**　　由第四段可得到答案。

Passage 2

6. **the main point**　　由第一段第一句 "The first paragraph of a typical business letter is used to state the main point of the letter." 可得到答案。

7. **the purpose**　　由第一段第二句 "Begin with a friendly opening; then a quick transition to the purpose of your letter." 可得到答案。

8. **the second paragraph**　　由第二段第一句 "Beginning with the second paragraph, state the supporting details to justify your purpose." 可得到答案。

9. **first-hand accounts**　　由第二段第二句 "These may take the form of background information, statistics or first-hand accounts." 可得到答案。

10. contact information
由第三段第二句 "If the purpose of your letter is employment related, consider ending your letter with your contact information." 可得到答案。

Passage 3

11. a projection screen
由第二段第一句 "Equipment in the room: there are 5 tables, 25 chairs, 1 very small white board, and a projection screen." 可得到答案。

12. 48 hours
由第五段第一句 "Reservation requests must be made at least 48 hours in advance of the day and time that the room is needed." 可得到答案。

13. a telephone call
由第五段第二句 "You will receive an e-mail or a telephone call confirming your reservation of the available room." 可得到答案。

14. doors of
由第八段 "A weekly schedule of upcoming classes will be posted both on the doors of the room, and on the Library's website in the Library Instruction section." 可得到答案。

15. 285-723
由最后一段 "Reservations can be made during the academic year by contacting Sondra Bentz, Jen Boone, or Mary Dennison at: 285-723." 可得到答案。

Passage 4

16. Public Service
由文章的题头 "The *Wall Street Journal* Honored with Two Pulitzer Prizes in 2007: Public Service and International Reporting" 可得到答案。

17. unearth issues
由第一段 "The *Wall Street Journal* takes great pride in our belief that we serve a public trust — that our highest calling as a news organization is to unearth issues so that they can be effectively addressed." 可得到答案。

18. investigative and analytic
由第二段 "That mission was once again rewarded with two Pulitzer Prizes in 2007: one for Public Service (for the brilliant investigative and analytic work on stock options backdating)…" 可得到答案。

19. Paul Steiger
由第三段第一句 "These awards represent the 15th and 16th Pulitzer Prizes the Journal's news department has received under Paul Steiger, who became managing editor in 1991." 可得到答案。

20. 33
由第三段第二句 "The *Wall Street Journal* has received 33 Pulitzers to date." 可得到答案。

Passage 5

21. **NEC Electronics** 由第一段第一句 "NEC Electronics has developed the MP211, …" 得到答案。

22. **an application processor** 由第一段第一句 "NEC Electronics has developed the MP211, an application processor for mobile phones that features three CPUs and a DSP on a single chip, …" 可得到答案。

23. **Proprietary software** 由第一段第二句 "Proprietary software technology allows the CPU cores to perform processing in parallel, …" 可得到答案。

24. **power consumption** 由第二段第一句 "Further reductions in power consumption have been achieved by optimizing the MP211 for cellular phone terminals, …" 可得到答案。

25. **digital signal processor** 由第三段第一句 "The MP211 also features a high-performance DSP designed based on the digital signal processor technology accumulated over many years by NEC Electronics." 可得到答案。

Part IV Translation

《基本要求》对 A 级翻译（英译汉）的要求是：能借助词典将中等难度、一般体裁的文字材料和对外交往的一般业务材料译成汉语。在翻译生词超过总词数 5% 的实用文字材料时，笔译速度每小时 250 个英语单词。本部分试题满分为 20 分。主要考查考生准确理解内容或结构较复杂的英语材料的能力，要求译文准确、完整、通顺并符合汉语的习惯。考生要取得较好的成绩，不仅要具有较高的阅读能力，较强的汉语表达能力，还要有一些翻译的基本技能和技巧。A 级试卷的第四部分为翻译，包括英译汉（4 题）和汉译英（1 题）。

1 翻译题的解题思路及技巧

单句翻译的解题思路

翻译题的前四道题是单句翻译，题型为多项选择，即给出四个选项，其中一个最佳答案、一个较好答案、一个较差答案和一个最差答案，这四个选项按等级的得分别为：2 分 – 1.5 分 – 1 分 – 0 分。

● **正确理解原文，准确用词**

理解原文要求准确无误。通过查看该句子的词（或词性）与词、词与句子之间的语法关系及逻辑关系准确地理解原题所表达的意思。例如：

1. When you turn down an invitation, you'd better give an explanation. 你拒绝别人邀请时最好能做出解释。

[解析] turn down 这个词组有 "调低" 和 "拒绝" 的意思，根据上下文，此处只能译为 "拒绝"。

2. It has been ten years since my father was a teacher. 我爸爸不当老师已有十年了。

[解析] was a teacher 的状态已结束。

● **分析语法，掌握结构**

在较长的英语句子中存在着比较复杂的关系，很难按顺序用一句汉语表达出来。要抓关键，理结构，看词序，看语态。找出主句和从句的骨干结构及其修饰成分，同时要注意是否有省略的地方，要注意介词短语、不定式短语、分词短语、动名词短语的各种语法功能。例如：

1. There are some kinds of rays from the sun, which would burn us to death if we were not protected from them.

[解析] 正确译文：如果我们不是受到（大气层的）保护的话，来自太阳的某些种类的射线就会把我们烧死。（…if we were not protected 是被动语态，是一个虚拟条件句。）

误译为：如果我们不是防备的话，来自太阳的某些种类的射线就会把我们烧死。

2. She advised me not to say anything until asked.

[解析] 正确译文：她劝我别说什么，除非有人要我说。（这个句子省略了 …until I was asked。）

误译为：她劝我别说什么，除非我想问。

● **英汉对照，忠实原文**

在英译汉的过程中，有些句子可以逐字对译，有些句子由于英汉两种语言的表达方式不同，不能用直译的方法对译，所以我们在翻译时，应做一些相应的调整和改变，使中文译文通顺、自然。例如：

1. Every life has its roses and thorns. 人生有苦有乐。

2. He is the last person for such a job. 他最不配做这件事。

单句翻译的技巧

● **语序的颠倒**

中、英文句子的排列和组成顺序千差万别，因此翻译时，必须做一些调整，才能使译文成为流畅生动的中文。例如：

1. 词和词组的颠倒

tough-minded 意志坚强；northeast 东北

2. 句子的颠倒

1) There is an English book on the desk. 书桌上有一本英语书。

2) I shall feel obliged if you will favor me with a call. 如果你能尽早给我回电话，我将非常感激。

● **文字的增减**

　　为了让译文符合汉语的习惯和表达规律，我们在翻译时要按意义上（或修辞上）和句法的需要增加一些词来更忠实、更通顺地表达原文的内容。例如：

1. Before the meeting and super, he would visit his parents. 在开会和吃晚饭前，他还要看望他的父母。（增加动词）

2. The play moved the audience to enthusiasm. 这出戏激发起观众极大的热情。（增加形容词）

3. My mother worked in a school; she is now a doctor in this hospital. 我妈妈过去在一个学校工作，现在是这个医院的医生。（增加表示时态的词）

● **句子的分句、合句法**

　　分句法和合句法是改变原文句子结构的两种重要方法。所谓分句法是把原文的一个简单句在翻译时译成两个或两个以上的句子，而合句法则反之。例如：

1. How can I apologize for missing our date yesterday? 昨天未能赴约，我该怎么向你道歉呢？（分句法）

2. The boy crashed down on a protesting chair. 那个男孩猛地坐在一把椅子上，椅子被压得吱吱作响，好像是提出抗议一般。（分句法）

3. Surprisingly, none of the children showed any sign of fear in face of terrorists. 令人惊讶的是这些小孩面对恐怖分子毫无惧色。（合句法）

4. In case the air moves, there will be a breeze. 空气的缓慢流动会产生微风。（合句法）

● **转换译法**

　　英语和汉语不仅用词、造句的方法不同，而且表达意思的方式也不同，因此，在忠实于原文的前提下，翻译时有时需要进行转换，对一些词和语法成分也需要作适当的调整。例如：

1. We cannot estimate the value of modern science too much. 对现代科学的价值无论怎样重视也不为过。（否定转译为肯定）

2. He is as strong as a horse. 他力大如牛。（其他转译，此句中不能译为"马"）

● **定语从句的翻译**

　　定语从句可分为限定性和非限定性定语从句，一般说来，定语句子较长的，可译为"……的"结构的定语，放在先行词之前，从而将复合句译成单句。如果定语从句的结构比较复杂，译成含"的"字的定语从句显得长而不符合汉语的习惯，可以采取分译法。例如：

1. Air is the mixture that we know best. 空气是我们最熟悉的混合物。

2. It was a young man, tall and handsome, though a little tired, on whom her eye fell when she stopped and turned. 她站住，转过身来，定睛一看，是一个年青的小伙子，他个子很高，虽然有点疲倦但十分英俊。

● **被动语态的翻译**

　　在科技文章中，英语大量采用被动语态，我们可以采用以下技巧来正确翻译被动语态的句子。

1. 保留原文的主语用"被……"。例如：

Louis was sent to the school by his parents when he was seven. 路易斯 7 岁时被父母送到这所学校。

2. 把被动语态译为"是……的"、"由……的"等。例如：

The flowers in the garden were watered by those old men this morning.

花园里的这些花和树是那些老人今天早晨浇的。

3. 使用无主句。例如：

You are asked to reply this letter. 请你回复此信。

4. 增添"人们"、"大家"作汉语的主语。例如：

It will be noted that their suggestion is reasonable to a certain degree.

人们将注意到，他们的建议在某种程度上是合理的。

● **长句的翻译**

1. 顺序法。例如：

The shops in Chicago are really wonderful and you will find most of them in the area which is called the loop. 芝加哥的商店确实令人眼花缭乱，而且你会发现这些商店大部分都集中在市里所谓的"商业区"。

2. 逆序法。例如：

A film can slow down the formation of crystals so that the students can study the process.

为了能让学生研究这一过程，电影可以放慢演示晶体形成的过程。

3. 分译法。例如：

We would like you to hasten shipment receipt of this letter. 我方希望贵公司收到此信后，尽快交货。

4. 综合法。例如：

Modern scientific and technical books, especially textbooks, require revision at short intervals if their authors wish to keep pace with new ideas, observations and discoveries. 对于现代书籍，特别是教科书来说，要是作者希望自己的内容能与新概念、新观察到的事实和新发现同步发展的话，那么就应该每隔一段时间，将书中的内容重新修改。

段落翻译的解题思路

　　英汉翻译中的第二部分为一段 70 词左右的英文段落，要求考生将其译成较通顺的汉语。内容全是应用文，包括广告、告示、报告片段、说明书片段、合同片段、招 / 投标书片段、规章片段等。本部分分值 12 分。

● **正确理解段落翻译的内容**

段落翻译属于主观题型,理解是前提,有了正确的理解,还得有符合汉语习惯的表达。既需要对原文的正确理解,还要有对原文语言和译文语言的驾驭能力。翻译时首先把握句子结构和词语用法,还要注意上下文意思的连贯性以及句与句之间的语法和逻辑关系,弄清代词的指代意思,分析所要翻译的句子中的词汇、结构和习惯用法。做到先理解,再翻译。既要忠实原作的内容和风格,又要对原作的内容、风格、语体、语言有全面的照顾,不拘泥于原文的形式。例如:

1. In June this year we place the order for electric heaters. The deadline of October 31 has passed and there is still no indication of when delivery is to be expected. Please reply immediately with reasons for delay and inform us of when and how the goods will be shipped. If we don't hear from you soon, we shall have to cancel the order.

[译文]:今年六月我们订购了电热器,如今 10 月 31 日的最后期限已过,但我们仍不知货物何时能到达。请即刻来信告知货物因何故耽搁,以及将于何时以何种方式发货。如无回函,我们将取消订单。

[解析]:这封责问信措辞严厉,弄清前后句与句之间的逻辑关系和意思的连贯性是翻译这类信件的关键。原委—提出责问的原因—要求对方采取行动—后果。

关键词:place an order, cancel an order, delivery

2. Normally speaking, China is now only at the beginning stage of producing its own fax machines, and the products can at best compete with the low-grade imported ones in the U.S. market. Great efforts are needed to master and apply new and high technologies for the development of new famous brand fax model so as to win a great market share.

[译文]:总的来说,中国自产传真机尚处于初级阶段。其产品最多也只能与美国市场上低档次的进口传真机相媲美。为了获得更大的市场份额,还要花大力气掌握和运用高新技术来开发传真机的新的著名品牌。

[解析]:第一、二句说明情况,第三句指出目标。第三句较长,翻译时先把握句子结构,并按照汉语习惯,把目的状语放在前面,读起来更自然顺口。

关键词:at best, low-grade, market share, fax machine

段落翻译的技巧

准确和流畅是衡量翻译好坏的质量标准,准确就是译文要与原文的思想内容、文字风格相一致。流畅则指译文要通俗易懂。为达到二者的和谐统一,要采用直译和意译的方法。

● **直译**

在语言条件许可下,译文不仅传递原文的内容,还保留原文的修辞风格和组句形式。例如:

谁知盘中餐,粒粒皆辛苦。Who knows that every grain in the bowl is the fruit of so much pain and toil?

● 意译

有些原文的内容或形式不宜用汉语直接表达，而是经过解析后用另一种语言表达出来，也就是更注重意思的翻译，而不拘泥于表面文字。需要深入钻研原文，达到融会贯通，方能抓住要点。例如：

1. He is the last man I want to see. 他是我想见的最后一个人。（意译：他是我最不想见的人。）

2. The photo flatters him. 他本人长得没有照片上那么帅。（词意的引申）

● 正反译

由于英汉思维方式的不同，英汉语言的表达习惯也不尽相同，英语和汉语都有从正面或反面来表达一种概念的现象。翻译时，原文从正面表达的句子，译文可以从反面来表达。反之亦然。这种表达方式不仅使语言更生动流畅，且效果更佳。例如：

1. Keep off the grass. 请勿践踏草坪。（离开草坪）

2. I love you more than I can say. 我说不出我有多爱你。（我爱你超过我能说的）

3. I can't agree more about it. 我对此非常赞同。

4. Don't lose time in posting the letter. 赶快把这封信寄出去。

● 增译

翻译既是语言的翻译，也是思维的翻译。为使意思更加清晰，可在译文中增加名词、副词、语气助词等。例如：

1. The difference between a brain and a computer can be expressed in a single word: complexity. 电脑与人脑的差异，可用一句话来表达：人脑比电脑更复杂。（complexity 如只译作"复杂性"就不易理解。这里采用了增译法）

2. This shopping mall's major focus is on women's fashion, priced in the middle range and affordable to all consumers. 此购物中心以经营女式服装为主，价格以中档为主，所有的顾客在这里都能够找到他们能消费得起的商品。

② 翻译题的练习及解析

单句翻译

1. If this ring were antique and not modern, the silver and workmanship would be much better.

   A. 这枚戒指如果不是新式的，而是古色古香的，那么，银的成色与工艺就会更好。

   B. 如果这枚戒指不时尚的话，那么，银戒指的工艺就会更好。

   C. 这枚戒指如果不是老式的而是新的，那银的成色与工艺就会更好。

   D. 那枚银戒指的成色和工艺，因为是古色古香的而显得更好。

2. Only members of the company are entitled to use these facilities.

    A. 只要获得光荣称号的职工，才能用这些设备。

    B. 只有该公司的职工才有资格使用这些设备。

    C. 只有该公司的职工才懂得怎样使用这些设备。

    D. 这些设备是为该公司的职工专门设计的。

3. The explorer lost his way, so he climbed to the top of the hill to locate himself.

    A. 这个探险者爬上山顶发现自己迷路了。

    B. 这个探险者沿着别人走的路一直走到山顶。

    C. 这个探险者迷了路，于是他爬上山顶以便确认自己所在的位置。

    D. 这个探险者迷了路，于是他爬上山顶以便扎营住下。

4. Children from pet owning families have strong immune system and are ill less frequently than other youngsters; research has shown...

    A. 那些把孩子当成宠物来养的家庭比其他家庭在研究方面更具有系统性和抗病的能力。

    B. 研究表明，宠物的孩子比家庭养的孩子更具有免疫能力，也不容易生病。

    C. 不养宠物的孩子比养宠物家庭的孩子更具有系统性和抗病的能力。

    D. 研究表明，那些家庭里饲养宠物的孩子比其他孩子来说具有更强免疫系统，也更不容易生病。

5. A criminal entrapped an elderly man in a bad investment and stole his money.

    A. 犯罪分子使一位老人陷入投资的陷阱，偷走了他的钱。

    B. 犯罪分子诱骗一位老人帮助他们进行错误的投资，并偷走了他的钱。

    C. 犯罪分子诱骗一位老人从事错误的投资，骗走了他的钱。

    D. 犯罪分子使一位老人进行了一次糟糕的投资，并偷走了他的钱。

6. She began at the entry level as a clerk and worked her way up the ladder to become president of the company.

    A. 她从职员岗位开始，后来，一步一步地向上爬，当上了公司的总裁。

    B. 她从底楼的入门职员开始工作，后来，借助一把楼梯，爬上了公司总统的办公室。

    C. 她从入门当职员开始，后来，逐步晋升，当上了公司的总统。

    D. 她从最低岗位的职员开始，后来，逐步晋升，当上了公司的总裁。

7. A good book at bedtime may be as effective as a late night cheese in making peculiar dreams.

    A. 睡觉前，床边放一本好书，你们会像晚餐时吃的奶酪一样，做一些特殊的梦。

    B. 睡觉前读一本书，可能会像晚餐时吃的奶酪一样回味无穷。

    C. 睡觉前读一本书，可能会在梦里做一些像晚餐时吃的奶酪一样的好梦。

    D. 睡觉前读一本书，可能会像在梦里吃的奶酪一样回味无穷。

8. After the fight, the police arrested us, it was a bad trip.

    A. 斗殴之后，警方逮捕了我们，那是一个不幸的局面。

    B. 我们有一个不幸的旅游，因为打架后，警察把我们抓了。

C. 斗殴之后，警方逮捕了我们，那是一个糟糕的短途旅游。

D. 一次不幸的短时间斗殴之后，警方要逮捕我们。

9. I can't come to your wedding but I'll be there in spirit.

A. 我不能参加你们的婚礼，但是我衷心祝愿你们幸福。

B. 我虽能加你们的婚礼，但并不是说你们就幸福。

C. 我不能参加你们的婚礼，但到时候我的心会和你们在一起的

D. 我不能参加你们的婚礼，但是我的灵魂和你们在一起。

10. The woman stopped outside the shop, and was joined by her husband who began to talk to her in a low voice, begging her to excuse him.

A. 那个妇女走到店门口时，她丈夫加入了她，开始低声地和她说话，并祈求她原谅。

B. 那个妇女走到店门口停下来，她丈夫朝她走过来，开始低声地和她说话，并祈求她原谅。

C. 那个妇女走到店门口停下来，她丈夫朝她走过来，并轻轻地说你要给我道歉。

D. 她丈夫说只有她走到店门口停下来，他才会低声地祈求那个妇女的原谅。

11. Present day traffic destroyed much of the peace of the city.

A. 现代的交通大大地破坏了市中心的宁静。

B. 现代的交通车都是在市中心出事，我们没有了宁静。

C. 市中心的宁静是现代交通造成的。

D. 白天的交通在很大程度上地破坏了市中心的宁静。

12. Both Li Hua and I treasure our many years of happiness together. And we are grateful, too, for the many good friends like you we have had along the way.

A. 李华和我都十分珍惜像你一样的好朋友，因为我们共同在一起幸福地生活了好几年。

B. 我和李华都十分珍惜我们共同度过的这些岁月，当然，对于像你一样的许多好朋友也都心存感激。

C. 我和李华都十分珍惜像你一样的好朋友，同时，也对在路上遇到你们而感到高兴。

D. 我和李华共同在一起幸福地生活了好几年，都十分珍惜像你一样的好朋友。

13. I was so pleased to hear of your graduation (this year). My hearty congratulations, and I hope that you will find your career a source of great joy and happiness.

A. 很高兴得到你大学毕业的消息，谨向你表示衷心的祝贺，并希望你在今后的工作中愉快幸福。

B. 很高兴得到你大学毕业的消息，我从心里表示祝贺，并希望你有一个愉快的工作。

C. 我很高兴你大学毕业了，并希望你能有一个我能表示衷心祝贺的工作。

D. 你大学毕业的消息让我很高兴，谨向你表示衷心的祝贺，并希望你在今后的工作中能愉快幸福。

14. The output of chemical fiber in this county has been increased five times as against 1995.

A. 这个县的化纤产量是1995年的3倍。

B. 这个县的化纤产量比1995年增加了4倍。

C. 这个县的化纤产量是1995年的4倍。

D. 这个县的化纤产量比1995年增加了5倍。

15. We ask you to accept our apologies for the delay in delivery and the trouble and inconvenience this caused both you and your clients.

    A. 对这次延误交货给我们带来的不便与麻烦，你们应该给我们道歉，并接受批评。

    B. 对这次延误交货并由此对你方以及你方客户带来的所有麻烦与不便，我们深表歉意。

    C. 对这次延误交货出现的麻烦，请你们给我们的客户道歉，并接受批评。

    D. 对这次延误交货带来的不便，我们要向你们的客户道歉，并承认是我们的错。

16. Rather than squeezing your own oranges, have you tried buying packs of orange juice?

    A. 你是否试过买几盒橙汁，而不是自己榨。

    B. 你宁愿自己榨橙汁，也不试着去买几盒。

    C. 你自己榨橙汁了，还要试着去买几盒吗？

    D. 你宁愿买几盒橙汁，也不想试着自己榨。

17. The book was originally thought to be too shocking to be published.

    A. 这本书最初被认为会使人大吃一惊，因此得以出版。

    B. 出版这本书，是由于人们认为它会有一种原始的震撼力。

    C. 这本书写的太过分了，因此，这本书不可能出版。

    D. 这本书原先被认为过于离谱，不能出版。

18. Out in the fresh air, she quickly regained sense.

    A. 远离新鲜空气，她很快就恢复了精神。

    B. 她在室外呼吸点新鲜空气，很快就有了意识。

    C. 远离新鲜空气，她很快就有了新的感受。

    D. 她在室外呼吸点新鲜空气，很快就恢复精神了。

19. I was ambitious and wanted to rise above such a life.

    A. 我是一个有野心的人，我想超越自己的生活。

    B. 我雄心勃勃，希望过上天堂般的生活。

    C. 我雄心勃勃，不安于这种生活。

    D. 我的雄心壮志是要过一种超越普通人的生活。

20. Perhaps more importantly, our exploration of space has taught us to view the earth, the universe and ourselves in a new way.

    A. 也许更为重要的是，我们在太空的探索和从新的角度看待我们自己、看待地球和宇宙又有了一条新路。

    B. 也许更为重要的是，我们对太空的探索教会了我们如何从新的角度看待我们自己，看待地球和宇宙。

    C. 也许更为重要的是，我们从新的角度看待我们自己，看待地球和宇宙的方法，教会了我们一条对太空的探索之路。

    D. 也许更为重要的是，当我们从新的角度看待我们自己，看待地球和宇宙时，我们就会放弃对太空的探索。

答案与解析

1. 各项得分为：A（2分），D（1.5分），C（1分），B（0分）
   这是一个虚拟语气的句子。antique: 古董，workmanship: 工艺

2. 各项得分为：B（2分），C（1.5分），A（1分），D（0分）
   这是一个被动语态的句子。be entitled: 被授予……权利

3. 各项得分为：C（2分），D（1.5分），A（1分），B（0分）
   这是一个由 so 引导的状语从句，不定式 to locate himself 作状语，表目的。

4. 各项得分为：D（2分），C（1.5分），B（1分），A（0分）
   from pet owning families 作定语修饰 children，本句翻译时要加词"不养宠物的孩子"，这样句子才完整。

5. 各项得分为：C（2分），A（1.5分），D（1分），B（0分）
   entrap someone in something 意思是"诱骗某人上当"，根据题意不能译为"偷"。

6. 各项得分为：D（2分），A（1.5分），C（1分），B（0分）
   entry level: 最低要求，begin… as: 从当……开始

7. 各项得分为：B（2分），C（1.5分），D（1分），A（0分）
   这一句用转换法翻译，译为"睡觉前读一本好书"。从整个句子来理解，making peculiar dream 译为"回味无穷"才能成为正确和生动的中文。

8. 各项得分为：A（2分），B（1.5分），C（1分），D（0分）
   从前面句子的内容来理解，a bad trip 意思是"一个不幸的局面"，不能译为"旅行"。

9. 各项得分为：C（2分），D（1.5分），A（1分），B（0分）
   in spirit: 在内心，在精神上；根据上文的内容和汉语的表达法，译为"我的心……"。

10. 各项得分为：B（2分），A（1.5分），C（1分），D（0分）
    who 引导的定语从句修饰 her husband，begging 引导的分词短语作伴随状语。

11. 各项得分为：A（2分），D（1.5分），B（1分），C（0分）
    present day 意为"现代的"，不能译为"目前"。

12. 各项得分为：B（2分），D（1.5分），A（1分），C（0分）
    many years of happiness together 增加"我们共同度过的"使句子通顺。we have had along the way 是定语从句，修饰 friends。

13. 各项得分为：A（2分），B（1.5分），D（1分），C（0分）
    本句应采用转换法来翻译，将名词短语 my hearty congratulations 转为句子来翻译，source of great joy and happiness 是宾语补语。

14. 各项得分为：B（2分），C（1.5分），A（1分），D（0分）
    increased five times 增长4倍，不是5倍。译为：这个县的化纤产量比1995年增加了4倍，或翻译为：这个县的化纤产量是1995年的5倍。

15. 各项得分为：B（2分），D（1.5分），C（1分），A（0分）
    apology for 意思为"表示歉意"，this caused both you and your clients 是定语从句，修饰 trouble and inconvenience。

16. 各项得分为：A（2分），B（1.5分），C（1分），D（0分）

rather than 意思为"不是……而是"。

17. 各项得分为：D（2分），B（1.5分），A（1分），C（0分）

too shocking to 是主语补语，too...to... 意思为"太……以至于不能……"。

18. 各项得分为：D（2分），B（1.5分），C（1分），A（0分）

out in the fresh air 作状语，regain sense 意思为"恢复精神"。

19. 各项得分为：C（2分），D（1.5分），B（1分），A（0分）

句中 ambitious 是形容自己，应取其褒义解释,应译为"雄心勃勃",不能译为"有野心"。

20. 各项得分为：B（2分），C（1.5分），A（1分），D（0分）

to...in a new way 是宾语补足语。

段落翻译

1. A four-star tourist hotel, Xi Yuan Hotel is situated at Sanlihe Road, next to the Import-export Building and the Capital Gymnasium. It has an elegant environment and is accessible to transportation. Xi Yuan Hotel boasts 900 guest rooms and suites, all well-equipped with modern facilities. There are all together 9 restaurants and bars. The hotel is equipped with modern communication means and may provide its customers with such services as fax, IDDD（国际直拨电话）and amusing activities.

2. Haier Group is the world's fourth largest white-goods manufacturer and one of China's Top one hundred electronics and IT companies. Haier has thirty design centers, plants and trade companies and more than 50,000 employees throughout the world. Haier's fifteen leading products, including refrigerators, air conditioners, washing machines, televisions, water heaters, personal computer, mobile phones and kitchen facilities have been considered as China's famous brand.

3. Safe Deposit Boxes for the safe keeping of money and other valuables. They are provided at your disposal free of charge. The hotel can not be held responsible for valuables left in guest rooms. Safe Deposit Boxes are available on request at the Front Desk Cashier's at no charge. The hotel is not responsible for any loss or damage of the valuables left in rooms.

4. The Chinese Export Commodities Fair is held twice a year in the city of Guangzhou. Tens and thousands of foreign businessmen come to the fair from all over the world. They are attracted by various kinds of goods on display. The fair itself is a mirror of China's economy. Chinese primary commodities, such as silk, tea and coal sell well on the world market. Light industry and weaving products, including clothing and machinery items are also well received in many countries.

5. With the rapid development of science and technology, the mobile phone has got more and more functions. It can be used not only to communicate and get access to the web, but also to play MP3, watch television, play electronic games and take pictures. Besides, it can perform the functions of weather forecast, recording, the notebook, the calendar, the alarm clock and the calculator. There have been lots of changes in the designing. For instance, the colored screens have replaced the black and white ones. And even the smart phone has been put into use now.

答案与解析

1. 西苑饭店是一座四星级酒店，位于北京三里河路，与进出口贸易大楼、首都体育馆相毗邻，环境优美，交通便利。饭店共有客房 900 套，均配备了现代化的便利设施。饭店共设餐厅、酒吧 9 个。饭店还有传真、国际直拨电话等现代化通讯设备及各种娱乐设施可以为每位客户提供优质服务。

   关键词语：boast: 以拥有……而自豪；communication means: 通讯工具；be accessible to: 易接近的，易进入的（译成中文时，考虑汉语表达的习惯，译成"交通便利"）；provide sb. with sth.: 给某人提供某物。

2. 海尔集团是世界第四大白色家电制造商，也是中国电子信息百强企业之首。在全球建有 30 个设计中心，制造基地和贸易公司，员工超过 5 万人，海尔的 15 个主导产品包括电冰箱、空调、洗衣机、电视、热水器、个人电脑、手机和厨房设施被评为中国名牌产品。

   关键词语：be considerd as: 被视为……；top one hundred companies: 百强企业之首；IT = information technology；including… 为分词短语，作定语修饰 leading products（主导产品）。

3. 贵重物品保险箱：为了您的钱和其他贵重物品的安全，本酒店设有贵重物品保险箱免费供您使用。酒店对客人放在客房内的贵重物品不负看管的责任。前台收银处有免费的保险箱可供使用。酒店对客人放在客房内的贵重物品的丢失和损坏概不负责。

   关键词语：Front Desk Cashier's: 前台收银处；left in guest rooms 是过去分词短语，修饰 valuables，译为"放在客房内的贵重物品"。

4. 中国出口商品交易会每年在广州举行两次。届时成千上万的外国客商从世界各地汇集到广州。他们被参展的各种各样的商品所吸引。广交会本身就是反映中国经济的一面镜子。中国的主要产品如丝绸、茶叶、煤等在国际市场很畅销，轻纺产品包括服装在许多国家很受欢迎。

   关键词语：weaving products: 纺织产品；well received: 很受欢迎

5. 随着科技的迅速发展，手机具有越来越多的功能。它不仅可以用来通讯和上网，还可以用来播放 MP3、看电视、玩电子游戏和摄影。此外，手机还具有天气预报、录音、记事本、日历、闹钟、计算器等功能。手机的设计也发生了许多变化。例如，彩屏代替了黑白屏。时至今日智能手机也已投入使用。

   关键词语：smart phone: 智能电话

第二部分　模拟试题

Test One

Part I　Listening Comprehension (15 minutes)

Directions: *This part is to test your listening ability. It consists of 3 sections.*

Section A

Directions: *This section is to test your ability to understand short dialogues. There are 5 recorded dialogues in it. After each dialogue, there is a recorded question. Both the dialogues and questions will be spoken only once. When you hear a question, you should decide on the correct answer from the 4 choices marked A, B, C and D given below.*

Example: *You will hear: W: Are you catching the 13:15 flight to New York?*

M: No. I'll leave this evening.

Q: What are the two people talking about?

You will read: A. New York City.

B. An Evening Party.

C. An air trip.

D. The man's job.

From the dialogue we learn that the man is to take a flight to New York. Therefore, "C. An air trip" is the correct answer. Now the test will begin.

1. A. It was satisfactory.　　　　　　　　　　B. It was just so so.
   C. It was disappointing.　　　　　　　　　　D. It was untrue.
2. A. 7:20 p.m.　　　B. 7:30 p.m.　　　　C. 7:40 p.m.　　　　D. 7:50 p.m.
3. A. At a hotel.　　　　　　　　　　　　　　B. At the man's house.
   C. At a garden.　　　　　　　　　　　　　　D. At the woman's house.
4. A. Manager and waitress.　　　　　　　　　B. Customer and waitress.
   C. Customer and manager.　　　　　　　　　D. Husband and wife.
5. A. Does her homework.　　　　　　　　　　B. Washes clothes.
   C. Cleans the back yard.　　　　　　　　　　D. Enjoys the beautiful day.

Section B

Directions: *This section is to test your ability to understand short conversations. There are 2 recorded conversations in it. After each conversation, there are some recorded questions. Both the conversations and questions will be spoken two times. When you hear a question, you should decide on the correct answer from the 4 choices marked A, B, C and D given in your test paper.*

Conversation 1

6. A. Renting an apartment.　　　　　B. Buying a house.

   C. Asking for help.　　　　　　　　D. Repairing the house.

7. A. $1,200.　　B. $1,300.　　C. $1,400.　　D. $1,500.

8. A. Two kilometers.　　　　　　　　B. One kilometer.

   C. Less than a kilometer.　　　　　D. More than a kilometer.

Conversation 2

9. A. She has experience of office work.

   B. She likes young people, and wants to get some experience on teaching.

   C. She likes working independently.

   D. The salary is very attractive.

10. A. The woman likes working on her own.

    B. The woman likes working with others.

    C. The woman is a well-experienced.

    D. The manager is quite dissatisfied with the woman.

Section C

Directions: *This section is to test your ability to comprehend short passages. You will hear a recorded passage. After that, you will hear 5 questions. Both the passage and questions will be read two times. When you hear a question, you should complete an answer to it with a word or a short phrase (**in no more than 3 words**). The questions and incomplete answers are printed on your test paper. You should write your answers correspondingly. Now the passage will begin.*

11. How many ways of going on holiday are there at present?

    At present there are _____ ways of going on holiday.

12. Where do holidaymakers of the first type go when they go on holiday?

    They always go to _____ or mountain resorts when they go on holiday.

13. What do holidaymakers of the first type enjoy?

    They just enjoy _____ and play the sports they like.

14. What does going on holiday mean to holidaymakers of the other type?

For them, going on holiday _____.

15. What do holidaymakers of the other type do if they come to a place?

They will stay until they get a proper feeling of it or fully enjoy the local food, wine and _____.

Part II   Structure (15 minutes)

Directions: *This part is to test your ability to construct grammatically correct sentences. It consists of 2 sections.*

Section A

Directions: *In this section, there are 10 incomplete sentences. You are required to complete each one by deciding on the most appropriate word or words from the 4 choices marked A, B, C and D.*

16. The flood has caused _____ to this village.

A. many damages 　　　　　　　　B. much damages

C. much damage 　　　　　　　　　D. few damages

17. He was informed that it was_____ who wanted the interview.

A. I 　　　　　B. me 　　　　　C. myself 　　　　　D. mine

18. I don't think he can buy spare parts for this car, _____?

A. can't he 　　　B. can he 　　　C. am I 　　　D. am not I

19. He tried to make up _____ the lost time _____ staying up late.

A. with...with 　　B. with...by 　　C. for...with 　　D. for...by

20. Hardly had I _____ when the play began.

A. seated 　　　B. been sat 　　　C. sited 　　　D. been seated

21. You look smart in this new jacket. That old one _____ thrown away many years ago.

A. ought to be 　　　　　　　　　B. ought to have been

C. would be 　　　　　　　　　　D. would have been

22. "The ground is wet." "Yes, didn't you know? _____ for the last 20 minutes."

A. It's raining 　　　　　　　　　B. It was raining

C. It's been raining 　　　　　　　D. It has rained

23. The form _____ in and returned within three weeks.

A. is to be filled 　　　　　　　　B. will fill

C. is to fill 　　　　　　　　　　D. are going to be filled

24. The stronger the coffee is, _____ now.

A. the more I like 　　　　　　　　B. the better I like

C. the more better I like it 　　　　　D. the better I like it

25. Were it not for the debt, we _____ a happy life.

    A. are living   B. would live   C. were living   D. will live

Section B

Directions: *There are 10 incomplete statements here. You should fill in each blank with the proper form of the word given in the brackets. Write the word or words in the corresponding space.*

26. I'm sorry, some of the books in your list are not (avail) _____ at the time being.

27. She was under great financial (stressful) _____, so she had to find another part-time job.

28. The sinking of the ship is due to its (load) _____.

29. He passed the examination; all of us give our (congratulate) _____ to him.

30. Roger's (refuse) _____ to pay the fine got him into trouble.

31. Soon the employees became very (skill) _____ in doing such jobs.

32. It's high time that you (pay) _____ more attention to your pronunciation.

33. Do the results of the study have any practical (apply) _____?

34. It is Mary who (sing) _____ the song.

35. What a (self) _____ girl you are; let the other children share your toys.

Part III   Reading Comprehension (40 minutes)

Directions: *This part is to test your reading ability. There are 5 tasks for you to fulfill. You should read the reading materials carefully and do the tasks as you are instructed.*

Task 1

Directions: *After reading the following passage, you will find 5 questions or unfinished statements, numbered 36 to 40. For each question or statement there are 4 choices marked A, B, C and D given in your test paper. You should choose the correct choice.*

    In our system of education today, examinations are a common feature. Our present education system has often been criticized as too examination-oriented (以考试为导向的). However, one must remember that in offices and other areas of work, examinations still feature clearly. There is no doubt that the fear and influence of examination cause much preparation work. So it therefore appears that examinations whether considered good or bad would stay for a while as a test of human knowledge.

    Examinations are meant to test the intellect of a person, how much he knows or how he has learnt from a particular course. It is designed to make students study, which should be their immediate mission in life. In our competitive world of today, examinations have a highly selecting or <u>filtering</u>

（筛选）role. In the university, students have to pass annual examinations before they are allowed to continue, or study a harder syllabus（教学大纲）. Moreover, for entrance into a university, pre-university examination results would provide a guide as to whether a student has the minimum qualifications necessary.

In offices either government or private ones, examination results show clearly whether a person is fit for promotion. The results indicate how much he knows about the work.

In all these cases, examinations inculcate（灌输）a spirit of hard work and competition. Students or office workers can refresh their mind again and again on what they have learnt. This maintains a certain individual and overall standard of knowledge.

36. The first paragraph mainly indicates that _____.

A. although criticized, examinations are still widely used

B. examinations play a bad role in education

C. one should take an argument in favor of examinations

D. examinations serve as a test of human knowledge

37. The function of examinations in offices is that their results _____.

A. show clearly how well a person is prepared for the examinations

B. show clearly whether a person is fit for promotion

C. suggest the way in which the employees deal with routine work

D. indicate whether an employee has minimum qualifications necessary

38. Which of the following statements is NOT mentioned in the passage?

A. Examinations can motivate people to work hard and to be competitive.

B. Examinations involve much preparation work.

C. Through examinations, excellent people can be selected.

D. Examinations have produced many people capable of their own field.

39. The underlined word "filtering" in Paragraph 2 means _____.

A. passing   B. purifying by using a filter

C. motivating   D. encouraging

40. The author's attitude to examination seems to be _____.

A. uncertain   B. neutral   C. positive   D. partial

Task 2

Directions: *This task is the same as Task 1. The 5 questions or unfinished statements are numbered 41 to 45.*

The hotel uses a reservation confirmation system to verify the room requests and personal information of guests. When a reservation inquiry comes over the phone, reservation agents provide a confirmation number on the spot. Later, a letter is sent out to confirm the telephone request. The letter of confirmation contains vital information such as reservation dates, roommate, type of accommodation, number of guest, and any special needs. The confirmation should also clearly indicate whether the reservation is guaranteed or non-guaranteed.

Simply having received a confirmation from the hotel does not ensure a guest that space will be available. The reservation is usually guaranteed with a credit card number. If the reservation is guaranteed, then the confirmation letter should indicate this classification. Guests are expected to show the confirmation letter to the front desk agents upon arrival at the hotel.

When guests change their reservations, the hotel sends out updated confirmation notice. Updated notices can be mailed only if changes do not take place too close to the date of arrival. In the case of cancellations, the hotel may issue a cancellation number to protect both guests and the hotel. Without such numbers, guests would have difficulty challenging no-show charges made to their credit card number.

41. What does a reservation confirmation system work in the hotel?
    A. To verify room requests.
    B. To check personal information on guests.
    C. To indicate the reservation status.
    D. All of the above.

42. The confirmation letter contains vital information as the following EXCEPT _____.
    A. reservation dates   B. type of accommodation
    C. any special need   D. a confirmation number

43. What should a guest do with the letter of confirmation?
    A. Mail it back to the hotel.
    B. Show it to the front desk agents when arriving.
    C. Leave it at home while traveling.
    D. Read it and then throw it away.

44. Hotels send out an updated confirmation notice to a guest when _____.
    A. a cancellation is made
    B. the change is too close to the arrival date
    C. a previous reservation is changed
    D. All of the above

45. What can a cancellation number mean?
    A. To protect both hotel and guests.
    B. To guarantee no-show charges to a credit card account.
    C. To prevent an increase in cancellation requests.
    D. To challenge a no-show status on the reservation record.

Task 3

Directions: *The following is an introduction to getting hired. After reading it, you are required to complete the outline below it (No. 46 to No. 50). You should write your answers briefly (**in no more than 3 words**) correspondingly.*

My uncle runs a manufacturing company with 400 employees, and he often does the interviewing and hiring himself. He says there are four keys to getting hired:

Firstly, prepare to win. Getting hired is no longer an once-in-a-lifetime experience. Employment experts believe that today's graduates could face as many as ten job changes during their careers. That may sound like a lot of pressure. But if you're prepared, the pressure is on the other folks. Secondly, never stop learning. Work on your weaknesses and develop your strengths. To be able to compete, you've got to keep learning all your life. And then, believe in yourself, even when no one else does. Don't ever let anyone tell you that you can't accomplish your goals. Who says you're not tougher, harder working and more able than your competitors? At last, find a way to make a difference.

Four Keys to Getting Hired

The writer's uncle is the boss of a company who often does the _____46_____ himself. As he says, there are four keys to getting hired:

1) Prepare _____47_____. Getting hired isn't an once-in-a-lifetime experience.
2) Never stop learning. Work on _____48_____ and develop your strengths.
3) Believe in yourself. Don't ever let anyone tell you that you can't _____49_____.
4) Find a way to _____50_____.

Task 4

Directions: *The following is a list of terms used in Olympic Games. After reading it, you are required to find the items equivalent to (与……相同的) those given in Chinese in the table below. Then you should put the corresponding letters in the brackets numbered 51 to 55.*

A. — stadium
B. — boxing
C. — bungee jumping
D. — discus
E. — diving
F. — relay race
G. — high jump
H. — javelin
I. — shot-put

J. — long jump

K. — soccer/football

L. — weight lifting

M. — fencing

N. — track and field

O. — hurdles

P. — arena

Example: (A) 体育馆   (D) 铁饼

51. ( ) 拳击	( ) 跨栏赛跑
52. ( ) 击剑	( ) 赛场
53. ( ) 举重	( ) 田径
54. ( ) 跳水	( ) 跳远
55. ( ) 跳远	( ) 蹦极

Task 5

Directions: *There is a passage below here. After reading it you should give brief answers to the 5 questions (No. 56 to No. 60) that follow. The answers (**in no more than 3 words**) should be written after the corresponding numbers.*

How can you write a good proposal? *A Practical Guide for Writing Proposals* is the best choice for you.

First, the guide tells you that the general purpose of any proposal is to persuade the readers to do something, either to persuade a potential customer to purchase goods and/or services, or to persuade your employer to fund a project or to implement a program that you would like to launch.

Secondly, the guide tells you that any proposal offers a plan to fill a need, and your reader will evaluate your plan according to how well your written presentation answers questions about WHAT you are proposing, HOW you plan to do it, WHEN you plan to do it, and HOW MUCH it is going to cost. To do this you must make sure the level of knowledge possessed by your audience and take the positions of all your readers into account. You must also make sure whether your readers will be members of your technical community, of your technical speech community, or of both, and then use the appropriate materials and language to attract both. You might provide, for those outside of your specific area of expertise (专业知识), an exclusive summary written in non-technical (easily accessible) language, or you might include a glossary (词汇表) of terms that explain technical language used in the body of the proposal, and/or attach appendices (附录) that explain technical information in generally understood language.

56. What is the best choice for you to write a good proposal?

_____ for Writing Proposals.

57. Who will be persuaded to purchase goods or services?

_____

58. How many suggestions does the guide tell you?

_____ .

59. What must you make sure to answer the four questions?

To do this you must make sure the _____ possessed by your audience.

60. What's the function of a glossary of terms?

To _____ used in the proposal.

Part IV   Translation — English to Chinese (25 minutes)

Directions: *This part, numbered 61 through 65, is to test your ability to translate English to Chinese. After each of the sentences numbered 61 to 64, you will read four choices of suggested translation. You should choose the best translation and mark the corresponding letter. And for the paragraph numbered 65, write your translation in the corresponding space.*

61. When the above commodities are available for export, please let us know by telex.

A. 当上述货物生产出口的话，请发电报给我们。

B. 如果以上商品有货可供出口的话，请发传真通知我们。

C. 如果以上商品可供出口的话，请发电报告诉我们。

D. 当上述货物有货提供出口的话，请发传真通知我们。

62. In terms of solving their problems, social scientists encounter greater resistance than physical scientists.

A. 在解决问题时，科学家比物理学家还要有更大的阻力。

B. 为了解决问题，社会学家同物理学家一起遇到了相当大的阻力。

C. 在探索如何解决他们的问题时，社会科学家比物理学家有了更伟大的发现。

D. 说到解决问题，社会学家比物理学家遇到的阻力更大。

63. The development in the information industry enhances and encourages the total technological growth.

A. 信息业的发展增进并刺激整个技术发展。

B. 信息工业的发展增加和鼓励科技的发展。

C. 在信息工业发展的幅度中，提高和鼓励使得整个技术发展成长了。

D. 信息产业的发展幅度增进和刺激技术的总增长。

64. He spoke hopefully of the success of concert.

A. 他充满希望地谈到音乐会的成功。

B. 他抱着希望说这项活动会成功。

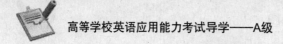

C. 他满怀希望地谈到音乐会会取得成功。

D. 他说希望这个活动成功。

65. Most meetings have an agenda. For a formal meeting, this document may be handed out in advance to all participants. For an informal meeting, the agenda may be simply a list of the points to be dealt with. The purpose of an agenda is to speed up the meeting and keep everyone to the point.

_____

_____

_____

_____

Part V Writing (25 minutes)

Directions: *This part is to test your ability to do practical writing. You are required to fill in the following Time Deposit Certificate based on the information given below. You should write your answer in the following chart.*

Time Deposit Certificate
Bank of China

No.: _____   Fixed Deposit Receipt

Date: _____   Account No.: _____

In Figures _____   Not Transferable

Received From _____

　　　　　　The Sum of _____

As deposit for a period

　　　　　Bearing interest at the rate of _____

　　　　　　　　Payable _____

Bank of China

The account holder's name: Liu Li

The account number: 5194120002033347

The depository bank name: Bank of China, No. 8542786693052

Fixed deposit: $8,000

Date: July 8, 2007

Interest rate: 1.3

Test Two

Part I Listening Comprehension (15 minutes)

Directions: *This part is to test your listening ability. It consists of 3 sections.*

Section A

Directions: *This section is to test your ability to understand short dialogues. There are 5 recorded dialogues in it. After each dialogue, there is a recorded question. Both the dialogues and questions will be spoken only once. When you hear a question, you should decide on the correct answer from the 4 choices marked A, B, C and D given below.*

Example: You will hear: W: Are you catching the 13:15 flight to New York?

       M: No. I'll leave this evening.

       Q: What are the two people talking about?

   You will read: A. New York City.

         B. An evening Party.

         C. An air trip.

         D. The man's job.

  From the dialogue we learn that the man is to take a flight to New York. Therefore, "C. An air trip" is the correct answer. Now the test will begin.

1. A. She will probably pay 26 dollars for the gloves.

 B. She will probably buy the leather gloves.

 C. She will probably buy both of gloves.

 D. She will probably buy the silk gloves.

2. A. The secretary is not very efficient.

 B. The secretary is a man.

 C. The secretary has not been working there very long.

 D. The secretary is married.

3. A. Her English is quite good.

 B. Her pronunciation is very bad.

 C. Her spelling is very bad.

 D. Her spelling is very good.

4. A. He is going to wash his face.

 B. He is going to water the flowers.

 C. He is doing his homework.

 D. He is helping his mother.

5. A. He wants to have a rest for a few days.

   B. He wants to do some shopping with his mother.

   C. The final exams he took were easy.

   D. It is too early for him to make plans.

Section B

Directions: *This section is to test your ability to understand short conversations. There are 2 recorded conversations in it. After each conversation, there are some recorded questions. Both the conversations and questions will be spoken two times. When you hear a question, you should decide on the correct answer from the 4 choices marked A, B, C and D given in your test paper.*

Conversation 1

6. A. In the park.   B. In the zoo.

   C. At the office.   D. At home.

7. A. She was attracted by some food.   B. She was chasing a monkey.

   C. She heard a loud noise.   D. She saw a monkey.

Conversation 2

8. A. E-mails.   B. Calls and short messages.

   C. Cellphones.   D. Letters.

9. A. A short message.   B. An E-mail.

   C. A letter.   D. A cellphone.

10. A. An E-mail.   B. A short message.

    C. A videophone.   D. A cellphone.

Section C

Directions: *This section is to test your ability to comprehend short passages. You will hear a recorded passage. After that, you will hear 5 questions. Both the passage and questions will be read two times. When you hear a question, you should complete an answer to it with a word or a short phrase (**in no more than 3 words**). The questions and incomplete answers are printed on your test paper. You should write your answers correspondingly. Now the passage will begin.*

11. How was the first newspaper written?

    It was written _____.

12. Where and when was the earliest daily newspaper started?

    It was started in _____ in _____.

13. When was the first regular English newspaper printed?

It was printed _____.

14. When did the first daily English newspaper come out?

It came out in _____.

15. Do English language newspapers have the largest circulations （发行量） in the world?

_____ / _____.

Part II   Structure (15 minutes)

Directions: *This part is to test your ability to construct grammatically correct sentences. It consists of 2 sections.*

Section A

Directions: *In this section, there are 10 incomplete sentences. You are required to complete each one by deciding on the most appropriate word or words from the 4 choices marked A, B, C and D.*

16. Smith _____ a book about China last year, but I don't know whether he has finished it.

A. has wrote   B. wrote   C. had written   D. was writing

17. —How long _____ each other before they _____ married?

—For about a year.

A. have they known; get   B. have they known; were going to get

C. do they know; are going to get   D. had they known; got

18. _____, they would certainly come and help us.

A. Had they time   B. Do they have time

C. Had they have time   D. Did they had time

19. Many people agree that _____ knowledge of English is a must in _____ international trade today.

A. a; /   B. the; an   C. the; the   D. /; the

20. _____ his father had come, his face lit up.

A. Having learned   B. When he learned

C. Hearing   D. When learning

21. Her daughter was admitted into college _____ we had hoped.

A. which   B. that   C. as   D. like

22. Shall we stay at school or _____ to the park?

A. to go   B. go   C. going   D. went

23. The problem will be fully discussed at the meeting _____ the next day.

A. hold   B. holding   C. to be held   D. held

24. It is not until 1997 _____ he entered university.

    A. which   B. that   C. when   D. since

25. They will be back home _____.

    A. a week later   B. after a week   C. in a week   D. a week

Section B

Directions: *There are 10 incomplete statements here. You should fill in each blank with the proper form of the word given in the brackets. Write the word or words in the corresponding space.*

26. After (interview) _____ for the job, you will be required to take an English test.

27. The question is now (close) _____ and there will be no further discussion.

28. (Keep) _____ away from my friends and relations, I felt very lonely.

29. Gardening is a pleasant (employ) _____ for a Sunday afternoon.

30. I'll get my secretary (copy) _____ the letter for you.

31. I'd rather you (attend) _____ the meeting now.

32. The main pine of this house needs (repair) _____.

33. The police (be) _____ searching for the thief everywhere.

34. The fireman rushed into the burning home, (mind) _____ of the danger.

35. There has been a total technological change in the (organize) _____ of society.

Part III   Reading Comprehension (40 minutes)

Directions: *This part is to test your reading ability. There are 5 tasks for you to fulfill. You should read the reading materials carefully and do the tasks as you are instructed.*

Task 1

Directions: *After reading the following passage, you will find 5 questions or unfinished statements, numbered 36 to 40. For each question or statement there are 4 choices marked A, B, C and D given in your test paper. You should choose the correct choice.*

For years, students were assured that with a college degree in hand they could acquire an excellent job. However, in recent years, several developments have signaled the beginning of a change in the supply-demand relationship in the services of education. Teachers with terminal degrees far outnumber the available teaching positions in many disciplines. The chairman of a science department today may receive three to four hundred applications for a position that once attracted only half a dozen. States are closing down some colleges and requiring others to **cut back on** undergraduate and graduate programs. Higher education is well into a buyer's market.

With the realization that higher education has lost its boasted position in the eyes of the public, administrations of colleges and universities must be prepared to enter into competition with all other supplies of products and services. Private institutions in the long run, have no alternative but to satisfy their customers. Today's students are in touch with the reality of the world, and they realize that while a degree may obtain the first job for them, keeping the job and advancing depend upon the education behind the degree.

36. Which statement is TRUE according to the passage?

    A. Students still believe they can get a good job if they have a college degree now.

    B. Students believed they were sure to get a good job if they had a college degree in hand.

    C. Good jobs are only given to the people who have college degrees.

    D. Many good jobs have disappeared in recent years.

37. Teachers with terminal degrees _____.

    A. are easy to find a job

    B. lack certain knowledge for teaching

    C. are given positions in many small towns

    D. are greater in number than they are needed

38. The phrase **cut back on** means _____ in the passage.

    A. cut short   B. reduce   C. return to   D. turn back

39. Higher education has lost its boasted position because _____.

    A. it is into a buyer's market

    B. it has produced a lot of products

    C. it can't compete with the private institutes

    D. its services are not good enough to satisfy their customers

40. If you want to keep a job and advance you should _____ according to the passage.

    A. obtain a degree

    B. get in touch with the reality of the world

    C. learn a lot of things besides a degree

    D. involve in graduate programs

Task 2

Directions: *This task is the same as Task 1. The 5 questions or unfinished statements are numbered 41 to 45.*

Yesterday we discussed the problem of prices, or, in the economist's term, inflation. We noted that during periods of inflation all prices and incomes do not rise at the same rate. Some incomes rise more slowly than the cost of living, and a few do not rise at all. Other incomes rise more rapidly than the cost of living.

We concluded that persons with fixed incomes, as for example, the elderly who depend upon pensions, and persons with slow-rising incomes as, for example, an employee with a salary agreed to in a long-term contract, will be most seriously affected by inflation. Please recall that while their dollar incomes stay the same, the cost of goods and services rise, and in effect, real income decreases; that is, they are able to purchase less with the same amount of money.

We also talked about the fact that stockholders and persons with business interests and investments would probably benefit most from inflation, since high prices would increase sales receipts, and profits would likely rise faster than the cost of living.

And now before we begin today's lecture, are there any questions about the term inflation or any of the examples given in our discussion so far?

41. What is the main purpose of the talk?

    A. To introduce the concept of inflation.

    B. To discuss the causes of inflation.

    C. To review yesterday's lecture on inflation.

    D. To argue in favor of inflation.

42. According to the lecture, what does "inflation" mean?

    A. Rising prices.   B. Fixed income.

    C. Real income.   D. Cost of living.

43. Who benefit most from inflation?

    A. Persons who have salaries agreed to in long-term contracts.

    B. Persons who own businesses.

    C. Persons with pensions.

    D. Persons with slow-rising incomes.

44. What happens when income rises more slowly than the cost of living?

    A. Inflation is controlled.   B. Real income decreases.

    C. Purchasing power stays the same.   D. Dollar income increases.

45. According to the passage, which statement is NOT true?

    A. The day before the problem of rising prices was discussed.

    B. The old people with pension will be seriously affected by inflation.

    C. During periods of inflation people can't buy the same things with the same amount of money.

    D. During periods of inflation, all prices will rise at the same rate.

Task 3

Directions: *The following is an advertisement. After reading it, you are required to complete the outline below it (No. 46 to No. 50). You should write your answers briefly (**in no more than 3 words**) correspondingly.*

WE MAKE ENGLISH EASY

We're American Language Institute at New York University's School of Continuing Education. We help people speak, read and write English with greater confidence and great ease.

There are classes during the day, in the evening, and on weekends—for beginning, intermediate, and advanced students.

We also offer courses in accent correction, public speaking, and English for business. To insure proper placement, the institute will evaluate you and guide you to the most appropriate courses.

For more information call (212) 998-7040 or write to:

International Student Admissions

American Language Institute

New York University

Washington Square North, Room 10

New York, NY 10003

New York University

School of Continuing Education

WE MAKE ENGLISH EASY

We help people ____46____, _____ and _____ English with greater confidence and great ease.

We provide classes for beginning, ____47____, and advanced students.

The institute will ____48____ you and guide you to the suitable courses.

You can call ____49____ to get more information.

Our institute's address is Washington Square North, Room 10, ____50____, NY 10003.

Task 4

Directions: *The following is a list of terms used in insurance. After reading it, you are required to find the items equivalent to (与……相同的) those given in Chinese in the table below. Then you should put the corresponding letters in the brackets numbered 51 to 55.*

A. — Health Insurance

B. — Whole Life Insurance

C. — Full Insurance

D. — Flood Insurance

E. — Residence Insurance

F. — Endowment Insurance

G. — Casualty Insurance

H. — Liability Insurance

I. — Car Danger Insurance

J. — Cargo Insurance

K. — Third Person Injured Ability

L. — Motorcar Accident Report

M. — Evidence of Loss

N. — Adjustment

O. — Beneficiary

Example: （H）责任险　　　　　　（K）第三人伤害责任险

51. （　）养老险	（　）住家险
52. （　）理赔	（　）受益人
53. （　）车损险	（　）意外险
54. （　）健康险	（　）损失证明
55. （　）货物险	（　）汽车出险报告书

Task 5

Directions: *There is an application letter below here. After reading the letter you should give brief answers to the 5 questions (No. 56 to No. 60) that follow. The answers (**in no more than 3 words**) should be written after the corresponding numbers.*

HRD Director

Shanghai Office

Rohm and Hass China Inc.

488 Wuning Rd (S), Shanghai

Dear Mr. Director,

　　I have learned from the newspaper that you are employing an administrative secretary. I'm very much interested in this position.

　　I have worked as an administrative secretary for a chemical company in Shanghai for three years, so I have some understanding of the chemical industry. I graduated from Shanghai Jiaotong University in 2006, holding a bachelor degree. Having obtained certificates of CET-4 and CET-6, I find myself fluent in both spoken and written English. In addition, I'm also quite familiar with computer skills.

Enclosed forward to you is my resume.

Looking forward to your early reply.

Yours sincerely,

(signature)

Zhang Wen

56. Where did the writer learn that an administrative secretary was wanted?

The writer has learned _____.

57. How many years has the writer worked for a company in Shanghai?

The writer has worked for a company in Shanghai _____.

58. Why did the writer have some understanding of the chemical industry?

He has worked as _____ for a chemical company.

59. What certificates has the writer obtained?

He has obtained _____.

60. Where did the writer put his resume?

He put it _____.

Part IV Translation — English to Chinese (25 minutes)

Directions: *This part, numbered 61 through 65, is to test your ability to translate English to Chinese. After each of the sentences numbered 61 to 64, you will read four choices of suggested translation. You should choose the best translation and mark the corresponding letter. And for the paragraph numbered 65, write your translation in the corresponding space.*

61. They keep saying we'll get the money, but the reality is that there is none left.

A. 他们有保留地说我们会得到钱，但实际情况是根本没钱留下来。

B. 他们再三说我们会得到钱，但实际情况是根本没钱留下来。

C. 他们再三说我们不会得到钱的，但实际情况是有许多钱留了下来。

D. 他们再三说我们不会得到钱，但在现实生活中，他们没有钱留给我们。

62. His academic record was constantly maintained at the top level, which is resulted from his devotion to study and intelligent nature.

A. 他的学习成绩一直名列前茅，这归功于他对学习的投入和天生的聪慧。

B. 他的学术记录一直都放在最高处，这归功于他天生的聪慧和努力学习。

C. 他的学习成绩一直名列前茅，结果，他对学习的投入更大了。

D. 他的学习记录一直没人打破，这并不归功于他站的高看的远以及天生的聪慧。

63. The methods are tried and true, we used them for years and they have always worked for us.

 A. 这些方法的的确确地被试过，我们已经采用这些方法好几年了。

 B. 这些方法经过实验，证明可靠，我们已使用这些方法多年了。

 C. 这些方法试过，而且不太真实可信，虽然我们已经采用这些方法好几年了。

 D. 这些方法我们只采用了一年，因此，我们不能证明这些方法是可靠和可信的。

64. Their latest proposal to concentrate on primary education has met with some opposition.

 A. 他们最后的建议是集中精力抓好初等教育，但是遭到了一些反对。

 B. 集中精力抓好初等教育的最初建议，最后还是得到了一些人的赞成。

 C. 他们最近提出的集中全力于初等教育的提议，遭到了某些人的反对。

 D. 他们指出不集中精力抓好初等教育，就会遭到了一些反对意见。

65. Before placing a firm order, we should be glad if you would send us your products on fifteen day's approval. Any of the items unsold at the end of the period and which we decide not to keep as stock, would be returned at our expense. I'm looking forward to hearing from you soon.

 _____

 _____

 _____

 _____

Part V   Writing (25 minutes)

Directions: *This part is to test your ability to do practical writing. You are required to write an inquiry letter according to the information given below. You should write no less than 80 words.*

假如你方是一家电动自行车 (electrical bikes) 公司，收到某公司 5 月 29 日的询盘函 (An Inquiry Letter)。请写一封报盘函 (An Offer Letter)，告知对方相关的商品信息及价格优惠条件等。

Test Three

Part I   Listening Comprehension (15 minutes)

Directions: *This part is to test your listening ability. It consists of 3 sections.*

Section A

Directions: *This section is to test your ability to understand short dialogues. There are 5 recorded dialogues in it. After each dialogue, there is a recorded question. Both the dialogues and questions will be spoken only once. When you hear a question, you should decide on the correct answer from the 4 choices marked A, B, C and D given below.*

Example: *You will hear: W: Are you catching the 13:15 flight to New York?*

        M: No. I'll leave this evening.

        Q: What are the two people talking about?

   You will read: A. New York City.

          B. An evening Party.

          C. An air trip.

          D. The man's job.

  From the dialogue we learn that the man is to take a flight to New York. Therefore, "C. An air trip" is the correct answer. Now the test will begin.

1. A. She doesn't want to go with him.
   B. She will go because she likes the concert.
   C. She doesn't like the concert.
   D. She wants to go, but she can't.
2. A. $400.   B. $300.   C. $200.   D. $150.
3. A. At an airport.   B. At a railway station.
   C. In a hotel.   D. In a library.
4. A. Because her job is in the city.
   B. Because life in the city is less expensive.
   C. Because jobs are easier to find in the city.
   D. Because living in the suburbs costs a lot.
5. A. If he can help the woman.   B. If the woman will be late.
   C. If a complaint will really do any help.   D. If the servants need any help.

Section B

Directions: *This section is to test your ability to understand short conversations. There are 2 recorded conversations in it. After each conversation, there are some recorded questions. Both the conversations and questions will be spoken two times. When you hear a question, you should decide on the correct answer from the 4 choices marked A, B, C and D given in your test paper.*

Conversation 1

6. A. Six hours.　　　　　　　　　　B. Five hours.
   C. Four hours.　　　　　　　　　　D. Two and a half hours.

7. A. Because it's hot in the room.　　B. Because it's freezing in the room.
   C. Because it's snowing.　　　　　D. Because they want to go to a movie.

Conversation 2

8. A. Tom Smith.　　B. Tom White.　　C. Tom Green.　　D. Tom Addison.

9. A. $12.　　　　　B. $43.　　　　　C. $69.　　　　　D. $96.

10. A. Any time after 11:00 a.m.　　　B. Any time after supper.
    C. Any time before 11:00 a.m.　　D. Any time before supper.

Section C

Directions: *This section is to test your ability to comprehend short passages. You will hear a recorded passage. After that, you will hear 5 questions. Both the passage and questions will be read two times. When you hear a question, you should complete an answer to it with a word or a short phrase (**in no more than 3 words**). The questions and incomplete answers are printed on your test paper. You should write your answers correspondingly. Now the passage will begin.*

1. Where does the speaker give this talk?
   The speaker gives this talk _____.

2. What kind of program is it?
   It is a _____.

3. Where are the records for the audience from?
   The records for the audience are from classical Western music, _____ and pop.

4. In this broadcast, what shall we study?
   We shall study the _____ of music.

5. What shall we hear in tonight's broadcast?
   We'll hear a Beethoven piano piece and songs sung by a _____.

Part II   Structure (15 minutes)

Directions: *This part is to test your ability to construct grammatically correct sentences. It consists of 2 sections.*

Section A

Directions: *In this section, there are 10 incomplete sentences. You are required to complete each one by deciding on the most appropriate word or words from the 4 choices marked A, B, C and D.*

16. I prefer to live in the country rather than _____ in a city.

    A. to live   B. live   C. living   D. lived

17. I tried to make everybody _____ comfortable here.

    A. feel   B. felt   C. feeling   D. being felt

18. _____ at the airport, David found his friend had departed.

    A. When arrived   B. When having arrived

    C. When arriving   D. When arrived at

19. These insects can _____ the color of their surrounding.

    A. take after   B. take in   C. take down   D. take on

20. It is not urgent, so you may do it _____ your leisure.

    A. at   B. in   C. by   D. with

21. This book is designed for the learners _____ native languages are not English.

    A. whose   B. which   C. who   D. what

22. Though he _____ well prepared before the job interview, he failed to answer some important questions.

    A. will be   B. would be   C. has been   D. had been

23. It was because I wanted to buy a dictionary _____ I went downtown yesterday.

    A. but   B. and   C. why   D. that

24. It's said that the agreement _____ between the two companies last month will become effective from May 1.

    A. to sign   B. signed   C. to be signed   D. signing

25. Each penny, dime, and quarter _____ carefully by the bank teller.

    A. are counting   B. is counting   C. are counted   D. is counted

Section B

Directions: *There is an error in each of the following sentences marked with A, B, C and D. You are required to mark out the error. Then you should mark the corresponding letter.*

26. They did not feel <u>at ease</u> <u>after</u> their experiment <u>was proved</u> a <u>success</u>.
                    A   B   C   D

27. <u>In time</u>, he stopped his <u>dependence</u> on his father and learned to <u>stand</u> on his own <u>foot</u>.
       A   B   C   D

28. It is <u>demanded</u> that he <u>hands in</u> the <u>homework</u> <u>this</u> afternoon.
               A   B   C   D

29. He said <u>softly</u> that he would rather <u>stay</u> at home than <u>going</u> out <u>for</u> a walk.
               A   B   C   D

30. The <u>company's</u> training plan <u>designed</u> to help the employees <u>improve</u> their work habits and
              A   B   C

    <u>efficiency</u>.
       D

31. <u>Worst of all</u>, the "greenhouse effect" could cause polar ice caps <u>to melt</u>, <u>raising</u> sea level
       A   B   C

    <u>too high</u> that some cities would vanish.
       D

32. Those students expected <u>to offer</u> some jobs <u>on</u> campus <u>during</u> the <u>coming</u> summer.
                               A   B   C   D

33. <u>This is</u> the athlete <u>whom</u> everyone <u>says</u> will win the <u>gold</u> medal at the winter Olympic Games.
       A   B   C   D

34. Only <u>when</u> I got there <u>that I realized</u> how <u>badly</u> the house <u>had been damaged</u>.
            A   B   C   D

35. The more we <u>attempted</u> <u>to explain</u> our mistake, the <u>worst</u> our story <u>sounded</u>.
                A   B   C   D

Part III   Reading Comprehension (40 minutes)

Directions: *This part is to test your reading ability. There are 5 tasks for you to fulfill. You should read the reading materials carefully and do the tasks as you are instructed.*

Task 1

Directions: *After reading the following passage, you will find 5 questions or unfinished statements, numbered 36 to 40. For each question or statement there are 4 choices marked A, B, C and D given in your test paper. You should choose the correct choice.*

The American idea of customer service is to make each customer the center of attention. People going shopping in America can expect to be treated with respect from the very beginning. When customers get to the store, they are treated as honored guests. Customers don't usually find store clerks sitting around watching TV or playing cards. Instead, the clerks greet them warmly and offer to help them find what they want. In most stores, the signs that label each department make shopping a breeze (容易的事情). Customers usually don't have to ask how much items cost, since prices are clearly marked.

When customers are ready to check out, they find out nearest and shortest checkout lane. But as Murphy's Law would have it, whichever lane they get in, all the other lanes will mover faster. Good stores open new checkout lanes when the lanes get too long. Some even offer express lanes for customers with 10 items or less. After they pay for their purchases, customers receive a smile and a warm "thank you" from the clerk. Many stores even allow customers to take their shopping carts out to the parking lot. That way, they don't have to carry heavy bags out to the car.

In America, customer service continues long after the sale. Many products come with a money-back guarantee. If there is any problem with the product, customers can take it back. The customer service representative will often allow them to exchange the item or return it for a full refund.

36. From the passage we know in America the principle of customer service is to _____.

    A. be fast and convenient

    B. make customer the center of attention

    C. be the first in the world

    D. make the customer feel at home

37. When customers enter the store in the USA, they will _____.

    A. see store clerks sitting around watching TV

    B. receive warm greetings from clerks

    C. show their respects to clerks

    D. be given a pamphlet introducing the goods

38. Why do people in the USA feel shopping is a breeze?

    A. The price is very cheap.

    B. The products are good.

    C. The signs of departments are clear.

    D. The departments are large.

39. According to Murphy's Law, people feel _____.

    A. the lane they get in is faster than other lanes

    B. the lane they get in is slower than other lanes

    C. it's better to stand in a newly-opened lane

    D. it's better to find the nearest and shortest checkout lane

40. If there is a problem with the product, the customer may _____.
    A. have it repaired by others
    B. send the product to others
    C. ask the customer service representative to say sorry to him
    D. ask for a refund from the store

Task 2

Directions: *This task is the same as Task 1. The 5 questions or unfinished statements are numbered 41 to 45.*

Over the past years we offered advice to foreign students who want to attend an American college or university. Today we tell about a way to study through the International Students Exchange Program (ISEP) which was started in nineteen seventy-nine in the United States.

ISEP is a group of colleges and universities around the world. They cooperate to provide international educational experiences for their students. 260 schools in the United States and 35 in other countries are members of the program.

Students can study for up to one year in the United States or any of the other countries involved. They do not have to go through the usual application process to get into a school. And pay only what they would have to pay for a term at their own school at home.

To take part in the ISEP program, students must attend a member college or university. Each school has an ISEP coordinator who helps students apply to the ISEP office in Washington, D.C.

To be accepted, students must have good grades. They must also provide TOEFL scores. TOEFL is the Test of English as a Foreign Language. Students are asked to list up to ten choices of American schools they would like to attend.

ISEP officials say students should begin preparations at least one year before they want to experience the program. Applications must be sent to Washington by February of each year. The students accepted can then begin their year in the United States in September.

41. According to the passage, ISEP _____.
    A. provides international educational experiences
    B. is a college
    C. is in the United States
    D. is extremely difficult to be admitted

42. Which of the following is NOT true according to the passage?
    A. The International Students Exchange Program was started in 1979.
    B. Everyone must get into a school through the application process.
    C. The United States is one of the countries where students can study.
    D. The money paid for the program is the same as that at their own school.

43. In order to take part in the program, students have to do all of the following EXCEPT _____.

 A. attending a member college

 B. having good grades

 C. providing TOEFL scores

 D. providing information about financial condition

44. We can know from the passage that _____.

 A. It does not matter whether you send your application to Washington or not

 B. Students often prepare for the program in the first year of college

 C. It takes students about one year to prepare for the program

 D. Students can choose as many schools as they want

45. What is the passage mainly about?

 A. How to attend foreign schools.

 B. How to get good marks in ISEP.

 C. How to take part in the ISEP Program.

 D. How to take part in TOEFL.

Task 3

Directions: *The following is an introduction to application. After reading it, you are required to complete the outline below it (No. 46 to No. 50). You should write your answers briefly (**in no more than 3 words**) correspondingly.*

Every international application on entering Moon River College starts from APPLICATION. What you need to know about application is, firstly, to apply early. Because space is limited in every college program and not every program accepts international students. Applying six months in advance will help you secure a space for the next academic year. It will also provide you with the time that may be required to apply for a Canadian Study Permit allowing you to come to Canada to study at Moon River College.

You need to read the admissions criteria (准则) carefully. Each program has its own set of entrance requirements. Here is also the Special Selection Criteria: entrance testing, an orientation session can be required for entrance to some programs. Apply early to ensure that there is enough time to complete your application and meet all of the selection criteria for the program of your choice.

Payments of the Application Fee and Tuition Deposit can be made by Visa, Master Card, Money Order, Bank Draft or Wire transfer payable to Moon River College. Application submitted without the $400 will not be accepted.

For more detailed information on the application process please refer to the application form on the back pages of this View book.

Please note that the official transcripts (副本) or certifications must be originals or certified (合格) copies. They must indicate your academic standing and language proficiency. Certified

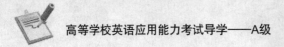

translations of all academic documents should be provided when the originals are written in a language other than English.

Applying to Study at Moon River College

The first important thing to be known while applying is _____46_____.

The information sources: _____47_____.

Money paid when submitting application: _____48_____.

Requirements for official transcripts or certificates: _____49_____ and _____50_____.

Task 4

Directions: *The following are some terms of positions. After reading it, you are required to find the items equivalent to (与……相同的) those given in Chinese in the table below. Then you should put the corresponding letters in the brackets numbered 51 to 55.*

A. — Commander-in-Chief

B. — Chief Judge

C. — General Manager

D. — Governor of the Chinese People's Bank

E. — President of the Higher People's Court

F. — Chairman of the Board of Directors

G. — Dean of English Department

H. — Director of the Department of Asian Affairs

I. — Police Commissioner

J. — Executive Secretary

K. — Senior Editor

L. — Prime Minister

M. — Provincial Governor

N. — State Councilor

O. — Financial Controller

Examples: (F) 公司董事长   (C) 总经理

51. ( ) 亚洲司司长	( ) 执行秘书
52. ( ) 总理	( ) 审判长
53. ( ) 总司令	( ) 省长
54. ( ) 中国人民银行行长	( ) 国务委员
55. ( ) 高级编辑	( ) 财务总监

Task 5

Directions: *There are two letters below here. After reading it, you should give brief answers to the 5 questions (No. 56 to No. 60) that follow. The answers (**in no more than 3 words**) should be written after the corresponding numbers.*

Invitation and Reply

Letter 1

Guangdong Chemical Products Co., Ltd.

Guangzhou, Guangdong, China

June 8

John & Carry Co., Ltd.

32 Gavery Avenue

Washington

United States

Dear Sir or Madam,

We should like to invite your company to attend the 2000 International Fair which will be held from August 29 to September 4 at the above address. Full details on the Fair will be sent in a week.

We look forward to hearing from you soon, and hope that you will be able to attend.

Yours faithfully

Zhang Qing

Letter 2

John & Carry Co., Ltd.32

Gavery Avenue, Washington

United States

June 12

Guangdong Chemical Products Co., Ltd.

Guangzhou, Guangdong, China

Dear Ms Zhang,

Thank you very much for your invitation to attend the 2000 International Fair. As we are going to open a repair shop in your city at that time, we are sorry that we shall not be able to come.

We hope to see you on some future occasion.

Yours faithfully

David Stevenson

56. Which company does David Stevenson work for?

    _____.

57. What does Ms Zhang invite them to do?

    She invites them to attend the _____.

58. Why can't they accept the invitation?

    Because they are going to open _____ in the city at that time.

59. When will the fair be held?

    From August 29 to _____.

60. What will Ms Zhang do if David Stevenson accepts the invitation?

    She will send _____ on the Fair in a week.

Part IV   Translation — English to Chinese (25 minutes)

Directions: *This part, numbered 61 through 65, is to test your ability to translate English to Chinese. After each of the sentences numbered 61 to 64, you will read four choices of suggested translation. You should choose the best translation and mark the corresponding letter. And for the paragraph numbered 65, write your translation in the corresponding space.*

61. Both sides have virtually done nothing to maintain the lasting peace.

    A. 双方均未就维持持久和平作出实质性努力。

    B. 为了维持持久和平，双方实质上什么也没有做。

    C. 实际上不是双方都做了维持永久和平的事情。

    D. 双方均未就维持过去的和平作出实际努力。

62. Bargaining is not common in shops, and customers are expected to pay the marked price for goods.

    A. 讨价还价在商店里是不平常的，并且顾客应按市场价付款。

    B. 讨价还价在商店里是不普通的，顾客期望是按标明的货价付款。

    C. 讨价还价在商店里是不常见的，顾客被期望按标明价买货物。

    D. 讨价还价在商店里是不常见的，顾客应按标明的货价付款。

63. We are proud to have him on our staff and are sure he will be able to give you the kind of service you have come to expect.

    A. 我们很高兴他将会成为我们中的一员，我们相信，他会尽可能完成你所预期的服务。

    B. 我们为他是我们中的一员而感到自豪，同时，我们相信他能够提供给您所期待的服务。

    C. 我们很荣幸他是我们中的成员，相信他定会为您提供优质服务，满足你们的要求。

    D. 我们证明他会加入我们员工的行列，相信他会尽可能完成你上次来时所期待的服务。

64. It's quite natural that all the terms and conditions agreed upon between us during the negotiation should be indicated in the sales confirmation or the contracts.

　　A. 理所当然，通过谈判所达成的条件都应在合同和销售确认书当中体现出来。

　　B. 理所当然，我们经过协商一致同意合同和销售确认书中的所有条件。

　　C. 理所当然，经过协商所同意的合同和销售确认书中的条款应写下来。

　　D. 理所当然，我们应该通过谈判来确认合同和销售的条款。

65. "Lucky" Brand Chocolates are made of superior raw materials by up-to-date scientific method. The product is allowed to leave the factory only after strict examination of its quality. Owing to the influence of tropical climate on raw materials used, white spots may occasionally appear on the surface of the product, but the quality remains unchanged in that event.

　　_____

　　_____

　　_____

　　_____

Part V　Writing　(25 minutes)

Directions: *This part is to test your ability to do practical writing. You are required to write an e-mail including the following information. Remember to write the message in the corresponding space on the Translation/Composition Sheet.*

以李敏的名义给王丽发一封电子邮件：

李敏的电子信箱：Limin@hotmail.com

王丽的电子信箱：Wangli@sina.com

发邮件日期：2005 年 7 月 16 日

邮件内容：自大学毕业后，好久未曾相聚。在海外学习的好友马虹回昆明，想邀请王丽于 7 月 23 日晚 7:00 在花园酒店共进晚餐。

Test Four

Part I   Listening Comprehension (15 minutes)

Directions: *This part is to test your listening ability. It consists of 3 sections.*

Section A

Directions: *This section is to test your ability to understand short dialogues. There are 5 recorded dialogues in it. After each dialogue, there is a recorded question. Both the dialogues and questions will be spoken only once. When you hear a question, you should decide on the correct answer from the 4 choices marked A, B, C and D given below.*

Example: *You will hear: W: Are you catching the 13:15 flight to New York?*

M: No. I'll leave this evening.

Q: What are the two people talking about?

You will read: A. New York City.

B. An evening Party.

C. An air trip.

D. The man's job.

From the dialogue we learn that the man is to take a flight to New York. Therefore, "C. An air trip" is the correct answer. Now the test will begin.

1. A. He agrees to lend her his dictionary.

   B. He put his dictionary on the desk.

   C. He doesn't know where his dictionary is.

   D. He doesn't want to lend his dictionary to the woman.

2. A. Because she will wash the dishes.　　B. Because she will clean the backyard.

   C. Because she will wash the clothes.　　D. Because she feels hot outside.

3. A. Four dollars.　　B. Five dollars.　　C. Six dollars.　　D. Ten dollars.

4. A. At a post office.　　　　　　　　B. In a bank.

   C. At a supermarket.　　　　　　　D. At a school.

5. A. She should think about becoming a teacher.

   B. She really needs a full-time job.

   C. She should work hard for the school.

   D. She needs to spend her time studying.

Section B

Directions: *This section is to test your ability to understand short conversations. There are 2 recorded conversations in it. After each conversation, there are some recorded questions. Both the conversations and questions will be spoken two times. When you hear a question, you should decide on the correct answer from the 4 choices marked A, B, C and D given in your test paper.*

Conversation 1

6. A. By plane.   B. By train.   C. By ship.   D. By car.

7. A. Friends.   B. Holiday guides.   C. Relatives.   D. Schoolmates.

Conversation 2

8. A. A close friend of the woman.   B. A regular patient of Dr. Anderson.

   C. A new patient of Dr. Anderson.   D. An old friend of Dr. Anderson.

9. A. A friend of the man recommended Dr. Anderson to him.

   B. The man would like to have one of his teeth pulled out.

   C. The man will go to work tomorrow.

   D. Dr. Anderson will have an important meeting to attend in the next two days.

10. A. At 9:00 a.m. tomorrow.   B. At 5:00 p.m. tomorrow.

   C. At 8:30 a.m. tomorrow.   D. At 8:30 p.m. tomorrow.

Section C

Directions: *This section is to test your ability to comprehend short passages. You will hear a recorded passage. After that, you will hear 5 questions. Both the passage and questions will be read two times. When you hear a question, you should complete an answer to it with a word or a short phrase (**in no more than 3 words**). The questions and incomplete answers are printed on your test paper. You should write your answers correspondingly. Now the passage will begin.*

11. What should be repeated when you accept an invitation over the telephone?

   You should repeat four things: the day of the week, _____, the time and the place.

12. What would you do if you do not know how to get to the host's home?

   You should ask for direction at once and _____.

13. What is necessary for you to do once you accept an invitation?

   It is necessary for you to _____ and to appear on the party punctually.

14. What is considered rude?

   It is considered rude to accept an invitation and then not to appear without _____ in advance.

15. What would you do if you can't attend the party?

You should make a call to explain the circumstances and _____ to your host or hostess before the party.

Part II   Structure (15 minutes)

Directions: *This part is to test your ability to construct grammatically correct sentences. It consists of 2 sections.*

Section A

Directions: *In this section, there are 10 incomplete sentences. You are required to complete each one by deciding on the most appropriate word or words from the 4 choices marked A, B, C and D.*

16. _____ the danger as she climbed up the stair and reached for the doll.

    A. Little the baby realized   B. The baby little realized

    C. Little the baby did realized   D. Little did the baby realize

17. Lucy _____ her homework this morning, but she didn't.

    A. may be doing   B. must have done

    C. should have done   D. can do

18. While _____ the museum, I encountered an old classmate.

    A. visit   B. visited   C. be visiting   D. visiting

19. Two hundred cars _____ since the beginning of the year.

    A. sell   B. are sold   C. have sold   D. have been sold

20. Had I known his telephone number, I _____ you to tell me.

    A. didn't ask   B. hadn't asked

    C. wouldn't have asked   D. mustn't have asked

21. It is high time the children _____.

    A. went to bed   B. go to bed

    C. will go to bed   D. should go to bed

22. Do you think that it is necessary to make yourself _____?

    A. understand   B. understood

    C. understanding   D. being understood

23. The fisherman together with his sons always _____ a lot of fish.

    A. catch   B. catches   C. catching   D. caught

24. By the end of next semester, we _____ more than three thousand new words.

    A. have learned   B. will learn

    C. will have learned   D. have been learning

25. You may use the room _____ you clean it afterward.

    A. as long as   B. because   C. so that   D. even though

Section B

Directions: *There is an error in each of the following sentences marked with A, B, C and D. You are required to mark out the error. Then you should mark the corresponding letter.*

26. I know <u>nothing</u> about the accident <u>except</u> <u>which</u> I read <u>in the newspaper</u>.
           A   B   C   D

27. She was very <u>surprising</u> to find <u>the laziest</u> student <u>did the best</u> <u>in</u> the examination.
               A   B   C D

28. The article <u>attracted</u> <u>considerate</u> interest from scientists <u>who</u> study <u>physics</u>.
           A   B   C   D

29. The world will be a better place <u>to live in</u> if we accept the principle <u>which</u> other animals have
                                  A   B

    equal rights <u>to live</u> as <u>ourselves</u>.
               C   D

30. I was very <u>angry</u>, since I <u>was made</u> <u>waiting</u> two hours for <u>an appointment</u>.
             A   B   C   D

31. It is <u>believed</u> that trees can warn <u>each other</u> to danger by releasing <u>chemicals</u> into the air.
       A   B   C   D

32. <u>Many children</u> in the United States <u>spend</u> <u>most of</u> their time <u>to watch</u> TV.
      A   B   C   D

33. <u>It</u> is because he is <u>too</u> inexperienced <u>therefore</u> he does not now <u>how</u> to deal with this problem.
  A   B   C   D

34. <u>Hundreds of</u> <u>woman doctors</u> <u>took part in</u> the construction <u>of</u> the hospital after the earthquake.
      A   B   C   D

35. The <u>surroundings</u> which a child <u>grows up</u> in usually <u>has</u> an effect on his <u>development</u>.
         A   B   C   D

Part III   Reading Comprehension (40 minutes)

Directions: *This part is to test your reading ability. There are 5 tasks for you to fulfill. You should read the reading materials carefully and do the tasks as you are instructed.*

Task 1

Directions: *After reading the following passage, you will find 5 questions or unfinished statements, numbered 36 to 40. For each question or statement there are 4 choices marked A, B, C and D given in your test paper. You should choose the correct choice.*

Nearly all children have trouble getting along with their parents. They know their parents love them and have done much for them, but they find it hard to communicate or obey their parents' rules. Arguments such as these as well as other kinds of family conflicts can be resolved by following principles of communication, respect, and consideration.

The most important element of any relationship is good communication. When parents make a rule for their children, they will usually explain the reason for their rule. For example, "I don't want you to be out after 10 o'clock at night because I don't think it is safe." Perhaps the child disagrees with this rule. The child should communicate by expressing his or her opinion politely. Talking through a disagreement can often help parents and children understand each other.

Then, respect is important. Even if a child disagrees with the final decision of the parent, he or she should still show love and respect in word, action, and attitude. Often, the child becomes angry or complains when he does not get his way. Children who want to be treated like adults should act in a responsible and trustworthy manner.

Third, it is important to consider the needs and rights of the other person. Caring for others requires resisting pride and selfishness. If a child helps with housework and thanks his parents often, the parents will appreciate it, and their relationship might be better.

These principles can be applied to any relationship. A person who communicates well and shows respect and consideration should have little trouble in relationship with parents or others.

36. Regarding parent-child conflict, the author thinks _____ .

    A. at one time or another all parents and children have conflicts

    B. parents and children should never have conflicts

    C. conflicts between parents and children can never be resolved

    D. unresolved conflicts will cause more conflicts later in life

37. Which of the following would be the best title for this article?

    A. Obey Your Parents' Rules   B. Respect for Your Parents

    C. Caring for Others   D. Getting Along with Parents

38. In the sentence "Often, the child becomes angry or complains when he does not get his way." (Para. 3), what does "get his way" mean?

 A. Make himself understood.

 B. Gain what he wants.

 C. Have a friendly relationship with his parents.

 D. Find the way to his home.

39. The children can show their consideration to their parents by the following EXCEPT _____.

 A. resisting pride and selfishness

 B. helping with housework

 C. thanking their parents often

 D. disagreeing with parents' final decision

40. In the last paragraph, the author suggests that _____.

 A. it is impossible for a child to get along well with his/her parents

 B. developing the skills to get along well with parents can also help with other relationships

 C. a person who is good at communicating with others may also have trouble in parent-child relationship

 D. if a person cannot get along well with others, he will never get along well with his/her parents

Task 2

Directions: *This task is the same as Task 1. The 5 questions or unfinished statements are numbered 41 to 45.*

Taking up a job through competition, many Japanese don't sleep well, and this affect their live quality and practical work, showed a poll released on Tuesday. The survey by the National Sleep Organization found that Japanese adults get an average of 6.5 hours of sleep a night, short of the 6—8 hours the Organization suggests.

"Half of the country sleeps pretty well—the other half has problems," the organization's chief executive said in a statement.

Of the 1,506 adults interviewed over telephone between Sept. 20 and Nov. 7, 2004, 75 percent were found having a sleep problem, mostly snoring (打鼾). Other sleep problems include having difficulty falling asleep, waking many times during the night and waking up too early. However, the report said, 76 percent said they do not believe they have sleep problem. About one fourth of adults said sleep problems have some effect on their daily lives. About one fourth of people said they drank at least four caffeinated (添加咖啡因的) drinks, such as coffee, tea or cola, each day for energy.

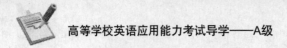

41. According to the National Sleep Organization, how long should adults sleep a night?

    A. 10—9 hours.   B. 5—6 hours.   C. 4—8hours.   D. 6—8 hours.

42. The National Sleep Organization found many Japanese sleep poorly by _____.

    A. telephoning them   B. communicating with them face to face

    C. using the Internet   D. asking their doctors

43. The sleep problems many Japanese were found having, do NOT include _____.

    A. having difficulty falling asleep   B. waking many times during the night

    C. snoring   D. dozing

44. How many people do they believe have sleep problems according to the report?

    A. About 50 percent.   B. About 76 percent.   C. About 30 percent.   D. About 25 percent.

45. The main idea of this passage is _____.

    A. why Japanese have sleep problems   B. how to deal with sleep problems

    C. that many Japanese sleep poorly   D. how to sleep well

Task 3

Directions: *The following is an introduction to reading newspapers. After reading it, you are required to complete the information below it (No. 46 to No. 50). You should write your answers briefly (**in no more than 3 words**) correspondingly.*

How to Read Newspapers

    The headline of a newspaper presents the heart of the news in brief form. Because of space limitations headline writers tend to use short verbs and nouns. Scanning the headlines gives a hasty look at the major news of the day. Headlines are often presented in steps. Each Section adds to the news presented in the top headline. If you have only a little time, you may wish to read the headlines and follow up only a few stories you are particularly interested in.

    The first paragraph or lead of a news story answers certain questions that might be asked by a reader. A lead answers some or all of these questions: "Who? What? When? Where? Why? How?" Once again, if you are pressed for time, you can get a great deal of information by reading just the lead.

    The news article develops the information presented in the headline and the lead. Since news columns must fit the space provided, putting the most important information at the beginning makes sense. You will not, of course, read every news item every day.

How to Read Newspapers

1) _____46_____ help you to get the major news of the day.

2) If you haven't enough time, you are advised to read the headlines and follow up only _____47_____ that you are interested in.

3) Once again, if you are pressed for time, you can get a lot of information by _____48_____.

4) You must bear it in mind that the _____49_____ is always put at the beginning of news column.

5) It is impossible that you can read _____50_____ every day.

Task 4

Directions: *The following is a list of Chinese festivals. After reading, you are required to find the items equivalent to (与……相同的) those given in Chinese in the table below. Then you should put the corresponding letters in the brackets numbered 51 to 55.*

A. — the Beginning of Spring

B. — the Waking of Insects

C. — Pure Brightness

D. — Grain Rain

E. — the Summer Solstice

F. — Slight Heat

G. — White Dew

H. — the Autumnal Equinox

I. — Frost's Descent

J. — Great Snow

K. — Rain Water

L. — the Beginning of Winter

M.— Cold Dew

N. — the Winter Solstice

O. — the Spring Equinox

Examples: （N）冬至 　　　　　　　（J）大雪

51. （ ）立冬	（ ）寒露
52. （ ）清明	（ ）谷雨
53. （ ）惊蛰	（ ）雨水
54. （ ）夏至	（ ）春分
55. （ ）小暑	（ ）霜降

Task 5

Directions: *There is a business letter below here. After reading the letter you should give brief answers to the 5 questions (No. 56 to No. 60) that follow. The answers* **(in no more than 3 words)** *should be written after the corresponding numbers.*

Dear Sirs,

We are sure that you would be interested in the new "Housewife" Vacuum Cleaner which is to be placed on the market soon. Most of the good points of the earlier types have been incorporated into the machine which possessed several novel features that have been perfected by years of scientific research.

You will find that a special contrivance（装置）enables it to run slightly more than half the current required by machine of equal capability. Furthermore, most of the working parts are readily interchangeable and, in the event of their being damaged, they are thus easy to be replaced.

The special advantages it offers will make it a quick-selling line, and we are also ready to cooperate with you, by launching a national advertising campaign. Moreover, we are ready to assist to the extent of half the cost of any local advertising.

Bearing in mind the rapid turnover which is likely to result, you will agree that the 5 percent commission（佣金）we are prepared to offer you is extremely generous.

You will find enclosed leaflets（样页）describing this vacuum cleaner and we look forward to your agreeing to handle our product as the sole agent in your district.

Yours faithfully,

Zhang Hua

56. What does the writer recommend in this letter?

_____ is to be placed on the market.

57. What is the advantage of the working parts in the machine?

In the event of their being damaged, the working parts are _____.

58. How will the seller cooperate with the buyer in a national advertising campaign?

The seller is ready to assist to the extent of half the cost of _____.

59. What else does the writer enclose with the letter?

_____ describing this vacuum cleaner.

60. For what purpose is the letter probably written?

In order to find _____ to handle their product.

Part IV Translation — English to Chinese (25 minutes)

Directions: *This part, numbered 61 through 65, is to test your ability to translate English to Chinese. After each of the sentences numbered 61 to 64, you will read four choices of suggested translation. You should choose the best translation and mark the corresponding letter. And for the paragraph numbered 65, write your translation in the corresponding space.*

61. That bad-tempered old lady has no sense of humor and takes everything that is said too seriously.

 A. 那个坏脾气的老妇人缺乏幽默感，并对所听到的一切太过较真。

 B. 那个古怪的老妇人没有意识到幽默，并对所听到的一切太过较真。

 C. 那个坏脾气的老妇人没有感受到其中的幽默,并太过严肃地带走了所说的全部材料。

 D. 那个古怪的老妇人没有意识到幽默，很严肃地采纳了所说的内容。

62. The newly broadened road is two times wider than the previous one.

 A. 新扩建的道路是扩建前的两倍。

 B. 新拓宽的道路比前一条宽出两倍。

 C. 新拓宽的道路是前一条宽度的三倍。

 D. 新扩建的道路是前一次扩建的三倍。

63. We are now seeking a pretty as well as experienced English secretary to assist the general manager.

 A. 我们正在招聘一位漂亮且老练的英文秘书来管理总经理的工作。

 B. 我们正在面试一位漂亮且有经验的英文秘书来协助总经理使其做好工作。

 C. 我们正在招聘一位漂亮且有经验的英文秘书来协助总经理的工作。

 D. 我们正在寻找一位漂亮且老练的英文秘书来担任总经理的职位。

64. It is my great honor to have received your invitation, but I'm terribly sorry for not being able to accept it.

 A. 收到你的邀请我非常光荣，但是很抱歉不能接受它。

 B. 我非常光荣地收到了你的请柬，但是很糟糕，我没有能力接受它。

 C. 收到你的邀请我倍感荣幸，但是非常抱歉我不能接受这个邀请。

 D. 收到你的请柬我很光荣，但是我不能接受它，十分对不起你。

65. Fly non-stop to Australia on a plane. When Ansett Australia expended into Asia, we created a new standard of international air travel. We not only introduced the world's most spacious aircraft, but the quality of in-flight service for our guest that is unsurpassed.

 _____

 _____

 _____

 _____

Part V   Writing (25 minutes)

Directions: *This part is to test your ability to do practical writing. You're required to write a*
BUSINESS ADVERTISEMENT of China Daily *according to the information given*
below.

CHINA DAILY（《中国日报》）是中国最有权威的英语报纸，为国内外读者提供最新的政治、经济、文化及教育方面的信息。《中国日报》有12版，并不定期地出版特别增刊。该报发行至全国所有省份和主要城市，以及世界上150多个国家和地区。

海外读者订阅资费为：3个月105美元，6个月200美元，12个月380美元（含航空邮费）。

Words for reference: 有权威的 authoritative   增刊 supplement   发行 distribute
订阅 subscription

Test Five

Part I   Listening Comprehension (15 minutes)

Directions: *This part is to test your listening ability. It consists of 3 sections.*

Section A

Directions: *This section is to test your ability to understand short dialogues. There are 5*
recorded dialogues in it. After each dialogue, there is a recorded question. Both the
dialogues and questions will be spoken only once. When you hear a question, you
should decide on the correct answer from the 4 choices marked A, B, C and D given
below.

Example: *You will hear: W: Are you catching the 13:15 flight to New York?*
M: No. I'll leave this evening.
Q: What are the two people talking about?
You will read: A. New York City.
B. An evening Party.
C. An air trip.
D. The man's job.

From the dialogue we learn that the man is to take a flight to New York. Therefore, "C. An
air trip" is the correct answer. Now the test will begin.

1. A. At a restaurant.   B. At a hotel.
   C. At a post office.   D. At a café.

2. A. The man didn't like the TV program.

   B. The woman enjoyed this TV program.

   C. The man wanted to listen to some music.

   D. The woman didn't want to listen to music.

3. A. She is going to see a play.

   B. She is going to have dinner with the man.

   C. She is going to have a meeting.

   D. She is going to attend a party.

4. A. Teacher and student.   B. Guest and waiter.

   C. Customer and shop assistant.   D. Father and daughter.

5. A. 8:00 p.m.   B. 8:05 p.m.   C. 8:10 p.m.   D. 8:50 p.m.

Section B

Directions: *This section is to test your ability to understand short conversations. There are 2 recorded conversations in it. After each conversation, there are some recorded questions. Both the conversations and questions will be spoken two times. When you hear a question, you should decide on the correct answer from the 4 choices marked A, B, C and D given in your test paper.*

Conversation 1

6. A. Have dinner with the woman.   B. Meet his brother at the airport.

   C. Give a birthday party.   D. Go shopping.

7. A. Invite him to her birthday party.   B. Go shopping.

   C. Travel together.   D. See a film.

Conversation 2

8. A. In a post office.   B. In a store.

   C. In a library.   D. In a laboratory.

9. A. Because her nephew will enter college soon.

   B. Because it will be her nephew's birthday soon.

   C. Because she likes her nephew very much.

   D. Because her nephew will graduate from college soon.

10. A. A pen.   B. A pencil.

    C. A hand ball set.   D. A chess set.

Section C

Directions: *This section is to test your ability to comprehend short passages. You will hear a recorded passage. After that, you will hear 5 questions. Both the passage and questions will be read two times. When you hear a question, you should complete an answer to it with a word or a short phrase (**in no more than 3 words**). The questions and incomplete answers are printed on your test paper. You should write your answers correspondingly. Now the passage will begin.*

11. Who do you think is speaking?

_____ is speaking.

12. Where does the speech occur?

The speech occurs _____.

13. What houses can the tourists see in Victoria Park?

The tourists can have a special view of houses of all shapes, _____ and colors.

14. In late autumn and winter, what can tourists do in this park?

This park is the best place for _____.

15. When should the tourists come back to the bus?

The tourists should come back to the bus _____.

Part II   Structure (15 minutes)

Directions: *This part is to test your ability to construct grammatically correct sentences. It consists of 2 sections.*

Section A

Directions: *In this section, there are 10 incomplete sentences. You are required to complete each one by deciding on the most appropriate word or words from the 4 choices marked A, B, C and D.*

16. There are so many restaurants along the street that I'm not sure which one _____.

A. to be eating at   B. to eat at   C. eating at   D. for eating at

17. He told me how he had given me shelter and protection without which I _____ of hunger and cold.

A. would be died   B. would have died

C. would die   D. will have died

18. _____ you are familiar with the author's ideas, try reading all the sections as quickly as you possibly can.

A. Now that   B. Ever since   C. So that   D. As long as

19. No matter how frequently _____, the works of Beethoven always attracts large audience.

   A. performing
   B. performed
   C. to be performed
   D. being performed

20. I walked too much yesterday and _____ are still aching now.

   A. my leg muscles
   B. my leg's muscles
   C. my muscles of leg
   D. my muscles of the leg

21. The room is in a terrible mess; it _____ cleaned.

   A. mustn't have been
   B. shouldn't have been
   C. can't have been
   D. wouldn't have been

22. Hardly _____ when a loud explosion was heard.

   A. the train had started
   B. the train had been started
   C. had the train started
   D. did the train start

23. _____ new employee feels insecure during _____ first few weeks on the job.

   A. Many …their
   B. Many…his or her
   C. Many a …their
   D. Many a…his or her

24. So little _____ about mathematics that the lecture was completely beyond me.

   A. I know
   B. I knew
   C. do I know
   D. did I know

25. _____ from the hill, the sense of pride suddenly appeared in our mind.

   A. When we saw it
   B. Having seen
   C. Seeing
   D. Seen

Section B

Directions: *There are 10 incomplete statements here. You should fill in each blank with the proper form of the word given in the brackets. Write the word or words in the corresponding space.*

26. I dreamed of becoming an (engine) _____ while my father wanted me to be a doctor.

27. He was often (patient) _____ with his employees and as a result they decided not to work for him any longer.

28. As is known to us all, Hainan is the second (large) _____ island in our country.

29. The (appear) _____ of the headmaster at the party didn't seem to be welcomed.

30. The math teacher raised a series of questions (consider) _____ after the next class.

31. The secretary worked late into the night, (prepare) _____ a long speech for the president.

32. (Short) _____ after she graduated from the university, she moved to another city with her family.

33. My father told me that he was considered too difficult a student (teach) _____ when he was young.

34. His mother being very worried, he regrets (tell) _____ her that he has lost his job.

35. As good friends, he couldn't avoid (influence) _____ by Xiao Li.

Part III Reading Comprehension (40 minutes)

Directions: *This part is to test your reading ability. There are 5 tasks for you to fulfill. You should read the reading materials carefully and do the tasks as you are instructed.*

Task 1

Directions: *After reading the following passage, you will find 5 questions or unfinished statements, numbered 36 to 40. For each question or statement there are 4 choices marked A, B, C and D given in your test paper. You should choose the correct choice.*

Women's roles have changed throughout the world in recent years, but nowhere so obviously as in America. In many American homes today, it is more and more common to find that the children are left in day-care centers or nursery schools while both parents work. The woman may earn as much or more money than her husband. At home, household duties are shared in varying degrees by all family members. It is not unusual to find father cooking dinner, cleaning the living room or charging the baby. Mother might be outside mowing the lawn or washing the car. Children have responsibilities, too. One of the goals of the Women's Liberation Movement has been to have both men and women share in childcare, housework and financial responsibility. Today many American women will not marry a man who is not willing to participate equally in household responsibilities.

The high cost of living has made it necessary for many women to have jobs outside the home, but women often choose to have jobs in order to use their skills and education or to seek a more fulfilling and interesting life. Many American women enjoy the independence that an outside job and the salary give them. Although women have made advances toward equality, sex discrimination (歧视) still exists. Men-employers and even some women-employers sometimes are not for women working outside the home, and in some cases, a woman might be paid less than a man who performs the same job. American women, however, have met challenges since pioneer days, and they continue to work for true equality.

36. In the article the author implies that little children in America used to stay_____.

    A. in nurseries   B. in day-care centers

    C. at home   D. at school

37. Many American women go out to work in order to _____.

    A. earn enough money to support the family

    B. make their husbands share in the housework

C. enjoy independence

D. get more money than their husbands

38. Men have learned to _____.

A. go to work with their wives

B. do some of the house work

C. be the bread winners of their families

D. be left alone at home while their wives go out to work

39. By saying that "sex discrimination still exists", the author means _____.

A. women are still treated unequally

B. women can not find jobs as men can

C. men approve of women working outside the home

D. some women themselves do not like working outside the home

40. The article tells us women's roles have changed a lot throughout the world, but _____.

A. it is impossible for the women to win true equality

B. it is not difficult for the women to win true equality

C. it is greatly successful for the women to win true equality

D. it takes a long time for the women to win true equality

Task 2

Directions: *This task is the same as Task 1. The 5 questions or unfinished statements are numbered 41 to 45.*

Advertising has become a very specialized activity in modern times. In the business world of today, supply is usually greater than demand. There is great competition between different manufacturers of the same kind of product to persuade customers to buy their own particular brand. They always have to remind the consumer of the name and the qualities of their product. They do this by advertising. The manufacturer advertises in the newspapers and on posters. He sometimes pays for songs about his product in commercial radio programs. He employs attractive salesgirls to distribute samples of it. He organizes competitions, with prizes for the winners. He often advertises on the screens of local cinemas. Most important of all, in countries that have television he has advertisements put into programs that will accept them. Manufacturers often spend large sums of money on advertisements. We buy a particular product because we think that it is the best. We usually think so because of the advertisements that say so. Some people never pause to ask themselves if the advertisements are telling the truth.

41. How many kinds of advertisements are mentioned in the passage?

A. 7.   B. 5.   C. 4.   D. 8.

42. According to the passage, which of the following is NOT true?

    A. Some people never have any doubts about what advertisements tell them.

    B. Great competition exists between different manufacturers of the same products.

    C. The customer usually demands more than the manufacturer can supply.

    D. The manufacturer wants to persuade customers to buy his own brand.

43. Which of the following advertisements is the most important one?

    A. Advertising in the newspapers.

    B. Putting advertisements into TV programs.

    C. Distributing samples by attractive salesgirls.

    D. Organizing competitions with prizes for the winners.

44. The passage tells us that the customer usually buys a particular brand because he thinks that _____.

    A. he can get a prize

    B. it is the cheapest

    C. there is great competition between customers for the same brand

    D. it is the best

45. _____ could be the title of the passage.

    A. Advertising

    B. Supply and Demand

    C. The Manufacturer and the Customer

    D. The Result of Advertisements

Task 3

Directions: *The following is a job advertisement. After reading it, you are required to complete the outline below it (No. 46 to No. 50). You should write your answers briefly (**in no more than 3 words**) correspondingly.*

Assistant to Public Relations Manager

Business Press is the world's most respected publisher of business news. PR and publicity (宣传) play an essential part in ensuring our continued success, and this is an outstanding opportunity that could also be the start of a career in Public Relations.

Reporting directly to our PR Manager, you will run her office and learn quickly to do just about everything. Filling documents, taking calls from journalists and answering their questions are all included in this. You will also help to organize events and visits, prepare reports every month and generally help to run an efficient press office.

The perfect candidate (候选人) will have a high standard of education, strong communication skills and an excellent telephone manner. Professional secretarial qualifications are an advantage. A minimum (最小的) to two years' experience, which should be within a busy office, is essential.

You will be confident, have a smart professional appearance and be in a hurry to "get things done".

> **Assistant to Public Relations Manager**
>
> Assistant to Public Relations Manager will help to organize events and visits, prepare reports ____46____. The candidates are required to have strong ____47____ skills and an excellent ____48____, and have at least ____49____ years' experience. At last, the candidates should have a smart ____50____ appearance.

Task 4

Directions: *The following is a list of products advertisement. After reading it, you are required to find the items equivalent to（与……相同的）those given in Chinese in the table below. Then you should put the corresponding letters in the brackets numbered 51 to 55.*

A. — fashionable and attractive packages

B. — a wide selection of colors and designs

C. — reasonable price

D. — quality assured

E. — with a long standing reputation

F. — economy and durability

G. — have a long history in production and marketing

H. — fine craftsmanship

I. — rank first among similar products

J. — timely delivery guaranteed

K. — popular both at home and abroad

L. — excellent in quality

M. — various styles

N. — complete in specifications

O. — sophisticated technologies

Examples: （O）工艺精良 　　　　　　　　（N）规格齐全

51.（　）驰名中外	（　）品质优良
52.（　）技艺精湛	（　）居同类产品之首
53.（　）包装新颖美观	（　）久负盛名
54.（　）产销历史悠久	（　）价格公道
55.（　）花色繁多	（　）保证质量

Task 5

Directions: *The following is a Lucky Promotion. After reading it you should give brief answers to the 5 questions (No. 56 to No. 60) that follow. The answers (**in no more than 3 words**) should be written after the corresponding numbers.*

Lucky Promotion

Fly with Singapore airlines to Canada and you could win free tickets. There is a winner every day from November 1 to December 30, 2006.

Fly between November 1 to December 30, 2006, and you could win free tickets daily, plus a chance to win one of the 2 great prizes:

First prize: one pair of first class return tickets on Singapore airlines to any of our destinations in Canada, 5 night's accommodation (住宿) in a five-star hotel and US$2,000 cash.

Second prize: one pair of business class return tickets on Singapore airlines to any of our destinations in Canada, 3 nights' accommodation in a five-star hotel.

Plan your holiday to Canada on Singapore airlines now and try your luck for the good chance!

For more information, contact the Singapore Airlines Office at your place or visit our websites at www.singaporeair.com.

56. How long does the lucky promotion last?

From November 1 to _____, 2006.

57. What could you win if you fly with Singapore airlines within the period mentioned?

You could win _____ every day, plus a chance to win great prizes.

58. How many first class return tickets can you get if you win the first prize?

_____ return tickets.

59. What kind of hotel can you stay in free of charge if you win a second prize?

A _____.

60. How can you get more information about the promotion?

Contact the _____ or visit its websites.

Part IV　Translation — English to Chinese　(25 minutes)

Directions: *This part, numbered 61 through 65, is to test your ability to translate English to Chinese. After each of the sentences numbered 61 to 64, you will read four choices of suggested translation. You should choose the best translation and mark the corresponding letter. And for the paragraph numbered 65, write your translation in the corresponding space.*

61. I was so impressed by these words that I used them immediately for a Christmas card and later for a moving novel.

    A. 我被这些话打动了，马上把它们用到了圣诞卡上，后来又写进一部感人的小说中。

    B. 这些语句对我来说印象太深了，以至于我立即把它们用到了圣诞卡上，后来又用到了一部感人的小说中。

    C. 我记住了这些话语，当场把它们写到圣诞卡上，后来又写进一部可以活动的小说中。

    D. 我对这些词汇留下了很好的印象，迅速写到了一张圣诞卡上，然后又写了一部动人的小说。

62. It is announced that a child under four years of age not occupying a separate seat is charged 10% of the adult fare.

    A. 据通知，不到四岁的孩子是不能占位的，否则按 10% 的票价收取费用。

    B. 接到通知，不到四岁的孩子不能单独占位，按成人的 10% 收取费用。

    C. 通知说，不分开占位的四岁以下儿童，其票价是大人票价的 10%。

    D. 有通知，未满四周岁的儿童不独占一座位，按成人票价的 10% 买票。

63. If I had taken the doctor's advice and rested for a few days, I should have completely recovered by now.

    A. 假如我听医生的劝告，歇息几天，我应该现在就已经完全康复。

    B. 要是我听了医生的劝告，休息几天，现在就能完全康复了。

    C. 如果我能听医生的话，休息几日，早就应该完全康复了。

    D. 只要我肯听医生的话，休息几日，就一定能够完全康复。

64. It is agreed that remaining in a bad relationship not only causes continual stress but may even be physically harmful.

    A. 坏关系只会造成继续的压力，但不会引起物理上的危害，没人会反对这一点。

    B. 呆在一个坏的环境中不仅会带来巨大的压力，而且还会精神衰弱，这已是共识。

    C. 长期恶劣的人际关系不但会引起精神持续紧张，甚至还可能危害身体健康，这是大家公认的。

    D. 僵硬的人际关系不仅引起持续的压力，而且引起身体的危害，大家都同意这一点。

65. All car makers in China were involved in hot price wars last year to achieve high sales targets, but most of them failed due to customers' wait-and-see attitudes. But car prices are likely to drop by bigger range in the second half than in the first half due to car makers' increased sales targets and many new products competition.

_____

_____

_____

_____

Part V　Writing (25 minutes)

Directions: *This part is to test your ability to do practical writing. You are required to write an indication according to the following information given in Chinese.*

某制药厂研制了一种医治胃病的新药。请你为该药写一份 100 词左右的英语使用说明书。内容应包括：

(1) 本产品为传统中药，对胃病的治疗与保健有显著效果；

(2) 常量：每日三次，成人一次两粒，儿童一次一粒。胃不舒服时可加服一次一粒；

(3) 服药后可能出现轻微的恶心、欲呕吐、困倦等症状，属正常现象，停药后该现象自动消失；

(4) 本药品应置于阴凉干燥、儿童不能接触处；

(5) 使用本药品还应严格听从医嘱。

　　注意：不要逐条翻译，要写成短文。

Words for reference:

粒：pill；保健：health care；症状：symptom；说明：indications

Test Six

Part I　Listening Comprehension (15 minutes)

Directions: *This part is to test your listening ability. It consists of 3 sections.*

Section A

Directions: *This section is to test your ability to understand short dialogues. There are 5 recorded dialogues in it. After each dialogue, there is a recorded question. Both the dialogues and questions will be spoken only once. When you hear a question, you should decide on the correct answer from the 4 choices marked A, B, C and D given below.*

Example: *You will hear: W: Are you catching the 13:15 flight to New York?*

M: No. I'll leave this evening.

Q: What are the two people talking about?

You will read: A. New York City.

B. An evening Party.

C. An air trip.

D. The man's job.

From the dialogue we learn that the man is to take a flight to New York. Therefore, "C. An air trip" is the correct answer. Now the test will begin.

1. A. $4.　　　　B. $6.　　　　C. $7.　　　　D. $11.

2. A. To the school.　　　　　B. To the post office.

   C. To a friend's house.　　　D. To a restaurant.

3. A. Stop and take a rest.

   B. Take another path to the hill.

   C. Wait for the rest of people to catch up.

   D. Continue on to the top of the hill.

4. A. Meet her mum at the airport.

   B. Say Bye-bye to her mum at the airport.

   C. Fly to another city with her mum.

   D. Go to the movie with her mum.

5. A. Her exams have already begun.

   B. She has finished two papers.

   C. She's trying to complete her papers.

   D. She's too busy to work on her papers.

Section B

Directions: *This section is to test your ability to understand short conversations. There are two recorded conversations in it. After each conversation, there are some recorded questions. Both the conversations and questions will be spoken two times. When you hear a question, you should decide on the correct answer from the 4 choices marked A, B, C and D given in your test paper.*

Conversation 1

6. A. To tell Bob he won't be free tonight.

   B. To ask whether Bob has left or not.

   C. To tell Bob there will be a lecture tomorrow afternoon.

   D. To ask Bob whether he will be free tonight.

7. A. At 1:00 p.m.　　　　　B. At 1:30 p.m.

   C. At 2:00 p.m.　　　　　D. At 2:30 p.m.

Conversation 2

8. A. In a farm house.　　　　B. In the open.

   C. At a hotel.　　　　　　D. At home.

9. A. It snowed a lot.　　　　B. It rained nearly every day.

   C. There was a lot of sunshine.　D. It was foggy.

10. A. They were tall.　　　　B. They were strange.

    C. They were friendly.　　　D. They were cold.

Section C

Directions: *This section is to test your ability to comprehend short passages. You will hear a recorded passage. After that you will hear 5 questions. Both the passage and the questions will be read two times. When you hear a question, you should complete the answer to it with a word or a short phrase (**in no more than 3 words**). The questions and incomplete answers are printed in your test paper. You should write your answers correspondingly. Now the passage will begin.*

11. When will the exam take place?

    The exam will take place _____.

12. What should students bring with them to the exams?

    Students should bring _____ with them.

13. What will be the format of the exam?

    The exam mainly consists of _____.

14. What does the teacher suggest students to review?

    The teacher suggests students to review midterms as well as the textbook and _____.

15. When is this talk most probably being given?

    The talk is most probably being given _____ before exam.

Part II   Structure (15 minutes)

Directions: *This part is to test your ability to construct grammatically correct sentences. It consists of 2 sections.*

Section A

Directions: *In this section, there are 10 incomplete sentences. You are required to complete each one by deciding on the most appropriate word or words from the 4 choices marked A, B, C and D.*

16. It was not until 1920 _____ regular radio broadcasts began.

    A. while   B. which   C. that   D. since

17. —How did you think of your visit to the museum?

    —I thoroughly enjoyed it. It was _____ than I expected.

    A. far more interesting   B. even much interesting

    C. so more interesting   D. a lot much interesting

18. I would have come sooner but I _____ that you were waiting for me.

    A. didn't know   B. don't know

    C. hadn't know   D. haven't known

19. Not only I but also Jane and Mary _____ tired of having one exam after another.

    A. is   B. are   C. am   D. be

20. Robert and his songs _____ were famous in the United States are also popular in China.

    A. which   B. who   C. that   D. as

21. It's no good _____ problems with a man like him.

    A. to discuss   B. being discussed

    C. discussing   D. to be discussed

22. The little girl _____ dance before so many guests, _____ she?

    A. doesn't dare to; dare   B. daren't does; does

    C. dares not; dare   D. daren't; dare

23. The water will be further polluted unless some measures _____.

    A. will be taken   B. are taken

    C. were taken   D. had been taken

24. After the new technique was introduced, the factory produced _____ tractors in 1998 than the year before.

    A. as twice many   B. as many twice

    C. twice as many   D. twice many as

25. When Jack arrived, he learned Mary _____ for almost an hour.

    A. had gone   B. had set off

    C. had left   D. had been away

Section B

Directions: *There are 10 incomplete statements here. You should fill in each blank with the proper form of the word given in the brackets. Write the word or words in the corresponding space.*

26. It is necessary that he _____ (send) to the hospital at once.

27. The tourists took with them full camping _____ (equip), including tents, lights, quilts, and a sleeping bag.

28. The more challenging the journey is, the more _____ (excite) the young people will feel.

29. He had inside _____ (inform) as to what was going on in the U.S. Central Intelligence Agency (CIA).

30. As a rule, primary school students and all teenagers _____ (not allow) to enter the net bar.

31. She is _____ (fortune) enough to enjoy good health.

32. He found it _____ (increase) difficult to read, for his eyes were failing.

33. In _____ (add) to a cowboy movie, we also saw a Mickey Mouse cartoon.

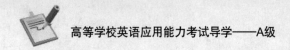
34. Neither the clerks nor the manager _____ (know) anything about the accident now.

35. I'd like to have my house (decorate) _____ before I move in.

Part III   Reading Comprehension   (40 minutes)

Directions: *This part is to test your reading ability. There are 5 tasks for you to fulfill. You should read the reading materials carefully and do the tasks as you are instructed.*

Task 1

Directions: *After reading the following passage, you will find 5 questions or unfinished statements, numbered 36 to 40. For each question or statement there are 4 choices marked A, B, C and D. You should choose the correct choice.*

A major part of managing stress is to recognize those situations you can change, and to learn to accept those you can't change. When you can separate those situations that you have control over from those you don't, then you will know when to take action and when to "let go" of problems you can't resolve.

Often pressures from outside sources can cause stress. We have two **options**: we can either change the demands on us or change the way we think and react to the demands. Sometimes we have to acknowledge that the demands are unreasonable. Then we either accept them or work to change the demands. For example, let's say a teacher gives you homework with a deadline. Given your other obligations (责任，义务), you first think that the task is unreasonable; you think you need more time to complete the assignment. You have two possible choices. You can try to change the demand, e.g. ask the teacher for an extension (延期), or you can accept the situation by changing your perception of it, e.g. by thinking that the assignment is simple. In the latter case, you may need to re-evaluate and change your other obligations. By recognizing that you have a choice—to either change the demands on you or change your perception and reaction to the demands—you will feel that you are in control.

As you read through your list of stressors, identify one or two things in your life that you can change easily and that will **make a difference** to you. Take action on those couple of things that will have the biggest positive impacts on your life with the least amount of effort. Resolving even a couple of things in your life may bring much relief.

36. The word "option" in the second paragraph can be replaced by _____.

    A. choice   B. reason

    C. problem   D. situation

37. When you meet some difficulties, you'd better _____.

    A. change them   B. accept them

    C. give them up   D. identify them

38. What's the usual reason for stress?

    A. Unsettled problems.   B. Limited capability.

    C. Pressures from outside sources.   D. Personality.

39. The phrase "make a difference" in the last paragraph means _____.

    A. differentiate   B. influence   C. change   D. resolve

40. Which of the following would be the best title of this passage?

    A. The Varieties of Stress   B. Managing Stress

    C. The Recognition of Stress   D. How to accept Stress

Task 2

Directions: *This task is the same as Task 1. The 5 questions or unfinished statements are numbered 41 to 45.*

Fire Instructions

The Person Discovering a Fire Will:

1) Operate the nearest fire alarm. (This will cause the Alarm Bells to ring, and also send a signal to the telephone switchboard operator who will immediately call the fire Brigade).

2) Attack the fire with available equipment, if it is safe to do so.

Fire Alarm Bells

The Fire Alarm Bells will ring either in the area of A block (workshops and Administration Offices) or in the area of B Block (Teaching) and C Block (Sports Hall). Those in the area where the Alarm Bells are ringing should take action as indicated below. Others should continue with their work.

On Hearing Your Fire Alarm:

1) Those in class: will go to the Assembly Area under the instructions given by the teacher.

2) Those elsewhere: will go to the Assembly Area by the most sensible route, and stay near the head of their Department.

Assembly Area

The Assembly area is the playing field which is south of Sports Hall. Here names will be checked.

Procedure

1) Move quietly.

2) Do NOT stop to collect your personal belongings.

3) Do NOT attempt to pass others on your way to Assembly Area.

4) Do NOT use the lift.

Fire Alarms

Fire Alarms are situated as follows:

1) Administrative Block

At the Reception Desk, at the end of connecting corridor, outside the kitchen door, back of the stage in the Main Hall.

2) Teaching Block

At the bottom of both stairways and on each landing.

3) Workshops

Outside Machine Shop No.1: Engineering Machine Shop No.2.

4) Sports Hall

Inside Entrance Lobby

41. This passage consists of advice on fire safety primarily for _____.

    A. people using a new kind of equipment

    B. workers in an engineering factory

    C. teachers

    D. students

42. When a person discovers a fire, what is the first thing he should do?

    A. Attempt to put it out.

    B. Telephone the switchboard operator.

    C. Start the alarm bells ringing.

    D. Contact the fire brigade.

43. People in the block where the fire bell has rung must gather for a check of names _____.

    A. in another block　　　　　　　　B. in the administration office

    C. in one of the playing fields　　　D. in the sports hall

44. Imagine you are in the administration office, when a fire breaks out in the sports hall, what should you do according to the fire instructions?

    A. Look for the fire-fighting equipment.

    B. Go quickly to the Assembly area.

    C. Go to the Reception Desk.

    D. Carry on with the work you are doing.

45. According to the instructions, what is a teacher supposed to do first in case of a fire?

    A. To check the names of your students from a list.

    B. To lead your students out of the building.

    C. To get detailed instructions from your Head of Department.

    D. To patrol the stairways and landings.

Task 3

Directions: *The following is an article about computer virus. After reading the following material, you are required to complete the outline below it (No. 46 to NO. 50). You should write your answers briefly (**in not more than 3 words**) correspondingly.*

Computer Virus and Virus Scan

A computer virus is a software program that attaches itself to another program in computer memory or on a disk, and spreads from one program to another. Viruses can damage data, cause computers to crash, display offending or bothersome messages, or lie dormant (保持静止的状态) until such time they are set to "awaken". In today's industry, scanning is no longer considered to be an extravagance—but a necessity. Computer viruses no longer attack your computing environment only but all other computing environments which you contact. Computer viruses can attach themselves to the files being used and later propagate (复制) themselves through disks and files. Important information and hardware losses could plague (瘟疫, 烦扰) your computing environment should you not take the proper precautions.

Many anti-virus products, such as Virus Scan, hold up the list of proper precautions. Scheduled periodic scans of your computing environment can offer you that added assurance that you are practicing "safe computing".

Means of spreading:	A computer virus often attaches itself to another program or hides itself on computer ____46____, and then duplicates themselves through ____47____.
Measures taken:	The main device to prevent important information and hardware being damaged is to ____48____. Now among many anti-virus products, ____49____ are regarded as good software to provide proper precautions.
	To add assurance for your computer, ____50____ of your computer environment is necessary for you.

Task 4

Directions: *The following is a list of terms for movies. After reading it, you are required to find the items equivalent to (与……相同的) those given in Chinese in the table below. Then you should put the corresponding letters in brackets numbered 51 to 55.*

A. — Computer graphics
B. — Feature movie
C. — Box-office flop
D. — Box-office hit
E. — Child star
F. — Cameo roles
G. — Location
H. — Musical
I. — Out-take
J. — Postproduction
K. — Screen test
L. — Short movie
M. — Silent movie
N. — Slapstick
O. — Sitcom
P. — Sound stage
Q. — Splatter movie
R. — Star-studded team
S. — Wide screen movie

Examples: (N) 闹剧　　　　　　　　(C) 低票房

51. ( ) 电脑动画		( ) 情景喜剧
52. ( ) 外景拍摄地		( ) 后期制作
53. ( ) 童星		( ) 故事片
54. ( ) 试镜		( ) 摄影棚
55. ( ) 宽银幕影片		( ) 全明星阵容

Task 5

Directions: *The following is a sales letter. After reading it, you should give brief answers to the 5 questions (No. 56 to No. 60) that follow. The answers (**in not more than 3 words**) should be written after the corresponding numbers.*

A Sales Letter

Jilin Electric Appliances Import & Export Corp.

Changchun, China

March 7, 2006

Smith Trading Co.

New York

U.S.A.

Dear Sirs,

We appreciate very much your confidence in the range of our electric appliances.

There is an exceptionally high demand for electric heaters owing to the cold weather during the season. The brand you ordered is now out of stock. However, the manufacturer has promised us a further supply by the end of this month if you could wait until then, we would deliver promptly the goods you need.

For over fifty years, our company has manufactured electric products which have enjoyed increasing markets in many countries and has built a reputation for service and quality. We are committed to being the best appliance supplier in some areas. Under separate cover, we send you our latest sample book of similar electric items we have recently produced. As one of our regular customers, you will be allowed a special discount of 2.5% provided we could receive your order before March 20th.

We stand ready to serve you—and welcome your call.

Sincerely yours,

× × ×

1. What are they thankful for?

They are thankful for ___56___ in the range of their electric appliances.

2. What causes the running short of the electric heaters?

It is mainly ___57___.

3. What is their company famous for?

It is famous for its ___58___.

4. What does this company send to its customers recently?

The company sends ___59___.

5. On what condition can their customer be offered a special discount of 2.5%?

The customers can be offered a special discount on the condition that the company can ___60___ before March 20th.

Part IV   Translation —— English into Chinese (15 minutes)

Directions: *This part, numbered 61 through 65, is to test your ability to translate English into Chinese. After each of the sentences numbered 61 to 64, you will read four choices of suggested translation. You should choose the best translation and mark the corresponding letter. And for the paragraph numbered 65, write your translation in the corresponding space.*

61. Metal has many useful properties, of which strength is the most important.
    A. 金属在诸多特性中以强度最为重要。
    B. 具有强度的金属有多种用途。
    C. 金属有许多有用性能，其中强度最为重要。
    D. 金属坚硬耐磨才是其最重要的性能。

62. No area could be expected to survive both as a true nature reserve and as a tourist attraction.
    A. 不能指望一个地方既成为真正的自然保护区，又成为旅游胜地。
    B. 任何地方都能既成为真正的自然保护区，又成为旅游胜地。
    C. 这一地区既不能成为真正的自然保护区，又成为旅游胜地。
    D. 一个地方不能既成为真正的自然保护区，又成为旅游胜地。

63. We regret to inform you that we'll have to cancel our order on account of your failure to deliver the goods punctually.
    A. 我们抱歉通知你们为了及时交货，我们将取消在你们失误账面上的订货。
    B. 我们遗憾地通知贵方，由于你们的失误，未能及时交货，我们只好取消订货。
    C. 我们遗憾地通知你们，由于贵方未能及时交货，我方只得取消订货。
    D. 我们抱歉通知你，为了保证及时送货，我们不得不取消让你修改错误账面的命令。

64. If you desire an interview, I shall be most happy to call in person, on the day and at any time you may appoint.
    A. 如你渴望面试，我一定遵照所约定之时日，前往拜访。
    B. 如你有意面试，我会很高兴在你约定的任何日期时间去拜访你。
    C. 如贵公司有意面试，本人一定遵照所约定之时日，前往拜访。
    D. 如你渴望面试，我会很高兴在你约定的任何日期时间亲自给你打电话。

65. As requested we enclose our latest catalogue and price list. I'm certain that our autumn products will be interesting to your customers as they are of latest design and space age material. With the global warming trend, such light decoration stuffs are getting more and more popular.

    _____

    _____

    _____

    _____

Part V   Writing (15 minutes)

Directions: *This part is to test your ability to do practical writing. You are required to write a contract according to the following information given in Chinese below.*

要点如下：

中华人民共和国湖北省 XX 工业大学（Industrial University of Hubei Province of the People's Republic of China）和美国科罗拉多州 (Colorado state) XX 工业大学，为促进 (promote) 两校之间的科学技术交流 (exchange) 与合作，经过诚挚友好的讨论，达成 (reach) 以下协定。

1) 双方将互相提供科学技术资料，交换有关情报，互相学习。

2) 双方互相派遣学者 (scholar)，专家互访，进行参观学习，做学术演讲。

3) 双方每年互相交换学生 10-20 人。

4) 本协定有效 (valid) 期为 5 年。

中华人民共和国湖北省 XX 工业大学

_____（签字）

美国科罗拉多州 XX 理工学院

_____（签字）

一、专项训练听力原文（Listening Scripts）

Listening Comprehension

Section A Short Dialogues

● 逻辑推理题

1. W: I'm looking for John's apartment. Am I on the right floor?

   M: No. He lives on the third floor. You can take the stairs up.

   Q: Where will the woman find John's apartment?

2. M: You can keep the books one month only.

   W: OK, I'll return them on time.

   Q: Where does this conversation probably take place?

3. W: Good morning, sir. Can I help you?

   M: Yes. I'm leaving today. Can I have my bill settled? My name is John Smith and my room
   number is 1108.

   Q: Where does this conversation probably take place?

4. M: Did Bill have any plans to buy a house?

   W: Hardly any. You see, a house is beyond his means.

   Q: What is true about Bill?

5. W: What do you think of Paris?

   M: It's interesting. In almost every street, you can see buildings of different styles.

   Q: What is the man's opinion of Paris?

6. W: Hello, sir. May I take your order now?

   M: Sorry, I haven't decided yet. A friend of mine is coming.

   Q: What's the probable relationship between the two speakers?

7. W: Hi, John. I haven't seen you since we graduated from the university.

   M: That's right. You took business administration, didn't you?

   Q: What is the relationship between the two speakers?

8. W: Would you rather have the party on Tuesday morning or Friday afternoon?

 M: Whatever you decide will be fine about me.

 Q: What is the man telling the woman?

9. M: It's been very cold in the past two days.

 W: We haven't seen the worst of it yet. More snow is forecast next week together with strong winds.

 Q: What will the weather be like next week?

10. W: I agreed with your plan at the meeting. It was a good idea.

 M: You should back me up then.

 Q: What does the man mean?

● 判断题

11. M: Is this the Service Department? I'd like to speak to the manager, please.

 W: If you hold the line, I'll get Mr. Robbins for you.

 Q: What do you think the man is going to do?

12. M: Would you like to go with me to see Peter? He's ill.

 W: Yes, I would, but first I have to visit Professor John.

 Q: What is the woman going to do now?

13. W: I heard that this film is very good. Did you enjoy it?

 M: No, I think it showed too much unnecessary violence.

 Q: How does the man feel about this movie?

14. M: I'm afraid Smith won't be back until 12:00 o'clock. Shall I take a message for him?

 W: Oh, yeah. Please ask him to give me a call when he gets back.

 Q: What does the woman want the man to do?

15. M: Did you get any message about the meeting on Wednesday?

 W: Yes, I did. But I'm still not quite sure what the meeting is about.

 Q: What does the woman want to know?

16. W: Tom is not good at English. Maybe he needs a tutor to get him through the exam.

 M: That could be true, but I think we should talk with him first.

 Q: What are the two people probably going to do?

17. M: Could you help me type these papers some time tomorrow, Jane?

 W: I'm afraid I can't. The meeting is said to last the whole day.

 Q: What will Jane do tomorrow?

18. M: How about the tour to the island?

 W: It was worth neither the time nor the money.

 Q: What did the woman mean?

19. M: I'm told that Alice is trying to find a job in an electronics company.

W: As far as I know, she is good at anything but electronics.

Q: What does the woman mean?

20. W: We are informed that the 11:30 train is late again.

M: Why did the railway company even bother to print the schedule?

Q: What do we learn from the conversation?

● 数字及计算

21. W: Can I help you?

M: Yes, I want to borrow these two novels and this one as well.

Q: How many books does the man want to borrow?

22. W: How long does it take you to drive home when there is not much traffic?

M: Only 25 minutes. But if I can't leave my office before 5:30 p.m., it sometimes takes me 50 minutes.

Q: How long does it take the man to drive home during the rush hour?

23. W: I'll have these shoes. Please tell me how much I owe you.

M: They are 40 dollars a pair, and 3 pairs make a total of 120, but today we offer a 10% discount.

Q: How much does the woman have to pay?

24. M: How many students are there in your class?

W: Altogether there are 100 students. A quarter of them are from the United States, and the rest are from Europe.

Q: How many students are from Europe?

25. W: Excuse me, when will the 7:15 train arrive?

M: It will be delayed for two hours because a bridge has broken.

Q: When will the train arrive?

26. M: What time does the meeting start?

W: At 8:30. We have 15 minutes to get there.

Q: What time is it now?

27. W: I thought it cost $8 to post an express letter.

M: It used to, but the price has gone up by $4.

Q: How much does it cost to post an express letter now?

28. W: Do you sell T-shirts, sir?

M: Yes, we do. They are on special sale this month, and one for $28, two for 50.

Q: How much does one T-shirt cost?

29. M: Will Dr. Smith's lecture begin at 1:40 or 2 o'clock?

W: It will begin at 1:50 and finish in two hours.

Q: When will the lecture begin?

30. M: How much does it cost?

    W: You are very lucky, sir. The shoes are on sale today. It is only $39.95 now. Yesterday it was $45.

    Q: How much are the shoes today?

● 因果关系

31. W: What did you think about the President's speech on TV yesterday evening?

    M: Unfortunately, I got home too late to watch it.

    Q: Why didn't the man watch TV?

32. M: Would you like to go to the movie with me? I have got an extra ticket.

    W: I wish I could, but I have to get to the station to meet my sister.

    Q: Why can't the woman accept the invitation?

33. W: Henry, have you finished your research paper for chemistry?

    M: Not yet, it seems that I always put things off until the last minute.

    Q: Why hasn't the man finished his research paper?

34. W: Will you go with us to Hangzhou? It's a beautiful place.

    M: Oh, I'm afraid I don't have enough money.

    Q: Why won't the man go with them?

35. M: I had no idea that you could type so fast.

    W: My mother began to teach me typing when I was six years old.

    Q: Why does the woman type so fast?

36. W: I wish you had told me your departure time earlier.

    M: I'm sorry. I thought my wife had already told you.

    Q: Why is the woman angry?

37. W: I hear you are moving to a new apartment next month.

    M: Yes. My roommate plays the radio all night long, and I can't sleep well.

    Q: Why is the man going to move?

38. W: How do you like this skirt?

    M: The style is good, but the color seems too dark to match your age.

    Q: Why doesn't the man like this skirt?

39. W: What happens in the first part of the film?

    M: To tell you the truth, I don't exactly remember because it almost put me to sleep.

    Q: Why can't the man remember exactly?

40. W: Mike, you haven't finished your homework today, have you?

    M: No. My mother has been ill for several days and I have to look after my sister.

    Q: Why hasn't Mike finished his homework today?

● 建议及请求

41. M: I left my umbrella in my room. Wait while I go back to get it.

    W: Don't bother. The weather report said it would clear up by noon.

    Q: What is the woman's suggestion for the man?

42. W: I'm really angry with John. He never listens to me.

    M: Take it easy, Allena. Things will work out.

    Q: What does the man suggest Allena do?

43. M: I'm looking for a job, but what should I do?

    W: Why not have a look at the advertisement?

    Q: What is the woman's suggestion for the man?

44. W: Tom, what game shall we have for our children?

    M: Why don't we leave that to themselves?

    Q: What is the man's suggestion?

45. M: Excuse me, Madam, could I leave this here for a few hours, please?

    W: Why not go to the luggage office over there?

    Q: What does the man ask the woman to do?

46. W: The movie starts in 10 minutes and there are too many people.

    M: Why don't we come back for the next show? Maybe it would be less crowded.

    Q: What is the man's suggestion?

47. W: It's a lovely day. Why don't we go sightseeing?

    M: Would you like to wait for me a few minutes? I have to finish this letter.

    Q: What do you think the man will do?

48. M: I'm going to invite a few of my classmates to my birthday party.

    W: You can't just invite a few. The others will be angry.

    Q: What does the woman suggest the man do?

49. M: Shall we have something special for a change?

    W: How about Chinese food? I know a famous restaurant.

    Q: What are the two speakers probably going to do?

50. W: Excuse me, could you tell me how to get to the bookstore?

    M: Certainly, but it's quite a long way.

    Q: What does the man mean?

Section B Short Conversations

Conversation 1

W: The house I just rented is beautiful. We're so lucky.

M: Tell me about it.

W: Well, it's in a small town, 20 miles south of the capital city.

M: Good location. But how's the house itself?

W: It looks quite new from outside.

M: What about the inside?

W: Well, it has a nice living room, a dining room and two large bedrooms. One for us and the other for the kids.

M: It sounds wonderful. What about the kitchen?

W: It's quite modern. It has a new refrigerator, and an electric stove. It also has a nice dishwasher.

M: Is there any furniture yet?

W: No. We can go shopping tomorrow.

M: How about the rent?

W: $1,500 per month.

M: That's not too bad.

Questions:

1. What are the man and woman doing?

2. What are the man and woman going to do next?

3. What is the probable relationship between the man and the woman?

Conversation 2

A man got into a train sitting opposite a woman who seemed to be about forty years old and they began talking to each other.

M: Do you have a family?

W: Yes, I have one son.

M: Oh, really? Does he smoke?

W: No, he's never touched a cigarette.

M: That's good. I don't smoke either. Tobacco is very bad to one's health. And does your son drink wine?

W: Oh, no. He's never drunk a drop of it.

M: Then I congratulate you, ma'am. And does he ever come home late at night?

W: No, he never does. He goes to bed immediately after dinner every night.

M: He's a wise young man. How old is he?

W: He's six months old today. But he'll grow up to be a gentleman.

Questions:

4. How does the woman feel about her son?

5. Which of the following probably best describes the man's feeling at the end of the conversation?

Conversation 3

M: Hello. 152376.

W: Hello. Is Cathy there?

M: No, I'm sorry, Cathy is out.

W: Is that you, Leo?

M: No, I'm not Leo.

W: Oh! I'm sorry…er…, well, could you please leave Cathy a message for me?

M: Sure. What is it?

W: Well, I'm supposed to be meeting Cathy for tea at my home. Would you ask her to see if she has my English dictionary? If she does, tell her to bring it along.

M: All right. And where are you calling from?

W: 130, Rose Avenue. I'm Cathy's friend Patty.

M: OK, Patty.

W: Thank you.

Questions:

6. Where is Patty calling from?

7. Why can't Patty speak to her friend?

8. Why is Patty calling?

Conversation 4

W: How soon do I have to leave my room?

M: Normally it's by 12 o'clock at noon on the day of your departure.

W: Well, you see, my plane doesn't go till half past five tomorrow afternoon.

M: Which room is it, Madam?

W: Room 611, the name is Browning.

M: Ah yes, Mrs. Browning. You may keep your room then untill 2 p.m., if you wish.

W: Oh, that's nice. By the way, how long will it take to get to the airport from here?

M: It's usually a 90-minute ride. But you'd better start off at 2:30 in case there is a traffic jam on the way.

W: Thank you very much.

M: With pleasure.

Questions:

9. Who is the woman?

10. Where does the conversation most likely take place?

Conversation 5

M: What's the matter, Mary? You don't look very happy.

W: I'm not. I'm worried about my English.

M: What's the problem?

W: I'm not practicing enough.

M: Why not?

W: Well, I seldom have the chance to meet English people.

M: You should go out more.

W: Where should I go?

M: You should go to pubs, and you should join a club.

W: But... English people never speak to me.

M: Ah, you should speak first.

W: What can I talk about?

M: The weather! English people are always interested in talking about the weather.

Questions:

11. Why doesn't Mary look very happy?

12. Why does Mary say that English people never speak to her?

13. What can we learn from the dialogue?

Conversation 6

W: I've been trying to get that book for some time.

M: Well, I'm sorry but it is still not available now...uh... we can order it for you.

W: How long will it take to get it?

M: About a week.

W: All right.

M: Now, what is the title?

W: *Teaching Reading Skills in a Foreign Language*.

M: Do you happen to know the name of the author?

W: Yes, it's Christine Nuttall.

M: Can I have your telephone number, madam?

W: 535178.

M: Thank you. As soon as it comes in, I'll ring you.

W: Thank you very much.

Questions:

14. What is the woman trying to do?

15. Where does the conversation probably take place?

Conversation 7

M: When is your vacation going to start, Barbara?

W: I'll be leaving on the third of July.

M: Oh, that's only a few days from now. How long are you going to be away?

W: Three weeks.

M: Where are you going?

W: This time I'd like to go to the beach. I need a real rest.

M: Have you made your hotel reservation yet?

W: Oh, I don't need to do that. I'll be staying with my friends.

M: You're lucky, Barbara. It's hard to find a place to stay at the beach in July.

W: Just think, in a few days I'll be swimming every day, playing beach ball, and lying in the sun.

M: Don't tell me about that! It sounds so great!

W: What about you, Ken? Where are you planning to take your vacation?

M: I don't know. I should think about it now.

Questions:

16. When will Barbara's vacation start?

17. Why does Barbara prefer the beach?

18. Where is Ken going to have his vacation?

Conversation 8

W: It was a heavy storm last night, wasn't it?

M: It certainly was. The wind broke several windows. What weather!

W: Do you know that big tree in front of my house? One of the biggest branches came down in the night.

M: Really? Did it do any damage to your house?

W: Thank goodness! It is far away from that.

M: I really hate storms. It's about time we had some nice spring weather.

W: It's April, you know. The flowers are beginning to blossom.

M: Yes, that's true. But I still think the weather is terrible.

W: I suppose we should not complain. We had a fine March after all.

Questions:

19. What happened to the tree in front of the woman's house?

20. What was the weather like in March?

Conversation 9

M: I hear you and Adam are engaged at last.

W: Yes, we are.

M: When are you getting married?

W: In the spring.

M: That's wonderful. Where's the wedding going to be?

W: We're not sure yet. Perhaps in San Francisco.

M: Oh, yes. I remember Adam's parents live there, don't they?

W: Yes, that's right.

M: Where are you going to live?

W: We're going to buy a flat or a small house somewhere in the south.

Questions:

21. When is the woman getting married?

22. Where's the wedding probably going to take place?

23. Why does the woman want to choose San Francisco for the wedding?

Conversation 10

M: Hello, Louisa. Are you coming to my birthday party?

W: Yes, I'm. How do I get to your house from the station?

M: Well, call me when you get to the station and I'll pick you up there.

W: Are you sure it won't be too much trouble?

M: It's no trouble at all. It only takes about 20 minutes.

W: Oh, I want to check your phone number. Is it 538816?

M: No. It's 518816.

W: Oh, really? I'm glad I checked.

M: What time do you plan to arrive at the station?

W: I plan to get there around 7:30 p.m.

M: OK. See you then.

W: See you. Goodbye.

Questions:

24. How can the woman get to the man's house?

25. When does the woman plan to get to the station?

Conversation 11

M: Can I have breakfast in my room?

W: Certainly, sir. Breakfast is served in your room from 6 a.m until 9 a.m. Here's the menu.

M: I'd like to have Italian breakfast.

W: Yes, sir. And at what time would you like it?

M: About half past eight, I think.

W: Very good, sir. And what kind of fruit juice would you like?

M: I'd like lemonade, please.

W: Lemonade. And would you prefer tea or coffee?

M: Coffee, please. Thank you very much.

W: Good night.

Questions:

26. Where does this conversation probably take place?

27. What does the man want?

28. At what time does the man want his food served?

Conversation 12

W: Excuse me. Are you Mr. Smith who comes from England?

M: Yes, I am. And this is my wife, Tina.

W: I'm Terry Wang, a friend of Mr. Mark Li. Mark is much occupied this morning, so he asked me to pick you up.

M: Oh, it's very kind of you. Thank you.

W: Did you have a good flight?

M: Yes, wonderful.

W: Let me help you with your luggage.

M: Thank you.

Questions:

29. Where does the conversation take place?

30. Why doesn't Mark come?

Conversation 13

M: I've got two tickets for a football match this afternoon. Why don't you come?

W: Uh, no, thanks. I'm not interested in it.

M: Oh, why not? Have you ever seen it played?

W: No, I haven't. But…

M: That's what I thought. You don't know what you're missing.

W: Don't I? Why?

M: Because it's very fast, with lots of action.

W: Really? Who're playing?

M: Two of the best men's teams in the world, one from England and the other from Belgium.

W: It sounds exciting. Hmm, well, perhaps I'll come after all.

Questions:

31. What're the two tickets for?

32. When is the match?

33. Why does the woman hesitate to accept the invitation to the match?

Conversation 14

W: Welcome to the mountain!

M: We're delighted to be here. It's really beautiful.

W: Yes, it is.

M: No pollution! Not many cars and in fact, not much traffic of any kind! How long have you been in this place?

W: Oh… about two years. I like the beautiful lake here most.

M: Did you build the cabin yourself?

W: Friends and family joined in. It took us one whole summer. We camped outside and used the lake water for drinking and washing.

M: Interesting, wasn't it?

W: Yes, it was.

Questions:

34. Where does the woman live?

35. Why does she live there?

Conversation 15

M: When did we visit this place last time?

W: It was on our 10th wedding anniversary, five years ago. I remember exactly.

M: How about swimming at the Long Beach again? We should relax.

W: Don't you think it might be a good idea to spend this weekend there? It will be our 15th wedding anniversary.

M: Great idea! It'll be just like old times.

W: The children will be excited.

M: So will I.

Questions:

36. What are they planning to do?

37. How special will that weekend be to the couple?

Conversation 16

M: Mum, here's a letter from Aunt Alice.

W: Give it to me… How wonderful! She is coming to visit us.

M: When is she coming?

W: She is coming by car on the 22nd and staying here until 26th.

M: Is she coming alone?

W: No, she is coming with Cynthia and Fay.

M: Mother, I don't remember them. How old are they?

W: Cynthia is 15. Fay is older, she is 17.

M: Mother, may we have a party?

W: If you like, but now we have to think about meals and other things.

M: Prepare the list, mother. I can go shopping. I can go to the small stores. Everyone knows me there.

Questions:

38. How long is Aunt Alice going to stay?

39. How old is Fay?

40. What will the son do immediately?

Conversation 17

W: Excuse me, sir.

M: Yes. What can I do for you, madam?

W: I bought this walkman here yesterday, but I don't know how to use it.

M: OK, let me show you. First, press OPEN button to open the door of the walkman. Put your cassette in and close the door.

W: And then?

M: Press POWER button. If the power is on, there will be a light indicated here, and after that, press PLAY and turn up the volume.

W: Oh, yes. Thank you.

Questions:

41. Where does the conversation take place?

42. What is the woman's problem?

Conversation 18

M: Sandy, what was your first job?

W: Well, when I graduated from the university in 2000, I worked first as a teacher in a primary school. That lasted for two years. Then I was promoted to deputy schoolmaster.

M: What were your duties?

W: I was responsible for all the teaching affairs.

M: Did you enjoy it?

W: Well, I like the job very well, but it was poorly paid.

M: And how long did you stay there?

W: Oh, about a year. I left because I wanted to apply for a position in the Sales Department of a company. That's where I'm working now.

Questions:

43. What was Sandy's first job?

44. Where does Sandy work now?

45. How long did Sandy stay in the primary school?

Conversation 19

M: Excuse me, madam.

W: Yes?

M: I bought this alarm clock this morning, but it doesn't work.

W: Oh, let's see what the problem is.

M: The alarm button doesn't work. When I press it in, the alarm doesn't stop.

W: You are right. I'll replace this one for you. Do you have your receipt with you?

M: No, I don't.

W: Sorry, we can't replace your clock without the receipt.

M: All right, I'll go back for it.

Questions:

46. What's wrong with the clock?

47. Why can't the clock be replaced?

Conversation 20

M: I'm thinking of buying a gift for my mother. Could you give me some advice?

W: Sure. What would you like to buy?

M: I'd like to buy some typical products here.

W: Then you can buy some silk products, such as tablecloths, handkerchiefs or blouses.

M: That's a good idea! Where can I buy them?

W: I suggest the First Department Store on Fifth Street.

M: Are the goods very expensive there?

W: No. The prices are very reasonable.

M: Great! Thank you.

W: It's my pleasure.

Questions:

48. For whom does the man want to buy a gift?

49. What gift will the man probably buy?

50. What about the prices for the goods in the First Department Store?

Section C Short Passages

Passage 1

    Almost in every case of job hunting, you are going to have an interview. An interview is an arranged chance for employers and employees to meet for the first time. An interview usually lasts for 15 to 30 minutes. The interviewer may ask the job applicants many questions, all concerned with the job advertised. The interviewer wants to know how well the applicants are trained, how much education they have received, what experience they have got, how they express themselves, and most important of all, what kind of person they are. There are some routine questions such as "Introduce yourself", "How much do you know about our company?", "Why do you want to work here?" and etc. If you once worked somewhere, they woud ask, "Why did you quit your job?" When taking an interview, remember to dress formally, talk politely, respond quickly and think wisely.

Questions:

1. What are the applicants going to have in almost every case of job hunting?

2. How long does an interview usually last?

3. What is the most important thing the interviewer wants to know about the applicants?

4. Which question will be asked if the applicants once worked somewhere?

5. What should the applicants remember to do when taking an interview?

Passage 2

A library is more than just a place where books are stored. A library is a source of information. That information may come from books such as fiction, nonfiction, or reference books, from periodicals such as newspapers, magazines, and journals, from audio-visual materials such as records, cassette microfilms, video tapes, etc. or even from a computer terminal.

Students go to the library to study and write research papers. The periodical room of a university library is where foreign students often find newspapers and magazines from their countries. In the reference room, they can find catalogues from many universities in the U.S. and other countries. If you want to buy a car, the reference librarian can show you the blue book, which lists the prices of new and used cars. People who need information in a hurry can telephone the reference room at many libraries.

Questions:

6. What is a library?

7. What can we get from libraries?

8. What kinds of books are available?

9. What do the students go to the library to do?

10. If one is in a hurry, how can he get the information?

Passage 3

It was a weekend in summer and all the lines of subway in the town were crowded. An old man was walking in the subway, looking for an empty seat. Suddenly he saw one and got in. A small bag was lying on the seat and a well-dressed gentleman was sitting beside it.

"Is this seat empty?" asked the old man.

"No, it is occupied by a man who has gone to buy a newspaper. He'll be back soon."

"Well," said the old man, "I'll sit here until he gets back." Ten minutes passed. The subway started. "He has missed the subway," said the old man, "but let him not lose his bag." With these words he took the bag and was about to throw it out of the window. The well-dressed gentleman jumped up and cried out, "Don't! It's my bag!"

Questions:

11. Why was the old man walking in the subway?

12. What did the old man see lying on the seat?

13. What did the old man ask?

14. What did the old man say when the subway started?

15. What did the old man want to do?

Passage 4

Sometimes people are confused about what type of food is healthy, and what kind of food may hurt their health.

A healthy diet is important for people. Everyone wants to live a long and healthy life. We know that the food we eat affects us in different ways. For instance, doctors believe that fruit and vegetables can usually prevent many different diseases. On the other hand, meat and other high-fat foods are bad for our health, which may lead to obesity. As a result of years of research, we know that too much fat is bad for our health, which may cause some diseases. To enjoy many years of healthy life, we should improve our diet now. We should eat more grains, fruit and vegetables, and eat fewer meat and milk products.

Questions:

16. What are people confused about?
17. What is important for people?
18. What kind of food can prevent many different diseases?
19. What's the result of eating more meat and other high-fat foods?
20. To enjoy many years of healthy life, what should we do?

Passage 5

The difference between life in one country and another is quite often not so great as the difference between city life and village life in the same country. In an English village, everybody knows everybody else; they know what time you get up, what time you go to bed and what you usually have for dinner. If you want any help, you will always get it and be glad to help anyone else in return. In a large city like London, there are many things to see and many places to go to. However, people often do not know each other well. It sometimes happens that you have never seen your next door neighbor, don't know his name or anything about him. People living in London are often very lonely, particularly after work. This is because the people they are with all day are scattered over large areas in the evenings and weekends. If you walk through the streets in the center of London on a Sunday, it is almost like an empty town.

Questions:

21. What's the difference between life in one country and another?
22. In an English village, what does a person know about his neighbors?
23. How about people in a large city like London?
24. How do people in London feel, particularly after work?
25. If people walk through the streets in the center of London on a Sunday, what is it like?

Passage 6

There are quite a few questions which you are not supposed to ask in the United States.

In the United States, one's income is top secret. People at the same office don't know how much each person earns, except the boss.

It is also considered impolite to inquire about one's property. If one of your American friends shows you something that he has just bought, you will, of course, say "What a nice skirt", "It looks beautiful", or something like that, but don't inquire about the price.

In the United States, one must not ask about the age of others. If you do, they will feel unhappy, especially ladies and the old. Americans hate to find they are getting old.

It is, therefore, advisable to get familiar with the American idea of personal privacy before going to the States, for people in China might have quite a different concept.

Questions:

26. In the United States, what question is top secret?

27. How do people think about inquiring about one's property?

28. What can't you ask when someone shows you something that he has bought?

29. What would people in the United States feel if you ask about their age?

30. What should we do before going to the States?

Passage 7

When you talk with a new friend, usually there are three parts in the conversation. The first part is greeting. In this part, you and your new friend will greet each other and tell each other your names or exchange name cards. The second part is the conversation itself. Sometimes the conversation is just a small talk. That is, you talk about unimportant matters, such as the weather, sports, entertainments and other interesting things. But it's not the time for you to ask about private or unpleasant things. Sometimes the conversation is about important matters like business affairs. The third part of the conversation is the leave-taking part. In this part, you tell your new friend that you are happy to have met him or her and then the conversation comes to an end.

Questions:

31. How many parts are there in the conversation when you talk with a new friend?

32. What's the first part?

33. In the second part, what can't you ask your new friend?

34. What's the third part of the conversation?

35. In the third part, what can we talk about with a new friend?

Passage 8

Advertising is part of our daily lives. To realize this fact, you have only to look through a magazine or newspaper. Most people see and hear several hundred advertising messages every day. In the advertising industry, selling products is the most important goal.

By advertising, messages can go around the world at high speed. But it is also true that there exists the problems of international advertising—problems of language and culture. To avoid problems in translation, international advertisers must choose different methods of advertising for different countries. Besides, they must also consider differences in laws and customs. Finally, there is the choice of what to advertise. The best advertisement in the world means nothing if the product is not suitable for the market. So knowing how to advertise in the world market can help companies to advertise successfully.

Questions:

36. What's the most important goal in the advertising industry?

37. How can the messages go around the world by advertising?

38. What're the problems of international advertising?

39. To avoid problems in translation, what must we consider?

40. What does an advertisement mean if the product is not suitable for the market?

Passage 9

Ladies and gentlemen, may I have your attention, please. First of all, let me give you a brief introduction to the Easy-Click, our newly-developed wireless mouse.

What makes this new product special is that it is wireless. From now on you are totally free from the trouble of connecting the device to your computer.

You will find this new model extremely easy to use, and that's why it's called the Easy-Click. Not only is the positioning accurate, but the shape just fits any size of human hands, no matter your hands are big or small, though it is small itself. The new material will ensure you a very special feel; once you have an Easy-Click, you'll never need other mouses. Buy one now at our chain stores and click easy!

Questions:

41. What kind of product is the salesman promoting?

42. What is the most outstanding feature of the new device?

43. Why is the new product called Easy-Click?

44. What do we know about the size of the new model?

45. Where are the products available?

Passage 10

Like any great buildings, the White House has an eventful history. The corner stone for it was laid in 1792, and it was completed in 1799. James Hoopen, an architect, designed the building. He based the design on 13 buildings he knew and admired. The first president living in the White House was John Adams in 1800. And since it was quite new, the house was unpleasant and cold and not very comfortable. On August 24, 1814, during the War of 1812, the English burnt the building and only the walls were left standing. Hoopen then rebuilt it following his original design. The gray stone walls were painted white to cover the smoke stains, and this explains the name it has—the White House.

Although this name was used for the building for some time, it did not become official until the administration of Theodore Roosevelt. The White House had been altered many times but the basic design remains. The main building is 117 feet wide and about 85 feet deep. Offices are in the three-story east wing and this is where the public enters to tour the White House.

Questions:

46. When was the White House completed?

47. Who was James Hoopen?

48. What happened to the building during the War of 1812?

49. Why were the walls painted white?

50. Who was the first president living in the White House?

二、模拟试题听力原文

Test One

Part I   Listening Comprehension

Section A

1. M: You look depressed today. Have you got the results of the test yet?

   W: Yes, but unfortunately, my grade should have been much better.

   Q: What does the woman think of her grade?

2. M: Hurry up, dear. The movie will start at 7:40 p.m. We only got ten minutes left.

   W: All right. We'd better take a taxi.

   Q: What's the time now?

3. M: How do you like the party held at the hotel last night?

   W: Well, the food was delicious and I had a good time there.

   Q: Where was the party held?

4. M: Waitress, I'll speak to your manager. I ordered fried chicken, but this is pickled.

   W: I'm terribly sorry, sir. I'll change it for you right away.

   Q: What's the probable relationship between the two speakers?

5. M: It's such a sunny day. Why not sit out in the backyard for a while and enjoy the sunshine?

   W: I'd love to. But there are a lot of assignments to do.

   Q: What will the woman probably do?

Section B

Conversation 1

W: Hello, is that 352088?

M: Yes, it is.

W: I'm inquiring about the apartment advertised in the morning paper.

M: Oh yes?

W: I wonder if you could tell me how much the rent is per month, please.

M: It's $1,500.

W: I see. Is it near the city center?

M: Yes, it's only about half a kilometer away.

W: Which floor is it on?

M: On the fourth floor.

W: I see. Would it be possible for me to see it tomorrow, say 6 p.m.?

M: Yes, certainly.

Questions:

6. What are the two speakers talking about?

7. How much is the rent per month?

8. How far is the apartment away from the city center?

Conversation 2

M: I've read your application form, and I'd like to ask you some questions.

W: Certainly.

M: Why do you want to apply for this job?

W: Well, I expect to get some teaching experience. And I like staying with young people.

M: The job requires a lot of paperwork. Can you manage it?

W: Yes. I have experience of office work. I'm sure that I can do it well.

M: Good. Could you work well in a group?

W: Yes, I like to work with others. But I'm very independent, too. I think I can also work well on my own.

M: Very good. You might be the right person for the job. We'll think about it.

W: When can I know the result?

M: We'll let you know within a week.

Questions:

 9. Why does the woman want the job?

10. Which of the following statements is NOT true?

Section C

At present there are more and more ways of going on holiday. In my opinion, there are two types of holidaymakers.

Holidaymakers of the first type always go to seaside towns or mountain resorts when they go on holiday. Their only aim is to relax. They just enjoy the local scenery and play the sports they like.

Holidaymakers of the other type go to foreign countries to increase their knowledge. For them, going on holiday is educational. If they come to a place, they will stay until they get a proper feeling of it or fully enjoy the local food, wine and their special culture.

Questions:

11. How many ways of going on holiday are there at present?
12. Where do holidaymakers of the first type go when they go on holiday?
13. What do holidaymakers of the first type enjoy?
14. What does going on holiday mean to holidaymakers of the other type?
15. What do holidaymakers of the other type do if they come to a place?

Test Two

Part I   Listening Comprehension

Section A

1. W: These silk gloves are quite a bit cheaper than the leather ones.

   M: I really like the leather, but I can't pay 26 dollars.

   Q: What will the man probably do?

2. W: Who's your new secretary, Tom?

   M: Miss Lisa. I'm very pleased with the work that she has done so far.

   Q: What do we know about the man's secretary?

3. W: Have you difficulty with pronunciation, Louis?

   M: No, I haven't much difficulty with the pronunciation; I can pronounce English quite well, but I can't spell most of the words right.

   Q: What is the problem with his English?

4. W: Why don't you wash your face and go to bed, Smith? It is too late.

   M: I have to finish my homework first.

   Q: What is Smith doing?

5. W: So Tom, now that your final exams are over, what are you going to do?

   M: I plan to take it easy for a few days or so.

   Q: What does Tom tell the woman?

Section B

Conversation 1

M: Excuse me, have you seen my little grey dog as you were walking through the park?

W: No, but I'll look before I leave. What's her name?

M: Her name? Actually, I call her Cinders because of her black color.

W: Why isn't she on a leash?

M: She saw a monkey and broke away before I could catch her.

W: Is she afraid of a monkey?

M: Yes, because the big monkey is running after her.

W: I see now.

Questions:

6: Where does the conversation most likely take place?

7: Why did the dog run away?

Conversation 2

M: How do you usually keep in touch with your friends, Sally?

W: I usually give them a call or send them a short message by my cellphone. Sometimes I send them an e-mail.

M: So do I. Cellphones are the most popular means in today's communication. Forty or fifty years ago, however, letters were widely used around the world.

W: That's it. My grandfather sent 100 letters back when he studied in England from 1950 to 1952.

M: Things have changed so much! Have you seen that there is a kind of telephone which is called videophone, with which you can see the person you are talking to?

W: Yes, I have. That is wonderful.

M: This is the advantage of modern life. Don't you think so?

Questions:

8. How does Sally usually keep in touch with her friends?

9. Which is the most popular means in modern communication?

10. If a man wants to see the person with whom he is talking, which of the following should he choose?

Section C

The first newspaper was written by hand and put on the walls in public places. The earliest daily newspaper was started in Rome in 59 B.C. In the 700's the world's first printed newspaper was published. Europe didn't have a regular newspaper until 1609, when one was started in Germany.

The first regular published newspaper in English was printed in Amsterdam in 1620. In 1621, an English newspaper was started in London and was published once a week. The first daily English newspaper was the *Daily Current*. It came out in March 1720.

Today, as a group, English language newspapers have the largest circulation in the world. But the largest circulation for a newspaper is that of the Japanese newspaper *Asahi Shimbum* (朝日新闻). It sells more than 11 million copies every year.

Questions:

11. How was the first newspaper written?

12. Where and when was the earliest daily newspaper started?

13. When was the first regular English newspaper printed?

14. When did the first daily English newspaper come out?

15. Do English language newspapers have the largest circulations in the world?

Test Three

Part I   Listening Comprehension

Section A

1. M: Would you like to go to the concert tonight?

   W: I'd like to, but I have to work.

   Q: What does the woman mean?

2. M: I bought this $400 TV set at half price.

   W: It's a good one. You're lucky.

   Q: How much did the man pay for the TV set?

3. W: Good morning, sir. Can I help you?

   M: Yes. Can I check out now? I'm leaving an hour later. My name is George Brown and my Room Number is 2009.

   Q: Where does this conversation most probably take place?

4. M: Have you decided where to live when you get married?

   W: I would like to live in the city near my office, but Tom wants a house in the suburbs to save on expenses.

   Q: Why does the woman want to live in the city?

5. W: I'm going to complain about the slow service here.

   M: Does it help?

   Q: What does the man want to know?

Section B
Conversation 1

W: It's freezing here. What's wrong with the heating anyway?

M: I've got an idea. Why don't we go out?

W: Out? In this weather? It's snowing!

M: I mean… let's go somewhere warm. We can go to a movie, for instance. I think *Gone with the Wind* is playing at the theatre down the street.

W: *Gone with the Wind*! It's six hours long.

M: Oh, Mary, it's only about four.

W: Really, George, I...

M: Come on, Mary. It'll be nice and warm in the theatre. Let's see... It's a quarter after seven now. Maybe there's a show soon. I'll call the theatre and find it out.

Questions:

6. How long is *Gone with the Wind*?

7. Why does the man advise the woman to go out?

Conversation 2

W: Good evening. Welcome to Village Green Inn. What can I do for you, sir?

M: I have a reservation with you.

W: May I have your name, please?

M: Tom Addison.

W: Yes, Mr. Addison. May I have a look at your passport, please?

M: OK. Here you are.

W: Would you please fill out the registration form?

M: All right. What is the rate for one person per night?

W: $69.

M: Do you accept traveler's check?

W: Sure. Here is the key card to Room 4312. The bellman will show you the way.

M: Thanks. I will be leaving tomorrow. When shall I check out?

W: Any time before 11:00 a.m.

M: All right. I'll remember that.

Questions:

8. What is the man's name?

9. What's the rate for one person per night?

10. When will the man check out?

Section C

   Good evening. Tonight's broadcast brings together music from different corners of the world. The records we have chosen for you are from classical Western music, folk songs and pop. In this broadcast we shall study the language of music. We shall try to find out how music expresses people's feelings. You'll hear a Beethoven piano piece and songs sung by a pop group and some black Americans. It will be natural if you like one more than the others. I shall be trying to explain why they are all good music. The feeling in each of the following compositions is sadness. You can find sadness in words, in paintings, and in music. Music is one form of art. It's like the spoken language, but uses sounds differently. I shall be saying a few words after each record. Now, the piece by Beethoven.

Questions:

11. Where does the speaker give this talk?

12. What kind of program is it?

13. Where are the records for the audience from?

14. In this broadcast, what shall we study?

15. What shall we hear in tonight's broadcast?

Test Four

Part I   Listening Comprehension

Section A

1. W: Do you mind if I borrow your English dictionary?

   M: No, of course not. It's on the shelf.

   Q: What does the man mean?

2. M: It's a sunny day today. Why not go out for a picnic?

   W: I'd love to, but there is a lot of laundry to do.

   Q: Why can't the woman go out?

3. M: These are very nice T-shirts. How much are they?

   W: Six dollars each. For two, ten dollars. They are on special sale today.

   Q: How much does one T-shirt cost if you buy two?

4. M: Excuse me, I want to send this parcel to Paris by air. How much is the postage?

   W: Please put it on the scale.

   Q: Where does this conversation most probably take place?

5. W: I'm getting a part-time job next week.

   M: Don't you think you should concentrate on doing your schoolwork instead?

   Q: What does the man suggest the woman do?

Section B

Conversation 1

W: Hello. When did you get back?

M: Um, this morning. Around 6 o'clock a.m..

W: Did you have a good time?

M: It was brilliant. Pretty good.

W: How did you go, by train?

M: No, I borrowed a car from my uncle, so I drove there.

W: Did you go to London?

M: Yes, I was in London the whole time.

W: Where did you stay in London?

M: With friends who had invited me to go and visit them. They showed me around London, and they were my holiday guides.

Questions:

6. How did the man go to London?

7. Whom did the man visit?

Conversation 2

W: Good morning. This is Dr. Anderson's Office. May I help you?

M: Good morning. I'm Johnson. My friend recommended Dr. Anderson to me. I'd like to make an appointment with him to have my teeth checked.

W: I can arrange for you to see the doctor two days from now.

M: Can't I come in tomorrow?

W: I'm afraid Dr. Anderson won't be able to see you then. He has a full schedule for the next couple of days.

M: Two days later? But… you see, my teeth…I can't bear them.

W: Yes, I see. Please wait a moment. I'll call the doctor.

(*After a minute.*)

W: You're so lucky. The doctor asks you to come here at around 8:30 tomorrow morning. Will that be all right?

M: Well, yes. But what time is the clinic open?

W: We start from 9:00 a.m. and close at 5:00 p.m. on weekdays. The doctor will look at your teeth before work.

M: Thanks. I'll come here at 8:30 tomorrow morning. Goodbye.

W: Goodbye!

Questions:

8. Who is Mr. Johnson?

9. Which of the following statements is true according to the conversation?

10. What time will the appointment be?

Section C

When accepting an invitation over the telephone, make it a habitual way to repeat four things: 1) the day of the week, 2) the date, 3) the time and 4) the place. Then you are sure you understand it correctly. If you do not know how to get to the host's home, this is the moment to ask for directions and to write them down. It is necessary for you to thank the host sincerely and to appear at the party punctually.

Since telephones are so widespread that communication is easy in the United States, it is considered rude to accept an invitation and then not to appear without phoning your regrets in advance. If something prevents you from attending, please telephone your host or hostess immediately. Explain the circumstances and express your apologies. Do it before the party, as far ahead of time as you can.

Questions:

11. What should be repeated when you accept an invitation over the telephone?

12. What would you do if you do not know how to get to the host's home?

13. What is necessary for you to do once you accept an invitation?

14. What is considered rude?

15. What would you do if you can't attend the party?

𝒯𝑒𝑠𝑡 𝓕𝒾𝓋𝑒

Part I Listening Comprehension

Section A

1. W: Can I have a single room for a night, please?

   M: Sorry, madam. All our rooms are occupied.

   Q: Where does this conversation probably take place?

2. M: I don't enjoy the TV program. Would you please turn it off for me?

   W: Certainly. Would you like to listen to some music instead?

   Q: What do we learn from the conversation?

3. M: Would you like to have dinner with me on Sunday?

   W: Thank you very much, but I'm going to the theater that evening.

   Q: What is the woman going to do on Sunday?

4. W: I'd like a blue dress please, one without a collar and belt.

   M: This one might suit you, madam. Try it on, please.

   Q: What is the relationship between the two speakers?

5. W: Mary left for London 10 minutes ago.

   M: That's right! It's now 8:15 p.m.

   Q: When did Mary leave for London?

Section B
Conversation 1

W: Hi, Bill. This is Nancy.

M: Oh, hi. How is everything going?

W: Just fine, thanks. How about you?

M: Pretty well.

W: Uh, I'm calling to see if you will be free on Saturday night.

M: Hmm, Saturday night? Let me think. Oh, I'm afraid not. My brother just called to say he was coming that night. I told him I would meet him at the airport.

W: Oh, that's too bad! It's my birthday and we are going to have a party at my place. I thought you would come then.

M: I'm really sorry, but I won't be able to make it.

Questions:

6. What is the man going to do on Saturday night?

7. Why does the woman call the man?

Conversation 2

M: May I help you?

W: Yes, my nephew is graduating from college next week and I'd like to get him a nice gift.

M: How much would you like to spend for the gift?

W: Well, I usually spend about 20 dollars on a gift. Do you have anything nice for that price?

M: How about a pen and a pencil?

W: No, my brother gave him that for his birthday last year.

M: Well, then would he enjoy a chess set?

W: No, he doesn't play chess, but he is quite athletic.

M: Then you could get him a handball set.

W: That's a good idea.

Questions:

8. Where does the conversation most probably take place?

9. Why does the woman buy a gift for her nephew?

10. What will she buy as a gift?

Section C

Ladies and gentlemen, your attention, please. Our bus will arrive at Victoria Park in a few minutes. You can feel the comfortable cool air coming from the lake on our left. This is a favorite place for tourists in summer, especially on a hot summer afternoon like today. This lake is one of the great wonders of nature. No one knows when and how it was formed, but people began to build houses around the lake a hundred years ago, so in this park you can have a special view of houses of all shapes, styles and colors. In late autumn and winter, this park is the best place for bird watching. School teachers like to bring children here and they just love it.

Now our bus is driving around the lake. You can sit back and enjoy the beauty of everything here. The bus will take us to a good spot, where you can take the most wonderful photos you have ever taken.

Here we are! Please get off and enjoy yourselves. Return to the bus in 30 minutes and then we will climb the mountain five miles away and have our dinner after that. See you!

Questions:

11. Who do you think is speaking?

12. Where does the speech occur?

13. What houses can the tourists see in Victoria Park?

14. In late autumn and winter, what can tourists do in this park?

15. When should the tourists come back to the bus?

Test Six

Part I   Listening Comprehension

Section A

1. M: The pen costs $13, but I only have $7.

   W: I have $6. Would you like to borrow it?

   Q: How much will the woman lend the man?

2. M: Can you stay for dinner?

   W: I'd love to, but I have to go and send some letters before picking up children from school.

   Q: Where will the woman go first?

3. M: Would you like to stop for a rest now?

   W: Oh, let's keep going. We are almost at the top of the hill.

   Q: What does the woman want to do?

4. M: Shall we go to the movie this evening?

   W: Oh, I'm sorry. I'm afraid I can't. I'm seeing my mum off at the airport at 7:30.

   Q: What will the woman do this evening?

5. W: Why does Linda have to spend so much time in the library?

   M: To finish her papers before exam begins.

   Q: What does the man say about Linda?

Section B

Conversation 1

M: Hello. May I speak to Bob?

W: I'm sorry, but he left a few minutes ago.

M: That's too bad.

W: Will you phone him again tonight?

M: I'm sorry, but I won't be free tonight.

W: Can I take a message?

M: It's very kind of you. There will be a lecture on English history by a famous professor at 2:30 tomorrow afternoon in the lecture hall. Please tell Bob not to be late.

W: Sure, bye.

M: Bye.

Questions:

6. Why does the man phone Bob?

7. When will the lecture be given?

Conversation 2

M: Morning, Sue. Did you enjoy your holiday in the country?

W: Yes, thanks. We had a great time. And some friends went with us.

M: Where did you stay? In a hotel?

W: No, we camped in the mountains, near Snowdon. We cooked all our meals over an open fire.

M: Sound wonderful. Was the weather good?

W: The sun shone nearly every day and it didn't rain at all.

M: Did you like the people there?

W: Yes, they were great. We met some farmers and had tea in their houses.

M: When did you get back? Last night?

W: No, this morning. You must think we are mad.

Questions:

8. Where did Sue spend the night in the country?

9. What was the weather like in the country?

10. What did Sue think of the people in the country?

Section C

Now I'd like to talk to you about the final exam. The exam will be held next Thursday, the last day of the exam week. Remember to bring along a few pens in case you run out of ink. Unlike the midterm exam, this test will not include multiple-choice questions. It will consist of short passages. You will have to answer three of the five passage questions. The exam includes all of the subject matter we have covered in class. So I would suggest you review your midterms as well as the textbook and your class notes. The final will take up 50 percent of your grade in the course; the research project will take up 20 percent, and the midterm 30 percent. I will be in my office almost all day on Thursday of next week. If you run into any problems, please feel free to stop by. Good luck with your studying and I'll see you on Thursday.

Questions:

11. When will the exam take place?

12. What should the students bring with them to the exam?

13. What will be the format of the exam?

14. What does the teacher suggest the students review?

15. When is this talk most probably given?

Test One

Part I　Listening Comprehension

Section A

1. **C**　推理题。男士问女士是否知道考试结果了，女士回答说成绩应当比这个结果好，此处用了虚拟语气，故选 C。

2. **B**　计算题。男士说电影 7:40 p.m. 开始，只有 10 分钟了，因此现在的时间是 7:30，故选 B。

3. **A**　由男士问话"昨晚在酒店举行的晚会怎样"可知举行晚会的地点在酒店，故选 A。

4. **B**　判断题。男士说到"服务员，我点的是炸鸡，给我上的却是腌制的"，由此可以判断他们的关系是客人和服务员，故选 B。

5. **A**　女士提到的 assignments 等同于 homework，表示"分配、布置的任务、功课"，故选 A。

Section B
Conversation 1

6. **A**　本题可根据一些关键词如 apartment, rent 判断出他们在谈论租房的事。故选 A。

7. **D**　每月的房租是多少？在男士的第三句话里得到了答案，故选 D。

8. **C**　问公寓离市中心的距离，回答是 about half a kilometer，故选 C。

Conversation 2

9. **B**　问为什么女士要应聘这份工作？对话第二句给出了此题的答案：我希望积累些教学经验，同时喜欢和年轻人在一起。故选 B。

10. **D**　在四个句子里，A、B、C 均是女士提到的，只有 D 不符合对话内容，故选 D。

Section C

11. **more and more**　文中第一句指出"目前，度假的方式越来越多"。

12. **seaside towns**　在第二段第一句里讲到，第一种度假者会去海边或山野度假村。

13. **the local scenery**　第二段第二句里说他们是到这些地方享受自然风光和做喜欢的运动。

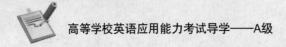

14. **is educational**　　第三段第二句说到第二类度假者的目的是接受文化熏陶。

15. **their special culture**　　文章最后一句说到第二类度假者度假的目的是享受美食、美酒和地方文化。

Part II　Structure

Section A

16. **C**　名词 damage 不可数，不能用 many 和 few 修饰。故选 C。

17. **A**　强调句型中强调的是句子的主语，用主格形式。故选 A。

18. **B**　本题考点：反意疑问句。主句以 suppose, think, believe, expect 等动词作谓语时，附加疑问部分要与宾语从句中的主语和谓语保持一致。当否定转移到此类句子的主句时，附加疑问用肯定形式。

19. **D**　固定搭配 make up for 意为"弥补"，介词 by 表示"通过某种方式"，D 符合题意，故选之。

20. **D**　sit 为瞬间性动词，不用于完成时态，be seated 表示"就座，坐下"，此处用其过去完成时形式，故选 D。

21. **B**　考查情态动词后接动词的情况，本句意为"你穿上这件新夹克很帅气，那件旧的在几年前就该扔了"。情态动词 ought to 后接完成形式表示"本该 / 应该……（但是却没有……）"，故选 B。

22. **C**　时间状语 for the last 20 minutes，表示的是过去的一段时间里完成的动作持续到现在并有可能继续下去，动词的时态应用现在完成进行时。故选 C。

23. **A**　时间状语 within three weeks，表示将来的一段时间。be to 表示将来一段时间内必定要进行的动作，而 be going to 表示"打算做某事"，故排除 D，同时不定式的逻辑主语是 form，动词形式用被动，排除 B 和 C，故选 A。

24. **D**　本题句型为"the + 比较级 …the + 比较级"，表示"越……就越……"。

25. **B**　省略 if 连接词的条件状语从句，因此助动词 were 提前放在句首。根据 were 可以判断这个句子是对现在情况进行假设的虚拟句，因此主句用"would + 动词原形"。故选 B。

Section B

26. **available**　　"买得到"，加形容词后缀 -able。

27. **stress**　　"压力"，用其名词形式。

28. **overload**　　加前缀 over- 表示"过量，超负荷"。

29. **congratulations**　　用名词形式，表示"祝贺，恭喜"用复数形式。

30. **refusal**　　"拒绝"，加名词后缀 -al。

31. **skillful**　　"熟练的"，用其形容词形式，加后缀 -ful。

32. **paid**　　根据句型"It's high time that…"，从句中的动词用过去形式。

33. **application**　　"运用"，用其名词形式，加后缀 -ation。

34. **is singing**　根据题意，应用动词的进行时态。
35. **selfish**　"自私的"，用其形容词形式，加后缀 -ish。

Part III　Reading Comprehension

Task 1

本文是一篇议论文，文章指出虽然许多人对考试不满，提出种种异议，但考试仍然为社会各界广泛运用，因为它能有效地选拔人才，促使人们努力工作和学习。

36. **A**　推理题。此题要求概括第一段大意。文中指出，虽然有人批评现代教育是以考试为导向，但仍然被广泛运用，故选 A。
37. **B**　细节题。根据文章第三段第一句可知，A 与 C 两项的内容文中没有涉及，D 项"说明雇员是否达到了所要求的最低水平"是干扰项，故选 B。
38. **D**　细节题。分别根据文章最后一段第一句话，第一段第四句，第二段第三句话，可排除 A、B、C。
39. **B**　语意题。filter 意为"过滤"，可根据 selecting 猜测出此意，故选之。
40. **C**　语气题。uncertain 意为"不确定"；neutral 意为"中立"；positive 意为"肯定"；partial 意为"片面"，根据文中内容可知作者对考试的态度是积极肯定的，故选 C。

Task 2

文章介绍了酒店使用房间预定确认系统来核实客人房间预定要求和个人信息。该系统通过确认信、更新确认通知等形式进行房间预定管理。

41. **D**　细节题。文章第一段第一句包括了 A、B 项的内容，第二句说到通过寄信给客人来确认房间预订情况，故选 D。
42. **D**　推理题。在文章的第一段第四句话里说到确认信里包含的信息，A、B、C 选项都属于提到的信息，故选 D。
43. **B**　细节题。文章第二段最后一句话说到客人有了确认信，在到达酒店后要先出示给前台的服务员，故选 B。
44. **C**　细节题。文章第三段第一句提到如果客人要改变预定，酒店要发出更新确认通知，故选 C。
45. **A**　推理题。文章最后一段第三句提到酒店会发给顾客一个取消预定的号码以保护双方的利益，故选 A。

Task 3

46. **interviewing and hiring**　从文章的第一句话可以得到答案。
47. **to win**　从第二段第一句话可知答案。
48. **your weakness**　从文章第二段可知第二点就是：Work on your weakness and develop your strengths.
49. **accomplish your goals**　从文中倒数第二行可找到答案。
50. **make a difference**　在最后一句中可找到答案。

Task 4

51. B, O   52. M, P   53. L, N   54. E, G   55. J, C

A. — stadium 体育馆

B. — boxing 拳击

C. — bungee jumping 蹦极跳

D. — discus 铁饼

E. — diving 跳水

F. — relay race 接力赛

G. — high jump 跳高

H. — javelin 标枪

I. — shot-put 铅球

J. — long jump 跳远

K. — soccer/football 足球

L. — weight lifting 举重

M. — fencing 击剑

N. — track and field 田径

O. — hurdles 跨栏赛跑

P. — arena 赛场

Task 5

　　介绍《建议书书写实用指南》一书作为写好建议书的最佳选择。首先《指南》会告诉你建议书的主要目的是劝说读者；其次，《指南》会告诉你，任何建议书都需要提供一个计划来满足要求。

56. *A Practical Guide*　　　　　　根据第一段，可知书的名字是：*A Practical Guide...*

57. **A potential customer**　　　　根据第二段后半句，可得到答案。

58. **Two**　　　　　　　　　　　　根据第二、三段开头，可知答案。

59. **level of knowledge**　　　　　根据第三段第二句，可知答案为 level of knowledge。

60. **explain technical language**　　词汇表的作用，根据第三段第四句，可得到答案。

Part IV　Translate English to Chinese

61. **B—D—C—A**　commodities: 商品；telex: 传真

62. **D—A—B—C**　in terms of: 说到，谈到；resistance: 阻力

63. **A—D—B—C**　information industry: 信息业；encourages: 刺激

64. **C—A—B—D**　spoke of: 谈到

65. 大多数会议都有一个议事日程。就一个正式会议来说，这一文件有可能提前交给与会者。对一个非正式会议来说，议事日程有可能只是列出需要处理的一些要点。议事日程的目的就是加快会议进行并使每个人都知道要点。

Part V   Writing

Time Deposit Certificate

Bank of China

No.: 8542786693052   Fixed Deposit Receipt

Date: July 8, 2007   Account No.: 5194120002033347

In Figures $8,000   Not Transferable

Received From Liu Li

The Sum of Eight Thousand Dollars

As deposit for a period

Bearing interest at the rate of 1.3%

Payable 8,104

Bank of China

Test Two

Part I   Listening Comprehension

Section A

1. **D**   推理题。根据 "…but I can't pay 26 dollars"（我不可能付 26 美元）推断出答案是 D。

2. **C**   推理题。根据 new secretary 推断出答案是 C。

3. **C**   推理题。根据 "…but I can't spell most of the words right"（但是，大多数的单词我都拼不对）推断出答案是 C。

4. **C**   细节题。根据 "I have to finish my homework first." 得出答案是 C。

5. **A**   推理题。根据 "I plan to take it easy for a few days or so." 推断出答案是 A。

Section B

6. **A**   细节题。根据 "…as you were walking through the park?" 得出答案是 A。

7. **D**   细节题。根据 She saw a monkey and broke away before I could catch her （她看见一只猴子，我还没抓住她，她就逃离了）得出答案是 D。

8. **B**   该题为细节题。会话一开始男士问 "How do you often keep in touch with your friends, Sally?"，女士回答 "I usually give them a call or send them a short message by my cellphone." 可知女士通常以打电话和用移动电话发短信和朋友保持联系，故正确答案为 B。

9. **D**   该题为细节题。会话中男士说 "Cellphones are the most popular way in today's communication."，可知移动电话是当今最盛行的通讯方式，故选 D。

10. **C** 该题为细节题。男士说到 "Have you seen that there is a kind of telephone which is called videophones with which you see the person you are talking with?"，可知视频电话是一种能看到通话对方的通讯工具，故选 C。

Section C

11. **by hand** 细节题。根据第一句 "The first newspaper was written by hand…" 可得出答案。

12. **Rome in 20 B.C.** 细节题。根据第二句 "The earliest daily newspaper was started in Rome in 59 B.C." 可得出答案。

13. **in 1620** 细节题。根据 "The first regular published newspaper in English was printed in Amsterdam in 1620." 可得出答案。

14. **March 1720** 细节题。根据 "The first daily English newspaper was the *Daily Current*. It came out in March 1720." 可得出答案。

15. **It does** 细节题。根据 "English language newspapers have the largest circulation in the world." 可得到答案。

Part II Structure

16. **B** 时态题。句中有 last year 只能用过去时。

17. **D** 谈论的是过去的事情，从句用一般过去时，主句动作发生在从句动作之前，用过去完成时。

18. **A** 这是一个 if 引导的条件从句的省略，如果包含 had, were, should, 或 could, if 的虚拟条件句省略时，就要将这些词放在主语前面作部分倒装。

19. **A** 抽象名词一般不与冠词连用，泛指一般概念意义，如：music, happiness, knowledge, 但是有些抽象名词可与不定冠词连用而具体化，如 a knowledge "一门学问"。international trade "国际贸易" 为泛指，不加冠词。故 A 正确。

20. **B** 主句的主语是 his face, 因此, 不能用分词短语，只能用状语从句。故 B 正确。

21. **C** as, which 都可以用于复合句中，但 as 常见于 as is known; as is said; as is reported; as is expected; as we had hoped; as often happens, as will be shown, as we know, as may be imagined; as we all can see 等搭配中。

22. **B** or 前面用的是动词原形，此处也用动词原形。

23. **C** "明天要举行的会议" 表示将来，又表示被动，故选 to be held。

24. **B** 这是一个强调句。强调句的句型是 "It is (was)… that (who)…"。

25. **C** "in + 一段时间", 表示说话时为起点的一段时间后，与一般将来时连用。"一段时间 + after", 表示某一具体时间或从某一事件算起的一段时间后。"after + 一段时间", 表示在……之后，用一般过去时，但时间为点时间时，只能用 after + 时间，用于各种时态。

Section B

26. **interviewing**　在介词后，要用动名词。

27. **closed**　此句用被动语态，be + done。

28. **Keeping**　keep away from 意为"使……远离"。

29. **employment**　用名词 employment（职业，工作）。

30. **to copy**　get sb. to do sth. 意为"促使某人做某事"。

31. **attended**　would rather + (not) do sth. 宁愿做（不做）……"。would rather sb. did sth. 意为"宁愿某人做某事"。谓语动词用虚拟语气，用一般过去时表示现在或将来要做的事，用过去完成时表示过去要做的事（would rather sb. had done sth.）。

32. **repairing**　need + to be done 或 need + doing 指"需要（某事）被做"。

33. **are**　police 是集合名词，如果所采取的行动是一致的，谓语动词用单数，若是分头行动，谓语动词用复数。原题是分头搜捕小偷，所以谓语动词用复数。这类集合名词还有 family，class，cattle 等。

34. **mindless**　mindless of 为"不考虑，不注意"的意思。

35. **organization**　在介词后需填写名词。organization of society 意为"社会结构，社会体制"。

Part III　Reading Comprehension

Task 1

　　本文阐述了大学学业与目前职场就业的一些情况，由于供求关系的改变，高等教育已经成为了买方市场。拥有文凭并不能拥有较好的工作，只有加强学习，才能保住这份工作并有所发展。

36. **B**　细节题。根据短文第一句。多年来学生们确信只要有大学文凭就可以找到一个好工作。

37. **D**　outnumber 意为"在数量上胜过"；discipline 意为"学科，科目"。有学位的老师，比实际的教学岗位多得多。

38. **B**　语意题。cut back to 意思是"缩小"。

39. **A**　细节题。根据 High education is well into buyer's market（高等教育已成为了买方市场）可得到答案。

40. **C**　推理题。根据短文最后一句。"他们意识到学位证书可以帮他们找到第一份工作，但是，要保住这份工作并有所发展，却取决于获得学位证书后的教育。"

Task 2

　　本文阐述了通货膨胀给社会和各阶层带来的影响。

41. **C**　细节题。根据短文第一句"昨天我们讨论了物价上涨的问题……"。

42. **A**　语意题。根据短文第一句"……或用经济学家的说法：通货膨胀"。

43. **B**　细节题。根据短文第三段第一句。

44. **B** 推理题。根据第二段最后一句。

45. **D** 推理题。根据第一段第一句"……我们注意到在通货膨胀期间，并不是所有的价格和收入以同等的比率上涨。"可推断出 D 项是错误的，因而选 D。

Task 3

本文是一则美国纽约语言大学招生广告，介绍了学校的宗旨、招生简章和所设课程。

46. **speak, read, write** 细节题。根据第一段第二句话 "We help people speak, read and write English…"

47. **intermediate** 细节题。根据第二段话中的 "…for beginning, intermediate and advanced students"

48. **evaluate** 细节题。根据第三段第二句话 "to insure proper placement, the institute will evaluate you and…."。

49. **(212) 998-7040** 细节题。根据 "For more information call (212) 998-7040 or…"

50. **New York** 细节题。根据 "New York, NY 10003"。

Task 4

51. F, E   52. N, O   53. I, G   54. A, M   55. J, L

A. — Health Insurance 健康险

B. — Whole Life Insurance 终身人寿险

C. — Full Insurance 全额保险

D. — Flood Insurance 洪水保险

E. — Residence Insurance 住家险

F. — Endowment Insurance 养老险

G. — Casualty Insurance 意外险

H. — Liability Insurance 责任险

I. — Car Danger Insurance 车损险

J. — Cargo Insurance 货物险

K. — Third Person Injured Ability 第三人伤害责任险

L. — Motorcar Accident Report 汽车出险报告书

M.— Evidence of Loss 损失证明

N. — Adjustment 理赔

O. — Beneficiary 受益人

Task 5

本文是一则个人求职信函，介绍了个人基本信息、所持证书、资历，并简略说明了求职意向。

56. **from a newspaper**　　　　　根据第一句得到答案。

57. **for three years**　　　　　根据第二段第一句"I have worked... for three years"。

58. **an administrative secretary**　根据第二段第一句"... so I have some understanding of the chemical company"。

59. **CET-4 and CET-6**　　　　根据第二段第三句"Having...CET-6"。

60. **with the letter**　　　　　根据"Enclosed forward to you is my resume"。

Part IV　Translation—English into Chinese

61. **B —A —D —C**　keep saying: 再三说；...none left: 根本没钱留下来

62. **A —B —C —D**　at the top level: 名列前茅；intelligent nature: 天生的聪慧

63. **B —A —C— D**　be tried and true: 经过实验证明可靠

64. **C —A —D—B**　latest proposal: 最近提议；concentrate on: 集中全力于

65. 在正式下订单之前，如果贵方同意给我们 15 天的试销期，我们将会感到很高兴。在试销期限结束时，任何未销出而我们又不准备库存的产品将退还给你们，退货费用由我方负担。我期待着早日收到你的回信。

提示： unsold（未销出的）是过去分词作后置定语；which we decide not to keep as stock 是定语从句；修饰 Any of the items（我们又不准备库存的产品）；at the end of the period 意为"在此期限结束时"；at our expense 意为"由我方负担"。

Part V　Writing

An Offer Letter

Jan. 20, 2008

Dear Sirs,

　　We welcome your inquiring of May 29th and thank you for your interest in our electrical bicycles. In reply to your inquiring, we have pleasure in enclosing our illustrated catalog and price list giving the details you ask for. All types can be supplied from stock.

　　As you will be able to see from our illustrated catalog, all the electrical bicycles we manufacture are of very high quality and are suitable for you purpose. The prices quoted are very competitive.

　　On regular purchase in quantities, we would allow you a 5% discount.

Sincerely yours,

(signature)

Test Three

Part I Listening Comprehension

Section A

1. **D** 推断题。从女士的回答中可知她想去，但不得不工作，故选 D。
2. **C** 计算题。听清问题是关键。问买电视机付了多少钱，$400 的一半是 $200，故选 C。
3. **C** 逻辑推理题。check out 和 room number 为这段话的关键。通过男士的回答可以推断出对话发生在宾馆，故选 C。
4. **A** 因果关系题。弄懂对话内容，才能做出正确选择。女士说她想生活在靠近她办公室的城市，所以她的工作在城市，故选 A。
5. **C** 男士回答的很简单，Does it help 表示他想知道投诉是否真的有用，故选 C。

Section B

Conversation 1

6. **C.** 数字题。问题问的是 *Gone with the Wind* 这部影片有多长？故选 C。
7. **B.** 因果关系题。问题：为什么男士劝告女士出去？原因是房间里极冷。故选 B。

Conversation 2

8. **D.** 问题问的是：这个男的叫什么？对话第五句给出了此题的答案：Tom Addison。
9. **C.** 推断题。男士问，一个人每晚多少费用？答案在对话第九行。故选 C。
10. **C.** 问题问退房的时间，文中明确提到，上午 11:00 以前的任何时候，故选 C。

Section C

11. **on the radio** 根据提示信息可知该题问的是说话者是在哪儿讲话，联系原文中的关键词，如 broadcast 可知这是一个收音机广播，所以正确答案为 on the radio。

12. **music program** 该题问的是这是什么节目，根据原文中的一些关键信息，如 classical，Western music, folk songs and pop，可知这是个音乐节目，所以正确答案为 music program。

13. **folk songs** 该题提问的是为听众挑选的唱片来自哪儿，根据原文中句子 The records we have chosen for you are from classical Western music, folk songs and pop，可知正确答案。

14. **language** 由问题和答案的其他部分可知这里要填入一个名词，来问答问题"在广播中我们将学习到什么"，根据原文中的句子 In this broadcast we shall study the language of music，可以直接写出答案。

15. **pop group** 该题问的是在今天的广播中我们将听到什么，根据提示信息 You'll hear a Beethoven piano piece and songs sung by a pop group，可知答案为 pop group。

Part II　Structure

Section A

16. **B**　固定句型 prefer to do sth. rather than do sth. 意为 "宁愿做某事而不愿做……"。

17. **A**　固定词组用法，make sb. do 意为 "使某人做某事"。故选 A。

18. **C**　when doing sth. 表示前后两个动作同时发生，且从句的动词与主句主语是主动关系。

19. **D**　take after: 脾气、模样像某人；take in 吸收，领会；take down: 记下，拆除；take on: 呈现。故选 D。

20. **A**　at one's leisure 意为 "某人有空时"，故选 A。

21. **A**　考查关系代词的用法。需用 whose 引导定语从句，修饰前面的 learners，故选 A。

22. **D**　考查时态。根据上下文，要用过去完成时。

23. **D**　考查句法结构 "It is…that" 强调句型。

24. **B**　考查过去分词的用法。sign 与 the agreement 的关系应用被动关系，即协议（the agreement）只能被签署（signed），又因为时间为上个月，故选 B。

25. **D**　关键词是 each，所以谓语动词要用单数形式；语态上是被动。故选 D。

Section B

26. **B**　此句子中时间状语从句为固定搭配 not…until，所以应把 after 改为 until。

27. **D**　根据题意，应把名词 foot 的单数形式改为复数形式 feet。

28. **B**　考查虚拟语气的用法。用 "should + 动词原形" 的形式，should 往往可以省略，因此用动词原形。把 hands in 改为 hand in。

29. **C**　固定句型 would rather do sth. than do sth. 意为 "宁愿做某事而不愿做……"。

30. **B**　依题意本句中的主语为 the company's training plan，因此考虑用被动语态形式。把 designed 改为 is designed。

31. **D**　本题的意思是海平线被提升得太高，以至于有的城市会被淹没，应用 so…that 句型。too high 应改为 so high。

32. **A**　在该题中，不定式作 expected 的宾语，而且主语是 students，应用被动语态，所以应把 to offer 改为 to be offered。

33. **B**　本题考察的是定语从句，其中 everyone says 为插入语。关系代词在定语从句中指人，作主语，要用 who。故把 whom 改为 who。

34. **B**　以 only 开头的句子，要用部分倒装结构，把 that I realized 改为 did I realize。

35. **C**　本题句型为 "the + 比较级 ... the + 比较级"，表示 "越……就越……"，前面有 the more，所以后面要用形容词比较级，把 worst 改为 worse。

Part III　Reading Comprehension

Task 1

本篇讲述的是在美国顾客服务的宗旨就是使每一个顾客成为关注的焦点，更好更方便地为客户服务是商家努力的目标。

36. **B** 主旨题。第一段第一句指出了"在美国顾客服务的宗旨就是使每一个顾客成为关注的焦点"。故选 B。

37. **B** 推断题。第一段第五句指出："相反的，店员会亲切地打招呼，并且协助顾客寻找需要的东西。"故选 B。

38. **C** 细节题。第一段倒数第二句指出了"大部分的商店里，每个商品分类区清楚的标识使购物成为一项轻松的乐事"。故选 C。

39. **B** 推断题。第二段第二句指出了"不过根据莫非定律的说法，不论你站在哪一排，其他排都会比你这排进行得快"。故选 B。

40. **D** 推断题。第三段的第三句和第四句指出了"如果产品有问题,顾客可以把它送回去。客户服务人员通常会为他们换商品或是全额退款"。故选 D。

Task 2

本文是一篇告诉学生如何去外国读书的文章,其中对入学要求和细节做了具体的陈述。

41. **A** 细节题。从文章第二段第二句可知, 提供国际教育经历。故选 A。

42. **B** 判断是非题。从文章的第三段第二句可知, 去外国读书, 不一定要通过通常的申请程序。故选 B。

43. **D** 细节题。从文中第四、五段可知, 没有提及提供经济状况。故选 D。

44. **C** 陈述事实的题目。从文章最后一段得知, 去外国读书, 一般建议提前一年准备。故选 C。

45. **C** 主旨题。文章告诉学生怎样去外国读书, 所以选 C。

Task 3

46. **to apply early**　　　　　根据第一段第一句, 可以得到答案。

47. **the admissions criteria**　根据第二段第一句, 可以得到答案。

48. **$400**　　　　　　　　　根据第三段的内容"若不支付 400 美元, 所提交的申请将不予受理"可以得到答案。

49. **originals**　　　　　　　根据最后一段的内容："正式的副本或证书一定是原件或合格的复印件"可以得到答案。

50. **certified copies**　　　　与 49 题相同。

Task 4

51. H, J　　　52. L, B　　　53. A, M　　　54. D, N　　　55. K, O

A. — Commander-in-Chief 总司令

B. — Chief Judge 审判长

C. — General Manager 总经理

D. — Governor of the Chinese People's Bank 中国人民银行行长

E. — President of the Higher People's Court 最高人民法院院长

F. — Chairman of the Board of Directors 公司董事长

G. — Dean of English Department 英语系主任

H. — Director of the Department of Asian Affairs 亚洲司司长

I. — Police Commissioner 公安局局长

J. — Executive Secretary 执行秘书

K. — Senior Editor 高级编辑

L. — Prime Minister 总理

M.— Provincial Governor 省长

N. — State Councilor 国务委员

O. — Financial Controller 财务总监

Task 5

56. **John & Carry Co., Ltd.** 考查对信件格式的掌握。询问单位地址，答案在两封信的信头部分。

57. **2000 International Fair** 推测题。推测写信人的目的，注意两封信的署名。答案在第一封信中可以找到。

58. **a repair shop** 细节理解题。不能接受邀请的原因。本题答案在第二封信中，可以找到相关信息。

59. **September 4** 细节理解题。交易会的举办时间。对时间提问，答案在第一封信中可找到。

60. **full details** 细节理解题。发出邀请方的计划。在第一封信中最后一句话。

Part IV　Translate English to Chinese

61. **A—D—B—C**　do nothing: 什么都没做；lasting peace: 持久和平

62. **D—A—C—B**　be expected to: 应该……

63. **B—C—A—D**　be proud to: 为……感到自豪

64. **A—C—B—D**　agree upon: 达成一致；negotiation: 谈判；confirmation: 确认书

65. "幸运牌"巧克力系用上等材料，以最新科学方法配制而成。其质量经过严格检测，始行出厂。由于巧克力原料品质受热带地区影响，偶尔出现有产品表面发白的情形，但其并未变质。

Part V   Writing

Date: July 16, 2005

From: Limin@hotmail.com

To: Wangli@sina.com

Subject: Invitation

Dear Wangli,

If you have no previous engagement at 7 p.m. on July 23rd, I want to invite you to dinner in the Garden Hotel.

We haven't enjoyed being together since we graduated from university, for everyone is too busy to have a reunion. I'd like to give you a pleasant surprise. Mahong, our best friend, arrived in Kunming the day before yesterday. We haven't met her for a whole year since she left for overseas study. Now she has come back for her summer vacation. Last night, she asked me to invite you to have dinner with her. We are looking forward to meeting together again.

Yours faithfully

Limin

Test Four

Part I   Listening Comprehension

Section A

1. **A**   推断题。女士向男士借英语词典，男士同意借给她，并告知词典放在书架上。

2. **C**   因果关系题。女士想要去野炊，但是有很多衣服要洗。laundry 是关键词，意思是"要洗的衣物"。

3. **B**   数字计算题。促销 T 恤衫，买一件 6 美元，买两件 10 美元。

4. **A**   逻辑推断题。针对地点提问，听出关键词 send this parcel（寄包裹），postage（邮费），scale（秤），可得出答案。

5. **D**   建议请求题。concentrate on 是"关注、集中注意力"的意思，男士的建议是女士应该集中注意力在学习上，而不是做兼职。

Section B

Conversation 1

6. **D**   男士提到他没有坐火车，而是借了一辆车，自己开车去伦敦。

7. **A**   根据 With friends who had invited me to go and visit them 一句得知，是朋友邀请男士拜访他们。

Conversation 2

8. **C** 听力材料中提到 "My friend recommended Dr. Anderson to me. I'd like to make an appointment with him to have my teeth checked"。由此可知，Mr. Johnson 是经朋友介绍，来找 Dr. Anderson 检查牙齿的新病人。

9. **A** 选项 C 和 D 在听力材料中没有出现，B 是干扰项，男士只提到要检查牙齿，而没有说要拔牙。

10. **C** 细节题。听到 "The doctor asks you to come here at around 8:30 tomorrow morning." 和 "I'll come here at 8:30 tomorrow morning." 即可做出正确判断。

Section C

11. **the date** 　　　　根据文中第一句话 "When accepting an invitation over the telephone, make it a habitual way to repeat four things: 1) the day of the week, 2) the date, 3) the time and 4) the place." 可得出正确答案。

12. **write them down** 　　根据原文 "If you do not know how to get to the host's home, this is the moment to ask for directions and to write them down." 可得出正确答案。

13. **thank the host** 　　根据原文 "It is necessary for you to thank the host sincerely and to appear at the party punctually." 作答，但是要注意答案不得多于 3 个单词，因此必须去掉副词 sincerely。

14. **phoning your regret** 　根据原文 "it is considered rude to accept an invitation and then not to appear without phoning your regret in advance." 可得出正确答案。

15. **express your apologies** 根据原文 "If something prevents you from attending, please telephone your host or hostess immediately. Explain the circumstances and express your apologies." 可得出正确答案。

Part II Structure

Section A

16. **D** 考点是倒装。当表示否定的副词 little 位于句首时，主谓部分倒装。

17. **C** 考情态动词。may be doing 表示对现在情况的推测；must have done 表示对过去情况的肯定推测；should have done 表示本该做某事，但实际没有做；can 表示具备做某事的能力。句意为：Lucy 今早本该做家庭作业，但是她没有做。故选 C。

18. **D** 考点为现在分词作时间状语，表示两个动作同时发生。

19. **D** 主语 car 和谓语 sell 之间是被动关系，"since + 时间点" 用于现在完成时态，因此本题要用现在完成时态的被动语态，"have/has been + V-ed" 结构。

20. **C** 考点是虚拟语气。表示与过去事实相反的情况时，主句要用"would (should, could, might) + have + V-ed"。

21. **A** 考虚拟语气。在 It is (about/high) time that 后的定语从句中,谓语动词用过去式（be 动词用 were）表示婉转的提议或建议。

22. **B** make sb. do sth. 意为"让某人做某事"。make sb./sth. done 意为"让某人 / 某事被……"。句中所表达的意思是让你自己被其他人所理解,因此用过去分词,表示被动。

23. **B** 考主谓一致。with, together with, as well as 连接并列的主语,谓语动词要与 with, together with, as well as 前的那个主语保持一致。

24. **C** 考动词时态,by the end of next semester 提示用将来完成时,结构为:will have + V-ed。

25. **A** 考点是状语从句的引导词。as long as 意为"只要", because 意为"因为", so that 意为"结果是", even though 意为"即使"。

Section B

26. **C** which 改为 what。what I read in the newspaper 译为"我在报纸上所读到的",what 做 read 的宾语。

27. **A** surprising 改为 surprised。surprising 意为"令人感到惊奇的", 通常修饰物; surprised 意为"感觉到惊奇", 通常修饰人。

28. **B** considerate 改为 considerable。considerate "体贴的,为别人着想的"; considerable "相当多的,可观的"。

29. **B** which 改为 that, that 引导同位语从句, 作 principle 的同位语。

30. **C** waiting 改为 to wait。动词 make 在主动语态中的用法:make sb. do sth., 宾补省略 to;改成被动语态后, to 要补充出来, sb. be made to do sth.。

31. **C** 把 to 改为 of, warn sb. of sth. 是固定搭配。

32. **D** to watch 改为 watching。spend some time doing sth. 是固定搭配。

33. **C** 把 therefore 改为 that。此句为 It is...that... 的强调句型。

34. **B** woman doctors 改为 women doctors。由 man, woman 构成的复合名词在变成复数时两部分都要变作复数。

35. **C** has 改为 have。主语 surroundings "环境", 谓语动词要用复数。

Part III Reading Comprehension

Task 1

本文讲述了父母与孩子相处中产生分歧时应注意的三个原则,即交流、尊重和考虑彼此的需要和权利。

36. **A** 文章第一句话明确指出,几乎所有的孩子在与父母相处过程中都会遇到困难。

37. **D** 主旨题。这篇文章讲的是如何与父母相处,A、B、C 过于片面,提到的是在与父母相处时的具体做法。

38. **B** 语意题。get one's way 是固定短语，根据上下文推断出 get his way 的意思是"得到他所想要的"。

39. **D** 细节题。参看原文第四段，A、B、C 在原文中都可以找到，而 disagreeing with parents' final decision 没有提到。

40. **B** 推断题。根据最后一段第一句 These principles can be applied to any relationship（与父母相处的原则能够运用到处理任何关系中），由此可推断出发展与父母相处的技巧能对处理其他人际关系有帮助。

Task 2

本文讲述的是经学者研究在目前的工作压力下，日本人的睡眠比较差，从而影响了人们的生活和工作质量。

41. **D** 根据第一段第二句 "The survey by the National Sleep Foundation found that American adults get an average of 6.5 hours of sleep a night, short of the 6—8 hours the Foundation suggests." 可以看出：基金会建议的日本成年人每晚的睡眠时间为 6—8 小时。故答案 D。

42. **A** 根据第三段第一句 "Of the 1,506 adults interviewed over telephone between..." 可以得知：是通过电话对人们进行的采访才发现人们的睡眠问题。故答案为 D。

43. **D** 根据第三段第一句和第二句 "...were found having a sleep problem, mostly snoring. Other sleep problems include having difficulty falling asleep, waking many times during the night and waking up too early." 可以得知：睡眠问题有 snoring, having difficulty falling asleep, waking many times during the night and waking up too early，而不包括 dozing。故答案为 D。

44. **D** 根据第三段 "... 76 percent said they do not believe they have sleep problem. About one fourth of adults said sleep problems have some effect on their daily lives." 可以得知，在调查的所有人中，有 76% 的人不相信自己有睡眠问题，约四分之一的成人说已经影响了他们的日常生活，故答案选 D。

45. **C** 根据全篇文章的含义可以得知本文主要讲述的是日本人的睡眠比较差。故答案为 C。

Task 3

46. **Scanning the headlines**　从原文中 Scanning the headlines gives a hasty look at the major news of the day 可找到答案。

47. **a few stories**　从句子 "If you have only a little time, you may wish to read the headlines and follow up only a few stories you are particularly interested in." 中可找到答案。

48. **reading the lead**　根据文章第二段最后一句 "Once again, if you are pressed for time, you can get a great deal of information by reading just the lead." 可找到答案。

49. **most important information**　　根据第三段中"Since news columns must fit the space provided, putting the most important information at the beginning makes sense." 一句，可以得知，最重要的信息放在新闻专栏的开头。

50. **every news item**　　根据最后一句话"You will not, of course, read every news item every day." 可找到答案。

Task 4

51. L, M　　　52. C, D　　　53. B, K　　　54. E, O　　　55. F, I

A. — the Beginning of Spring 立春

B. — the Waking of Insects 惊蛰

C. — Pure Brightness 清明

D. — Grain Rain 谷雨

E. — the Summer Solstice 夏至

F. — Slight Heat 小暑

G. — White Dew 白露

H. — the Autumnal Equinox 秋分

I. — Frost's Descent 霜降

J. — Great Snow 大雪

K. — Rain Water 雨水

L. — the Beginning of Winter 立冬

M. — Cold Dew 寒露

N. — the Winter Solstice 冬至

O. — the Spring Equinox 春分

Task 5

56. **"Housewife" Vacuum Cleaner**　　在信的第一句话"We are sure that you would be interested in the new 'Housewife' Vacuum Cleaner which is to be placed on the market soon." 中可找到答案。

57. **easy to be replaced**　　在信的第二段"Further, most of the working parts are readily interchangeable and, in the event of their being damaged, they are thus easy to be replaced." 中可找到答案。

58. **any local advertising**　　在信的第三段"Moreover, we are ready to assist to the extent of half the cost of any local advertising." 中可找到答案。

59. **The leaflets** 在信的最后一段 You will find enclosed leaflets describing this vacuum cleaner 中可找到答案。

60. **a sole agent** 在信的最后一段 "we look forward to your agreeing to handle our product as the sole agent in your district." 中可找到答案。

Part IV Translate Chinese to English

61. **A—B—D—C** sense of humor 意为"幽默感"；take sb./sth. seriously 意为"认真地对待某人 / 某事"。

62. **B—C—D—A** X times + 形容词比较级 + than… 意为"比……多了 X 倍，是……的 (X+1) 倍"。

63. **C—A—B—D** assist 是"协助"的意思。

64. **C—A—D—B** it 在句中作形式主语，真正的主语是 to have received your invitation；be able to do 能够做某事。

65. 乘飞机直飞澳大利亚。当安塞特澳大利亚航空公司业务拓展至亚洲，我们提供新标准的国际航空服务。我们不仅引进了世界上最宽敞的飞机，而且为乘客提供的舱内服务的质量也是无与伦比的。

Part V Writing

CHINA DAILY is China's most authoritative English-language newspaper. It offers readers both at home and abroad China's latest political, economic, cultural and educational news. *CHINA DAILY* is published in twelve-page broadsheets, plus unscheduled issues of special supplements. It is distributed in all provinces and major cities in China as well as 150 countries and regions all over the world.

Subscription rates for overseas readers: US$150 for 3 months, US$200 for 6 months, and US$380 for 12 months (Airmail postage included).

Test Five

Part I Listening Comprehension

Section A

1. **B** 推理题。从女士的问话中听到 single room，由此可推断出是在酒店订房间，故选 B。

2. **A** 判断题。男士说 I don't enjoy 和 turn it off，所以可以判断出男士不喜欢这个电视节目，故选 A。

3. **A** 因果关系。男士邀请女士周日共进晚餐，女士在答复时首先说 Thank you，但后面 but 就表示女士拒绝了邀请，并说明了理由是 going to the theater，故选 A。

4. **C**　推理题。女士想要一条裙子，而男士说 suit 和 try it on，可见两人的关系是顾客和售货员，故选 C。

5. **B**　计算题。玛丽 10 分钟前离开，现在是 8:15，所以玛丽应该是 8:05 分离开的，故选 B。

Section B
Conversation 1

6. **B**　在对话中男士提到那天晚上他哥哥要来，他要去机场接他，故选 B。

7. **A**　在对话中，刚开始女士提到 I'm calling to see if you will be free on Saturday night，后面女士又说到 It's my birthday and we are going to have a party，所以可以推断出女士想邀请男士去参加她的生日派对，故选 A。

Conversation 2

8. **B**　问事情发生的地点，第一句 May I help you? 是服务场所常见的。根据后面对话中提到的 I'd like to get him a nice gift 以及二人对所购买礼物的讨论，可以判断对话发生在商店里，故选 B。

9. **D**　考查对细节的理解，在对话第二句女士就提到了 my nephew is graduating from college next week and I'd like to get him a nice gift，因此可以推断因为她侄儿马上就要大学毕业了，所以女士想给他买件礼物表示祝贺，故选 D。

10. **C**　与售货员的对话谈到了购买 a pen and a pencil，a chess set 以及 a handball set，对男士最后一个建议，女士表示同意（That's a good idea），所以极有可能会买手球套，故选 C。

Section C

11. **A tourist guide**　从整篇文章可以看出本文是一个导游在旅游途中向游客介绍某景点，所以可以推断出是一个导游在说话。

12. **on a bus**　在第二句话中可以听到 our bus will arrive at，所以可以推断出是发生在汽车上。

13. **styles**　在文章中可以听到 "in this park you can have a special view of houses of all shapes, styles and colors."。

14. **bird watching**　在文中可以听到 "in late autumn and winter, this park is the best place for bird watching."。

15. **in 30 minutes**　文章最后一段提到 return to the bus in 30 minutes。

Part II　Structure

Section A

16. **B**　句中 which one 与不定式构成不定式的疑问结构，其中 one 指代的是前面的 restaurant，显然不是不定式中 eat 的宾语，因此要在不定式后面加相应的介词 at，作为 eat 的地点状语。

17. **B** 考虚拟语气。without 可引导含蓄条件句，常使用虚拟语气。此处 without 与 which 一起引导定语从句（其先行词为 shelter and protection），表示与过去事实相反的假设，应该用 "would have + 过去分词" 的虚拟语气。

18. **A** now that 意为 "既然"，指说话人已知的原因。

19. **B** 考让步状语从句。句首的让步状语从句完整的形式如下：No matter how frequently the works of Beethoven are performed。

20. **A** 表达 "腿部肌肉"，只能说 leg muscles，不能用 "'s" 或 "of" 所有格。因为腿不是肌肉的所有者，只表明肌肉的部位。

21. **C** 对过去否定的推测用 "can't have + 过去分词"。

22. **C** 句意：火车刚一开动，就听到了一声很响的爆炸声。hardly...when 意为 "刚一……就……"。hardly 后用过去完成时态，并且要倒装，when 后用一般过去时态。

23. **D** many, many a 都作 "许多" 解，但前者用于复数名词前，后者则用于单数名词前。句中的主语 employee 为单数名词，应用 many a，它的代词也应为单数形式。

24. **D** 考倒装。"so + 形容词或副词 + that" 结构通常引起部分倒装。故 A 和 B 不对，C 项 do I know 的时态与本题不符，只有 D 符合题意。

25. **A** 考查 when 引导的时间状语从句。having seen 为现在分词的完成式，seeing 为现在分词的一般式，seen 为过去分词，它们的逻辑主语都不是 the sense of pride，因此与本题不符，只能选择状语从句。

Section B

26. **engineer**	根据句意应指 "工程师"。	
27. **impatient**	根据句意是 "他经常很不耐烦地对待他的职员，结果他们决定不再为他工作了"。因此应该填 impatient。	
28. **largest**	此处空格后面有表示比较范围的 in 短语，前面有 the second 来限定，所以应该用其形容词最高级形式。	
29. **appearance**	此处空格为 appear 的词形转换，因为前面有定冠词 the，后面又有 of 短语修饰，所以应该用其名词形式。	
30. **to be considered**	此处空格为 questions 的宾语补足语，与宾语形成被动关系，又因为意思上表示将来，所以应该用其不定式的将来式。	
31. **preparing**	此处空格前面没有连词，又因为与前面 worked 的动作同时发生，且与主语 The secretary 为主动关系，作为伴随状语，应该用现在分词。	
32. **Shortly**	根据句意，这里应该用副词。	
33. **to teach**	此处属于 too...to 结构，所以应该用其不定式形式。	
34. **telling**	regret 后面可以接不定式或动名词，regret to do 意为 "因要做某事而遗憾"，regret doing 表示 "后悔做了某事"。根据句意，是指抱歉做过某事，所以应该用动名词形式。	
35. **being influenced**	avoid 后接动名词，而且根据题意，此句是指 "他不可避免要受到小李的影响"，是被动语态，所以要填动名词的被动式。	

Part III   Reading Comprehension

Task 1

本篇文章主要是讲美国妇女的角色发生了很大的改变。在大多数家庭中，丈夫不再是唯一的养家糊口者，妻子已成为职业女性，其收入亦相当可观。然而，社会对女性仍然存在着歧视。老板们不赞成妇女参加工作，干同样的工作，妇女的收入低于男性。要实现真正意义上的男女平等，女性还要继续为维护自己的权利而斗争。

36. **C** 推断题。从文章中的第二句话 "But it is more and more common to find that the children are left in day-care centers or nursery schools while both parents work." 可推断出以前的孩子通常是待在家里而不是上幼儿园。

37. **C** 细节题。妇女外出工作会有 A，B，D 提到的情况，但最后一段提到 "more fulfilling and interesting life; …enjoy the independence" 等细节是答题的依据。

38. **B** 细节题。第一段中提到虽然 "…the husband still carries on his traditional role of breadwinner," 但 "It is not unusual to find father cooking dinner, cleaning the living room of charging the baby"，因此 B 正确。

39. **A** 推断题。在文章最后部分作者说："Although women have made advances…; Employers…sometimes are not for women working outside the home, and in some cases, a woman might be paid less than a man who performs the same job." 这都说明了 sex discrimination 的含义，即 A 表达的内容。

40. **D** 主旨题。作者在第一段中讲述了妇女的地位在各个方面产生了变化，在第二段中作者也指出 they continue to work for true equality，说明真正达到男女平等需要很长时间的努力。

Task 2

本篇文章主要是关于做广告的原因、形式和作用。做广告已成为现代社会的一种专业活动。制造商之间存在着激烈竞争，他们争相利用广告说服消费者购买自己的商品。消费者也深受广告影响。

41. **A** 细节题。从文章第五行开始列举了以下做广告的形式：报纸、招贴、收音机节目、分发样品、组织竞赛、电影广告和电视广告。故选 A。

42. **C** 细节题。从文章的第二行可以看到："供通常是大于需。"选项 C "顾客需要的通常多于厂家所能供应的"是错误的。其他三项文中都已提到，故选 C。

43. **B** 细节题。从文章的 "Most important of all, in countries that have television he has advertisements put into programs"（最重要的是，在有电视的国家，厂家让人把广告插入节目）可知道答案。

44. **D** 细节题。根据 We buy a particular product because we think that it is the best（"我们购买某一产品是因为我们认为它是最好的"）判断 D 正确。

45. **A** 主旨题。整篇文章不断地提到厂家做广告的原因、形式和作用。故选 A。

Task 3

46. **every month**	根据第二段最后一句可知答案。
47. **communication**	根据第三段第一句可知答案。
48. **telephone manner**	同 47 题。
49. **two**	根据第三段第三句可知答案。
50. **professional**	根据第三段最后一句可知答案。

Task 4

51. K, L   52. H, I   53. A, E   54. G, C   55. B, D

A. — fashionable and attractive packages 包装新颖美观

B. — a wide selection of colors and designs 花色繁多

C. — reasonable price 价格公道

D. — quality assured 保证质量

E. — with a long standing reputation 久负盛名

F. — economy and durability 经济耐用

G. — have a long history in production and marketing 产销历史悠久

H. — fine craftsmanship 技艺精湛

I. — rank first among similar products 居同类产品之首

J. — timely delivery guaranteed 交货及时

K. — popular both at home and abroad 驰名中外

L. — excellent in quality 品质优良

M. — various styles 款式多样

N. — complete in specifications 规格齐全

O. — sophisticated technologies 工艺精良

Task 5

56. **December 30**	本题问时间，在文章第一段就可以找到答案。
57. **free tickets**	在第二段就可以找到答案。
58. **One pair of**	本题在文中第三段中可以找到信息。
59. **five-star hotel**	很明显，相关信息在第四段中。
60. **Singapore Airlines Office**	在文中最后一段，"For more information, contact the Singapore Airlines Office..."。

Part IV   Translation

61. **B—A—D—C**   be impressed by: 对……留下印象；moving: 感人的

62. **D—C—B—A**   separate: 单独的；charged: 收取费用；adult fare: 成人票价

63. **B—A—C—D**   advice: 劝告

64. **C—D—B—A**   it is agreed that…: 公认的；physically: 身体的；continual stress: 持续的压力

65. 去年，汽车制造商们为了获得更好的销售业绩，都卷入了价格战。但由于消费者采取了观望的态度，绝大部分汽车制造商都没有到达目的。但是由于汽车制造商提高了销售目标以及众多新款车型的相互竞争，今年下半年汽车价格下跌的幅度可能会比上半年更大。

Part V   Writing

Indications

This kind of traditional Chinese medicine is very good for the treatment and health care of stomachaches. It should be taken three times a day, two pills at a time for grown-ups and one pill for children. In case of continued stomachache, one more pill can be taken at a time. It might make you feel slightly sick and likely to throw up or sleepy after taking it, and the symptom will disappear by themselves after you stop taking the medicine. The medicine should be put in a cool and dry place, where children cannot reach it. Furthermore, it's better to strictly follow the doctor's instruction before taking it.

Test Six

Part I   Listening Comprehension

Section A

1. **B**   推断题。只要抓住数字，即可答对。"I have \$6. Would you borrow it?" 为信息句。
2. **B**   推断题。女的要先去寄信然后到学校接孩子。before 是关键。
3. **D**   细节题。重点考查 keep going 的含义。
4. **A**   细节题。重点是 "see…off at the airport" 表示到机场为某人送行。
5. **C**   推理题。"To finish her paper before exams." 是信息句，说明行为目的。

Section B
Conversation 1

6. **C**   细节题，对方说 "Can I take a message?" 然后我们听到的 "There will be a lecture on English history" 是关键。
7. **D**   细节题，根据 There will a lecture on English history by a famous professor at 2:30 tomorrow afternoon 可得出答案。

Conversation 2

8. **B**   细节题，题中的 camp 是"露营"，是关键词，考生不一定都能听懂，只要抓住 in the mountain 即可。
9. **C**   细节题，可从听到的原句 The sun shone nearly every day 中获得正确答案。
10. **C**   细节题，原文中有 they were great。

Section C

11. **next Thursday**　细节题，可直接听取。从一开始 The exam will be held next Thursday 便可获得。

12. **a few pens**　细节题，可直接听取，在 Remember to bring two or three pens in case you run out of ink. 中获得。

13. **short passages**　细节题，根据 It will consist of short passages. 得到答案。

14. **their class notes**　在文中倒数第五句。

15. **a week**　情节认定题，听到 "Now I'll talk to you about the final exam. The exam will be held next Thursday" 就可推出是考试前一周。

Part II　Structure

Section A

16. **C**　注意词组 not...until 用于强调句时，往往要写成 not until...that。

17. **A**　此句意思为：比我估计的有趣得多。常见的比较级修饰词如下：much, even, still, far, rather, a lot, a little, a great deal, by far。

18. **A**　表示对过去事实的客观陈述，前面是与过去有关的虚拟语气。

19. **B**　考查主谓就近一致的应用。谓语取 "与邻近主语保持一致" 的原则，类似的用法有：neither...nor...；either...or...；not only...but also...；...or...；there be...。

20. **C**　修饰人和物的定语从句用 that 引导。

21. **C**　熟练掌握 V-ing 作主语的以下句型：It's no good + V-ing；It's no use + V-ing；It's a waste of time + V-ing。

22. **D**　dare 和 need 一样，既可做情态动词，也可做实义动词。

23. **B**　考查时态。在时间和条件状语从句中，主句用将来时，从句用一般现在时。

24. **C**　考查倍数词的位置。比较级中的倍数词放在比较句型前。

25. **D**　时态为过去完成时。瞬间动词不能和表示一段时间的状语连用。

Section B

26. **be sent/should be sent**　在 "It is important (necessary, strange, better...) + 主语从句" 这类句式中，从句的动词用虚拟语气，其形式为 "(should) + 动词原形"。

27. **equipment**　考查词性转换，动词变为名词，词尾加 "-ment"。

28. **excited**　形容词比较级句型，"the more...the more..." 表示 "越……就越……"，主语是人，所以用 excited（感到激动）。

29. **information**　考查词性转换，动词变为名词，词尾加 "-ation"。

30. **are not allowed**　考查被动语态。

31. **fortunate**　考查词性转换，名词变形容词，enough 修饰形容词。

32. **increasingly**　考查词性转换，要用副词修饰形容词，将动词变副词，加 "-ly"。

33. **addition** 考查词性转换，动词变为名词，词尾加"-ition"。

34. **knows** 考查主谓语一致和时态，词组"neither...nor..."连接主语时，谓语须和就近的主语保持一致。

35. **decorated** 考查固定搭配。此句考点是 have sth. done 的用法。have my house decorated 表示"让别人来装饰我的房子"。

Part III Reading Comprehension

Task 1

本文就如何应对压力提出了建议：对能够改变的情况采取行动，学会接受那些无法改变的情况。

36. **A** 推理题。题干为"第二段中的 option 一词可用什么代替。"该词所在的句子为该段主题句，该段讲述了面临压力时可采取的两种做法，由此可判断，其意为"选择"，故选 A。

37. **D** 主旨题。题干为"遇到困难时，你最好……"。文章第一句告诉我们看看哪些情况你能改变，并学会接受那些你不能改变的。其中 recognize 的原意为识别，所以答案为 D。

38. **C** 细节题。题干意为"形成压力的原因通常是什么？"答案在第二段的第一句话：来自外部的压力经常会造成心理压力。故选 C。

39. **B** 在 make a difference 的后一句中"have a positive impact on..."可知其意思应是"有意义，有影响"。故选 B。

40. **B** 主旨题。题干为"下面哪个是本文的最佳题目"。文章自始至终在谈论如何应对压力。故选 B。

Task 2

实用文体部分的阅读大多数都是要求查找信息。本篇是一篇有关火灾安全的产品说明书。

41. **D** 要求查找出本文主要针对的对象的信息，可从 Fire Alarm Bells 部分中的 in the area of B Block (Teaching) 和 On Hearing Your Fire Alarm 部分中的"Those in class... given by the teacher."推出正确答案应该是学生。

42. **C** 细节题。提问发现火灾的人首先应该做的事情。在文章的开头就交代了"The person Discovering a Fire will: 1, Operate the nearest fire alarm"。

43. **C** 细节题。在 Assembly Area 部分。

44. **D** 逻辑推理题。Sports hall 在 C Block，根据 Fire Alarm Bell 里的内容，只有位于铃响区域的人才须采取行动，administration office 在 A block，所以不需要采取行动。

45. **B** 逻辑推理题。题干是"在面临火灾时，教师应该做的第一件事是什么？"根据文章中的火灾指令"Those in class: will go to the Assembly area under the instructions given by the teacher."可获知教师的首要任务是带领学生撤离。所以 B 为正确答案。

Task 3

　　本文介绍了计算机病毒与病毒扫描的有关知识。对病毒的传播途径以及它的危害做了详细介绍。最后介绍了新型抗病毒产品及预防措施。

46. **memory or disk** 　　　　　　病毒附着于其他程序中或藏于存储器或磁盘中。

47. **disks and files** 　　　　　　通过磁盘和文件进行复制。

48. **take proper precautions** 　采取适当的预防措施。

49. **Virus Scan** 　　　　　　　为抗病毒产品。

50. **scheduled periodic scans** 　定期扫描能为你的计算机增加一道保险。

Task 4

51. A, O 　　　52. G, J 　　　53. E, B 　　　54. K, P 　　　55. S, R

A. — Computer graphics 电脑动画

B. — Feature movie 故事片

C. — Box-office flop 低票房

D. — Box-office hit 高票房

E. — Child star 童星

F. — Cameo roles 客串演员

G. — Location 外景拍摄地

H. — Musical 音乐歌舞剧

I. — Out-take 拍摄花絮

J. — Postproduction 后期制作

K. — Screen test 试镜

L. — Short movie 短片

M.— Silent movie 无声电影

N. — Slapstick 闹剧

O. — Sitcom 情景喜剧

P. — Sound stage 摄影棚

Q. — Splatter movie 暴力片

R. — Star-studded team 全明星阵容

S. — Wide screen movie 宽银幕电影

Task 5

　　本文是一封商家给顾客的商务信函。首先对顾客的订货表示感谢，进而解释了商家缺货的原因，同时承诺给顾客优惠待遇。

56. **their confidence** 　　　根据第一段第一句可知答案。

57. **the cold weather** 　　　根据第一段第二句可知答案。

58. **service and quality** 　　根据第二段第一句可知答案。

59. **latest sample book**　　根据第二段可知答案。

60. **receive their orders**　　根据第二段最后一句可知答案。

Part IV　Translate English into Chinese

61. **C—A—D—B**　　此句含有一个定语从句，properties 是指性能。句型是本题翻译的关键。

62. **A—D—C—B**　　本句主要在于否定的翻译、否定词的转移和几个名词短语的翻译。

63. **C—B—A—D**　　关键是短语 on account of 和 failure to deliver... 的理解和翻译。On account of 表示"由于……"的意思；failure to do sth. 表示"没能……"的意思。

64. **C—B—A—D**　　本句的关键是定语从句的理解和翻译以及短语的翻译。

65. 应您的要求，寄上我公司最新的产品目录和价格表。我们相信由于我们采用了最新的设计和太空时代的新型材料，贵公司客户一定会对本公司的今秋产品感兴趣。随着全球变暖，这种轻型装饰材料也会日益受到青睐。

　　（这是一封普通的商务书信。第二句结构较为复杂，要注意里边含有一个原因状语从句，表示"由于……"。翻译此类信函时，要注意语气的把握。）

Part V　Writing

Agreement on Scientific and technological

Exchange and Cooperation

Between the X X Industrial University of Colorado State of U.S.A. and X X Industrial University of Hubei Province of the P.R.C.

Following sincere and friendly discussions, the X X Industrial University of Hubei Province of People's Republic of China and X X Industrial University of Colorado State of U.S.A. with a view to promoting scientific and technological exchange and cooperation between the two institutes, have reached the following Agreement.

　i.　The two Parties will provide each other with scientific and technological materials and exchange relevant information learning from each other.

　ii.　The two Parties will carry out a scholar exchange program; these experts will make report and give lectures.

　iii.　The two Parties will exchange 10-20 students each year.

　iv.　The present agreement is valid for five years.

　　……… (signed)

　　For the X X Industrial University of Hubei Province of the People's Republic of China

　　……… (signed)

　　For the X X Industrial University of Colorado State of the U.S.A.